THE R

FIVE

MARY BALOGH won the *Romantic Times* Award for Best Regency Author and the Reviewer's Choice Award for Best Regency Author in 1985, and the *Romantic Times* Award for Best Regency Author in 1989. She lives in Kipling, Saskatchewan, Canada.

SANDRA HEATH has lived and worked in both Holland and Germany. She now resides with her husband and young daughter in Gloucester, England.

EDITH LAYTON has won nine writing prizes including the 1987 *Romantic Times* Award for Best Regency Author. She lives in Jericho, New York.

MARY JO PUTNEY has won four writing prizes, and was the winner of the 1988 *Romantic Times* Award for Best Regency Author. She lives in Baltimore, Maryland.

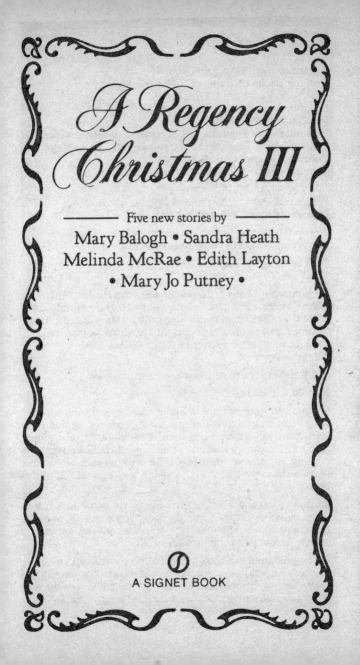

A Regency Christmas III

—— Five new stories by ——

Mary Balogh • Sandra Heath
Melinda McRae • Edith Layton
• Mary Jo Putney •

A SIGNET BOOK

SIGNET
Published by the Penguin Group
Penguin Books USA Inc., 375 Hudson Street,
New York, New York 10014, U.S.A.
Penguin Books Ltd, 27 Wrights Lane,
London W8 5TZ, England
Penguin Books Australia Ltd, Ringwood, Victoria, Australia
Penguin Books Canada Ltd, 10 Alcorn Ave., Suite 3000.
Toronto, Ontario, Canada M4V 3B2
Penguin Books (N.Z.) Ltd, 182-190 Wairau Road,
Auckland 10, New Zealand

Penguin Books Ltd, Registered Offices:
Harmondsworth, Middlesex, England

First published by Signet, an imprint of New American
Library,a division of Penguin Books USA Inc.

First Printing, November, 1991
10 9 8 7 6 5 4 3 2 1

Ⓟ REGISTERED TRADEMARK—MARCA REGISTRADA

Printed in the United States of America

BOOKS ARE AVAILABLE AT QUANTITY DISCOUNTS WHEN USED TO PRO-
MOTE PRODUCTS OR SERVICES. FOR INFORMATION PLEASE WRITE TO
PREMIUM MARKETING DIVISION, PENGUIN BOOKS USA INC., 375 HUDSON
STREET, NEW YORK, NEW YORK 10014.

Contents

Mistletoe and Folly

by

Sandra Heath

Sir Richard Curzon left Lady Finch's Christmas ball unexpectedly early. The diamond pin in his starched muslin neckcloth flashed in the light of a street lamp as he strolled slowly along the snowy Mayfair pavement of Pargeter Street. His fashionable Polish greatcoat was unbuttoned as he walked through the starry December night toward nearby Park Lane, and his town residence overlooking Hyde Park.

It had been Christmas Eve since the stroke of midnight, and the sounds of revelry followed him as London's *haut ton* danced the night away. They'd do the same the next night at the lavish masquerade to be held at Holland House, and Richard's name figured prominently on that guest list as well, but given the mood he was in at present he didn't know if it would be advisable to attend.

He breathed deeply of the keen winter air. The December of 1819 had been bitterly cold so far, almost as cold as the winter of 1814 when the Thames had frozen over, and somehow he didn't think it would improve before the new year. Lifting his cane he dashed some snow from an overhanging branch. Pargeter Street was a place of elegant mansions and high-walled gardens, and tonight it was filled with that air of excitement that always accompanied Christmas. A line of fine carriages was drawn up near Finch House, red-ribboned wreaths adorned all doorways, and more greenery could be seen through brightly lit windows, for it was as traditional to decorate one's house in Mayfair as it was any country cottage. Richard strolled on, feeling no excitement at all, just an unsettling restlessness, as if something of tremendous importance was about to happen to him.

His tall-crowned hat was tipped back on his blonde hair, and the astrakhan collar of his great-coat was turned up. Beneath the coat he wore the tight-fitting black velvet evening coat and white silk pantaloons that were *de rigueur* for a man of fashion, and altogether he presented the perfect picture of Bond Street elegance. He was handsome, charming, and much sought after in society, but tonight there was a pensive look in his blue eyes, and an unsmiling set to his fine lips.

The ball would continue until daylight, but he hadn't been enjoying the diversion, not even when he'd held Isabel in his arms for the waltz. Miss Isabel Hamilton was the woman he was to marry, and he loved her very much, but that hadn't prevented him from behaving aloofly all evening, so much so that in the end he'd felt obliged to remove himself. Isabel hadn't understood, indeed she'd been so displeased that she'd tossed her head in that willful but fascinating way of hers, and, much to the annoyance of that lord's shrew of a duchess, had promptly requested the good-looking young Duke of Laroche to partner her in a cotillion. She'd given Laroche her full and flattering attention, and hadn't glanced again at the fiancé who'd displeased her so.

With a sigh Richard jabbed his silver-tipped cane into the deep snow at the side of the pavement. Things weren't going well in his private life, for of late there'd been far too much friction and misunderstanding. Isabel was the belle of London, having taken society by storm when she'd arrived from her home in Scotland the year before. She had no title or fortune, but was very beautiful and from a good family, and she'd been besieged by admirers from the moment she arrived. With her shining short dark curls and melting brown eyes she was quite the most heartstoppingly lovely creature in the realm, and he was the envy of his many rivals for having won her hand. But as the months of the betrothal had passed he'd begun to see a side of her of which his rivals knew nothing. She could be flirtatious, capricious, selfish and untruthful, and these traits had rubbed a little of his happiness away. He still loved her, but deep in his heart he was beginning to have grave doubts about the wisdom of making her his wife.

But tonight he'd behaved boorishly, and she'd been perfectly justified in showing her displeasure. They were due to take a ride in Hyde Park in the morning, and he'd do his best to smooth her ruffled feathers. He'd do the same at the Holland House masquerade, which he reluctantly accepted he'd have to attend if he was to put matters entirely right with Isabel. But it all depended on his being able to shrug off this damned restlessness.

Something made him pause suddenly and whirl about to look swiftly back along the pavement. He had the strong feeling that he was being followed, but all he could see was the line of elegant carriages drawn up at the curbside outside Finch House, and the small groups of coachmen laughing and talking together as they whiled away the long hours of the ball. He continued to look back, for the feeling was so strong that every instinct told him someone was there, but there was nothing, just the empty pavement and the entrances to the mansions he'd passed. Someone could be hiding in one of those entrances. . . . For a moment he considered going back to look, but then decided against it. He had his cane and was well able to take care of himself against any footpad.

The sounds of the ball began to dwindle away behind him as he walked on again, but as the night became more quiet, there was a new sound as a travel-stained post-chaise turned the corner from Park Lane, driving toward him at the sort of weary trot that told of a long and arduous journey. The yellow-jacketed postboy scanned the houses on either side of the street until at last he saw the address he sought, and with relief maneuvered his tired horses to a standstill outside number forty-four, a few yards in front of Richard.

The owners of the house, Mr. and Mrs. Josiah Fitzhaven, were acquaintances of his, and he half-expected to see them in the chaise as he glanced toward it, but instead he saw two women, a rather elderly maid in a poke bonnet and prim brown mantle, and a young woman in a hooded crimson velvet cloak. He caught a glimpse of the latter's sweet profile by the light of a streep lamp opposite as she prepared to open the chaise door.

Instinctively Richard hastened forward to open it for her, extending his white-gloved hand to help her out. She slipped her fingers from the warm depths of her white swansdown muff, and as she accepted his hand he was conscious of the hardness of her wedding ring. The fragrance of lily-of-the-valley drifted over him as she stepped down to the snowy pavement; it was a perfume that evoked the past with a poignancy that was almost as tangible as her ring. Memories of a lost love were all around as she turned to thank him, and her hood fell back to reveal a face he'd never expected to see again.

His heart almost missed a beat. "Diana?" he whispered. "Diana, is it really you?"

With a gasp she stared at him, her magnificent green eyes wide with shock. "Richard?" she breathed, withdrawing her hand as if burned by his touch.

He gazed into the face he'd once adored to distraction. Her eyes were of a fathomless emerald, and she had a cascade of rich burnished chestnut curls which had always defied the efforts of pins to restrain them. She was that rarest of creatures, a flame-haired beauty with a flawless creamy-white complexion, and as he looked at her again, he knew there wasn't a woman on earth to compare with Miss Diana Laverick.

For the space of another heartbeat he was under her spell again, captivated by emotions he'd striven so desperately to deny since the last bitterly cold winter in 1814. But as he drank in the sweetly remembered face, the spell snapped suddenly, and reality rushed over him. She wasn't Miss Diana Laverick anymore, she was Mrs. Robert Beaumont, and she didn't deserve his love, she deserved his loathing.

All these years before in his home county of Cheshire, when he'd been a second son without hope of inheriting his father's wealth or title, he'd been unbelievably happy when he'd fallen in love with her. He'd been foolish enough to think she returned his love, but she was too ambitious and grasping to regard him as more than an idle fancy, and on Christmas Eve 1814 he'd learned of her sudden marriage to Robert Beaumont, a fabulously wealthy plantation owner who'd immediately swept her away to a life of luxury in Jamaica. She'd remained out of England ever since, and her heartbroken lover had at last managed to put his life in some sort of order again, but here she was on another Christmas Eve, stepping down to bring back all the torment he'd suffered at her hands. Perfidious, cold, calculating Diana, the bane of his life.

Bitter resentment gripped him anew, and his

blue eyes were suddenly icecold. "So, London is to be honored with your presence, is it? May I enquire if Mr. Beaumont is with you?"

She glanced back at the chaise, from which the elderly maid was alighting. "As you can see, Richard, Mr. Beaumont is not with me."

"Will he be joining you?"

"No." She gave the maid a warning look, as if to prevent her from saying something which might be out of turn.

The maid met her mistress's gaze, and remained silent, but she looked at Richard in an unsmiling way that conveyed her disapproval of him. He knew her, her name was Mary Keating, and she'd been in Diana's service for many years. She was a small, slight person with sharp gray eyes and a questing nose, and she always guarded her mistress as fiercely as any mother cat defending her kitten. In the past she hadn't disapproved of him, but she obviously did now.

Diana nodded at her. "See that Mr. and Mrs. Fitzhaven are informed of our arrival, and have their butler instruct some men to assist with the luggage."

"Yes, Miss Diana." Mary went to the door of the mansion, reaching up past the wreath of holly and mistletoe to rap the lion's head knocker.

Richard glanced at the house. "You're staying with the Fitzhavens?" he asked Diana.

"Very fleetingly."

"I had no idea you knew them."

"Mrs. Fitzhaven is my mother's second cousin, and she very kindly invited me to stay with them during my . . . She invited me to stay with them," she finished, as if deciding against a further explanation of her presence in London. She looked at him again. "I understand that you are now Sir Richard?"

"Yes."

"I was very sorry to learn that both your father and brother were lost on board the *Wanderer*."

He didn't reply.

"Are you married?" she asked.

"I'm betrothed to Miss Isabel Hamilton."

"The name means nothing to me." She gave the faintest of smiles. "As you may remember, I never left Cheshire before my marriage, and this is the first time I've been to London."

"I'm afraid I don't recall the details of your life, Mrs. Beaumont," he answered coolly. Anger bubbled beneath the surface of his calm. It was preposterous to be standing here exchanging pleasantries when he really wished to shake her and make her say she was sorry for all the hurt and anguish she'd caused him.

She couldn't ignore the chill in his voice, or the resentment in his eyes. "Richard, I'll only be here for a day or so, and I don't anticipate that you and I will meet again . . ."

"I sincerely trust not," he replied cuttingly.

The door of the house had been opened now, and light flooded out as footmen hastened to attend to the luggage at the rear of the chaise. Mary stood at the top of the steps, watching Richard and her mistress.

Diana gave him a ghost of a smile. "Given what you've just said, it would obviously be inappropriate to say that I'm glad we encountered each other like this."

"Very inappropriate indeed, madam." The rancor he felt was suddenly so great that he couldn't trust himself to prolong the meeting a moment more. "Goodbye, Mrs. Beaumont," he said tersely, "I trust this Christmas brings you everything you so richly deserve." Inclining his head in a gesture calculated to be insulting, he strolled on, his cane swinging as if nothing of any consequence had occurred.

Diana watched him until he turned the corner into Park Lane, where she remembered his town house was to be found. How full of resentment he still was, and how little he understood, even after all this time. Tears stung her eyes, and she blinked them back. He'd never forgive her, he'd made that plain enough when he'd ignored the letter she'd sent explaining her swift marriage to Robert. Oh, how sad Christmas always made her feel now, it was the time of year she dreaded most of all. She took a deep breath. The sooner all this was over and done with, the better for all concerned.

Mary came down the steps toward her. "Come inside out of the cold, Miss Diana."

"I'm coming, Mary."

"Mr. and Mrs. Fitzhaven have been called away unexpectedly because Mr. Fitzhaven's father is unwell, but they've left word that the house is entirely at your disposal."

Diana was about to reply when something made her look back along the pavement toward the crush of carriages outside Finch House. She'd heard a soft sound, a small scuffling noise as if someone was hiding in the shadows nearby.

"What is it, Miss Diana?" asked Mary, looking anxiously at her.

"I thought I heard something. Mary, I think there's someone watching us."

Mary shivered. "Then come inside straightaway, Miss Diana," she said firmly, ushering her mistress toward the steps.

Diana allowed herself to be drawn into the brightly lit entrance hall, where a kissing bunch of mistletoe, holly, red apples, and lighted candles was suspended low beneath two glittering chandeliers. The walls were a cool classical blue-and-white, and the floor patterned with black-and-white tiles. Two sapphire-blue brocade sofas were placed on either side of a white marble fireplace, where a huge yule log burned slowly in the hearth. Elegant console tables stood against the walls, each one presided over by a tall gilt-framed mirror adorned with girandoles, and at the far end a grand staircase led up to the floor above, vanishing between tall Corinthian columns that emphasised the spaciousness and grandeur of the house.

Mary led her across to some handsome white-and-gold double doors, opening them to show her into the sumptuous drawing room beyond. There was rose-pink silk on the walls, and gilded French furniture, and more chandeliers that cast a rich, warm glow over everything.

Mary relieved Diana of the crimson velvet cloak and the swansdown muff, and watched as she went to hold her hands out to the fire burning so brightly in the magnificent black marble fireplace. The maid's eyes were sad. "It will be over soon, Miss Diana, and then we can go home again."

"Home?" Diana turned to give her a rather wry smile.

"Well, it is, isn't it?"

"I suppose so."

Mary was worried about her, for she'd been through so much recently. The long journey hadn't helped, for although she, Mary, had been able to sleep when the chance arose, she knew that her mistress had had very little rest. "Miss Diana, I've asked the cook to prepare you a warm drink and a light supper, and there's a maid attending to your bedroom right now, so that when you've had some refreshment, you can get some sleep at last. I'm sure you'll feel a great deal better in the morning."

"In readiness for my fateful meeting with the lawyer in the afternoon," murmured Diana, thinking of how they'd traveled at breakneck speed from Falmouth in order to be in London in time.

"It may not be all bad news, Miss Diana," said Mary as reassuringly as she could.

"I wish I could feel that optimistic," replied Diana, turning to hold her cold hands out to the fire again.

Mary went sadly out, closing the doors softly behind her.

Diana gazed down into the hearth, but it wasn't the glow of flames that she saw, it was the ice in Sir Richard Curzon's blue eyes.

As the hired chaise at last pulled away from the curb outside, a secretive figure emerged stealthily from the shelter of some snowy laurels in front of a nearby house. The Honorable Geoffrey Hawksworth, son and heir of Viscount Hawksworth, cursed beneath his breath as snow slithered down the back of his neck and over his fashionable clothes. Standing on the pavement, he carefully brushed the black fur trimming on his elegant ankle-length redingote.

He was a tall young man, thin-faced and pale, with long-lashed hazel eyes and full lips. His curly brown hair was abundant, and cut in an extravagantly modish style. Beneath his redingote he too wore evening clothes, for he'd been following his adversary, Richard, from the ball when the intriguing encounter with the enigmatic Mrs. Beaumont had taken place.

As he looked up at the bright windows of number forty-four, there was a slyly thoughtful expression on his face. Pure chance had caused him to follow Richard, whose puzzling conduct tonight and sudden departure had aroused his curiosity; pure chance had also caused Mrs. Beaumont to step down from the chaise right in front of her old love. Geoffrey was one of the few people in London who knew about Diana, for he'd once been Richard's close friend, and Richard had told hardly a soul about his heartbreaking affair in Cheshire in the frozen winter of 1814, and he certainly hadn't told Isabel. He'd told his good friend Geoffrey, however, because Isabel hadn't entered their lives then, but when she'd arrived in London, and both men had fallen in love with her, they'd fallen out beyond all redemption. In the end she'd given her favor to Richard, but Geoffrey had never given up. Until she became Lady Curzon, the battle was far from over.

Geoffrey's hazel eyes glittered in the light from a street lamp as he pondered the engrossing encounter he'd just eavesdropped upon. The past had suddenly invaded Richard Curzon's present, and it was a past that still had the power to destroy that gentleman's equilibrium. Geoffrey had often wondered what his former friend's false-hearted Diana had looked like, and now he knew. She was bewitchingly beautiful, and if Richard's stung reaction had been any gauge, he was far from over her.

Turning, Geoffrey began to stroll back toward the ball, congratulating himself upon so fortuitously choosing to follow Richard. Diana Beaumont's arrival in town presented the perfect opportunity for driving a wedge between Richard and Isabel, whose dealings with each other hadn't been going sweetly of late. A plan was already forming in his scheming mind, a plan so simple that it could not possibly fail. He began to hum to himself, and his cane twirled as he walked. He gave no thought to Diana, whose marriage might be put in jeopardy by his machinations, he was only concerned with wresting Isabel from Richard.

Reaching Finch House, he left his top hat, gloves, cane, and redingote in the room provided, and then reentered the dazzling ballroom, where a sea of elegant, bejeweled guests danced beneath a canopy of chandeliers and Christmas garlands. No expense had been spared in the extravagant decorations, there were even German fir trees, their branches laden with tiers of colored wax candles, a continental fashion brought over by Lady Finch from her native Hanover.

Another waltz was playing, and Isabel was again dancing with Henry Daventry, Duke of Laroche. She wore a lowcut cerise silk gown, its hem modishly stiffened with rouleaux and bows, and there was a white feather boa trailing on the sandstrewn floor as she moved. Diamonds sparkled at her throat and trembled from her ears, and flouncy white ostrich plumes, her favorites, sprang from the circlet around her short dark hair. She was laughing at something Laroche had said, and her brown eyes were soft and teasing as she looked up into his good-looking face.

Geoffrey paused at the foot of the ballroom steps, toying with the lace spilling from his black velvet cuff. His adoring, intense gaze followed her every step, lingering on her exquisite face. Soon she would be his, he didn't doubt it for a moment now that he possessed such invaluable information about her loathed fiancé.

Stepping on to the crowded floor, he pushed his way toward her, tapping the duke on the shoulder. Laroche was an old acquaintance from school days, and no one ever called him by his first name, he was always simply Laroche. "Come now, Laroche, you're being greedy," said Geoffrey. "You mustn't hog the loveliest lady in the room, it's my turn now, besides, I've just seen your wife, she's looking for you. I suggest you adjourn to the card room, she's already searched there." It was a deliberate lie, for Geoffrey hadn't seen the duchess at all, but he knew the thought of his wife's approach would be sufficient to get rid of Laroche, whose dalliances outside the marriagebed had made the duchess an extremely jealous and suspicious woman.

Laroche swiftly relinquished Isabel to Geoffrey, and melted away into the press of guests. Isabel

pouted after him, and then gave Geoffrey a re-
proachful look.

"You haven't seen the duchess at all, have you?"
she said in her soft Scottish voice.

"Would I tell fibs at Christmas?" he replied,
whirling her away into the waltz.

"Yes, Geoffrey, you would, just as you'd tell fibs
on any other time of the year if it suited you," she
answered, smiling coquettishly.

"You look breathtakingly lovely tonight, Isabel,"
he whispered.

"Why, thank you, sir," she said in that teasingly
flirtatious way that always played havoc with him.
"It's so very agreeable to be paid compliments by an
admirer, instead of having to endure one's fiancé's
contrariness."

"Have you and Curzon quarreled again?"

"Not exactly, he's just seen fit to take himself
home. He was in a most beastly mood, quite the
surly bear, and I wish now that I'd told him not to
call on me again until he's improved his manners.
However, I didn't say any such thing, so he'll be
taking me riding in Hyde Park tomorrow morning,
and to the masquerade tomorrow night. Or should
I say tonight? It's Christmas Eve now, isn't it?"

"It is indeed," he replied, exulting not only in
the pleasure of holding her, but in the fact that she
was quite obviously very disenchanted indeed with
the man she was to marry. "Isabel, if you were
mine I'd never be a surly bear, and I'd certainly
never leave early."

"I know you wouldn't, Geoffrey, for you're the
most of an angel I ever knew."

"You should have chosen me."

"I know." She sighed, her lips pouting a little
again. "Richard's been so very hurtful of late, he's
even declined to buy me the little Christmas gift I
crave more than anything else in the world."

"Little Christmas gift?"

"It's only a little brooch, a golden sunburst that would look the very thing on the tartan sash I intend to wear with my new white silk gown, and he knows how much I want it, but this morning it was still in Cranford's window."

"Oh, my poor darling," murmured Geoffrey, drawing her just a little closer. His mind was racing, for he'd just thought of a way of adding to his plan in order to make it even more assured of success.

As dawn began to lighten the eastern sky, and Lady Finch's guests departed, Geoffrey's carriage drove slowly down Bond Street, drawing up outside the premises of Messrs Cranford, the fashionable jewelers. Stepping down, he looked in at the exquisite items shining in the light of a street lamp. The sunburst brooch reposed in a little red leather box, and, as Isabel had said, it would indeed look perfect with her tartan sash. Tartan accessories were all the rage now because of Sir Walter Scott's popular novels, and no one wore them to better advantage than Isabel.

Returning to the carriage, he instructed the coachman to drive to Piccadilly, and the premises of Messrs Duvall & Carrier, fanmakers and glovers to royalty. A few minutes later he alighted again, this time to study a window display of dainty gloves and fans of every description.

It wasn't long before his glance fell upon a fan that fitted his requirements in every way, for not only was it made of Isabel's adored white plumes, but it was also trimmed with little tartan bows. Next to it there was a small folding fan with gold-embroidered gray satin fixed upon sticks of gilded, carved ivory. He didn't know Mrs. Diana Beaumont, but intuition told him that she'd find such a fan very much to her liking.

He returned to the carriage again, and it drove

away along the virtually deserted street toward his Mayfair residence in North Street. It would be several hours yet before the shops opened for the hectic business of Christmas Eve, and in the meantime he had much to do. It would be a long time before he could get some sleep, but somehow he didn't feel even remotely tired, he had far too much on his mind for that.

As his carriage drove slowly along Park Lane, past Richard's imposing town house, the church bells of London began to strike seven.

The sound of the bells died away, but everything was quiet in the sumptuous green-and-gold drawing room where Richard had fallen asleep in a fireside chair, an almost empty cognac glass resting precariously in his hand.

The only light came from the fire, and shadows moved softly over the hand-painted Chinese silk on the walls, and over the rich green velvet curtains drawn across the tall windows overlooking Park Lane and Hyde Park. The whole room was in the Chinese style, with lifesize porcelain figures, pieces of jade, dragon- and chrysanthemum-embroidered chairs and sofas, and lotus-blossom carved on every wooden surface.

Richard didn't hear the church bells, for the windows were shuttered. His evening coat had been idly discarded on a nearby sofa, and his lace-edged shirt and white satin waistcoat had been partially unbuttoned. His crumpled neckcloth hung loose, and the diamond pin had been left on the marble mantelpiece amid the sprays of seasonal holly, mistletoe, ivy, and myrtle arranged with such care by the maids.

He was dreaming about Diana, and the Christmas five years before when he'd last held her in his arms. She'd been wearing a lilac gown, with a low neckline and long diaphanous sleeves gath-

ered in rich frills at her slender wrists. Her cloud
of chestnut hair had been brushed loose, tumbling
down about her shoulders in that wanton way he
loved so much. They'd slipped away from her family to the seclusion of the minstrels' gallery above
the great hall of her parents' Cheshire manor-
house, and masked mummers from the nearby village had been playing in the hall below. He and
Diana had been engrossed only in themselves as
they stood in each other's arms in the holly-
garlanded shadows. Her lips had tasted so sweet
as her supple body yielded against his, and she'd
felt so warm and alive through the soft stuff of her
gown. His love had never been stronger or more
sure than it had been in those magical minutes,
and yet within a day or so he was to learn of her
marriage to Robert Beaumont, a man of whose existence he knew nothing.

The fire shifted in the hearth, and the flames began to crackle loudly around a half-burned log.
Richard awoke with a start, and the glass fell from
his fingers, shattering on the polished fender. For
a moment he was confused, the tentacles of the
dream still coiling around him, but then it faded
away, and he remembered.

He leaned his head back wearily. Why had Diana
come back to torment him again? Why couldn't
she have stayed in Jamaica? He wished he'd been
able to put her firmly in the past, but now that he'd
seen her again, he knew that he'd never be able to
turn his back finally upon his first great love.

Getting up, he crossed to one of the windows,
drawing the curtains back and then folding the
shutters aside to look out at snowy Park Lane and
Hyde Park. A few tradesmen's carts were making
their way along the street toward the fashionable
shops of Oxford Street and Piccadilly, where soon
the most profitable day of the year would be in full
swing.

His gaze moved across to the park with its ghostly white trees. Would Isabel still be prepared to ride with him later on, or had he offended her too much? He wished now that he hadn't given in to his strange mood, but had remained at the ball, for then he'd have been spared the encounter with Diana. Damn her for coming back, and damn her even more for still being able to stop his heart with a glance.

In Pargeter Street, Diana was sleeping the sleep of the exhausted. Her flame-colored hair spilled over her pillow like molten copper, and there were no dreams to disturb her slumber. She had no idea of the stir her return was about to cause due to the underhanded intentions of one Geoffrey Hawksworth, who, the moment he'd entered his residence in North Street, had sat down at the great writing desk in his library with pen, ink, and many sheets of quality vellum upon which to perfect a more than passing resemblance to Sir Richard Curzon's rather distinctive writing. Letters had been exchanged during the days of the two men's friendship, and so Geoffrey did not lack examples from which to copy. It was painstaking work, but in the end he was satisfied that the only person who would be able to tell his work from the real thing would be Richard himself.

While this clandestine activity was taking place, Diana slept on, not waking until the ormulu clock on the mantelpiece struck nine, and Mary came in with a dish of morning tea, which she placed on the elegant marquetry table beside the four poster bed before going to draw back the curtains and fold the shutters aside.

It was a sunny morning, made brighter by all the snow, and the fresh light flooded into the bedroom, lying in sunbeamed shafts across the aquamarine-canopied bed, the brocade curtains of which were tied back with golden ropes. There was gray-and-white-striped silk on the walls, and a dressing table that was lavishly draped with frilled white muslin. A dressing room lined with wardrobes led off to one side, and a lacquered Chinese screen shielded the alcove where the washstand stood. There were two comfortable chairs by the fireplace, and above the mantelpiece was a mirror so large that Diana could see herself in the bed as she sat up.

Mary came to the foot of the bed. "Good morning, Miss Diana."

"Good morning, Mary," replied Diana, picking up the dish of tea and sipping it.

Mary went through into the dressing room, and emerged in a moment with a very odd assortment of clothes, an apricot velvet spencer, and a light-weight cherry wool riding habit.

Diana stared at the garments. "Mary, what are you thinking of . . . ?"

"It's not as foolish a choice as you may think, Miss Diana, for I've learned that there is an excellent riding school in the mews behind here, where fine horses can be hired for riding in Hyde Park. I know how much you like riding, and I also know that such exercise would do you good, so I've taken the liberty of ordering a saddle horse for you."

Diana stared at her in dismay. "Oh, Mary, the last thing I want to do is be seen somewhere as public and undoubtedly crowded as Rotten Row!"

"No one here knows you, except for Sir Richard Curzon, and it's doubtful if he would acknowledge you anyway." Mary draped the clothes over the back of one of the fireside chairs. "It's much colder here than in Jamaica, which is why I thought this spencer would go neatly under the coat of your riding habit. No one will know it's there, but it will keep you warm while you're out."

"Mary . . ." began Diana again, but the maid fixed her with a stern look.

"A ride will do you good, Miss Diana, you need a little diversion to take your mind off the appointment with the lawyer this afternoon."

For a moment Diana considered arguing, but she recognized that look, and knew it signified that Mary Keating would keep on until she gave in. "Oh, very well," she said with a sigh, "I'll go riding if you insist."

It was a decision that was to play right into Geoffrey Hawksworth's hands.

As Diana dressed for riding after breakfast, Geoffrey set off in his carriage, first of all for Messrs Duvall & Carrier in Piccadilly, and after that for Cranford's in Bond Street. The carriage blinds were lowered, for he didn't wish to be seen, and he wasn't alone in the vehicle, his reluctant valet was with him.

The carriage drew up at the curb in Piccadilly on the first part of the stratagem, and Geoffrey took a letter of authority, two sealed notes, and a fat purse from his pocket. He pushed them all into the valet's hands.

"I trust that by now you know exactly what you are to do. You are to tell the assistant that you are Sir Richard Curzon's man, and you are to hand over the letter of authority. It describes exactly the two fans in question, and it gives clear instructions as to the names and addresses of the two ladies to which they are to be sent. It also says that the fans are to be despatched without delay. You must be sure to give them the purse and see that they put the correct sealed note with the correct fan."

"Yes, sir."

The man's response was half-hearted, and Geoffrey gave him a testy look. "Is there something wrong?"

The valet swallowed, taking his courage in both hands in order to stand up to his master just a little. "Is it not just a little dishonest for me to pretend to be Sir Richard's man?"

Geoffrey's gaze was frozen. "If you wish to remain in my employ, I suggest you forget your conscience and just do as you're told."

"Yes, sir."

"Then get on with it!" snapped Geoffrey, leaning across to fling open the carriage door.

The noise of the busy street leapt in at them, a mixture of voices, footsteps, hooves, and wheels. A fiddler and a blind penny-whistler were playing *Good King Wenceslas,* a pieman was ringing his handbell and shouting the virtues of his hot pies, and a stagecoach was just leaving the nearby Gloucester Coffee House, its horn ringing out sharply. The valet climbed out, pausing on the pavement for a moment before turning to carefully close the carriage door again and then go into the shop.

Geoffrey held the blind slightly aside so that he could see what was happening. He could just make out the silhouette of the valet, and that of the young man behind the counter. The assistant was nodding, and then came to the window, opening the glass case and removing the two fans Geoffrey had selected at dawn.

A satisfied smile played on Geoffrey's full lips. It was going without a hitch. But then the smile was abruptly cancelled, for a formidable female face looked in through the carriage window barely inches away from him. He gave a start, drawing back and releasing the blind so that it fell back in place, but almost immediately the carriage door was opened, and the same fearsome face appeared again. It belonged to his great-aunt, his father's aunt, and a personage who was undoubtedly the scourge of the Hawksworth family, for she always demanded, and got, her own way. Small, rosy-faced and possessed of a curiously sweet smile, she was nevertheless a harpy of the highest order, and she seemed to take particular delight in imposing upon him whenever the mood took her. The mood had evidently taken her now.

"Ah, so it *is* you skulking in here like a felon, Geoffrey! What on earth are you up to?"

"Er, nothing in particular, Great-Aunt."

"No? Excellent, for that means that you can be of singular assistance to me."

"It does?" His heart sank. What did the old harridan want him to do? Whatever it was, he'd have to bow to her wishes, for she had considerable influence with his father, and therefore with the family pursestrings. Geoffrey had no intention of risking a reduction in his allowance simply because this medusa had been mildly offended.

"Yes," she said, opening the door fully and holding out her hand to him for assistance. "Well, help me in, sir, or would you see me struggle?"

Reluctantly he took the hand, and in a rustle of piped damson silk, she climbed in and took the seat opposite him. Her pelisse and matching gown were tightly fitted at the throat and cuffs, and her hands were plunged into a fur-lined muff of the same piped damson silk. She wore a plain black hat with a small black net veil through which her button-bright eyes were clearly seen. Her hair was tugged back in a knot at the back of her head, and she wore no jewelry at all.

As she made herself comfortable, Geoffrey was dismayed still further to see that she wasn't alone, but was accompanied by two maids carrying bundles of Christmas purchases. They proceeded to enter the carriage as well, taking up the two remaining seats. Now there wasn't any room left for his valet.

Geoffrey began to protest. "I say, Great-Aunt . . ."

"You said you weren't doing anything in partic-

ular, Geoffrey, and so I expect you to convey me
home to Hampstead. My fool of a coachman has
managed to break the wheel of my barouche on a
corner curbstone, and I require transport. I saw
your carriage waiting here, and knew that you'd
been heaven sent to assist me in my predica-
ment."

Geoffrey stared at her, too appalled to speak.
Hampstead was over four miles away, and uphill
through snow all the way! He still had Cranford's
to visit, but could hardly do that with the old biddy
watching his every move. Plague take her, for she
was interfering with his plans! For a moment he
considered getting out and leaving her the use of
his carriage, but almost immediately he dis-
counted such a course of action, for she'd regard it
as a slight, and his father would be regaled with
the tale of his son's disappointing manners.

The old lady's eyes were upon him. "Well, Geoffrey? Are we to remain here all day? Instruct the
coachman to take us to Hampstead."

There was nothing for it but to do as she ordered.
With ill grace, Geoffrey leaned out of the door to
tell the coachman what he was to do, and the carriage pulled away just as the valet emerged from
the shop, his errand completed. He stood on the
curb, staring after the carriage as it vanished amid
the crush of Piccadilly.

With a sigh, the valet turned to make his way
back to his master's residence in North Street. He'd
done all he'd been instructed to do, and soon the
two fans would be on their way. He didn't know
what his master was up to, but he did know that
it wasn't to any good.

While Geoffrey unwillingly commenced the short
but arduous journey to the heights of Hampstead,
Diana had set out on her ride in Hyde Park.

In spite of the snow, Rotten Row was a throng of

fashionable riders, both ladies and gentlemen.
Gleaming horses were handled with excellence,
and there was a display of high fashion that was
second to none as the *beau monde* rode to and fro
along the famous way where it was only the reign-
ing monarch's prerogative to drive in a carriage.

There was skating on the frozen Serpentine, and
nearby there was a great deal of interest in an
American horsedrawn sleigh driven with consum-
mate skill by a gentleman from Washington. A
party of mounted Bow Street Runners was making
its way west toward Kensington Palace, and nu-
merous people were simply taking in the air as
they strolled in the snow. Diana had at last gained
the measure of the bright chestnut horse provided
by the riding school. It had proved a surprisingly
mettlesome mount, tossing its head and capering
as if it would seize the very first opportunity to get
the better of her, but as she rode into Rotten Row,
she had it firmly under control.

She attracted many admiring glances from the
gentlemen, for she was very eyecatching in her
cherry wool riding habit, her flame-colored hair almost matching the sheen on her mount's chestnut
coat. There was a jaunty black beaver hat on her
head, black gloves on her hands, and she carried a
riding crop that she had no need to resort to. She
appeared to great advantage, and she knew it, and
under other circumstances she would have reveled
in all the admiration, but today her real wish was
to blend into the background, which was something she'd failed abysmally to achieve.

There was a second lady who looked particularly
delightful in Rotten Row that morning, for she was
beautifully turned out in a ruffed lime-green velvet
riding habit trimmed with black military frogging.
She rode a pretty strawberry roan mare, and her
lovely dark-eyed face was sweetly framed by the
lime-green gauze scarf encircling her little wide-

brimmed black hat. Miss Isabel Hamilton was used to being the center of attention in the park, and she was vain enough to deliberately incite her easy-going mount to dance around a little, in order to show off her riding skills.

She rode with Richard, with whom she'd at first been sulky and difficult when he'd called upon her at the Hanover Square house of the wealthy relatives with whom she lived, she most definitely being from the poor branch of the family. She'd been off hand and awkward whatever Richard had said, but it was virtually impossible to remain in a sulk with him when he was disposed to exert his immense charm. If he'd been in a strange mood at the ball, he was certainly endeavoring to make up for it now, for no gentleman could have been more gallant and attentive than he. If she hadn't known him better, she'd have concluded rather uncharitably and suspiciously that he had a guilty conscience, and *not* concerning his manners at the ball! But Richard wasn't the sort of man to play her false with another, and so she could only believe that the transformation this morning was due entirely to his acceptance that he'd behaved badly the night before.

At her side, Richard rode a large black Hanoverian that few others would have cared to take on, for it could be a savage beast at times, given to snapping its bared teeth at other nearby mounts. He had it under a tight rein, for he wished to concentrate upon sweetening Isabel, not upon the caprices of a disagreeable horse. He tipped his top hat back on his blonde hair, and took a deep breath of the icy morning air. He wore a pine-green coat and tight pale-gray breeches, and the shine on his top boots bore witness to his valet's devotion to duty. He was beginning to feel he'd smoothed the troubled waters of his dealings with Isabel, and no one could have been further from his thoughts than

Diana, who was at that very moment riding through the crowds toward him.

Isabel was talking about the masquerade that night. "What shall you wear, Richard? I think you would make a splendid cavalier."

"I think I'll just content myself with my ordinary evening wear and a mask," he replied, for if there was one thing he loathed it was dressing up. The invitation from Holland House hadn't stipulated fancy dress, and that was sufficient excuse for him. He smiled at her. "What do you intend to wear?"

"Oh, I haven't decided yet," she replied vaguely.

He was more than a little surprised. "You haven't decided? But I thought such matters were considered long before the actual day!"

"Well, I haven't made up my mind, and that's the end of it," she replied rather shortly.

He fell silent. It was strange that someone as particular as Isabel had yet to make up her mind about something she would normally have regarded as vitally important. Matters of clothing usually preoccupied her to the exclusion of all else.

It was Isabel who first became aware of the slight stir among the riders in front of them. The ladies looked far from pleased about something, and the gentlemen were equally far from being displeased. Then she saw the cause of it, a dainty red-haired figure in cherry, mounted on a spirited chestnut. Isabel's lips became set in a sour line, for the last thing she wanted was a rival in the beauty stakes, and this stranger was definitely as head-turning as she.

Diana rode toward them without realizing, but then something made her look directly at Richard, and with a gasp, she reined in. Her face became suddenly pale as she gazed at him. Her gloved hands tightened on the reins, and for a moment it seemed she would speak to him, but then her glance flickered toward Isabel, whose cold gaze was very pronounced. Diana kicked her heel, and urged her mount on past them, swiftly vanishing among the riders behind.

Isabel had reined in as well, and turned in the saddle to gaze after her. Then she looked sharply at Richard, whose discomfort was only too plain. "Who was she?" she demanded.

"Er, I believe her name is Beaumont, Mrs. Beaumont," he said lamely.

"I've never seen her before, and I don't believe I know the name. Do you know her well?"

"Hardly at all."

"Then don't you think her reaction to you was somewhat strange?" Suspicion burgeoned in Isabel's heart, for his responses were hardly reassuring. She wondered again about his remarkable attentiveness this morning. Was there something going on?

"I really have no idea why she behaved as she did," he said, meeting her eyes. "As I said, the woman is hardly known to me."

"I thought her rather vulgar, didn't you? So much red is hardly tasteful."

He didn't reply, for in truth he'd thought Diana looked magnificent, so magnificent that she'd stopped his breath with admiration. Oh, damn Diana, how he wished she'd stayed out of his life!

His silence displeased Isabel still more, and she too fell into a heavy silence as they rode on. A moment later they were joined by the familiar figure of Laroche, who presented a dashing sight on his highly bred bay Arabian horse, his greyhounds padding faithfully at the horse's heels. He wore a corbeau-colored riding coat and beige breeches, and he gave them both a lazily good-natured grin.

"*Eh, bien, mes enfants,* did you see the fair incognita on the chestnut? I vow several gentlemen turned their heads so sharply they almost severed them on their stocks!"

It wasn't a remark calculated to please Isabel, who gave him a stormy look. "Are you referring to the loud creature in scarlet? Richard knows her, he says her name is Mrs. Beaumont. Perhaps he also knows if she is indeed as brash as she looks. Is she, Richard?" There was a challenging note in her voice, and her dark eyes were accusing.

Richard's lips pressed angrily together for a moment. "Isabel, I told you, I hardly know her. As to her character, I promise you that it is of no interest to me."

Isabel searched his face, and evidently found something there she did not trust. "You're a liar, Richard Curzon!" she declared suddenly, in a tone loud enough to carry to several riders nearby. "That odious creature is known to you far more than you're saying!" Kicking her heels, she urged her startled mount away from them.

Richard made no move to follow her, and Laroche looked at him in surprise. "Hadn't you better make your peace with her, dear boy?"

"I don't think that at this precise moment she's open to reason, do you?"

Laroche pursed his lips, and then shrugged. "Richard, she's the loveliest woman in London, and you've snapped her up. You can't afford to rest on your laurels, not when the *monde*'s wolves are always prowling about."

"Isabel can be very unreasonable."

"But, in this particular instance, I wonder if her suspicions aren't just a little justified?" Laroche gave him a sly look. "How well *do* you know that proud Titania, eh?"

"There's nothing between Mrs. Beaumont and me, Laroche, and I'd thank you not to hint to the contrary!" replied Richard sharply.

"Alright, alright, don't bite my head off, I believe you!" protested Laroche, pretending to put up his hands in self-defense. "But if you love Isabel and wish to keep her, then I suggest you pay more attention to her wishes."

"Her wishes?"

"In matters such as that brooch she covets."

"So she's told you about that, has she?"

"She confides a great deal in me."

"Then let me explain that the brooch in Cranford's doesn't stand up to a close inspection, indeed it is somewhat inferior, which is why it still reposes in their window, and why I've taken the step of ordering an alternative which I intend to take delivery of this afternoon. I'll give it to her at the masquerade tonight, and when she sees it, I rather think she'll forget about the tawdry bauble she's convinced herself is essential to her happiness. I'm not an uncaring monster, Laroche, indeed I'm far from it."

Laroche looked at him for a long moment. "Do you love her, Richard?" he asked quietly.

Richard hesitated, and then lowered his eyes, for when he tried to picture Isabel's face, all he saw was Diana.

The silence was eloquent, and Laroche shifted uncomfortably in his saddle. "I, er, think I'd better be toddling along," he said, gathering his reins.

"No doubt I'll see you tonight at the masquerade."

"Er, no, I fear not. I have other plans."

Richard looked at him in surprise. "But I thought your wife was looking forward to it."

"She is, and as far as I'm concerned she can go, but I have something else to attend to." Laroche touched his top hat, and then urged his Arabian horse away. Followed by his greyhounds, he disappeared in the crush of riders.

Richard remained where he was, the only motionless figure in a moving sea of equestrians. Faced with the direct question about whether or not he loved Isabel, he hadn't been able to answer.

This morning he'd striven to placate her, but the moment Diana appeared . . . His thoughts trailed away in confusion. What in God's name *did* he feel?

Isabel rode furiously back to Hanover Square, thrusting the reins of her sweating horse into the hands of the groom who waited in front of the house, and then hurrying into the rather austere white marble entrance hall, where tall Doric columns rose toward a lofty ceiling. Following Lady Finch's lead, Isabel's aunt, Mrs. Graham, had had German fir trees placed on either side of the fireplace, their tiers of colored wax candles shining softly in the gloomy light cast down from the window above the main doorway. The Doric columns were festooned with seasonal branches, and an enormous bunch of mistletoe was suspended low from the ceiling, turning slowly in the draft caused by her entry.

There was a beautiful inlaid table standing in the center of the red-and-cream-tiled floor, and on it there was a large bowl of red-berried holly, and a silver dish for visiting cards. There was also a brown paper package, and Isabel was drawn to it like a pin to a magnet.

Putting her gloves on the table, she picked up the parcel, swiftly opening it as she saw that it was addressed to her. Oh, how she loved opening packages! Her breath caught with delight as she saw the fan inside, and she ran her fingertips over the soft white plumage and dainty tartan bows. It was the most perfect thing imaginable! Her glance fell on the sealed note that had fallen out on to the table, and her eyes softened a little as she recognized Richard's writing. Maybe he had some redeeming qualities after all . . .

Breaking the seal, she began to read the message inside. *My darling Diana, Words cannot say how*

*overjoyed I am that you are part of my life again,
nor can they convey the yearning I feel for the
moment I've set you up in a house where I may
visit you whenever I wish. My marriage will make
no difference to my love for you. You are my heart,
my mistress, and my life, and if you were free I'd
make you mine forever. I adore thee. Richard.*

Thunderstruck, Isabel stared at the note. His
darling Diana? A house? His mistress? The note
dropped to the table and she clutched the exquisite
fan to her breast, trying to gather her scattered
composure. So he *was* up to something behind her
back! Oh, the monster! He had a mistress and had
been found out because he'd made the foolish mistake of sending the wrong note to Hanover Square!

Fury seized her, and she flung the fan across the
floor where it came to rest at the foot of one of the
German fir trees. Her eyes flashed and her lips were
a thin line of rage. How dared he! How *dared* he!

Unbidden, a vision of the creature in the cherry
wool riding habit entered her head. Was that brazen Mrs. Beaumont his precious inamorata? If she
was it would certainly explain the odd way both
she and Richard had reacted on seeing each other.
Isabel hurried to retrieve the fan, examining the
handle as she searched for the maker's mark. She
soon found the name of Messrs Duvall & Carrier. If
she guessed correctly, then there had been a second fan, one intended for the unknown Diana, only
it contained the message intended for Hanover
Square! A visit to Piccadilly was most definitely
necessary in order to establish all the facts, before
Sir Richard Curzon could be faced with his vile in-
fidelity and deceit!

She called for a footman, and one emerged hastily
from the shadows, quailing a little at the blazing
fury in her eyes. "Yes, Miss Hamilton?"

"Have another horse saddled for me without delay!"

"Yes, Miss Hamilton." Turning, he almost ran from her presence.

She pulled on her gloves, flexing her fingers like the claws of a cat. So, Richard was making a fool of her, was he? He was keeping a mistress *and* paying court to the belle of London society! Well, he was about to find out that Miss Isabel Hamilton couldn't be treated like that. If anyone was going to be made a fool of, it was Richard himself!

With sudden decision she hurried through into the library, where she sat at the writing desk and dipped a quill in the ink. She wrote a very hasty note, and immediately sanded and sealed it, then she wrote a gentleman's name on it. She'd been hesitating about taking such a shocking course as the one she now intended, but Richard's duplicity had made her mind up for her. London was about to be scandalized, and Sir Richard Curzon would be left looking very foolish.

Reentering the hall, she found the footman waiting. "Have this delivered immediately," she said, giving him the note.

"Very well, Miss Hamilton. Your horse has been brought around to the front."

She nodded, but hesitated before going out. "See that the note is given to the gentleman himself, for it's important that it doesn't fall into the wrong hands."

"Very well, Miss Hamilton." The footman was the soul of discretion, giving no hint at all of his intense curiosity as to why she should be sending messages to such a gentleman.

A moment later she left the house again to ride to Piccadilly, and the premises of Messrs Duvall & Carrier.

No sooner had the sound of Isabel's horse died away in Hanover Square, than Diana returned to the riding stables in the mews behind Pargeter

Street. She walked back to the house through the garden at the rear, where a stone nymph stood in frozen nakedness in the center of an ice-covered pool. The trees were heavily laden with snow, and a robin redbreast sang his heart out from the wall, his bright eyes watching her as she made her way toward the house.

She was still thinking about the encounter in the park. The lady in lime-green must be the Miss Hamilton Richard was to marry. She was very beautiful indeed, and unnecessarily jealous and suspicious, for Richard hadn't been even remotely warm toward his former love, in fact he'd looked right through her. Diana sighed, recalling the chill in his gaze. If it hadn't been for that invisible barrier he'd placed so firmly between them, she'd have spoken to him, for what point was there in prolonging the bitterness of the past? But he'd given her no encouragement at all, and so she'd ridden on. But, oh, how she wished it could be different.

Entering the house, she found Mary waiting for her in the drawing room. "What is it, Mary?" she asked quickly, sensing that something had happened.

Mary went to a table and picked up a small brown paper package. "This was delivered a short while ago. It's addressed to you."

"To me?" Diana put her riding crop down, and began to tease off her gloves. "But who would send anything to me?"

"I don't know, Miss Diana," replied Mary unhappily, for every instinct told her that the package meant trouble.

Diana took the package and opened it, pausing in astonishment as she saw the exquisite gray silk fan inside. "Why, it's beautiful," she breathed, then she glanced down to the floor as the sealed note fell. Her face became still as she recognized Richard's writing.

Mary recognized the writing as well, for in the past she'd seen many letters written to her mistress by Sir Richard Curzon. Bending, she retrieved it. "It's from . . ."

"I know who it's from, Mary," replied Diana quietly, putting the fan and the brown paper wrapping on the table.

"But . . ."

"Mary, I've just encountered him in the park, and he looked through me so coldly that I could have turned to ice. Whatever this fan is, it isn't sent kindly, of that I can be sure."

"Perhaps you're wrong. Shouldn't you at least read the note?"

"I'm not wrong, but I'll read it," replied Diana, taking the note and breaking the seal. She read it aloud. *My beloved. Let this Christmas be the signal for a new future together. Let us forget the misunderstandings of the past and accept our undying love for each other. I will adore you throughout eternity. Richard.*

She dropped the note on to the fan, and began to wrap the package up again. "That Richard Curzon was resentful I've always known, but I didn't think he was also unspeakably petty and spiteful."

"Oh, Miss Diana . . ."

"I want this sent back to him at his Park Lane residence, with the message that I wish him to refrain from communicating with me again."

"Yes, Miss Diana."

Turning, Diana left the room, but as she hurried up the grand staircase there were tears in her eyes.

The church bells were sounding midday as Isabel reined her horse in by the doors of Messrs Duvall & Carrier. Giving the reins and a coin to a man selling mistletoe, she entered the dark confines of the exclusive establishment, and a superior young man came to assist her. He was dressed in a charcoal coat and starched blue-and-white-spotted silk neckcloth, and he placed his fingertips very precisely on the dark oak counter. He stood directly beneath a very pretty Christmas kissing bunch, and was so filled with a sense of his own importance that he made Isabel more furious than ever.

"May I be of assistance, madam?" he enquired.

"Possibly," she replied icily. "I have been sent a fan that was purchased at this establishment, but I believe there must have been a mistake made with the order, and that I've been sent the wrong fan."

"Mistake, madam?" He evinced amazement that anyone could believe such hallowed premises capable of perpetrating an error of any kind.

"Yes, sir, a mistake, sir," she said coldly. "The fan was purchased by Sir Richard Curzon."

"Ah, yes, I recall the order, indeed I handled it myself. Sir Richard sent his man to act on his behalf."

"And there were two fans concerned in the order?" She asked the question lightly, as if she already knew all about it and was just confirming the facts.

"Yes, madam, there were indeed two fans."

"As I thought, and you, sir, have sent the wrong one to me."

"Oh, that cannot possibly be so," he replied vainly, "for the letter of authority was quite specific."

"May I see it?"

He stared at her. "*See* the letter? Oh, I'm afraid that would be a little irregular."

"Then be irregular, sir, or else I shall make such a noise that you will very swiftly regret your obstinacy!"

He blinked, and then decided that discretion was the better part of valor, for she did indeed look as if she was capable of making a fuss to end all fusses. "Very well, madam, I'll go and get it now."

Turning, he went through a door at the rear of the shop, reemerging a moment later with the letter in his hand. As he held it out to her, she almost snatched it from him. Richard's telltale writing leapt out at her, as did the name of the recipient of the second fan: Mrs. Diana Beaumont. So, the creature in the park and his beloved Diana seemed to be one and the same, indeed the coincidence was too great for it to be otherwise. No wonder Richard had affected such vagueness in Rotten Row when they'd come face to face with his doxy! He must have thought himself undone! Well, he hadn't been undone then, but he most certainly was now!

Thrusting the letter back into the assistant's hand, she turned on her heel and marched out again, slamming the door so fiercely behind her that the little kissing bunch began to revolve on its scarlet ribbons. The mistletoe-seller saw the glint in her eyes and hastily held out the reins of her horse before retreating to what he felt was a safe distance. It was a wise move, for she mounted very swiftly, turning the horse actually on the pavement itself, much to the alarm of the unfortunate pedestrians nearby. Employing her riding crop on the horse's flank, she urged it away toward Park Lane, riding like a demon through the heavy Christmas traffic.

Piccadilly paused in amazement to watch the progress of the fury in the lime-green riding habit. She rode without any thought for others, weaving her nervous horse between the crowded vehicles and managing to knock a hamper and a brace of Christmas pheasants from the back of a stagecoach. She stopped some carolsingers in mid-song by cutting the corner into Park Lane and thus riding straight through them, and she was very nearly the cause of a spillage of yule logs all over the London street when she forced a heavily laden cart to swerve in order to get out of her way.

She reined in outside Richard's elegant town house, only just managing to control her lathered horse, which was now thoroughly upset. Dismounting, she dropped the reins and gathered her skirts to advance furiously on the front door.

Her angry knocking brought the butler as quickly as his legs could carry him, and he stood aside in astonishment as she strode in.

"M-Miss Hamilton . . . ?"

"Have someone attend to my horse," she answered shortly, glancing around the entrance hall with its Chinese paintings and lotus blossom chandeliers. "Where is Sir Richard?"

"In the conservatory, madam. Shall I announce . . . ?"

"That won't be necessary," she replied, marching away determinedly toward the rear of the house.

The butler gazed uneasily after her, for her mood didn't bode at all well for his master.

The conservatory was a lofty, spacious place, its many glass panes facing over the snowy gardens. Tropical leaves pressed all around, and the air was warm, fragrant, and damp. Richard was lounging on one of the white-painted wrought iron chairs set by a matching table. A decanter of cognac stood on the table, and he was sipping a glass as he glanced through a newspaper. Hearing her angry steps approaching, he put the glass and the newspaper down quickly, and rose to his feet.

"Isabel?"

"Good afternoon, sir."

A light passed through his eyes at her cold, angry tone. "Is something wrong?" he asked.

"Wrong, sir? Oh, yes, something is indeed wrong. You've been found out!"

"Found out? I don't understand . . ."

"I know all about your *belle de nuit!*"

He looked blankly at her. "I'm afraid I don't understand. What *belle de nuit?*"

"Your precious Mrs. Beaumont!" she snapped.

His eyes cleared. So that was it, somehow she'd found out about Diana's part in his past. "Isabel, I can explain all about Diana . . ."

She flashed him a look so bright and furious that it was as if her eyes were on fire. "So, you admit it! You *admit* she is more to you than a person with whom you are vaguely acquainted."

"Yes, I admit that much, but I assure you she . . ."

"Don't attempt to lie to me, sir, for it won't wash. You've been found out, and you have only yourself to blame. How foolish and careless of you to address the wrong note to me!"

He stared at her. "Isabel, what on earth are you talking about? What note?"

"I'm not a fool, sir, so don't treat me like one! You know perfectly well what note, for it can only be the one you penned to your vulgar little inamorata, but which you managed to send to me instead! How dare you deceive me, how *dare* you keep a mistress!"

His face became very still. "Isabel, I swear to you that I have no idea what you're talking about. I haven't written any notes, not to you or to anyone else!"

"And I suppose you didn't send your man to Duvall & Carrier's to purchase the two fans you'd picked out?" she replied frostily.

"No, damn it, I most certainly did not!" he snapped.

"Then the letter of authority in your handwriting just conjured itself out of nothing? As did the note for your precious Diana? No doubt she is at this very moment gazing upon the *billet doux* meant for me!"

For a long moment he was silent, then he spoke in a quietly incensed voice. "Are you telling me that someone has purchased two fans in my name, and had one sent to you and the other to Diana Beaumont?"

"Does it amuse you to ask something you know only too well, sir? Of *course* that's what I'm telling you! How long did you imagine you'd get away with it? Obviously you meant to continue keeping her after our marriage. . . ."

"Isabel, I am not keeping her, and I never have!"

"Monster! How can you face me and utter such manifest untruths!" she cried. "In the park earlier you said that she was hardly known to you, and yet now it's rather clear that that was a bare-faced lie. How long have you known her?"

"Over five years."

Isabel stared at him. "Are you telling me you've been keeping her all that time?"

"No, I'm just telling you how long I've known her. She was Diana Laverick then, and if I could have married her, I would, but she chose a wealthier husband and went with him to live in Jamaica. She returned to England yesterday, and that is the extent of my recent knowledge of her. She is not my mistress, I'd swear that on the Bible itself! Someone is up to something, Isabel, for I did not write any letter or any notes. I did not order any fans, and I did not send my man to Duvall & Carrier's."

"The note I received and the letter are both in your handwriting, sirrah."

"Then someone has forged my writing!" he replied shortly. "Damn it, Isabel, do you really imagine I'd conduct myself in such a way as to keep a mistress when I am betrothed to you? Do you honestly believe that I'd be so low and deceitful as to see someone else behind your back?"

She lowered her eyes. "Such things have been known, sir," she replied softly.

"You should trust me more, madam."

"Should I? Why, when you've lied already where that brazen doxy is concerned?"

"Isabel, Diana Beaumont is neither brazen nor a doxy, she is a respectably married woman who has done nothing to warrant being involved in this . . . this whatever it is. Someone has seen fit to meddle in our affairs, and I intend to find out who." He held her gaze. "Do you trust me, Isabel?" he asked softly.

She met his eyes, still remembering the encounter in the park. "No," she replied. "No, I don't trust you, sir."

"Then I think our betrothal must be at an end, don't you?" he said coldly.

"As you wish, sirrah," she replied, her chin raised proudly. For a moment she considered making the grand gesture of tossing his ring at him, but then she thought better of it, for the ring was very valuable, and she liked it a great deal. Conflicting emotions crossed her lovely face, but then she turned on her heel and left him. So, he thought to end the betrothal, did he? Well, she didn't intend to tell the world about it, she just intended to teach him the lesson of his life, and making him the laughing stock of society in the process! The shoe was about to be on the other foot, oh, *how* it was to be on the other foot!

As she flung from the conservatory, Richard turned to gaze angrily out at the snow-covered gardens. What was going on? Who was scheming against him like this? An obvious name came to mind, Geoffrey Hawksworth, but how would Geoffrey know about Diana? Then he remembered, in the days before Isabel, when he'd been intimate enough with Geoffrey to confide in him. Yes, Geoffrey knew all about Diana, and, coincidentally,

Geoffrey also happened to covet Isabel. If that same Geoffrey had somehow learned of Diana's return to England . . . Richard took a long breath. He'd lay odds that Geoffrey Hawksworth was behind all this, and the best way to start making enquiries was to adjourn to Messrs Duvall & Carrier to see what was what.

First things first, however, for there was the matter of setting Diana straight concerning the fan *she* had apparently received in his name. The lord alone knew what message had accompanied it, but . . .

"Sir Richard?"

He turned to see the butler standing there with a crumpled brown paper package in his hand. "Yes? What is it?"

"This has just been delivered from Mrs. Beaumont of Pargeter Street, sir."

Richard lowered his gaze to the package. "Indeed?" he murmured, going to take it. As he opened it, he saw the exquisite gray silk fan inside, and the note that purported to come from him. Oh, it was a clever forgery, that was for sure. No wonder Isabel believed it to have come from him. He read the brief but loving message. *My beloved. Let this Christmas be the signal for a new future together. Let us forget the misunderstandings of the past and accept our undying love for each other. I will adore you throughout eternity. Richard.*

He closed his eyes for a moment. Diana had received *this?*

The butler cleared his throat. "Sir, I fear there was an, er, communication from the lady."

"Communication?"

"The fellow who brought it said that he was instructed to say that Mrs. Beaumont does not wish to receive any further gifts, and that she wishes to be left alone." The man looked hugely embarrassed at having to repeat such a message.

Richard tossed the package and the note down on the table. "Have my horse saddled."

"Very well, sir."

"I won't be out for long, but if I'm needed urgently you'll find me either at Duvall & Carrier's in Piccadilly, or at 44 Pargeter Street."

"Yes, sir." The butler withdrew.

Richard stood looking down at the package. If Geoffrey Hawksworth was responsible for this, he'd pay dearly for such unwarranted meddling! Picking up his glass, Richard drained it of the cognac he'd been drinking before Isabel's arrival, but as he put it down on the table again, the incredulous realization flooded over him that his betrothal was at an end. He'd severed the engagement to the woman he'd pursued for so long, and he felt nothing, nothing at all.

Diana was at that moment leaving the house in Pargeter Street to enter the hired chaise that was to convey her, with Mary, to the lawyer's chambers in Lincoln's Inn. She wore a peach woolen mantle richly embellished with beaded black embroidery, and a wide-brimmed peach hat adorned with small black plumes. The distress caused by the arrival of the fan and its accompanying note had subsided a little now, and she was quite composed as the chaise drew away to set off east toward the city. Opposite her, Mary sat quietly in her corner seat thinking about Sir Richard Curzon. He'd taken refuge in his hurt pride five years before when he'd ignored Diana's long, tear-stained letter, and now he was exacting spiteful revenge. In the past Mary had believed him to be all that was right for her mistress, but she'd been forced to make a reappraisal of his character. That second opinion of him was now proving to be only too correct, for he was a mean-hearted, shabby toad to do such a monstrous thing to someone as sweet as Miss Diana.

The chaise drove swiftly eastward through the Christmas traffic, through streets that tingled with seasonal excitement and anticipation, but Diana kept her eyes downcast. She knew only too well what the lawyer was going to tell her, but she couldn't help, deep in her heart of hearts, hoping that there would be a little good news as well.

In Piccadilly, which was soon far behind the chaise, Richard reined his horse in outside Duvall & Carrier's, and, as chance would have it, tossed a coin to the same mistletoe-seller to look after the animal while he made enquiries inside. The very same assistant came to wait upon him, and evinced an ill-placed air of bewildered irritability on being asked yet again about the order for the fans.

"Sir, I am not at liberty to . . . !"

His words were choked in mid-sentence as Richard leaned across the counter to seize him by his immaculate blue-and-white-spotted neckcloth. "Now listen to me, my fine fellow," breathed Richard through clenched teeth, "someone has been playing fast and loose with my name, and I intend to get to the bottom of it. Either show me the letter I am supposed to have written, or I will suspend you from the ceiling alongside that damned kissing bunch! Do I make myself crystal clear?"

"Yes, sir!" squeaked the assistant, closing his eyes with relief as Richard relaxed his grip.

A moment later the letter had again been produced, and a nerve flickered angrily at Richard's temple as he read it. Geoffrey Hawksworth's name still came to mind, for somehow it had that sly gentleman's disagreeable mark all over it. He looked at the red-faced assistant, who was rubbing his throat as if he'd been half-strangled. "I understand my man is supposed to have brought this?"

"Yes, Sir Richard."

"Describe him to me."

"Well, sir, he was small and wiry, like a groom or a jockey, and . . ."

Hawksworth's valet to a tee! Without another word, Richard turned on his heel and strode out again, leaving the assistant to stare thankfully after him. The kissing bunch swayed a little in the draft from the doorway, and the man's eyes moved nervously toward it. There had been something in Sir Richard's tone that had suggested most strongly that the threat hadn't been uttered idly.

Richard rode to Geoffrey's residence in North Street, but was told that he wasn't at home. He was also told that Geoffrey's valet wasn't in the house, although if the truth were known that nervous fellow was at that very moment peeping down through the marble bannisters from the floor above, from whence he'd been about to descend with some of his master's clothes. Hearing Sir Richard Curzon's name announced, and detecting the anger in his voice, the valet had stayed wisely well out of sight. It was obvious that Sir Richard had put two and two together, and had come up with the correct answer, which meant that it had all suddenly become a little hazardous for the likes of the Honorable Geoffrey Hawksworth's unfortunate man.

Thanking his stars that the footman who'd answered the door really did believe him to be out of the house, the valet emerged from hiding as Richard rode away again. A gentleman in such a justifiable fury was to be avoided at all costs, so maybe now was the perfect moment to pay a visit to the family in Newmarket. The valet drew a long breath. Yes, London was a dangerous place now, and Newmarket a haven of peace and tranquility! He'd leave as soon as he possibly could.

At Pargeter Street, Richard's next destination, he was told that Diana was keeping an appointment with her lawyer in Lincoln's Inn and wouldn't be back for at least another hour, so he returned to Park Lane. As he entered his house, Geoffrey Hawksworth's carriage was at that very moment turning from Brook Street into Hanover Square, having at last returned from the lengthy and unwanted visit to Hampstead. His great-aunt hadn't been content with merely insisting upon being driven home, she'd made it plain that she'd be very displeased indeed if he didn't stay for a while. He'd therefore had to kick his heels drinking tea and nibbling wretched wafers until at last she'd relented and allowed him to leave. The Devil take the old tabby, for if ever there'd been a day when he'd wished her on another planet, this was that day!

But at least he'd now managed to complete the preparations for his stratagem, having stopped at Cranford's in Bond Street to attend to the business of the sunburst brooch. There hadn't been time to return to North Street for his valet, so he'd had to do it himself. He'd astonished his coachman by demanding the use of his box coat and wide-brimmed hat, but it was a necessary precaution in a shop where he'd recently made two purchases, and might be recognized. Disguising his voice, he'd pretended to be Richard's man, and had handed over a second letter of authority, together with a purse and another sealed note. The shop had readily agreed to despatch the brooch to the lady concerned, and now he was at liberty to proceed with the rest of his plan.

The afternoon light was just beginning to fade as the carriage turned the corner out of Brook Street. Geoffrey glanced out and was just in time to see a face he knew riding past on a gleaming Arabian horse. Swiftly lowering the glass, he leaned out.

"Laroche! I say, Laroche!"

The carriage halted, and Laroche turned in the

saddle, reining in as he recognized Geoffrey. He glanced back across Hanover Square, but then rode toward the carriage, followed by his greyhounds. "Good afternoon, Geoffrey."

"About last night at the ball . . ."

"Ah, yes, and the fact that you lied to me about my wife."

Geoffrey gave him an apologetic grin. "It was all I could think of to get you away from Isabel."

"And it worked handsomely."

"Forgive me. I promise not to resort to such trickery again tonight."

"Tonight?"

"The Holland House masquerade."

Laroche gave a slight smile. "Resort to whatever you wish tonight, dear boy, it's immaterial to me."

"Immaterial?"

"Because I will not be there. And now, if you have nothing further to say, I fear I have to be on my way. I've got a great deal to do before tonight."

"Oh, very well, if that's the way of it," replied Geoffrey. "Perhaps I'd better take this opportunity to wish you a very happy Christmas."

Laroche laughed. "My dear Geoffrey, I intend this to be the happiest Christmas of my life. Goodbye." Touching his top hat, he rode on into Brook Street, his greyhounds still padding at his horse's heels.

Shrugging at the fellow's somewhat odd manner, Geoffrey sat back again, and the carriage drove around Hanover Square, coming to a halt at the curb outside the Graham residence.

Geoffrey paused for a moment before alighting. Isabel must by now have received the fan and read the note, which meant that she'd have leapt to the conclusion that Richard was keeping Diana Beaumont as his secret mistress. What developments had there been? If it hadn't been for his old biddy of a great-aunt he'd have been here much sooner than this, and would have been able to manipulate things with a few well-chosen words here and there, but as it was he knew nothing about what may or may not have been going on, and he'd have to play it by ear.

Taking a deep breath, he climbed down from the carriage, looking up at the house. As the shadows lengthened, so the lights were being lit inside, and already the houses in the gracious square were bright for Christmas Eve. A girl was selling little kissing bunches on the pavement nearby, and her sweet, clear voice rang out. *Kissing bunches, kissing bunches for your sweetheart.*

Geoffrey smiled to himself, for if things went as he'd planned, he and Isabel would have no need of a kissing bunch to encourage them this Christmas . . .

He rapped his cane on the gleaming door, and the butler opened it almost immediately. "Ah, your grace, I was about to send your . . ." The man's face changed as he recognized Geoffrey. "Oh, forgive me, sir, I thought you were the Duke of Laroche returned for his riding crop."

Laroche had been here? Geoffrey was about to speak when Isabel herself appeared at the top of the grand staircase, looking delightful in a pink sprigged muslin gown that had a lavishly stiffened hem. A black-and-gold cashmere shawl trailed behind her as she hurried down the staircase, and there was a vivacious smile on her lips. She hesitated then, seeing Geoffrey.

"Oh, it's you," she said, her smile becoming a little fixed.

"Yes, it's me." He hardly noticed her lack of enthusiasm on seeing him, he was too surprised by her manner immediately prior to that. She'd looked positively blooming, and there was certainly no sign of the distress he'd expected. Had Duvall & Carrier failed to deliver the fan? It had to be something like that, for what else would explain her light-hearted manner? If she'd read his carefully worded note, she'd by now believe that Richard was Diana Beaumont's protector, and the last thing she'd be was light-hearted!

Geoffrey's mind raced in those few seconds, and he decided that there was nothing for it but to put the second part of his plan into action. He smiled at her. "I've come to take you to buy your Christmas gift."

"Christmas gift?" She returned the smile. "Why, Geoffrey, how sweet of you. What are you going to buy me?"

"That I will not say, but suffice it that it is something from Cranford's."

She clapped her hands in delight. "Oh, Geoffrey! You absolute darling! Are we going now?"

"I am at your disposal," he replied, sketching her a bow.

"I'll put some outdoor clothes on," she replied, gathering her skirts and hurrying back up the staircase, the shawl still dragging prettily behind her.

She returned a few minutes later wearing a gray three-quarter-length velvet pelisse over the pink muslin gown. A gray jockey bonnet rested on her shining dark curls, with a pink gauze scarf tied around the crown and hanging down to her hem at the back. Linking her little hand lightly through his proferred arm, she allowed him to lead her out into the increasingly dark late afternoon.

The streetseller's sweet cries rang out again. *Kissing bunches, kissing bunches for your sweetheart . . .*

In nearby Pargeter Street, Diana's hired chaise had just returned, and she and Mary had entered the drawing room. Diana teased off her gloves, and faced the maid.

"It was as bad as I always feared. Oh, why was I foolish enough to let myself hope . . . ?"

The butler came to the doors. "Begging your pardon, Mrs. Beaumont, but Sir Richard Curzon has called."

Without ceremony, Richard strode past him into the drawing room. "I wish to speak to you, madam," he said, tossing his hat, gloves, and cane on to a table.

Diana nodded at Mary. "That will be all for the moment, Mary."

"But, Miss Diana . . ."

"Please leave us."

Mary looked at her, and then gave Richard a cold glance, before going out. The butler closed the doors, and Diana was left alone with Richard. She turned away from him, for just being in the same room made her tremble. "We have nothing to say to each other, sir."

"On the contrary, madam, we have much to say, especially apropos the fan you are under the impression I sent to you."

"Under the impression? Sir, you *did* send it!" she cried, whirling to face him.

"No, madam, I did not," he replied shortly, but all the while he couldn't help thinking how exquisitely lovely she was.

"I recognized your writing, sir, and it may surprise you to know that I think you quite capable of malicious and spiteful acts."

"Malicious and spiteful? Is *that* how you see me?"

"How else? I wrote to you five years ago explaining my marriage to Robert, but you declined to acknowledge it in any way. I think you very shabby, sir, especially now that you've stooped to that cruel trick with the fan."

"I didn't receive any letter, madam, because you didn't send one. You tossed me aside be-

cause you found a better match, that's the beginning and end of the story." Bitterness rang
in his voice, and shone in his clear blue eyes as
he looked reproachfully at her.

Her green eyes were large and hurt. "You wrong
me, sir," she whispered, taking off her hat and
placing it gently on the table. Her hair, too heavy
for its pins, fell loose, tumbling down in a flame-
colored cascade. The fragrance of lily-of-the-valley
drifted sweetly over him, stirring the desire he'd
struggled so long to subdue. He still wanted her,
he still wanted her as much as ever . . .

She looked at him. "Please leave, Richard, for we
only hurt each other more all the time."

He turned to go, but before he knew it he'd
reached out to seize her, dragging her roughly into
his arms and kissing her on the lips. His fingers
curled in her hair, and he crushed her slender body
against his. Her perfume was all around him, al-
luring, beguiling, heartbreakingly poignant . . . He
bruised her lips with the force of his passion, but
nothing mattered except the sheer ecstasy of holding her again. She was the only woman he'd ever
wanted like this, the only woman who'd ever
pierced his heart and made him vulnerable. His
feelings for Isabel were as nothing compared to the
towering emotion Diana Beaumont could arouse in
him with just a glance.

She was struggling to escape, trying to beat her
fists against him, but he was too strong. Then sanity began to return. He was wrong to do this, wrong
to compel her by force . . . Abruptly he released
her, and she dealt him a stinging blow, leaving red
marks on his cheek. Her eyes were bright and full
of unspoken emotions. She didn't say anything,
but shook visibly as she again turned away from
him.

For a moment he could only stare at her, drinking in the way her hair fell in such heavy, curling

tresses, and the way her figure was outlined by the cut of her clothes. But he didn't say anything either, instead he snatched up his hat, gloves, and cane, and left the house.

In the drawing room, Diana hid her face in her hands, her lips still tingling from his kiss. Tears stung her eyes. "Oh, Richard," she whispered, "Richard I still love you so very much . . ."

Mary came in and found her. "Oh, Miss Diana . . ."

"I want to leave London as quickly as possible, Mary. Have the butler send out to see if a chaise can be hired."

"But it's Christmas Eve, Miss Diana, there won't be a chaise to be had anywhere. And with tomorrow being Christmas Day . . ."

"Just do it, Mary."

"Very well, Miss Diana." As Mary left the drawing room again, her thoughts of Sir Richard Curzon were very dark indeed. He had a great deal to answer for, a great deal.

The bell at Cranford's rang out prettily as Geoffrey ushered Isabel inside, and the proprietor himself came to assist them.

"May I be of service, sir, madam?" he enquired. He was a plump man with a balding head, and was much given to wearing bright blue clothes. Today he had on a sky-blue coat and matching cravat, with a frilled white shirt and indigo brocade waistcoat. He thought himself very much the thing, which indeed he was, being Mayfair's most exclusive and sought after jeweler.

Geoffrey leaned an elbow on the shining counter. "You have a brooch in the window, a sunburst made entirely of gold."

"Ah, you mean the one in the red leather box, sir?"

"Yes, that's the one."

"I fear it's already sold, sir. Sir Richard Curzon purchased it a short while ago, and it is just about to be delivered."

"Who to?" asked Isabel suddenly.

"Madam, I hardly think that that is information I am at liberty to divulge."

She glanced around, and her glance fell upon a silver-gilt bowl containing a bouquet of Christmas greenery, holly, mistletoe, ivy, and Christmas roses. Picking it up, she held it aloft, as if about to dash it to the stone-tiled floor. "Tell me, Mr. Cranford, or it will be the worst for your lovely bowl, which I'm surely will be greatly damaged if it accidentally falls."

The jeweler gaped at her, and then nodded quickly. "Very well, madam, I'll tell you. The brooch is to be delivered to Mrs. Beaumont at 44 Pargeter Street."

"Thank you," she replied, putting the bowl carefully back on the counter.

Geoffrey waited for the outburst of speechless fury, but it didn't come, instead Isabel was smiling at him. "What a shame about the brooch, Geoffrey, but I'm sure Mr. Cranford has more from which I can choose. Don't you, Mr. Cranford?"

"Oh, indeed so, madam," that gentleman replied with alacrity, producing a selection which he displayed swiftly before her.

Now it was Geoffrey who was speechless. She'd just learned that Richard had purchased for another woman the brooch *she* wanted, and yet she was dismissing it as being of no consequence! What was going on? It was inconceivable that Isabel should respond in such a fashion, and yet that was precisely what had happened.

A few minutes later they emerged from the shop, and Geoffrey's purse was measurably lighter as a consequence of purchasing a delightful little trinket studded with rubies. Isabel hadn't mentioned

Richard again, indeed it was as if he'd ceased to matter in any way. This impression was made more noticeable than ever when she smiled again on settling back in the carriage.

"Oh, Geoffrey, you're such a *darling* for giving me this little present. I must think of some way of rewarding you. I know, you shall escort me to the masquerade tonight!"

"Escort you to the masquerade? But what of Curzon?" He was utterly bewildered.

"Richard? Oh, I really have no idea." She pouted. "Don't you want to take me to Holland House tonight?"

"Yes, of course, it's just that . . ."

"Then it's settled, you will take me there. Come to the house at eight, yes, eight should about do it." She smiled again, fixing the brooch on to her pelisse.

Still utterly bewildered, Geoffrey said nothing more. He was completely at a loss to understand her, and totally at a loss for words.

Darkness had fallen, and the *beau monde* was preparing for the masquerade at Holland House. Fancy dress purchased specially for the Christmas Eve occasion was put out in readiness, and at Holland House itself Gunter's were attending to last minute details of the veritable banquet that was to be served to the hundreds of guests. The orchestra was tuning up, and the house was brilliantly illuminated, every single window boasting festive candles and festoons of yuletide leaves.

At 44 Pargeter Street, everything was quiet. Diana was in the drawing room endeavoring to read one of Sir Walter Scott's popular novels, and the only sound was the gentle fluttering of the fire in the hearth. She wore a dark green velvet gown, and gazed at the page without really seeing it, for all she could think about was Richard.

She heard someone knock at the front door, and then voices in the entrance hall. A moment later the butler brought her a small packet.

"This has just been delivered, madam," he said, giving it to her.

Her heart sank as she closed the book, for the arrival of this packet bore a marked similarity to the arrival of the fan a little earlier in the day. Reluctantly she opened the packet, and found the little red leather box inside. As she opened the box, she found herself gazing at a pretty sunburst brooch. There was, as she fully expected, another note in Richard's handwriting. *You're mine, my darling Diana, just as you always were and always will be. The future could be ours. Richard.*

Fresh tears stung her eyes, but she willed them back. She nodded at the butler. "Thank you, that will be all."

"Madam." He bowed and withdrew.

Diana put the brooch and its packing on the table next to her chair, and reopened the book. She wouldn't succumb to her tears again, she *wouldn't!* But the tears were stronger than she, welling hotly from her eyes and down her cheeks. She felt so unutterably wretched that she wished she were dead. She curled up in the chair, burying her face in the rich upholstery.

Mary came in shortly afterward, having learned of the brooch's delivery from the butler. Uneasy on her mistress's account, she'd hastened immediately to the drawing room, where her worst fears were realized as she found Diana weeping so heartbrokenly in the chair.

Diana was too distressed to even know the maid was there, and she knew nothing as Mary picked up the note that had come with the brooch, read it, and then replaced it. The maid's eyes were stormy as she withdrew from the room again. It was time that Sir Richard Curzon was set right on certain important points, and she, Mary Keating, was just the one to do it!

Five minutes later, clad in her plain but serviceable cloak, Mary left the house, stepping out into snowy darkness and making for Park Lane.

As Mary's angry, determined steps took her toward Richard's residence, Isabel was fully occupied in her apartment at the house in Hanover Square. The line of wardrobes in her dressing room were all open, and, together with her long-suffering maid, Isabel was surveying the array of garments inside.

"I'll take the salmon brocade, the white satin, and the plowman's gauze. No, not the plowman's gauze, I'm a little tired of it. I'll take the green organdy muslin instead."

"But, madam . . ."

"That takes care of the gowns," interrupted Isabel, not listening. "Now we come to the outer garments. I shall wear the black fur-lined cloak over my vermilion wool, but I shall also need the mantle, the pelisse, and probably the buttercup dimity paletot as well."

The maid was appalled. "But, madam, it's only a very small valise!"

"Not that small. Is it?" Isabel looked sharply at her. "Well? *Is* it that small?"

"Yes, madam, it is."

"Then we'll take a larger one."

The maid sighed inwardly. "Yes, madam."

"And of one thing we must be absolutely certain, we must not forget a single item of my jewelry."

"No, madam."

Isabel went through into her bedroom, and flung herself on her white silk bed, gazing up at the exquisitely draped canopy. Oh, what a cat was about to be set among the pigeons of Mayfair! And how very foolish Richard was going to look. It served

him right, for having the audacity to keep that
Beaumont demirep!

Mary was conducted to the conservatory, where
Richard received her. He was standing by the white
wrought iron table, and had been about to pour
himself another glass of cognac when his butler
had informed him that Mrs. Beaumont's maid was
insisting upon seeing him. One of the last people
on earth he wished to see was Mary Keating, who'd
have nothing pleasant to say to him, but he knew
he behaved more than badly when he'd called at
Pargeter Street earlier, and if Mary had come to
berate him, then it was no more than he war-
ranted.

He faced her, his blonde hair very golden in the
light from the solitary candelabrum standing on
the table. Leafy shadows pressed all around, and
outside the snowy garden looked almost gray-blue
in the night.

"You wished to speak to me, Mary?" he said.

Maid or not, in that moment she stood up to him
as his equal. "Yes, Sir Richard, I wish to speak to
you, and I trust you will hear me out to the end,
for it's important that you know the truth. You told
my mistress that you didn't receive her letter four
years ago . . ."

"I didn't."

"Then, since she will not tell you about it herself, it falls to me to do it for her. You didn't know
it, sir, but five years ago Miss Diana's father, Mr.
Laverick, was in very severe financial difficulties,
indeed he was an inch away from debtor's jail. His
debts had to be settled without delay, and they
were such that Miss Diana could not have turned
to you for help, for you were at that time your father's second son. Mr. Beaumont had been making
his interest known, and he somehow found out
about Mr. Laverick's debts. He offered to settle

them without delay, provided Miss Diana agreed to be his wife, and returned with him to his plantation in Jamaica. It broke her heart to agree to such a contract, Sir Richard, but she had to save her father. She wrote to you, because you'd come back here to London for a day or so, and it was a long, tear-stained letter that took a great deal of courage to send. She loved you with all her heart, she felt nothing for Mr. Beaumont, and yet she was prepared to spend the rest of her life as his wife." Mary held his gaze. "She wrote that letter, sir, and when she'd sealed it I took it to the letter carrier myself. I *know* it was sent."

"It didn't arrive."

"So you say, sir."

Anger stirred through him. "If I say it didn't arrive, then it didn't arrive!"

"You show wrath that someone should dare to cast doubt on your word, sir, and yet you think nothing of casting doubt on my mistress's word about that same letter."

He met her eyes, and then nodded. "The point is taken, Mary. Please proceed."

"You may think that Miss Diana has been enjoying a life of happiness and plenty since her marriage, Sir Richard, but that is not the case. Mr. Beaumont was a monster, he gambled heavily and drank still more heavily, and when he'd lost at the first and overindulged at the second, he was a very violent man. She endured it as best she could, for she'd meant her wedding vows, but he made it impossible. He was frittering away his fortune, and the plantation was in increasing difficulty. She had no one to turn to, no one to help her, and after one terrible night, when he'd drunk even more than usual, she knew that she couldn't go on anymore. She told him that she was leaving and coming home to England. In his fury he attacked her and tried to throw her down the stairs, but instead he lost his balance and fell down himself and was killed in an instant."

Richard stared at her. "Is all this true?" he breathed.

"Would I lie about such things, sir?"

"Tell me the rest."

"Well, as I said, on the night he died he'd been drinking far more than usual, and it turned out afterward that it was because he'd just gambled away his entire estate. Miss Diana was left with nothing at all, save her clothes, she had to sell what jewelry she had to settle bills he'd left outstanding. As soon as she could, she left Jamaica to come back here. She's going home to her parents in Cheshire, but first she had to come to London to see Mr. Beaumont's lawyer and finalize the remainder of his estate. She hoped there might be a small amount left at the end of it all, but there isn't. She's absolutely penniless, Sir Richard, but at least she's free of the man who made her so wretched for five long years. She vowed she wouldn't wear black for him, not even at his funeral, for he hadn't earned that tribute from one he'd used so shamelessly during their time together. Now she just wants to live her own life, Sir Richard, and she doesn't deserve to suffer all over again now, this time at your hands. You shouldn't keep sending her those gifts, sir, for such spite ill becomes you."

"Gifts? I only know of the fan I'm supposed to have sent."

"And the brooch, sir. It came tonight, and it upset her so much that that was when I decided to come to you."

"I didn't send the fan, and I didn't send the brooch, I swear that I didn't."

Mary searched his face, beginning to wonder if he was telling the truth after all.

"Mary, I'm innocent of all this, but I think I know who is behind it. There is someone who would move heaven and earth to win Miss Isabel Hamilton from me. He is also someone who happens to know of Diana's part in my past."

"Well, maybe this man is the guilty one, Sir Richard, I wouldn't know about that, but I do know that Miss Diana is already desperately unhappy, and is being made more unhappy."

He leaned his hands on the wrought iron table, his head bowed. "If only I'd known all this before, if only that damned letter hadn't gone astray . . ."

"Then you concede that there was a letter?"

He nodded. "I have no choice."

"Well, it's over and done with now, and you are about to marry Miss Hamilton . . ."

"No, Mary, I'm not marrying her. The betrothal was ended earlier today." He straightened, and looked at her. "There is only one woman who will ever really mean everything to me, and I looked into her eyes last night when I assisted her down from her chaise. I still love her, and I think I always will."

Mary stared at him. "Do you really mean that, sir?"

"With all my heart."

"Then tell her so yourself, I beg of you."

"Do you think she'll wish to hear?"

"I know she will." Mary smiled. "Come back with me now."

An unlit carriage waited in the mews lane behind Hanover Square. It was drawn up by the rear entrance of the Graham residence, and its blinds were lowered. The Christmas Eve night was bitterly cold, and there were clouds covering the stars. A few stray snowflakes fluttered silently down.

Suddenly the rear gate of the Graham house was quietly opened, and two women, a lady and her maid, emerged, the latter struggling with a heavy valise. The coachman clambered down to assist the

maid, and the lady hastened to the carriage door.
She wore a black fur-lined cloak over a vermilion
wool gown and matching pelisse, and there was a
stylish beaver hat on her short dark hair.

The carriage door opened, and the gentleman inside leaned out. "Isabel, my darling . . ." He
reached out to take her outstretched hand.

"Laroche," she whispered, allowing him to draw
her up into the vehicle, where she was soon en-
closed in his loving embrace.

"Oh, my darling," he breathed, his voice husky
with desire. "I thought you'd change your mind, I
thought Richard would win after all."

"Never, for my heart has always been yours,"
she murmured softly, her eyes dark.

"When I received your note today, I couldn't believe you'd decided to come away with me after
all."

"I'm not just another diversion, am I? Please tell
me that you love me."

"I love you," he replied immediately, just as he
had to other sweethearts since his marriage.

A moment later the carriage was driving away,
the maid seated up beside the coachman. Inside,
Isabel and Laroche were wrapped in each other's
arms, whispering sweet words. Isabel smiled to
herself in the darkness. Before the night was out
the whole of London would be talking about the
astonishing elopement of Miss Isabel Hamilton and
the married Duke of Laroche. She'd be notorious
for a while, but in the end she'd triumph, for Laroche had promised to divorce his wife and make
her his duchess. How important, wealthy and fine
a lady she'd be then, far more important and
wealthy than she'd have been as mere Lady Curzon. Her smile became sleek as she pondered Richard's reaction to the scandal. She'd turned the
tables on him, instead of he making a fool of her,

she'd made one of him! Oh, what a wonderful Christmas this was!

Diana was still curled up in the chair in the drawing room. Her tears had dried now, but her heart felt as if it had been shattered into a thousand unhappy fragments. She didn't hear the front door being opened, nor did she hear footsteps approaching the drawing room, she knew nothing until Mary spoke.

"Miss Diana?"

She looked up, her glance going immediately past the maid to where Richard stood. Slowly Diana rose to her feet. "Sir, I think we've said all there is to say."

Mary stood aside for him to enter, and then closed the doors upon them.

Richard halted a few feet away from Diana. "Mary has told me everything," he said quietly.

"She had no right." Diana turned away as hot color rushed into her cheeks.

"I wish you'd told me earlier, instead of letting me . . ."

"Would you have believed me? I think not, for you'd have preferred to continue thinking ill of me."

"Forgive me," he said softly, coming a little closer..

"Please go, sir, for I'm sure Miss Hamilton would not understand if she knew you were here."

"I'm no longer betrothed to her, Diana."

She turned. "Why?"

"We were ill-suited, and besides . . ."

"Yes?"

"Besides, I still love you."

She stared at him, her emerald eyes large and uncertain.

His heart tightened with love for her. "Diana, I

love you so much that I can't bear to think how you've suffered."

"Please don't toy with me, Richard, for I couldn't bear it."

"I'm not toying with you, I'm telling you the absolute truth. I love you, and I want you to be mine. I want the last four years to be wiped away, and for us to begin again."

Fresh tears shone in her eyes, and she took a hesitant step toward him. He needed no second bidding, but swept her into his arms, his lips seeking hers in a kiss so passionate and consuming that it was like a flame flaring through them both. Her perfume was all around, lily-of-the-valley, so delicate and exquisite that it seemed as if there was magic in the air. She was his again at last, returning his love just as he'd always dreamed.

Geoffrey's carriage drew up at the curb outside the Graham house in Hanover Square. He sat inside for a moment, adjusting his costume. He was dressed as Harlequin, and would have felt quite the thing had it not been for the unease caused by the discovery of Richard's angry visit to his residence. The fact that Richard had asked specifically if his valet was available was all the proof Geoffrey needed that Richard had discovered the truth, and as a consequence Geoffrey was very much in two minds about attending the Holland House masquerade. The thought of being confronted by a furious Richard was almost too alarming to contemplate, but now that Isabel was so nearly his, Geoffrey was very loath to forfeit the chance of escorting her. He was in a quandary, and so hesitated before alighting.

His glance fell on the wrist favor he'd purchased for her. It lay on the seat opposite, and was a delightful concoction of velvet mistletoe and holly, to be tied on with a dainty scarlet ribbon. It was such a pretty thing, and he'd been charmed with it the moment he saw it. He must take his courage in both hands, and risk the possibility of Richard's fury. Isabel was worth it all and more.

Taking a deep breath, he alighted, presenting a strangely lithe figure as he hurried up to the door of the house. Some carolsingers were on the corner, their lusty voices echoing around the elegant lamplit square, where a number of carriages were setting off for the masquerade. The singing was so very redolent of Christmas that Geoffrey turned for a moment to listen. *God rest ye merry, gentlemen, Let nothing you dismay . . .*

He rapped on the door, which in a moment was opened by a footman, but as Geoffrey made to step inside, the man shook his head. "I fear Miss Hamilton is no longer here, sir."

"Eh? What's that?" Geoffrey stared at him, for it was such an odd choice of words. No longer here? What was the fellow saying?

"She asked me to give you this note, sir," said the footman, holding out a sealed letter."

Puzzled, Geoffrey opened it and read. *Mr. Hawksworth. By the time you read this, I shall be long gone from London with the Duke of Laroche, whom I love with all my heart. He is to make me his duchess. Goodbye. Isabel Hamilton.*

Geoffrey stared at the letter, a thousand conflicting emotions tumbling through him. Isabel and *Laroche?* Numb, he looked at the footman, who was all civility.

"Will there be anything else, sir?"

"Er, no."

"Good night, sir, and the compliments of the season to you."

"Thank you. And to you." In a daze, Geoffrey turned away from the door. Isabel and *Laroche?* Oh, what a fool she'd made of him, and of Richard!

Richard. Suddenly Geoffrey thought again of the

awfulness of a confrontation with that gentleman. Perhaps now was the time to show discretion, rather than the proverbial valor. Yes, indeed, a Christmas visit to his family in Great Yarmouth would seem to be the wisest move under the circumstances.

Suddenly Geoffrey wished he hadn't been moved to meddle so. The old adage simply wasn't true, it *wasn't* all fair in love and war; it certainly wasn't fair to Geoffrey Hawksworth, that was for sure! With Isabel as his prize at the end of it, maybe it was worth the hazard, but now that she'd flitted off with that philanderer Laroche, it had all come to nothing!

The carolsingers were still in full voice on the corner as Geoffrey resumed his place in his carriage. As the vehicle drew away, his glance fell again on the pretty wrist favor. Mistletoe and holly? Mistletoe and *folly,* more like! He gave it a savage scowl, and then leaned his head back against the upholstery. Suddenly he wasn't enjoying Christmas at all, in fact it was the most disagreeable season of the entire year!

As the church bells struck midnight, and then began to peal out joyfully across London, Richard and Diana were locked in each other's arms in the house in Pargeter Street.

He drew back, putting his hand tenderly to her cheek. "It's Christmas Day," he whispered, "so will you make me the happiest man on earth by agreeing to be my wife?"

"Oh, Richard." Her eyes shone with joy.

"Will you?" he pressed.

"Yes, oh, yes."

"My darling . . ." He kissed her again, loving her so much that he felt weak. She was his forever now, and suddenly Christmas was a time of unbelievable happiness.

The Christmas Cuckoo

by

Mary Jo Putney

Jack Howard, late a major in the 51st Regiment, gave a depressed sigh as he folded his large frame into the chair nearest the fire. After 8 weeks of non-stop travel, he was rumpled, tired, and in dire need of a haircut and a shave. He had looked forward to reaching the Red Duck Inn so that he could eat, sleep the rest of the afternoon, eat again, then perhaps enjoy a spot of socializing in the taproom before retiring for the night. By morning he would have been sufficiently recovered from the rigors of travel to endure the ordeals ahead.

Instead, no sooner had Jack set foot from the stagecoach than he had been intercepted by a small gray clerk. The aptly named Mr. Weezle was secretary to the countess—everyone always called her "the countess," as if she were the only one in England—and he had been meeting the Portsmouth *Courier* every day for the last week. After the barest minimum of civil greetings, Mr. Weezle had swept Jack off to the coaching inn's private parlor, then pulled a paper from his pocket and begun reading through the items, ticking each off with a pencil. And the more the secretary talked, the more depressed Jack became.

Weezle punctuated his monologue by pulling a card case from his pocket and handing it to Jack. "The countess took the liberty of having new cards made for you."

"The countess has taken rather a lot of liber-
ties," Jack said dryly as he glanced at the top card
before slipping the flat gold case into the single
piece of baggage by his feet. At least the spelling
was correct. But then, it was hard to mistake a
name as common as John Howard.

Ignoring Jack's ungracious remark, Weezle adjusted the spectacles on his nose and consulted his
list again. "There are some people the countess
wishes you to call on before you leave London, but
of course you cannot do so until you are properly
attired. After we leave here, we will stop at Weston's. Though this is a busy time of year, Mr. Weston has promised to produce some decent clothing
for you overnight. Naturally, the garments won't
be done to his usual standards, but at least you
will be presentable. A more appropriate wardrobe
will be sent to Hazelwood within a week."

"Obliging of Mr. Weston," Jack said with a bale-
ful glance, "but I have no intention of visiting any
tailor this afternoon. When I do go to one, it will
probably be Scott."

"The countess would not like that," the secretary stated, as if that settled the matter. For him it
did. He frowned at his list. "Of course, you need a
valet, but it's impossible to hire decent servants at
this time of year. A pity you didn't reach London
last week, when you were supposed to. With
Christmas just three days away, there simply isn't
time to accomplish all that should be done before
going to Hazelwood. One of the countess's cousins
here in London has agreed to instruct you on how
to get on in society, but there will be time for only
a single lesson."

Among his friends Jack was famous for his im-
perturbable good nature, but Weezle's words trig-
gered a slow burn of anger. "No," he said flatly.
"My manners may be rough by her ladyship's
standards, but I'm too old to learn new ones."

Realizing that he had gone too far, Weezle peered
over his spectacles. "No one doubts that your manners are gentlemanlike," he said with a belated attempt at tact, "but since you've spent so many
years in the army, the countess thought that a bit
of polish would not go amiss. There will be a deal
of formal entertaining at Hazelwood."

Jack sighed, knowing that it was a waste of energy to be annoyed with the countess. She was his
great-aunt by marriage and he had known her
since he was in short coats; usually he had been
able to shrug off her domineering ways, so why
was he so irritated today? Perhaps because he'd
had no chance to eat since hastily swallowing a
slice of bread and a mouthful of ale at dawn. He
stood and walked across the room to ring for a servant so he could order food and drink.

The secretary's gaze fell on Jack's shabby top
boots and he pursed his lips disapprovingly.
"Those boots will have to go."

Jack stopped in his tracks, once again termi-
nally exasperated. "These are the most comfortable boots I have ever owned, and where they go,
I go."

Ignoring the remark, Weezle said, "Perhaps
Hoby can find time to fit you for new boots tomorrow morning."

"No."

Belatedly noticing Jack's dangerous tone, the
secretary said, "Would you prefer the afternoon?
Perhaps before visiting the countess's cousin."

"No, and no, and no again. I have no desire to
visit Hoby or Weston or any of the people on the
countess's list, nor to be drilled in etiquette like a
raw lad up from the country. All I want is a meal
and a hot bath and a decent night's sleep. Come
back tomorrow morning and we can talk about
your wretched list."

"Very well, if you insist," Weezle said stiffly.

"I've reserved rooms for you at the Clarendon. I'll summon the carriage to take us there."

"What is wrong with staying here?" Jack glanced around the inn's clean and thoroughly comfortable private parlor.

"This is hardly a suitable place for you."

Jack laughed, his good humor restored. "There have been nights when I've haggled with a cow for the right to share her straw, and been grateful to have that much."

Weezle's nose twitched like one of the lesser rodents'. "You must be most grateful to be returning to Hazelwood."

"Not particularly." His brief amusement fading, Jack said, "I'm not sure that I want to spend Christmas at Hazelwood."

Weezle looked shocked. "But the countess expects you."

"She may expect me," Jack said recklessly, "but she is not my commanding officer and has no power to order my presence."

"The countess said you might prove recalcitrant," the secretary said with ill-concealed irritation. "But where could you possibly spend the holiday except at Hazelwood?"

Until now Jack had intended to fall in with the countess's plans, but Weezle's remark was the last straw. "There is a whole world of possibilities out there"—he pulled his heavy greatcoat on, then stooped to pick up his bag—"and I'm going to discover what they are. Good-bye, Mr. Weezle. Tell the countess that I'll pay a call on her after the holidays."

Ignoring the secretary's outraged sputtering, Jack left the parlor and strode out into the courtyard. A fine, saturating rain was beginning to fall, and the bleak prospect made him hesitate while he considered what to do next. A pity he had no friends who would be in London this close to

Christmas. Winter gales had blown his packet from Lisbon several days off-course, the journey up to London had been made interminable by muddy roads, and Jack was heartily sick of traveling. All he wanted was to enjoy a little peace and warmth after too many years away from his homeland.

His brief burst of temper cooled and he was about to return to the inn to make his peace with Mr. Weezle. Then the secretary's sharp voice sounded from the doorway. "The countess will be *most* displeased if you don't come to Hazelwood."

Disapproval revived Jack's flagging resolve. He had no particular destination in mind, but he'd be damned if he would let himself be bullied by the countess and her minions. His gaze fell on a heavily loaded stagecoach that was preparing to leave, its team of Cleveland bays snorting restlessly. Impulsively he called to the guard, "Have you room for another passenger?"

The guard was busy stowing parcels in the front boot, but he paused to consult the waybill. "Aye, there's one outside place left." He shoved the waybill in his coat pocket and returned to his task. "But if you want it you'll have to move smartly, 'cause we're ready to roll."

As Jack turned toward the booking office, Mr. Weezle said, aghast, "You don't even know where that coach is going!"

"No, I don't," Jack said cheerfully. "But anywhere is bound to be better than the countess's demanding hospitality."

After hastily buying a ticket, Jack tossed his bag up to the guard, then began to ascend the ladder leading to the seats at the back of the carriage's roof. Even as he climbed, the vehicle lurched into motion, and Jack would have fallen if a helpful fellow passenger hadn't reached down to steady him. "Thanks," Jack gasped as he swung up to safety.

He turned and looked back, and the last thing he

saw as the coach left the yard was Mr. Weezle's slack-jawed face. The sight was almost worth the knowledge that Jack's grand gesture was going to cost him hours of cold, wet misery.

The seating consisted of two facing benches with room for three passengers in each. That is, there was room if one considered sixteen inches' width per passenger adequate, which it wasn't for most people, especially not men as large as Jack. As he squeezed into the middle place on the backward-facing seat, four of the other five passengers regarded him dourly, obviously regretting the amount of space the newcomer would occupy.

The fifth passenger, a rotund gentleman dressed as a farmer, was the one who had helped Jack up, and he offered the only friendly smile. "Going to be a cold ride to Bristol, brother."

"That it will," Jack agreed. So Bristol, where he didn't know a single soul, was his destination. He was going to spend hours in the freezing rain, squeezed as tight as a herring in a barrel, all for the dubious privilege of ending in another inn that would be no better than the Red Duck, and likely a good deal worse. Well, he thought philosophically, it wasn't the first time his stubborn streak had gotten him into trouble, and it certainly wouldn't be the last.

Silence reigned as the coach rumbled through the crowded city streets, swaying like a ship at sea. As they left London behind, Jack adjusted his hat in a vain attempt to keep rain from running down his neck. The raw cold bit to the bone. On the Continent, severe winters prevented coaches from having outside seats. Fortunate Britain, whose milder climate wouldn't kill outside passengers. At least, not quite.

An hour later Jack was thinking that he hadn't felt so cold since the retreat to Corunna when the rotund farmer reached inside his coat and pulled out a flat flask. "Me name's Jem," he said, addressing his words to all of his companions. "Anyone care to join me in some Christmas cheer?"

Four of the passengers fastidiously ignored the offer, but Jack said, "Don't mind if I do." He knew that drinking on an empty stomach was a mistake, but it was a little late in the day to start acting rationally. As he accepted the flask, he added, "My name is Jack."

Expecting brandy and water, Jack took a deep swig, then burst into strangled coughing as raw fire scalded his throat.

"Prime stuff, ain't it, Jack?" Jem said cheerfully.

"Quite unlike anything I've ever drunk before," Jack said with absolute truth. After a more cautious sip, he decided that the beverage was undiluted whiskey of a potency that should have dissolved the container. "Certainly takes the chill off," he remarked as he returned the flask.

Jem took a swig, then passed the whiskey back to Jack. "This is nothing compared to the winter of eighty-six. Why, I remember . . ."

Jack settled back contentedly. Cold and wet he might be, but Jem was certainly better company than Mr. Weezle.

The striking of the kitchen clock informed Meg Lambert that she couldn't delay any longer. She glanced at the kitchen window, where rain had drummed relentlessly since midafternoon. Ordinarily Meg did not mind bad weather, for the contrast made her appreciate the comfort of her farmhouse even more. Tonight, however, when sensible people were staying by their fires, she must go out into the storm.

She drained the last of her tea and set the cup down, then ordered, "Out of the way, Ginger." When the calico cat ignored her, Meg unceremoniously jerked her brother's letter out from under the furry feline rump. Ginger raised her head and gave the mistress of the house an injured glance, then tucked her nose under her tail and returned to slumber.

Meg scanned the letter once more, wishing the contents might have magically changed, but no such luck. It still said:

Dear Meg,
Please excuse my hasty scrawl, but the courier is waiting for this and impatient to leave. I'm most dreadfully sorry to say that I will be delayed and won't be home in time to meet Jack Howard myself. The colonel has asked me to perform a commission for him, and one doesn't refuse one's colonel!

Jack will be arriving in Chippenham on December 22 on the evening coach from London. You won't have any trouble recognizing him—he's tall and dark and handsome and looks just as an officer ought. I expect Phoebe to be most impressed with him. (And vice versa, of course!) Jack is a great gun and will fit right in. I swear I will be home as soon as possible, though I fear it won't be until after Christmas. Save me some of your special pudding and say all that is proper to Jack.

Love to all,
Jeremy

As Meg folded the single sheet again, her younger sister floated into the kitchen. Phoebe didn't walk like normal females; she had the drifting grace, ebony hair, and porcelain features of a woodland fairy.

"I'm going to take the gig into Chippenham now," Meg said. "I imagine the little girls are asleep, but you should probably look in on them later. And keep the fire up—I'm sure that Captain Howard and I will need it when we return."

Phoebe went to the window and peered out, her blue eyes concerned. "With a storm like this, perhaps Captain Howard has been delayed and won't arrive tonight."

"Perhaps not," Meg admitted, "but I still must go as long as there is any chance that he will be there."

Her sister frowned. "You shouldn't be driving alone on a night like this. Since Philip isn't home, I'll go with you."

"Thank you, darling, but there's no need," Meg replied. "It's scarcely three miles, and Clover and I have made the trip hundreds of times. Besides, you're just recovering from one chill—it would be foolish to risk coming down with another one."

Phoebe started to protest, then stopped. "I expect you're right. But be careful."

Swaddled in cloak, bonnet, scarf, and gloves, Meg squashed her way to the barn, her pattens sinking into the mud as sheets of icy water swept across the farmyard and wind rattled the branches of the nearby trees. She should have left earlier, for it would be a slow trip into town.

It took only a few minutes to harness Clover. Before climbing into the gig, Meg pulled a carrot from her pocket and gave it to the pony. "You'll get another when we're home again."

The pony flicked his ears back in acknowledgment of the bribe and they set off for Chippenham. Fortunately Meg knew the route well, for the slashing rain made it hard to see even the hedgerows that lined the lane.

The farmhouse stood on top of a large gradually inclined hill with a brook winding around the base. Usually the water was scarcely more than a trickle, but now the ford was over a foot deep and a strong current rocked the gig as it splashed through the water. The lane beyond was soggy, and soon one wheel bogged down in the mud.

Meg sighed as she climbed down to push the vehicle free. Everything was going wrong, which was what always happened when one wanted matters to be exactly right. Even to herself, Meg hated to admit how much hope she had pinned on this visit of Jeremy's friend. Phoebe was twenty and it was high time she married, but it was hard for a girl to find a husband when she never met any suitable young men. Given the disastrous state of the family finances, Phoebe would never have the London Season she deserved, and Meg had been deeply concerned about her sister's future. Then fate took a hand when her brother wrote that he would be able to come home on leave at Christmas, and he had invited his best friend to join them.

Judging by Jeremy's letters, Captain Howard was the answer to Meg's prayers: honorable, good-tempered, and from a well-to-do family in the Midlands. Now, if the captain would just cooperate and fall in love with Phoebe . . . There was an excellent chance that he would, for the girl was so beautiful and sweet-natured that any normal young man was bound to lose his heart to her.

Phoebe herself always greeted Jeremy's letters with an excitement that was more than sisterly fondness. Though the sisters had never discussed the matter, Meg suspected that the younger girl was halfway to being in love with her brother's friend. Yes, Meg had high hopes for Captain Howard's visit.

A branch slapped Meg's face, stinging her cheek and jerking her out of her reverie. As she batted the branch away, she thought wryly that Jack Howard had better be at the George, for she would feel most provoked if this journey proved fruitless.

* * *

"Chippenham! Twenny minutes fer dinner afore
we go on to Bristol!" the guard bawled.

There was a stampede of passengers to reach the
ground. Jack yawned and stayed where he was,
grateful to have room to stretch his legs after hours
of cramping. Not that he was feeling much discomfort; in fact, he felt nothing at all. Solemnly he pondered the question of whether he was numb with
cold or paralyzed by his companion's whiskey.
Probably both.

Before Jack could drift into full sleep, Jem
tugged on his sleeve. "Come along, brother," the
farmer said briskly. "You shouldn't stay out here
in the rain."

It *was* rather wet. Obediently Jack stood and followed the older man down the ladder. The ground
showed a distressing tendency to rise up to meet
him, and he watched it with interest.

Jem grabbed Jack's arm and steered him into
the inn. "You'll be better for some food in your
belly."

Jack hiccuped. "Very likely."

The warmth of the inn hit him like a steaming
blanket and he began wavering again. Tolerantly
Jem steered Jack through the main taproom into
a smaller room beyond, then deposited him on an
inglenook bench by the fire. "I'll bring you something to eat."

"Much obliged." Jack hazily pulled a coin from
his pockets and pressed it into the farmer's hand.
Then he lay back on the bench and promptly fell
asleep.

Jem took the silver crown and went to order food.
More than ten minutes passed before he managed to
purchase two hot meat pies from the busy hosts.
Munching on one, Jem returned to his companion.
"Here you go, lad, a nice pork pie."

Sublimely unaware, Jack slept on.

Next door the guard shouted, "Time to board the *Express!*"

Jem swallowed the rest of his pie and shook the sleeping man. "Look lively or you'll miss the coach."

Jack batted at the insistent hand, then subsided again.

Deciding stronger measures were needed, Jem tried to pull the other man off the bench, thinking that would wake him up.

Instead, Jack made a swift movement with his arm and Jem found himself polishing the floor with his breeches five feet away. Unhurt, he said admiringly, "Wish you were awake enough to teach me that trick, brother."

The guard yelled again, "Last call!"

Torn, Jem gazed at Jack and tried to decide what to do. Didn't look like the lad wanted to go anywhere, and Jem didn't want to learn what would happen to the next man who tried to wake him. Coming to a decision, Jem scrambled to his feet and dashed outside, where the coachman and guard were taking their seats.

"The gent who got on at the Red Duck at the last minute don't want to go no farther," Jem said breathlessly. "Toss down his bag. I'll take it inside and be right back."

The coachman growled, "Time we was leaving."

Knowing the infallible way to ensure cooperation, Jem gave each of the men a half-crown. "For your trouble."

The guard turned and rooted in the luggage, then handed the bag down to Jem. "Mind you hurry right back, or we'll leave without you."

Jem raced inside and tucked the bag under Jack's bench, then gave another half-crown to the landlord, who was regarding the sleeping man disapprovingly. "Let the lad spend the night here."

The landlord pocketed the coin. "Very well. I suppose there's no harm in it."

Jem still held the second pork pie, so he took a bite. "Have a happy Christmas, Jack," he said, his voice muffled with flaky pastry. Then, secure in the knowledge of his good deed, he dashed outside and boarded the coach that would return him to his own comfortable hearth before the night was over.

Tired and splashed with mud, Meg tethered Clover inside the stable of the George. She guessed that the coach from London had already come and gone, and sure enough, inside the inn the landlord and his wife were clearing away plates left by hasty passengers. Meg removed her dripping bonnet and shook out her damp curls. "Good evening, Mr. Bragg."

The landlord glanced up, surprised. "What brings you here on such a nasty night, Miss Lambert?"

"A friend of Jeremy's was supposed to arrive on the London coach." Seeing only a handful of locals drinking ale by the fire, she asked, "Didn't any passengers get off here?"

"Well, there's a gent in the other room," Mr. Bragg said dubiously, "but I doubt he's the one you're looking for."

Hoping the landlord was wrong, Meg crossed the main taproom to the smaller chamber beyond, then halted in surprise, wondering if the room's sole occupant could possibly be the right man, for her mental image of Jack Howard was quite different.

Unconsciously she had assumed that Jeremy's friend would be in the same mold as her brother: slim and young and elegant. Instead, the man sprawled along the bench was very large, very shaggy, and not at all elegant. Wisps of steam rose

gently from his worn coat, and his hat had fallen
to the flagged floor and rolled under the bench.
Jeremy had mentioned that his friend was a bit
older, but Meg has assumed Jack Howard would
still be somewhere in his mid-twenties, while the
man in front of her appeared to be at least a decade
her brother's senior.

Systematically Meg compared the stranger
against Jeremy's comments. Tall? Yes, definitely
tall. Dark? She studied the long unruly hair. She
would have called it brown rather than dark, but
certainly it wasn't fair.

How about handsome? Critically she examined
the sleeping face, where several days' worth of
beard darkened the long jaw. Even worn by fatigue
it was a pleasant countenance, but "handsome"
did seem rather an overstatement. Still, one tended
to think one's friends were attractive, and Jeremy
and Jack were very good friends. Meg just hoped
that Phoebe wouldn't be disappointed.

Deciding that she was wasting time, Meg bent
over the recumbent form. Then she stopped and
wrinkled her nose. The gentleman smelled as if he
had been held prisoner in a distillery. Not the most
proper behavior for a man visiting friends, but fortunately Meg was not easily offended. Besides, on
a night like tonight, spirits were a sensible way to
counter the cold and damp. Softly she said, "Captain Howard?"

When there was no reply, she tried again, raising
her voice. This time his lids fluttered open, reveal-
ing intensely blue eyes. Meg caught her breath,
understanding why someone would describe this
man as handsome. However, since those gorgeous
blue eyes were blank with incomprehension, she
asked, "Are you Captain Howard?"

Hearing a military rank penetrated Jack's
whiskey-aided exhaustion as nothing else would
have, for a soldier who wanted to die in his bed

learned to respond to emergencies no matter what his state. But what kind of emergency had a voice like spring flowers?

Blinking, he said, "Not captain. Major."

The voice said with apparent pleasure, "I didn't know you had received a promotion. Congratulations, Major." Then, uncertainly, "You *are* Jack Howard?"

"I was last time I looked, but it has been rather a long day." Wanting to see the face that went with that delicious voice, Jack concentrated until her features came into focus one by one. A riot of bright brown curls. Thoughtful hazel eyes with green flecks. A scattering of freckles across cheeks rosy with good health. And an extremely kissable mouth. His gaze fixed on that last feature, he asked hopefully, "Do I know you?"

"I am Miss Lambert," she explained, as if that would instantly clarify his confusion.

Jack frowned, trying to recall the name. "Miss Lambert?"

"Margaret Lambert, Jeremy's older sister, though if he ever mentioned me, he would have called me Meg. Everyone does."

Margaret. Jeremy. Meg. Who were these people? He would never have forgotten this lady's face. For that matter, Jack thought as he raised a vague hand to his head, where the devil was he and how had he gotten here?

"Where is Jeremy?" he asked. He knew several men by that name; if he recognized Miss Lambert's Jeremy, this conversation might make more sense.

The mobile face above him showed regret. "Jeremy has been delayed for a few days and won't be home until after Christmas. He asked me to apologize for his absence."

Jack sighed; no enlightenment there. Doggedly he tried to recall what had happened. Ah, yes, the irritating interview with Mr. Weezle that had driven Jack to board the coach to Bristol. What then? With a faint shudder he remembered the friendly farmer with the lethal flask of spirits.

After a brief survey of his surroundings, Jack concluded that he was in a tavern. Either he had liked the place and decided to stay or he had been incapable of further travel. But none of that explained how this appealing lady knew him.

As Jack racked his brain, the lady said helpfully, "Were you expecting to be met by Phoebe? No doubt Jeremy spoke more of her, for she's the family beauty. I don't look at all like her or Jeremy, for I'm only a half-sister."

"You look quite whole to me." He surveyed her from muddy toes to curly hair, missing nothing in between. "Women like you are why men will fight and die to defend home and hearth."

Miss Lambert blushed prettily. "I can see why Jeremy said you were charming, but don't waste your flattery on me. Phoebe is a much more suitable object."

Jack started to shake his head, then stopped hastily when the world began spinning. "Not flattery. God's own truth." Belatedly recognizing his impropriety, he added, "Begging your pardon for the language, Miss Lambert."

"Quite all right. One can't expect a man who is foxed to have perfect control over his tongue."

"Not foxed." It occurred to Jack that a gentleman did not converse with a lady while lying on his back, so he sat up, exercising great care. "P'haps a trifle well-to-go." Being upright gave him a better view of the lady, and it was well worth it. She was of medium height and her cloaked figure was agreeably round in all the right places, not like one of those skinny fashionable wenches.

Miss Lambert said briskly, "If you're feeling more the thing, it is time we set off. The weather is dreadful and it will be nearly midnight before we get home."

"Home?" Jack asked, startled. For the first time he wondered if he was dreaming; in normal life, well-bred, wholesome young ladies did not invite strange men home with them. Or perhaps she wasn't a lady? What a splendid thought.

"Of course," she said, for the first time showing a hint of impatience. "I certainly don't want to spend the night here. Can you manage to walk to the stables?"

Foxed he might be, but Jack knew a good offer when he heard one. "Be delighted to go home with you."

He stood, swaying slightly, then pulled his bag out from under the bench. Though she might not be quite a lady, she wasn't a tavern wench either; her home would be much better. There was a danger that he would be in no shape to perform when he got there, but he would certainly try. He gave her a sweeping bow. "For the honor of the regiment!"

Meg laughed. "For the honor of the regiment." Though the major did not make much sense in his present condition, she couldn't help liking him.

Taking her guest's arm, Meg guided him through the inn. To her surprise, he put his arm around her shoulders when they stepped outside, but she guessed that he needed a bit of steadying. She didn't mind if he used her for a cane; in return he was good protection from the wind and rain.

However, even the most liberal of interpretations could not excuse what happened in the stables. Meg untethered the pony and sacrificed half of her remaining carrot to reward Clover for his earlier endeavors. Then, after stroking his velvety nose and saying a few appreciative words, she turned to her guest, who had loaded his bag and was stand-

ing by the gig. "Will you open the doors so I can
drive outside, Major?"

He nodded but made no move toward the entrance. Thinking that he intended to help her into
the gig, Meg put her hand in his. But instead of
assisting her up as a gentleman should, Jack Howard gave a slight tug that pulled Meg against his
broad chest.

Startled, she glanced up to find the major's face
descending. When his warm mouth encompassed
hers, Meg gasped, then began cooperating from
sheer surprise. No one had stolen a kiss from practical Miss Lambert since her salad days. And none
of the Chippenham lads had *ever* kissed like this.

The major's hands did interesting things that
made Meg's knees weaken so that she had to cling
to his large frame for support. She had forgotten
just how pleasant a kiss could be. . . .

But how dare Jeremy invite such a dangerous
man to stay under the same roof as his sisters! she
thought with a flash of indignation. Immediately
she realized that her brother would not knowingly
have invited a rake home, so Jeremy must be ig-
norant of the major's disgraceful behavior. Well, if
Jack Howard was a rake, Meg decided, he simply
would not do for Phoebe.

Having reached that wise conclusion, she suddenly realized that all the time she had been
weighing the major's scandalous misconduct, she
had continued kissing him. In fact, her arms were
twined around him like ivy.

Shocked more by herself than by him, she pulled
her head back and exclaimed in freezing accents,
"Major Howard!"

As an elder sister, Meg had developed an exceedingly peremptory voice; the major instantly released her and jumped back as if she were made of
red-hot iron. "B-beg your pardon, Miss Lambert,"
he stammered. "Don't know what came over me."

He did not look at all rakish; in fact, his confused, guilty expression reminded Meg of a hound
that had just been caught snatching food from the
table.

Disarmed, she almost laughed. In truth, she was
more flattered than angry. Men never noticed Meg
when Phoebe was in the room, so she felt a secret
guilty pleasure in the knowledge that the major
had found her worth kissing. Suppressing her
amusement, she said frostily, "We shall both forget that happened." She climbed into the gig—
without help—and lifted the reins. "Please open the
stable doors, Major Howard."

Hastily he complied. Meg drove outside, then
waited while her guest closed and latched the doors
behind her. Silently he climbed into the carriage
and settled himself as far from her as possible,
which wasn't very far in a gig.

The storm soon quenched Meg's amusement, for
driving demanded all her attention. As she concentrated on avoiding the worst of the ruts, the major
slouched beside her, so quiet that she might have
thought he was sleeping or passed out from drink.

However, her passenger came alive whenever the
gig bogged down in the mud, which happened
about every ten minutes. No sooner would they
shudder to a halt than the major jumped down,
wordlessly freed the light vehicle from the rut, then
climbed back in and returned to his torpor. Meg
found it fascinating to watch him; clearly a sea-
soned soldier could do whatever was necessary,
even when half-seas-over.

The drive home seemed much longer than the
trip to town, and by the time they reached the ford,
Meg was tense with strain. Pulling Clover to a halt,
she studied the rushing water, which was wider
and deeper than it had been earlier. Briefly she
considered returning to Chippenham, but she
hated to give up when they were so close to home.

Besides, Phoebe would worry if they didn't return.
The water was a little high, but the streambed was
firm and they should be able to cross safely.

Clover was less sure, and it took all Meg's pow-
ers of persuasion to convince him to move forward.
As the gig entered the water, the current battered
the wheels and the pony stopped, whickering nervously.

"Steady, Clover," Meg murmured, her hands
firm on the reins. Clover started forward again and
in another minute he reached the far bank and began scrambling out of the water.

Then disaster struck with shocking suddenness.
One moment Meg was holding the reins and in
control of the gig. The next moment something
smashed into the vehicle, knocking it over and
pitching the passengers into the roiling stream.

Meg opened her mouth to cry out and found herself choking on icy water as her heavy cloak
dragged her below the surface. There was a deep
pool to the left of the ford, and the current tumbled
her into it. Helpless, drowning in the pitiless
depths, Meg succumbed to blind panic, striking out
hysterically as she fought for air.

One of her flailing feet kicked a yielding object,
and an instant later strong hands seized her and
pulled her to the surface. The major was tall
enough to stand on the bottom of the stream, and
his powerful arms held her securely against his
chest as dark water swirled around them.

Unable to touch bottom herself, Meg clutched her
rescuer desperately as she broke into convulsive
coughing. Finally air reached her anguished lungs,
but even though the danger was past, panic
drummed through her with every beat of her
pounding heart.

Then Major Howard murmured in her ear, his
voice warm and amused, "That was quite fun.
Shall we do it again?"

Meg choked in momentary outrage. Then laughter dissolved her terror. "You absurd man," she gasped, incongruously aware of the scent of wet wool and warm male. "If that is your idea of fun, perhaps I should take you back to the George."

"Oh, don't do that. This is much more amusing." The major bent and lifted Meg in his arms, then carried her through the water to the bank and set her on her feet, keeping his arm around her waist until it was clear that she could stand alone. Suddenly serious, he asked, "How much farther to your house?"

"J-just up the hill." Meg wrapped her arms around herself in a futile attempt to find warmth as the icy wind bit through her saturated clothing. "Do you know what caused the accident?"

"I think a floating tree trunk hit the gig and knocked it over. Your pony is over there, unhappy but unharmed."

Following the direction of his gesture, Meg saw Clover stamping about nervously, confused and distinctly disapproving. A tangle of harness attached him to the damaged carriage, which was snarled in a bush.

Major Howard guided Meg to the gig, then swiftly disconnected the harness and freed Clover. "Can you stay on the pony long enough to reach home?"

"I th-think so."

He put his hands around Meg's waist and lifted her to Clover's back, setting her sideways. Then he took off his greatcoat and draped it around her shoulders. "A pity this isn't dry, but at least it will block some of the wind."

The coat did help, but Meg protested, "You'll freeze!"

"Not as quickly as you will."

When Meg opened her mouth to argue further, the major barked, "No arguments, soldier!"

Stunned, Meg closed her mouth and obediently

curled her numb fingers around the leather harness straps. Was her companion joking or so drunk that he wasn't quite sure where he was? No matter, he certainly knew what to do.

They began to climb the hill, the major guiding the pony with one hand and using the other to steady Meg. Eager to return to his own stall, Clover moved briskly, and in less than five minutes they reached the old farmhouse.

"This is it," Meg said, her voice a croak.

"Here?" he asked, a note of surprise in his voice.

Apparently Jeremy had not explained the family circumstances to his friend, and the major had expected something grander. Too drained to explain, Meg merely said, "Around the house to the left. We'll go in the back."

They rounded the building and found light streaming through the kitchen windows. The major stopped at the door, then reached up and lifted Meg's shivering body from her perch. "You go inside and I'll stable the pony," he said as he set her on the ground. "I'll be along in a few minutes."

"But you're a guest," Meg protested through chattering teeth. "I'll take care of Clover."

He took her shoulders and turned her to the door. "Never disobey a superior officer. Now, *march.*"

Too cold to argue further, Meg fumbled with the latch. Almost immediately the door swung open and Phoebe was standing there, a lamp held high in one hand, her exquisite face warm with concern. With a small twinge, Meg knew that Jack Howard must be falling in love with her on the spot.

Oblivious of the dramatic picture she presented, Phoebe exclaimed, "Thank heaven you're home! I was getting worried. Don't just stand there, Meg, come inside—you're soaking wet." Then she looked over her sister's shoulder, her eyes narrowed as she peered into the darkness. "Welcome to Brook Farm, Captain Howard. Please, come in right away. You look as wet as Meg."

"He's a major now, Phoebe." Meg took off the greatcoat and handed it to her guest.

"This is not the time for formal introductions," the major said briskly as he draped the coat over his shoulders. "There was an accident and Miss Lambert is freezing. Put her next to the fire and warm her up. I'll be along as soon as the pony has been bedded down for the night."

Brought to an understanding of the circumstances, Phoebe made a shocked sound and ushered her older sister into the house. Once in the warm kitchen, Meg peeled off her cloak, briefly described the accident, then went to change into dry clothing while Phoebe set tea to brewing.

Still shivering, Meg returned to the kitchen and gratefully accepted a mug of tea fortified with brandy. "Major Howard hasn't come in yet?" she asked, wondering if some combination of drink, fatigue, and cold might have overcome him in the barn.

Before Phoebe could reply, the outside door swung open. A moment later, their guest—large, unkempt, and gently dripping water from his soaking garments—appeared in the doorway between hall and kitchen. Now that the danger had passed, his decisiveness was gone and he had lapsed back into dazed confusion, his blank gaze wandering from one object to another.

Meg stepped forward and handed him the other mug of fortified tea. "Drink this," she ordered.

It took him a moment to comprehend her command. Then he took the mug and downed the contents in one long swallow that must have scorched his mouth and throat.

Meg examined her guest critically; he looked dead on his feet, his blue eyes opaque with exhaustion. To be honest, she didn't feel much better, though at least she was sober.

Phoebe took over, seating both orphans of the storm by the fire, then feeding them potato-cabbage soup hot from the hob. Warmed both inside and out, Meg felt considerably better and assumed that the major did too, though he did not speak, simply ate his soup with clumsy hands and an unfocused gaze.

When he was done, Meg said, "Time for bed." Taking his hand, she led him upstairs as if he were a child. "Leave your wet clothes outside the door and we'll dry them tonight."

Reaching the bedroom that had been assigned to the guest, Meg opened the door and gave the major a gentle push. "Put your wet clothes outside," she repeated, hoping he understood.

Before Meg could leave, the major peeled off his blue coat and dropped it on the floor. It landed with a wet, squishy sound and was joined by his shirt a moment later.

Meg's mouth dropped open in astonishment. He really was a splendid specimen of masculinity, she thought, her gaze riveted to her guest's muscular torso and the dark hair that patterned his broad chest.

Then, oblivious of his shocking impropriety, the major began to unbutton his trousers.

Released from her paralysis, Meg blushed scarlet and beat a hasty retreat. "There are towels on the washstand," she called over her shoulder before shutting the door.

Downstairs in the kitchen, Phoebe waited, her expression doubtful. "He isn't at all what I expected. And . . . and is it possible he has been drinking?"

"I'm afraid so," Meg admitted as she went to stand in front of the fire. "But in spite of that, he has been very gentlemanly. He also just saved me from drowning." Remembering how important it was for Phoebe to like their guest, Meg spent the next ten minutes giving a glowing description of the major's virtues.

All the while, she listened for the sound of the bedroom door, but upstairs there was only silence. Finally Meg sighed. "He must have fallen asleep right away. I'd better get his clothing so it can dry. Perhaps we can find his baggage in the daylight, but if not, the major has nothing to wear but what he had on. Jeremy's things certainly aren't large enough."

"Let me do it," Phoebe offered. "You should be in bed."

Meg was tired enough to be tempted to accept. Then a vivid memory of Major Howard unbuttoning his trousers made her shake her head. There was no telling what condition their guest was in, and Meg was not about to let her innocent young sister find out. Lifting the lamp again, she said, "This will take just a moment. While I'm upstairs, will you make me another cup of tea?"

"Of course."

Meg was unsurprised when there was no answer to her knock. Steeling herself, she opened the door and was greatly relieved to find the major in bed and mostly covered.

The wet garments lay scattered across the room, but before collecting them, Meg found herself walking quietly to the bed and looking down at her guest. The blankets were drawn only to mid-chest, as if he had been too tired to finish covering himself, so Meg pulled them up around his throat. In spite of his ruffianly appearance, he looked exhausted and vulnerable.

With a surge of tenderness, she brushed back his thick brown hair, as she would have done with a slumbering child. "Sleep well, Jack Howard," she whispered.

As Meg made her way downstairs again, she thought that it would certainly be an interesting Christmas.

For a long time Jack hovered in the twilight area between sleep and waking, instinctively knowing that full awareness would not be a desirable state this morning. Then a bloodcurdling shriek shattered the last remnants of slumber.

Reflexively he opened his eyes and started to sit up, then subsided as a wave of nausea swept over him. He fell back against the pillows, heart pounding and eyes closed against the sunlight streaming through the window. Though it had been at least a decade since he had experienced this particular kind of wretchedness, Jack recognized it immediately as the aftermath of a truly appalling carouse.

The shriek sounded from outside again, the noise stabbing his throbbing temples. After identifying the sound as avian and presumably harmless, Jack dismissed it from his mind. Far more important was coming to terms with the events of the previous night, which he recalled with painful accuracy. London. The wet, freezing ride on the stage to Bristol. Jem. Then the coaching inn, where the delightful Miss Lambert had approached and greeted him. She had wanted a Jack Howard, and in his befuddled state he had been more than willing to oblige.

He winced as he remembered what had happened in the stable. Even three sheets to the wind, he should have known that a female so refined and well-spoken could only be a lady. Instead he had believed her a lightskirt and had lunged at her like a sailor just home from a year at sea. Though in fact she had not seemed to mind, at least not at first. . . .

Recalling that kiss in detail briefly mitigated

Jack's misery. Then the faint sound of voices downstairs brought him back to the present.

Now that he was sober, Jack could hazard a guess about what had happened; though the two men had never met, there was another officer named Jack Howard, a captain of the 45th Regiment. Lord, probably there were a half a dozen Jack Howards in the army; the name was common enough. And one of them was the friend of Miss Lambert's brother, but it wasn't the Jack Howard presently lying naked in bed in this pleasant farmhouse. That thought led him to offer a swift prayer that he had been conscious enough to undress himself, for the alternative did not bear thinking about.

Jack groaned as he considered the dreadful bind he had gotten himself into. How the devil was he going to tell Miss Lambert that he was an unintentional impostor? Last night she had been remarkably tolerant of his disgraceful condition, but the news that she had been misled would make those lovely hazel eyes flash with fury. It was a most distressing thought.

Immersed in his dilemma, Jack failed to hear the soft knock at the door, so Miss Lambert's entry into the bedroom caught him by surprise. He cast one horrified look at her, then behaved like any proper military hero would under such conditions. He dived under the covers and pulled a pillow over his head.

Unlike the shrieking bird that had awakened him, Miss Lambert's voice was soft and soothing. "Forgive me for disturbing you, Major Howard, but are you feeling all right?"

"Better than I deserve," Jack said in a strangled voice.

The pillow was tugged from his clutching fingers. "Sorry, I can't hear you clearly," she said.

"Were you injured in the accident? Or did you take a chill from falling in the water?"

Turtle-style, Jack poked his head out from under the covers. Miss Lambert looked as bright and honest as a summer day. She was also remarkably self-possessed, given the fact that she was in the bedroom of a strange man. A man who was in fact considerably stranger than she knew. "The only thing wrong with me is just punishment for my sins."

"I thought you would be suffering the effects of intemperance." She motioned toward the tray she had set on the bedside table. "That's why I brought up a pot of coffee. Would you like some?"

"Miss Lambert," Jack said fervently as his head emerged from its cocoon, "you are a woman in a thousand. A million."

Though he would not be fully recovered before the next day, the large mug of steaming hot coffee went a long way toward restoring Jack's raveled nerves. It also reminded him of the impropriety of this situation. "Miss Lambert," he said, setting down the empty mug, "you should not be here. Have a care for your reputation."

She laughed and poured him more coffee. "I've been on the shelf far too long to need to worry about my reputation—at least, I won't worry when I am under my own roof with my brother's best friend." She gave him a sudden sharp look. "Of course, it's different with Phoebe, who is of marriageable age. I've always taken care to see that she is properly chaperoned."

Ah, yes, Phoebe, the very pretty, very young female who had let them in the night before. Jack dismissed Phoebe and her perfections without a thought; it was Miss Lambert's good graces he craved, and was about to lose. Taking a deep breath, he said, "Miss Lambert, I owe you a profound apology."

A hint of color showed in her face and her gaze flickered away from his. "Please, say no more about what happened. You were not yourself last night."

He *had* been himself; that was the whole problem. While Jack was trying to find the words to explain, Miss Lambert continued, "I assume that you imbibed a bit too much when warding off the cold. Consider the episode forgotten."

Once more Jack braced himself to confess his underlying crime, which was far worse than stealing a kiss. "There is something I must tell you, Miss Lambert."

"Call me Meg. I'd like to think of you as one of the family. By the way, do you remember my telling you that Jeremy won't be home until after Christmas?"

Jack nodded. Meg gave him a rueful smile. "The household is at sixes and sevens just now. Besides Jeremy being delayed, Phoebe is recovering from a chill, Philip is visiting friends in Gloucester and won't be back until this afternoon, and my two goddaughters are here for Christmas because their older brothers have the measles and their mama asked me to take the girls until everyone is well again. And as if that weren't enough, our maid asked for a fortnight's holiday to visit her mother, who is ailing. I hope you'll forgive the disorganization."

"All soldiers become accustomed to disorganization."

Meg chuckled and knelt on the hearth. "I imagine you'll want to bathe, since falling in a stream is not quite the same thing. I'll build a fire and bring up some hot water."

Jack sat up, protesting, "I'll do that. You shouldn't be acting as a servant for me."

"Major Howard!" she said, blushing. "If you

don't stay where you are, I am going to be very embarrassed in a moment."

Abruptly remembering his nakedness, Jack slid down and pulled the covers to his chin. "I'm sorry," he said in confusion. "You are going to think me a complete lackwit."

She smiled. "Having raised two younger brothers, I am not easily shocked by male impulsiveness."

"You raised your brothers?"

"To a large extent." His hostess struck a spark into the nest of twigs she had laid, then watched while tiny flames began licking around the wood. "I don't suppose Jeremy ever explained the family situation?"

"He never told me a word," Jack said with perfect truth and a guilty pang. It was hardly the act of a gentleman to listen to her confidences, but he was curious to learn why people of obvious gentility were living in such reduced circumstances.

Meg sat back on her heels, a distant expression on her face. "We lived at Peacock Hill, a manor about a mile west of here. The estate has been in the Lambert family for generations, and Jeremy expected to inherit it even though Lord Mason, our local *nobleman*"—her voice became heavily sarcastic—"tried to buy the property several times. Peacock Hill adjoins Lord Mason's estate, and his lordship has coveted it for years, but of course Papa never considered selling.

"Then, five years ago, my father died quite unexpectedly and I was left as guardian of the younger children. The day after the funeral, Lord Mason called and informed me that Papa had lost the manor to him in a card game several months earlier."

Jack sat up in the bed, remembering just in time to pull the blankets up to cover his bare chest. "Did

Lord Mason have any proof of such an outrageous statement?"

"He had a deed, plus a vowel that he claimed Papa had written. It said that if Papa did not repay twenty thousand pounds to Lord Mason, Peacock Hill would go to his lordship on my father's death."

"You say 'claimed.' Were the documents false?"

She grimaced. "I think so, but I can't prove it, for the handwriting was very like my father's. When I told Lord Mason that I thought they were forgeries, he challenged me to produce a real deed. We searched through all of Papa's papers and everywhere else we could think of, but without success, so perhaps the deed he showed us is the real one."

"Was your father the sort of man who could have gambled away his children's inheritance?"

"It's not quite impossible," Meg said reluctantly. "Papa and Lord Mason were friends of sorts, and they did play cards occasionally. In a mad mood Papa might have wagered far beyond his means. If he did and lost, he would have been ashamed to tell anyone what he had done. Since he seemed to be in good health, he would have assumed there was time for him to repay the debt to Lord Mason, perhaps by taking out a mortgage."

Jack's mouth twisted. Miss Lambert had had to take responsibility for her family when she was not much more than a girl herself. "It's an infamous story. Since you thought the papers forged, did you consider taking the matter to law?"

For the first time a note of bitterness was audible in her soft voice. "I hired a lawyer. Lord Mason hired three. What chance does a poor person have to win justice from a rich aristocrat?" Her hands, which had been lying quietly on her knees, suddenly clenched. "I despise the nobility."

Jack flinched back from her intensity, not that

he blamed her for being angry. "Is this farm another family property?"

Meg's face eased. "No, Brook Farm belongs to me. My mother was the only child of an old yeoman family that has been here even longer than the Lamberts. Neither set of parents was enthralled when she and Papa fell in love, but the farm adjoins Peacock Hill and it made a decent dowry even though my mother's birth was inferior."

Using tongs, Meg laid several small pieces of coal on the fledgling fire. "My mother died when I was three, and two years later Papa married again. My stepmother was a wonderful woman and quite wellborn, but she was dowerless and left nothing to her children. So, when Lord Mason claimed Peacock Hill, Brook Farm was all we had left to keep us. A neighboring farmer works most of the land and the rent he pays is enough to support the family. Fortunately Papa had left enough money to buy Jeremy a commission. If Jeremy hadn't gone away, I think he would have gone mad with frustration."

"So you are devoting your life and your inheritance to caring for your family. You are very generous."

"It is not generous to perform what is both one's duty and one's pleasure," Meg replied in a matter-of-fact voice. Then her hazel eyes clouded. "Jeremy and Philip can make their own way, but I worry so about Phoebe. She deserves the opportunity to go to London, to see the world and find a man worthy of her."

"Even if the paragon proved to be a nobleman?"

"I doubt that there are any worthy noblemen," Meg said dryly. Her expression became earnest. "What I want for her is a man of character who will appreciate her sweet disposition as well as her

beauty. He needn't be rich, just have sufficient fortune so that she will be cared for."

Jack blinked, irresistibly reminded of a horse
coper, though Phoebe was a much prettier piece of
merchandise than a horse. It wasn't hard to de-
duce that Meg cherished hopes that her brother's
friend might form a *tendre* for her sister. Jack
shifted uneasily under his blankets. He should
have confessed earlier, before Meg Lambert had
told him all the family secrets. Now he would have
to wait a few hours, until a time when there wasn't
such a feeling of closeness between the two of
them. Not wanting to talk about Phoebe, he said,
"Your concern for your family is admirable, but
what do you want for yourself? A London Season?
A husband and children of your own?"

"Heavens, no!" Meg laughed. "No reasonable
man would want me, for I'm the managing sort.
As for a London Season . . ." She looked a little
wistful. "Even if I could have made my come-out,
I wouldn't have 'taken' in society. I'm not beautiful
like Phoebe, nor as wellborn, and owning one small
farm hardly qualifies me as an heiress. No, I'm
plain and practical and opinionated, and I belong
here."

"I think you underestimate the popularity you
might have had," Jack remarked, his tone warm.
"Females who are attractive, charming, and intelligent are always in short supply."

Coloring again, Meg stood and brushed dust from
her hands with quick, nervous movements. "I
looked at the wrecked gig this morning, and for a
wonder, your bag was still safely inside—it was
only the passengers who went in the water. I'll
bring the bag up, along with your clothes. They're
a bit the worse for wear, I'm afraid, but at least
everything is dry."

As she disappeared out the door, Jack folded his
hands beneath his head and thoughtfully regarded

the ceiling. What a splendid young woman she was, as pretty as she was kind and sensible. He envied the younger Lamberts for being the beneficiaries of her warmth and caring.

Jack sighed, knowing that he would have to leave Brook Farm as soon as he confessed that he was an impostor. A pity he had to reveal the truth, for a solitary holiday in an inn was not what he would have chosen for his first English Christmas in many years. It would be far more pleasant to stay right where he was.

Perhaps he shouldn't tell Meg that he was the wrong man.

To his regret, Jack found that he was nowhere near as shocked by the thought as he should be. Too many years of military pragmatism had eroded his higher sensibilities; having found a comfortable billet, he was loath to leave, even though his presence was based on a deception.

Even if he were shameless enough to conceal the truth, doing so was impractical, for Jeremy Lambert would be home in a few days. Worse, the real Captain Howard could walk in the door at any moment, and when that happened Jack would be in dire trouble.

Jack winced as he remembered how Meg Lambert had railed at the nobility. The lady had a temper, and she would feel hurt and betrayed by his abuse of her hospitality. At least if he confessed voluntarily, she might forgive his accidental transgression enough to let him call on her in the future.

Jack fervently hoped that she would.

After washing, shaving, and rendering himself as presentable as possible, Jack went downstairs, prepared to confess all to his hostess and throw himself on her mercy.

Unfortunately, the only person in the kitchen

was Phoebe Lambert, who sat by the fire doing
mending. Since she had not heard his footsteps,
Jack paused in the doorway, struck by the room's
welcoming warmth. The previous night he had
been too exhausted to notice his surroundings, but
now he saw that the old-fashioned kitchen was rich
with the unpretentious beauty of utility. Delicious
scents filled the air, clusters of dried herbs and onions hung from the beamed ceiling, and comfortable wooden chairs circled the scrubbed deal table.

Jack guessed that the Lamberts did most of their
living and laughing here. No formal drawing room
would ever be the heart of a home the way this
kitchen was the heart of Brook Farm.

As he examined the room, he blinked, realizing
that Phoebe was not the only inhabitant. A tabby
cat was curled on the girl's lap, a large black cat
sprawled pantherlike on top of the cupboard, legs
and long tail drooping over the edge, and a plump
calico was tucked in on herself on one of the Windsor chairs. Jack chuckled at the sight. Trust cats
to find a snug spot; the kitchen made him want to
curl up and purr too.

Hearing his sound of amusement, Phoebe looked
up and became quite still for a moment. Then she
set aside both cat and mending and came across
the room to greet him, her eyes bright as the copper pans that hung on the walls. "I hope you have
taken no harm from the accident, Major Howard.
Meg told me how you risked your life to save her."

"I don't think the situation was quite that
grave," Jack said uncomfortably. "While the water was over her head in that one spot, I think it
likely that Miss Lambert would have been able to
save herself if I hadn't been on the scene."

Phoebe smiled. "You are too modest, Major.
Would you like a cup of tea? Meg is outside feeding
the animals, but when she returns we will have
lunch."

While Phoebe brewed the tea, Jack sat in a Windsor chair. The calico cat materialized at his feet with a speculative look, then sprang onto his lap, landing with an impact that proved that she didn't miss any meals. Jack felt honored by her company.

As they chatted over their tea, Jack could not escape the feeling that Phoebe was disappointed in him, though her manner was entirely gracious. He suspected that she, too, had had hopes of Jack Howard, and was reluctantly letting go of them now that she was confronted with a real man rather than the image created by her brother's letters. If so, Jack was glad, for it would be a nuisance to have her become enamored of him simply because he was a new face—particularly since he was an impostor. Perhaps the real Captain Howard would please her more.

Jack had reached that point in his thinking when his hostess returned. She was accompanied by two miniature blond charmers and a shaggy dog of dubious breeding but noteworthy enthusiasm.

"I'm glad to see you so restored from the rigors of travel, Major." Meg deftly removed cloak and bonnet from the smaller child. "You haven't met my goddaughters yet, have you?" She gestured to the taller girl. "This is Tizzie." Then to the smaller: "And this is Lizzie. Girls, this is Major Howard."

Both girls curtsied gravely. While Tizzie shyly studied the stranger, Lizzie, a brazen little hussy, climbed into Jack's lap, which had been vacated by the prudent calico.

Lizzie regarded him soulfully. "I been feeding the chickens with Miss Meg. She has the fanciest chickens in the world."

Not to be outdone, Tizzie piped up, " 'N I helped milk the cows."

"How clever of you. Miss Meg is very fortunate to have such good helpers," Jack said admiringly, thinking that it was quite pleasant to have a warm, trusting armful of little girl on his lap. Glancing up, he said, "If I am to call you Meg and Phoebe, you must both call me Jack."

"Fair enough. You'll have noticed that this is not a very formal household." Meg removed her own bonnet and shook out her bright tumbling curls. "The girls have been a wonderful help. They are going to help me with the Christmas baking."

Visions of nuts and fruit in his head, Jack said hopefully, "Can I help too?"

"Of course. The more the merrier. But I think I'll postpone the baking until this evening. There's a hint of snow in the air, so we had best take advantage of the good weather to gather the evergreens this afternoon."

As the dog trotted over to the visitor and rested his jaw on Jack's knee, Meg added, "That's Rugger. He's a variety hound."

Jack smiled at the description and reached down to ruffle Rugger's ears. Snow? Surely that would delay Captain Howard. Perhaps it was safe to postpone his confession a bit longer.

The door opened again, and fickle Rugger bolted off to greet the handsome youth who entered.

Meg welcomed the newcomer with an affectionate hug. "What wonderful timing, Philip! We were just about to eat lunch. I suppose you were dreadfully underfed in Gloucester."

"Dreadfully," he agreed, laughing.

Taking her brother by the arm, Meg brought him over to Jack. "As you see, our guest has arrived, though Jeremy has been delayed for several days. Jack, I'm sure you could pick Philip out of a crowd as Jeremy's brother. They're as like as peas in a pod."

"A pleasure to meet you, Philip." Jack offered his hand without standing, since Lizzie showed no inclination to leave.

"It's a real privilege to have you here, sir." Philip

accepted Jack's hand enthusiastically. He was a
handsome youth of fourteen or fifteen, with Phoebe's
dark good looks.

"It is I who am privileged. Your sisters have been
making me feel very welcome."

Meg was pleased to hear the sincerity in Jack
Howard's voice. She had worried that her brother's
friend might be disconcerted by the modest way
they lived, for she knew that he had been raised in
much grander circumstances. But the tall major
seemed perfectly at home. In fact, she thought with
amusement as Tizzie came to lean against his
knee, he seemed to attract children and animals
like honey attracts bees.

The major cleaned up exceedingly well; as she
had suspected, that square jaw was most attractive now that it was shaved. She hoped Phoebe was
suitably impressed.

Bundled and basketed, the greens-gathering ex-
pedition set out. The weather was clear and cold,
with only the softness of the earth as a reminder
of the previous day's rain. Jack drew a deep breath
of crisp fresh air and decided that Meg was right
about the possibility of snow.

The party was passing the barn when another
one of the avian shrieks rent the air. Jack jumped,
then blinked in surprise as a large shimmeringly
colorful bird whirled past. "Good Lord, is that a
peacock?"

"It is indeed—one of what Lizzie calls my fancy
chickens. The silly beast has escaped again," Meg
said with resignation. "Philip, will you catch Lord
Feathers and return him to his pen?"

"Yes, but it will take a few minutes," her brother
said cheerfully. "Here, Phoebe, you carry my basket. I'll catch up with you once that imbecile bird
is back where he belongs."

Minus Philip, the party proceeded, with Phoebe

walking ahead with Tizzie, Lizzie, and Rugger, while the older members of the party followed. Jack cocked an eye at his hostess. "Peacocks?"

"They came from Peacock Hill, of course," Meg explained. "Since they weren't technically part of the manor, we brought them with us. They're quite useless, but we thought that the least we could do was make Lord Mason buy his own peafowl." She glanced up at Jack, guilty amusement in her eyes. "The entrance to Peacock Hill has always been flanked by two magnificent topiary peacocks. The week after we removed to Brook Farm, someone cut off the tail feathers of both. I suspect that Jeremy and Philip did it, though I never dared ask."

"It was a relatively harmless way of expressing some of their anger. And topiary tail feathers will grow back."

"They have," Meg agreed. "It's more than Lord Mason deserves." They had been climbing steadily, and finally reached a summit that yielded a magnificent view of the rolling countryside. As the younger members of the party skipped ahead, Meg halted and pointed into the middle distance. "There is Peacock Hill. Since Lord Mason wanted only the land, the house is empty now. A pity, when it was always such a happy place."

Through the leafless winter trees Jack was able to distinguish the outlines of a lovely Cotswold-stone manor. In the pale solstice sunshine, it seemed magical, a dream kingdom from which the Lamberts had been banished.

Meg said apologetically, "I don't usually dwell on the past as I'm doing today. We're very fortunate we had Brook Farm to fall back on, and I'm proud of the way the younger ones adjusted to living in a farmhouse. After we moved in, there was never a complaint from any of them."

"Perhaps it was because you set them a good example."

As the major's gaze met hers, Meg found herself momentarily immobilized by the admiration in the dark blue depths of his eyes. He really shouldn't look at her like that, she thought weakly, as if she were as young and attractive as Phoebe. It was enough to make even a sober spinster lose her head.

Fortunately Philip chose that moment to catch up with them. As they resumed walking toward the clump of holly bushes, he said with shy eagerness, "Sir, Jeremy wrote us of what you did at the Battle of Vittoria—he said that he had never seen such courage in his life. If you don't mind speaking of it, we would greatly appreciate your describing the battle to us."

Jack Howard looked disconcerted. "I do mind, actually."

Coaxingly Philip said, "Your modesty does you credit, sir, but I may never get another chance to meet a real hero, and I'd like to hear what happened in your own words."

Meg opened her mouth to reprove her brother for pestering their guest, but Jack's answer cut her off.

"War heroics are a sham, Philip," he said quietly. "Oh, sometimes soldiers act from great courage, but more often they do what they do because they have no choice—because it is safer to charge than to turn and run, or because they fear appearing cowardly, or because they are so tired of being afraid that death seems a welcome alternative. For real bravery, look at a widow struggling to raise her children alone or a doctor going into a plague-stricken city to treat the dying."

"Of course there are many kinds of courage," Philip said, a little taken aback, "but there is something splendid and glorious about risking death for one's country."

His voice edged, Jack replied, "Death may sometimes be necessary, but it is never glorious. For years my fondest ambition has been to die at home in my own bed."

Philip stared at their guest, shock and disillusion clearly visible on his handsome young face. Then, too polite to criticize the major for his unheroic attitude, Philip said stiffly, "I'd best retrieve my basket from Phoebe—the holly is just over there." Turning, he bolted off to join the others.

For several long moments there was silence between Meg and her guest. Then Jack turned to her and said harshly, "Meg, I'm not the man you think I am."

Far more than her brother, Meg could guess at the bleak experience that lay behind his words. "Who of us is what others think? Certainly I am not the strong, generous woman you think I am, for I too have done what I have because I had no choice," she said softly. "Don't condemn yourself for not living up to a boy's ideals, for Philip is too young to understand that nothing is simple, least of all courage."

"I know that, for I was no wiser at his age." The major drew a deep breath, his large frame rigid with tension. "But that is not all I meant—what I'm trying to say is that I am not Jeremy's heroic Jack Howard."

"Please, don't say anything more—words are never adequate for the deepest truths." Wanting to remove the shadows from Jack's anguished blue eyes, she laid an earnest gloved hand on his arm. "My trials have been different from yours, but I have learned that heroism lies beyond despair. And while it is certainly admirable, it is never glorious."

"You say that words are inadequate, yet you have just said something vitally true far more clearly than I could have." He covered her hand

with his, fingers gripping tightly. "But you are
making confession very difficult."

For an instant, as their gazes met, Meg felt dis-
oriented. The farm, the crisp winter day, her
nearby family, all fell away, no longer important.
Reality was the man in front of her, and the feeling
of profound intimacy between them.

Shaken, Meg disengaged her hand from his.
"Christmas is no time for confessions," she said,
striving to keep her voice light. "This is the season
for hope. Forget the past and your own imagined
failings and simply enjoy the moment."

Jack opened his mouth, then closed it again
without speaking. Then, abruptly, his tension disappeared as clearly as milk flowing from a spilled
jug. "You make it easy for me to yield to my less
admirable impulses, Meg," he said with a shaky
laugh. "Please don't judge me too harshly when
you find out what a weak, deceitful fellow I am."

She shook her head. "I'm sure that you are far
too hard on yourself." She grinned suddenly, remembering how he had barked at her after pulling
her from the flooded brook. "You're under orders,
soldier, to relax and enjoy the holiday."

Their laughter was interrupted by a distressed
wail, so they hastened down to the holly bushes,
where Lizzie was sucking fingers pricked by the
spiky holly leaves. Meg quickly soothed her
wounds, and the rest of the afternoon passed in
simple pleasures, with no dark shadows. Working
with leather-gloved care, they collected basket-
fuls of bright-berried holly, then added glossy ivy.
Philip, his earlier discomfiture forgotten, scrambled up an oak tree and cut a large handful of
mistletoe.

Lizzie tired on the walk home, so Jack transferred his evergreens to the others and carried her
the rest of the way, her drowsy blond head nestled
on his shoulder. He felt quite absurdly at peace.

When Meg had commanded him to relax and enjoy the present, he had surrendered all common sense and scruples. Of course he was a fool to continue his pretense, for there would inevitably be a reckoning, but he refused to worry about it. For whatever reason, fate had sent him to this warm and welcoming place, and fate could jolly well help him cope with the inevitable explosion when the truth came out. In the meantime, he intended to savor every glowing moment.

Dusk was falling fast when the party reached the house. Since it was unlucky to bring the evergreens inside before Christmas Eve, the prickly bounty was left in a shed before they proceeded into the kitchen.

After everyone had shared tea and currant cakes, Meg said, "Come along, girls, it's time for a nap."

"No!" her goddaughters said in chorus. Tizzie added hopefully, "We c'n help fix dinner, Miss Meg."

"It is very good of you to offer," Meg said seriously, "but if you don't nap now, I'm afraid you'll be too tired to help with the baking later, and I need your assistance for that more than I do for dinner."

The girls looked horrified, so Phoebe seized the moment and their hands and led them off to the small room they shared.

Jack watched them go fondly. "Is her name really Tizzie?"

"Actually it's Thomasina," Meg explained, "but Lizzie couldn't pronounce that, and calling them Tizzie and Lizzie proved irresistible."

Philip interjected, "I'm going out to feed the animals now, before it becomes dark."

"Will you see if there are any fresh eggs?" Meg lifted an apron from a peg and tied it around her trim waist. "I'll be using a lot of them tonight, and we'll need more for breakfast."

Philip nodded as he lit a lantern to take outside.

Rather hesitantly Jack said, "Can I help with the chores?"

"Of course, sir, if you wish to," Philip said, his face expressionless.

Outside the temperature was dropping and a few errant flakes of snow drifted about aimlessly. As they crossed the yard, Jack said, "I'm sorry to prove such a disappointment, Philip."

The youth turned his head quickly to the visitor. "Please, sir, it is I who should be apologizing. Ever since you spoke to me, I've been thinking. Jeremy used to talk like I did, but when I remembered the letters he's written, I realized that they changed after he had been in Spain for a few months. He stopped writing about the war and mentioned fighting in only the briefest way, usually just to assure us that he was all right. Instead, his letters are about his friends, like you, and about amusing things that happen. I didn't really notice at the time, but now I think I understand better how war changes a man."

"That it does." Jack swung open the barn door and let his companion proceed in with the lantern. "Congratulations, Philip. You are learning wisdom much more quickly than I did. Is it your ambition to be a soldier?"

Philip shook his head as he hung the lantern on a hook so it illuminated stalls containing three horses and four cows. "I'll leave that to Jeremy. One of my father's cousins is in the East India Company, and he said he'll get me an apprenticeship when I reach sixteen. Someone in this family needs to make money if my sisters are going to be taken care of."

Clearly Meg wasn't the only practical Lambert, Jack thought, impressed by Philip's clear, unself-

ish thinking. "I imagine Phoebe will find a husband if she wants one. But why has Meg never
married—have the men of Wiltshire no sense?"

Philip lifted a pitchfork and began transferring
hay to the stalls. "An aunt offered to sponsor Meg
for a London come-out. I was very small, but I remember how excited she was. Then my mother
became ill and Meg canceled her plans. She's been
taking care of us ever since, and now she's almost
thirty." He shoved his pitchfork into the haystack
with unnecessary force. "That's why I want to be
in a position to look after her."

Mildly nettled, Jack said, "Is it so unthinkable
that Meg might still marry? She is hardly ancient."

There was nothing wrong with Philip's understanding. Abruptly resting the tines of the pitchfork on the plank floor, he regarded Jack with stern
blue eyes. "Since Jeremy isn't here, it is my duty
to ask if you have intentions toward my sister. And
if so, whether they are honorable."

Perhaps it should have been humorous to see
a boy so young challenging a man over twice his
age, but Jack was moved rather than amused.
And with all his heart, he envied the Lamberts
the love that bound them together. "Perhaps it is
early to declare intentions," he said carefully, "but
if I develop any, I assure you that they will be
honorable."

Philip relaxed and said with a combination of
mischief and warning, "Good. I'd hate to have to
put a pitchfork through you."

Jack chuckled. "Being a devout coward, I assure
you that I won't risk such a fate. Meg is lucky to
have such defenders."

"Even Tizzie and Lizzie would attack anyone
who hurt Meg, and believe me, those two can bite
when sufficiently provoked," Philip said with feeling. Abandoning solemnity, he continued, "Do you

want to help me feed cabbage to the peafowl? Believe me, it's quite an experience."

In perfect charity they finished the chores in the stables, then went off together to the poultry shed.

Meg took the bubbling steak-and-kidney pie from the oven and set it on the wooden chopping block, then regarded the crumbly golden crust with satisfaction. The pie was just plain country food, but it did her no discredit. When Jeremy had first asked permission to bring his friend for Christmas, Meg had confronted the limitations of house and budget, then decided that Jack Howard would have to take them as they were or not at all. Fortunately, in spite of his privileged background, the major had accepted everything with cheerful goodwill. He looked like a man who would enjoy a good steak-and-kidney pie.

From across the kitchen Phoebe asked, "Is it time to start boiling the Brussels sprouts?"

"Wait until Philip and Jack come in." Meg wiped her hands on her apron, then gave the soup pot a stir. It was bean soup tonight, rich and savory. "There is nothing worse than gray, overcooked Brussels sprouts." Glancing up at her sister, she asked hopefully, "What do you think of Major Howard now that you've had time to become a little better acquainted?"

Phoebe made a rueful face. "I'm sorry, Meg, I know you were hoping that he and I might form an attachment, and I must admit that I had certain hopes in that direction myself. But I'm afraid it just won't do."

Meg frowned. "Don't you like him?"

"I like him very well," Phoebe assured her. "The major is kind and good-natured and there's something wonderfully *solid* about him. But he's much older than I expected, and not at all dashing—more like a large shaggy bear. I just can't imagine falling

in love with him, and he certainly shows no disposition to fall in love with me." She gave her sister a teasing smile. "I know that you're concerned
about my future, but I'm not at my last prayers
yet. Rather than casting lures to Major Howard, I'm
prepared to wait and see if someone better comes
along."

As Phoebe talked, Meg felt a surge of relief so
intense that it shocked her. Good Lord, could she
possibly be yearning for the major herself? The
idea was so nonsensical that she could feel color
rise in her cheeks. To conceal her expression from
Phoebe's interested gaze, Meg scooped up a spoon-
ful of soup and sampled it, scorching her tongue.
She gasped and waved her hand in a vain attempt
to cool her mouth. "Needs more salt," she said
when she could speak again.

As she reached for a salt cellar, Meg decided that
soup was really a safer subject than men, for a
burned mouth would heal much faster than a
burned heart. As she added a large pinch of salt to
the pot, she reminded herself firmly that the fact
that Phoebe wasn't interested in the major did not
mean that he was available for her. Then she reminded herself again. And again.

The household Jack had grown up in had treated
him with sufferance rather than affection, so he
had never known the kind of holiday happiness he
discovered that evening. Baking proved to be a
family affair, with Philip and Phoebe chopping nuts
and dried fruit, Jack assigned to grind lumps of
sugar to powder fineness, and Tizzie and Lizzie
aiding Meg in ways that seemed to involve squeal-
ing and covering all three of them with flour. The
cats and Rugger made periodic patrols under the
tables, hoping that all this activity would produce
tangible benefits for them.

Under Meg's direction they made a vast quantity

of tiny mince pies, enough so that everyone at Brook Farm could have one on each of the twelve days of Christmas, to ensure luck for the coming year. Then came gingerbread; Meg had everyone help her cut it into the shapes of stars before baking.

As the house filled with irresistibly spicy scents, Phoebe unexpectedly broke into song. To Jack's surprise, everyone else joined in, as if singing "While Shepherds Watched Their Flocks by Night" were the most natural thing in the world. For the Lamberts, it clearly was. Phoebe was a soprano, her voice a little weak because of her recent cold, but very sweet. Meg had a rich contralto and Philip a very passable tenor. Even Tizzie and Lizzie chimed in, their high clear voices like cherubim.

After the song was done, Meg looked up from the hazelnut-and-chocolate pudding she was mixing. "Do you sing, Jack?" she asked with a bewitching smile. "We could use a baritone."

As he looked into her warm hazel eyes, Jack felt something very strange happen deep in his chest. It wasn't the kitchen that was the heart of the Lambert household, it was Meg herself. And more than anything else on earth, he wanted to spend the rest of his life within the circle of her warmth. If they had been alone, he would have said as much.

Instead, Jack cleared his throat gruffly. "If you don't mind hearing a voice that has been described as capable of stopping a bull in its tracks, I'll be happy to join in."

This time it was Philip who started a song, choosing "The Holly and the Ivy," and for the next hour they sang all the Christmas carols they knew. Jack even taught them a simple Spanish song that he had learned on the Peninsula.

The party broke up gradually, first the little girls being taken off to bed, then the adults yawning and conceding fatigue. As Jack drifted toward sleep with the calico cat sprawled on his stomach, he knew that he had never felt so much a part of a family in his life.

"You may enter the parlor now!" Phoebe announced grandly.

It was Christmas Eve and Phoebe had insisted on total privacy while she decorated the kissing bough. Tizzie and Lizzie had been excited to near-speechlessness by the secrecy and would periodically peer into the parlor, attempting to steal a glimpse.

Caught up in the holiday mood, Jack had felt as much anticipation as the little girls. After doing the farm chores, he and Philip had brought in the Yule log. Then they all sat in the kitchen and turned the evergreens they had collected into yards and yards of garlands while Meg produced more delicacies for the Christmas feast.

Summoned by Phoebe, everyone solemnly entered the parlor to see the results of the girl's handiwork. Jack was prepared to admire whatever she had made, but in the event, it was quite unnecessary to counterfeit enthusiasm.

As Tizzie and Lizzie squealed rapturously, Meg lifted the kissing bough and exclaimed, "Oh, Phoebe! What a wonderful idea to use peacock feathers. I never thought of such a thing."

The kissing bough was a double hoop of dried vine and traditionally was decorated with evergreens, scarlet berries, candles, and mistletoe. That was quite enough to make it pretty, but bows of silver ribbon and the gleaming, colorful tips of peacock feathers made this one absolutely breathtaking.

"It *was* rather a stroke of genius, wasn't it?" Phoebe agreed. Clearly she was no believer in false modesty.

Taking the kissing bough from Meg, Philip gave his other sister a wicked grin. "Considering that you're as vain as a peacock, you should have thought of this years ago."

For a moment Phoebe teetered between behaving like a mature lady and giving in to her natural instincts. Instinct won and she threw a handful of feather scraps at her brother. "Beast! You should talk—it wasn't me who asked if I looked like that picture of Lord Byron."

"You don't have to—you look more like him than I do," Philip retorted, then retreated hastily across the parlor as Phoebe began stalking him with wrath in her eyes.

"Children, children," Meg said indulgently. "What will Major Howard think?"

Laughing, Jack replied, "Major Howard thinks that the Lamberts know how to have a good time."

Phoebe ceased chasing her brother and gave a wistful sigh. "I do so wish Jeremy was here. For weeks I've been looking forward to having him home for Christmas."

"We all have," Meg agreed, "but he'll be home soon, and that is almost as good." She smiled at their guest. "We're fortunate to have Jack here even though Jeremy was delayed."

Jack felt a massive stab of guilt at his deception, particularly knowing that if Jeremy were here, Jack would not be. With complete honesty he said, "The good fortune is mine."

Meg gave him one of her sweet, sweet smiles, then scooped Lizzie up in her arms. "It's time to put up the rest of the decorations. Shall we set this little angel on the mantelpiece?"

Lizzie shrieked with delight as Jack took her from Meg and perched her on the mantel, then put Tizzie by her side. With their bright blond hair, they made very fine angels for about one minute, after which the small sisters demanded to be taken down so they could help Phoebe weave bright bits of peacock feather into the garlands.

The mantel was decorated with candles and evergreens and ribbons, and the garlands were hung, filling the room with a tangy forest fragrance. Then Philip hung the kissing bough from the chandelier. As he lit the candles, all around the room feathers shimmered with iridescent blues and greens and silver bows sparkled to life. There was a soft collective intake of breath as everyone admired the effect. Outside it was dark and a bitter wind rattled the windows, but the parlor glowed with warmth and color and love. Most of all, love.

Then Philip pulled Tizzie under the bough and gave her a smacking kiss on the cheek. "There!" he said with a grin. "That's what kissing boughs are for."

As Tizzie gazed at him adoringly, Lizzie moved in for her kiss, followed by Philip's smiling sisters.

A quick learner, Tizzie seized Jack's hand, tugged him under the mistletoe, then waited hopefully. He laughed and obliged her, thinking how much a child's delight added to the magic of the season. Of course Lizzie also had to be kissed, and after that Phoebe presented herself with as little self-consciousness as the little girls.

After receiving Jack's playful kiss, Phoebe said gaily, "Your turn, Meg."

Jack gave Meg an appalled glance. As plainly as if it were written on the wall in letters of flame, he knew that they were both thinking of the kiss in the stable at Chippenham. So much for her comment that they should forget what had happened. Jack recalled with absolute precision how her soft body had molded against him, how she had tasted, and how she had responded. Remembering that, it was impossible to kiss her casually now.

Just before the silence became embarrassingly obvious, Meg stepped up and presented her cheek with a determined let's-get-this-over-with expression. Jack gave her a quick, awkward peck. Her creamy skin was silky smooth beneath his lips. Then the moment was over, to Jack's immense relief.

The evening's program was simple but rewarding for all ages. They dined, then danced as Meg and Phoebe took turns playing the old spinet. There was wassail for the adults and hot spiced cider for the little girls, and games like snapdragon and puss in the corner—once played with a real puss.

Eventually Tizzie and Lizzie curled up together in a ball, snoozing like kittens, and had to be carried off to bed. Then the adults relaxed around the fire, the Lamberts reminiscing about notable Christmases of the past. Jack said very little, though he several times compared this evening with what he would have had to endure at the countess's hands. As he sipped wassail, he gave thanks to the fate that had sent him here.

Finally Philip rose and clasped both of Phoebe's hands. "Time for bed, sleepyhead," he said, hauling his sister to her feet. "You'll have to walk because you're too heavy to carry."

"But I don't want to go to bed yet," she protested.

Her brother directed a meaningful glance from Meg to Jack. "Yes, you do."

Phoebe's eyes widened. Then she gave an exaggerated yawn. "For once you're right. I *am* rather tired."

As Philip tugged Phoebe from the room, he gave Jack a conspiratorial smile. Jack almost laughed; clearly he had acquired an enthusiastic ally.

As her brother and sister left the room, Meg murmured, "I should go to bed too. It will be a busy day tomorrow. There's the goose to prepare in the morning, and church, and a thousand other things." But she made no move to rise.

Curled up on the sofa with two cats, a dreamy smile, and tousled curls that glowed in the firelight, Meg looked good enough to eat, even though Jack should not be hungry after all the food he had put away. If he had any sense, he would also go to bed and leave his hostess in safe solitude, but these moments of peaceful togetherness were too precious to end quickly.

Needing something to keep his hands busy and off his hostess, Jack put his glass down and wandered over to the large Black Forest clock that hung on the wall, sprigs of holly fastened on top. "I've always had a fondness for cuckoo clocks. Is this one broken or has it just run down because you've been too busy to tend it?"

"There is a story to that clock. My father bought it in Munich when he was on his grand tour. He was always very fond of the clock and kept it in his study at Peacock Hill." Meg raised her glass and drained the last of her wassail. "He died in that study. It was very sudden—the doctor said his heart failed. The clock stopped that day and never ran again."

Intrigued, Jack ran appreciative fingers over the silky, beautifully carved wood. The hands had stopped at 11:27. "Did you decide to leave it like this as a memorial to your father?"

"Not really. It was just that so much happened after my father died—losing Peacock Hill, having to move. There was neither time nor money to have the clock fixed." Meg smiled wryly. "I suppose that I should see to it. Jeremy won't have Peacock Hill, but at least he can have Papa's clock, and it will be much more useful to him if it works."

"Shall I take a look at it?" Jack offered. "I'm a fair hand with things mechanical. Even if I can't fix it, at least I should be able to find out what's wrong.''

Since Meg looked doubtful, he said coaxingly, ''Please? I didn't bring any real Christmas presents, so fixing the clock can be my gift to you. I promise I won't leave it in worse condition than I found it.''

Meg smiled. ''Very well, if you don't mind. I'm fond of the clock, though I've always thought cuckoos quite dishonorable for their habit of laying their eggs in the nests of other birds. The poor host birds become fagged to death raising the cuckoos' ravenous offspring.''

Meg's words struck so unexpectedly close to the bone that Jack almost dropped the clock as he moved it to a table by the fire. What was he himself but a Christmas cuckoo who had ended up in the wrong nest? He uttered a brief prayer that Meg would prove more tolerant of him than of the despised cuckoo.

As he opened the clock, he remarked, ''A cuckoo is not that different from aristocratic parents who give their children to nurses to raise.''

''Another reason to despise the nobility,'' Meg retorted, ''though at least nurses are paid, unlike the poor victims of the cuckoos' deceit.''

Jack concentrated on the clock. He had the uneasy feeling that Meg was going to require a great deal of persuasion to see him in the light of an acceptable suitor. Perhaps he should confess now, when she was mellow with contentment and wassail.

Resolved, he opened his mouth to speak, then frowned as his probing fingertips touched something unexpected inside the clock case. ''There is some kind of obstruction—paper, I think. Could one of the children have stuffed something inside?''

''I suppose so,'' Meg said without much interest.

"There were always children in and out of Peacock Hill. Be grateful that it is paper and not something dreadful like a petrified frog."

Jack managed to pull the paper out without ripping it. There was one large sheet, bulky and yellow-gray with age. Curious, he opened it and flattened the sheet on the table, then peered at the faded writing in the flickering firelight.

The words were in Latin and it took time to puzzle out the old legal phrases. Then he gasped, his heart speeding up like a galloping horse. "Meg, come look at this."

Startled by his tone, she set her glass aside and came to peer over his shoulder.

"I hope to God I'm not raising false hopes," Jack said in a choked voice, "but I think this is the deed to Peacock Hill."

Meg felt the blood drain from her face. Snatching the paper up, she tilted it toward the fire. "Merciful heaven," she whispered. "You're right, this *is* the deed. Not long before he died, Papa waved it at me when he said that Lord Mason would give a fortune to possess this piece of paper." She ran trembling, awestruck fingers over the old lettering. "How on earth do you think it came to be inside the clock?"

Jack considered. "You say that your father died in his study. When he was stricken, he may have become confused and felt that he had to put the deed somewhere safe, where Mason couldn't get it. The clock was right there and had always been special to him, so he shoved the deed inside, jamming the mechanism. We'll never know, of course, but that seems a plausible explanation."

"But how did Lord Mason know that we would be unable to find the deed?" she asked in bewilderment.

Jack thought some more. "Perhaps your father once told Mason that the deed was hidden safe away. Then, when he died so suddenly, Mason decided to gamble on the remote chance that no one would know where your father had left it."

"It's the sort of thing Lord Mason might do, for he is a famous gamester," Meg said thoughtfully. "He had little to lose by trying, and his gamble paid off spectacularly well. The despicable wretch."

"His gamester's luck has run out," Jack said with deep satisfaction. "Not only can you reclaim Peacock Hill, but you can file a suit for fraud against Lord Mason. He'll probably pay a handsome settlement to keep the case from going to court and becoming public knowledge. I doubt he will want to be known as someone who stole the inheritance of a family of orphans."

Meg was too happy to be concerned with retribution. "You know what this means?" she said, bubbling with joy. "Jeremy will be able to sell out and come back to Peacock Hill and marry his sweetheart, Anne Marshall. I'm sorry, Jack, I know you'll miss him, but we need him more here. And Phoebe will be able to make her come-out and Philip won't have to go to India unless he really wants to . . ." Distractedly she brushed her hair back as she tried to think of all the implications. "You've given us all a Christmas present beyond our wildest dreams. I know the words are feeble, but thank you, Jack, from the bottom of my heart. I must go tell Philip and Phoebe."

"Let them sleep. The deed has waited for five years, it can wait until morning." Jack stood and put a hand under her chin, lifting it so that her gaze met his. "You always say 'we' and 'us,' Meg." Then, as he had once before, he asked, "Isn't there anything that you want just for yourself?"

As Meg looked into Jack's intense blue eyes, she caught her breath, feeling a shiver that started in her toes and tingled through her entire body. She made no protest when he drew her into an embrace under the kissing bough. His lips met hers in a warm, wise, leisurely exploration that bore no resemblance to the chaste kiss he had given her earlier.

Delirious with happiness and desire, Meg kissed him back. As Phoebe had said, there was something wonderfully solid about Jack Howard. But he was also, based on the evidence of her curling toes, the most intoxicatingly attractive man she had ever known. Best of all, he made Meg feel as irresistible as Helen of Troy. She almost dropped the precious deed.

Abruptly Jack set Meg away from him, though fortunately he kept his hands firmly on her waist or she might have folded down to the floor. "Tomorrow, after breakfast and church and all the rest, I have something very important to say to you," he said huskily. "You—not Phoebe or Philip or Tizzie and Lizzie, but you. Then I'm going to ask you a question. You know what it will be, don't you, Meg?"

"Yes, Jack." On this magical night, Meg knew that anything was possible, even that this delicious man might fancy an old spinster like her.

"Good. Then think about your answer." He bent his head and gave her a quick, expert kiss in case she had forgotten in the last sixty seconds. "Just be sure that the answer is yes."

"Yes, Jack," Meg said obediently. She knew that her eyes must be shining like the Star of Bethlehem.

Turning her around, he gave her a gentle slap on the backside. "Now, go to bed, Miss Lambert, or tonight might end in a way that would make Philip feel honor-bound to put a pitchfork through me."

Meg floated across the room, then turned in the doorway. "Good night, Jack." She blew him a kiss. "I love you, Jack."

When he took a step toward her, his face glowing
with joy, Meg whirled and dashed across the hall
and through the kitchen to her room on the other
side. The only thing that kept her from expiring
with embarrassment at her forwardness was the
knowledge that she had spoken the plain truth.

Her bedroom was freezing, so Meg set the deed
on the table and quickly undressed. Then she
moved the tabby cat, Striper, to the foot of the bed
and slid under the covers. Wrapping her arms
around a pillow, she whispered again, "I love you,
Jack."

Life was perfect.

It was very early when Meg woke, only the
faintest hint of dawn coloring the eastern sky. She
stretched luxuriously, feeling marvelous in spite of
the short night's sleep. Could she possibly have
dreamed the events of the previous night? No, on
her table the deed was visible, a pale rectangle in
the gloom.

Jack had said that he had something to ask her,
and that she should answer yes. With wonder, Meg
touched her lips, where the memory of his kiss lingered. The lovely, kind man upstairs actually
wanted to marry her. When she was younger, she
had twice refused two suitors who wanted her but
regarded her family as an unpleasant necessity.
Jack was different, for he fitted into her family as
if there had been a Jack-size vacancy just waiting
for him. There would be no problem giving him the
answer he wanted.

Meg was too full of energy to stay in bed, so she
threw back the covers and dressed, then went into
the kitchen and built up the fire. After stuffing the
goose for roasting, she started readying potatoes,
onions, bacon, and eggs for the hearty dish that
was the traditional Lambert Christmas breakfast.

Breakfast preparations complete, Meg glanced

out and saw that it was almost full light. A couple
of inches of feathery snow had fallen in the night,
enough to make snow cream. Tizzie and Lizzie
would enjoy that. Jack probably would too.

Thinking of Jack, Meg was gazing out the window with a foolish smile on her face when she
heard the outside door open into the hall next to
the kitchen. For a moment she was startled and a
little alarmed. Then she realized that there could
be only one person arriving so early on Christmas
morning.

She raced across the kitchen. "Jeremy?" she
called softly, not wanting to wake the others. "Is
that you?"

A lean, snow-dusted figure appeared in the
kitchen door. "It is indeed, Meg," said a familiar
beloved voice. "Cold, hungry, and ready to be
pampered."

With a squeal that would have done credit to
Lizzie, Meg hurled herself into her brother's arms.
As she did, footsteps sounded on the stairs and
Philip appeared, dark hair wild and clothes hastily
thrown on. "Jeremy—you finally made it!"

"Now, this is what I call a proper welcome!" Jeremy said, hugging his sister so hard that he lifted
her from her feet. Setting her down, he added,
"You've shrunk, big sister."

Turning, he wrapped an affectionate arm around
his younger brother's shoulders. "And you've
grown."

Meg studied Jeremy's tired but happy face. He
looked older, of course, and stronger. Her little
brother had become a man. Voice breaking, Meg
said, "Oh, Jeremy, it only needed you to make
Christmas perfect."

"Not quite." Smiling, Jeremy stepped back and
motioned toward a tall black-haired young man
who waited just inside the door. Meg had not noticed him, for the stranger had tactfully stayed in

the background during the family greetings. "Look who else is here."

Meg was only momentarily off-balance. So Jeremy had brought another friend. Fortunately it was a large goose. She gave the newcomer an approving glance. Like Jeremy, he was travel-stained and bristle-chinned, but he was still very attractive.

"I'm very pleased to meet you. Do you mind if I call you Meg?" the newcomer said. "Jeremy has told me so much about his family that I feel as if I know you all."

"Please do. And what is your name?" Meg replied, thinking that the young man had a charming smile. Phoebe would like him.

Jeremy laughed. "This is Jack Howard, of course."

With a flourish the newcomer kissed Meg's proffered hand. "I'm sorry that I was unable to notify you that I wouldn't reach Chippenham three days ago," he said apologetically. "The packet I was on was blown off-course and I reached London about the same time Jeremy did. By the sheerest coincidence, we met at the coaching inn last night. The coach was full, so we hired a chaise and drove all night to be here for Christmas."

Meg gasped. "But you're not Jack Howard."

"I assure you that I am," he said, gray eyes twinkling. "No doubt you were expecting someone a bit more presentable, but Jeremy will vouch for me."

Meg felt as if she had been turned into a marble statue. Then her gaze turned to meet Philip's shocked stare. It took her two tries to croak out the words, *"If you're Jack Howard, then who is the man sleeping upstairs in Jeremy's bed?"*

The calico cat woke Jack, nuzzling his cheek in a bid for attention. Absently he scratched her furry head, his thoughts on Meg. He hoped she would agree to an early wedding date.

He heard sounds downstairs and guessed that it

was Meg, up early and working. Quietly he rose and dressed, thinking that he could either help her in the kitchen or compromise her, whichever seemed most appropriate.

He went into the corridor to the top of the stairs and was just starting down when he heard the fatal words, *"If you're Jack Howard, then who is the man sleeping upstairs in Jeremy's bed?"*

Jack froze, one hand on the banister, his stomach curdling. He had become so convinced that fortune was favoring his cause that he had forgotten that the sword of Damocles hung over his head—and the supporting thread had just broken.

He almost bolted, but it was too late. A board shifted under his foot and the four people down in the hall turned to gaze up at him. There was Philip and a frowning, older version of him, a tall black-haired young man with puzzlement on his face, and Meg—his darling Meg, who stared as if Jack were something she had just found under a dead leaf.

With a groan, Jack sank down onto the steps and buried his face in his hands, wondering how on earth to explain himself.

Before he had a chance to try, a white-faced Meg snapped, "Just who the devil are you?"

Jack looked up. "My name *is* Jack Howard," he said simply. "I'm just not the Jack Howard you were expecting."

Ignoring the others, Meg asked in an edged voice, "Are you really a major?"

When Jack nodded, there was a soft murmur of surprise from below. Jeremy asked incredulously, "Are you Major Jack Howard of the 51st? 'Mad Jack' Howard, the hero of Badajoz?"

Jack winced. "For my sins, yes."

The black-haired man exclaimed, "Good God, Mad Jack Howard! It's a great pleasure to meet you, sir. I wish I had a guinea for every man who offered to buy me a drink, thinking I was you. I believe we are distantly related."

"Very likely," Jack agreed, distracted. "I have a great-aunt who would be able to explain the connection."

He saw that Philip had recovered quickly from his surprise and was now studying the fraudulent guest curiously, doubtless trying to reconcile Jack's diatribe on heroism with his ridiculous nickname. Meg, however, looked as if she had been stabbed through the heart.

Jeremy's brows drew together. "But I recently heard that you had sold out because you'd inherited the earldom of Winstoke?" he said, his rising tone making it a question.

Jack sighed. "You're well-informed, Captain Lambert."

Jack's answer was the last straw for Meg. Face stricken, she whirled and fled down the hall.

"Meg!" Jack called out despairingly. "Please give me a chance to explain." Abandoning his efforts to make polite conversation, he bolted down the stairs, past the startled group of young men, and followed Meg into the parlor.

As the parlor door banged shut, Jeremy Lambert turned to his younger brother. "Would you kindly tell me what the devil has been going on here?"

Philip grinned wickedly. "Meg found him at the George in Chippenham. He followed her home and, if I'm not mistaken, she had just about decided that she wanted to keep him. Unfortunately, she's a bit disconcerted to discover that he may be a tiger rather than a tabby cat."

"You mean that Major Howard—sorry, Lord Winstoke—wants to marry our Meg?" Jeremy asked in amazement.

"I think so. Not that anyone tells me anything."

A clear voice sounded from above. "Jeremy, is that you?"

Phoebe scampered down the stairs, resplendent in a scarlet robe, her dark hair curling deliciously around her face. Just like her older sister, she leapt into her brother's arms. "Oh, marvelous, you made it home in time for Christmas!"

"Indeed." Jeremy laughed. "Though I'm beginning to wonder if I've landed in Bedlam instead." Taking Phoebe's arm, he turned her to his companion. "This is my friend Jack Howard . . . *Captain* Howard of the 45th, not to be confused with *Major* Howard of the 51st, though apparently he was."

As she tried to sort out her brother's words, Phoebe automatically offered her hand, then gasped as she focused on the captain. "You—you look exactly as I thought Jeremy's friend would," she said stupidly.

The captain kissed her hand, then straightened without relinquishing his grip. "You are Phoebe. You couldn't be anyone else." He had the stupefied look of a man who has just hit a stone wall at speed. "You can't imagine how much I've looked forward to meeting you."

Philip rolled his eyes. Fearing that they would continue making sheep's eyes indefinitely, he gave his sister a light pinch on the rump. "Go put some decent clothes on, Pheebles—you are quite putting me to the blush."

It was Phoebe who blushed as she remembered her state of dishabillé. She released the captain's hand, shooting Philip a dagger look and whispering under her breath, "Don't you dare use that appalling nickname again—Phippy."

"Pax!" He grinned. "No nicknames."

As the entranced captain's gaze followed Phoebe up the stairs, Philip decided that it was time to play the host. "Jeremy, Captain Howard, you must be cold and famished. Why not come into the kitchen for some hot tea and breakfast?"

The two travelers accepted with alacrity, and Philip ushered them into the kitchen with a philosophical sigh. It would be a bit confusing if they ended up with two brothers-in-law named Jack Howard, but no doubt they'd learn to cope.

The fact that Jack had followed her into the parlor was the only thing that kept Meg from dissolving in tears. She retreated to the far corner of the room. "Your game is over, and I think it is time for you to leave, Lord . . . What was it, Winsmoke?"

"Winstoke, and I'm not leaving until I've said my piece." He looked at her pleadingly. "Later today I was going to tell you the truth—in fact, I tried to confess earlier, and you kept telling me not to say any more. I admit that I should not have left it at that, but I honestly did attempt to explain."

Meg gave a brittle laugh. "So you were being literal when you said you weren't the man I thought you were. Foolish me—I thought you meant something profound and mysterious. I didn't understand much, did I?"

"You understood a great deal more than I was able to say, Meg," he said quietly. "Please, try to understand now."

His words silenced Meg. As she thought back over the three days the major had been at Brook Farm, she realized that it was true that several times he had started to tell her something, but the conversation had always gone astray. And there had been other clues; he had never spoken of Jeremy or the regiment or any other aspect of his background. Thinking that they knew who he was, the Lamberts had noticed nothing unusual in his behavior.

Meg's face burned as she realized how she had misunderstood him from beginning to end. Particularly last night; he couldn't possibly have meant that he wanted to marry her, not with him being an earl. God only knew what he had meant. Her hands clenched spasmodically. "Why did you come home with me?"

"I wouldn't have been so brazen if I was sober, but you seemed to know me, and you were so lovely and kind. I would have followed you anywhere," he said simply.

Meg shivered. He didn't look like an earl or a legendary war hero; he still looked like Jack, large and shaggy, with an unpredictable mixture of shyness and humor and those blue, blue eyes that were so misleadingly honest. "Why were you in the George at all? Surely the Earl of Winspoke had someplace better to be for Christmas."

"Winstoke. And no, I definitely did not have a better place to be." He gave a faint, humorless smile. "In fact, when you met me, I was running away from my great-aunt by marriage, the dowager Countess of Winstoke, the most terrifying old dragon you could ever hope not to meet." His voice softened. "You're freezing, Meg. I'll build a fire and you'll feel better."

Meg *was* freezing, but she maintained a wary distance while he knelt at the hearth and efficiently laid a new fire. Abruptly she asked, "Why were you running away?"

He struck a spark, then sat back on his heels and watched as the shredded paper began to burn. "Do you want the short reason or the long reason?"

"The long one."

Still looking down, Jack said, "I was never supposed to inherit an earldom. I was an orphaned second cousin with half a dozen heirs between me and the title. With my parents dead, my great-uncle, the third earl, took responsibility for raising me. The dragon dowager was his wife. Just like you, they knew their duty to family and were quite punctilious about discharging their obligations. But, unlike you, they performed their duty with all the warmth and charm of a pair of testy hedge-hogs.''

He sighed and ran a hand through his brown hair, leaving it hopelessly disordered. "I don't mean that anyone was cruel to me. It was just that the Winstokes were very busy and I was very . . . insignificant, living in the margins of Hazelwood like a mouse in the larder. I was sent to school, though not Eton, of course. Eton was for heirs.

"I spent holidays at Hazelwood because there was nowhere else to go. I was given an allowance, a modest one, so I wouldn't get any ideas above my station, and a commission was purchased for me when I was old enough to be sent into the world. No one bothered to invite me to come back for a visit, although, to be fair, if I had visited, no one would have dreamed of asking me to leave. As a Howard, I had a right to be there. But that isn't quite the same thing as being welcome."

Reluctantly Meg felt a tug at her heart. There was no self-pity in Jack's voice. Just flat acceptance masking a sadness as large as all outdoors. She took a few steps toward the fire. "But now you're the master of Hazelwood. Surely that will make a difference."

He shrugged. "I will be obeyed, of course, but hardly loved. There was never enough love to go around at Hazelwood, and my becoming the master won't instantly change that. I fell out of touch with the family and didn't realize how close I stood to the title. It was a shock to be summoned back to England to take up my responsibilities when my cousin, the fifth earl, died. I'm still not quite accustomed to the idea of being the head of the family." He chuckled suddenly. "The way you railed against the nobility made it even harder to confess my sins."

Meg bit her lip; she *had* sounded rather fishwifish. "You've only just arrived back in England from the Peninsula?"

"The very day I met you. The dowager countess arranged everything, but characteristically forgot to consult me about my wishes. Her secretary met me in London and presented me with a list of things I must do to avoid disgracing my new station. He couldn't bring himself to call me Lord Winstoke—in fact, he barely managed common civility. After half an hour of that, I succumbed to an attack of rebelliousness and walked out of the inn and got on the first coach I saw. It happened to be going to Bristol. The rest you know."

Meg perched on the edge of the sofa and held her hands toward the fire. She felt much warmer. "The countess sounds like a proper tartar."

"She is," Jack agreed. "Mind you, this is no easier for her than for me. Her own son and grandson have died—seeing me in their place will be a bitter pill to swallow. But she will accept and help me because that is her duty. I've no doubt that she and I will learn to rub along tolerably, but it was not a bad thing to refuse to spend Christmas at Hazelwood. She needs to know that I won't let her bully me."

Meg shivered again; there must be a draft. "So Brook Farm was merely a convenient place to hide from the countess."

"When I reached the George, I was running away, and any inn would have done." His grave blue eyes met hers. "But as soon as I saw you, I had something to run *to*. As I said at the time, I knew you were everything men fight for: home, warmth, love."

Meg linked her hands tightly in her lap. "You weren't secretly laughing at our rural simplicity?"

"Good God, Meg, no!" he said, horrified. "I was so moved, so grateful, for the way you and your family welcomed me. I felt as if I'd come home after a lifetime of wandering. Meeting you seemed like fate. Nothing else could explain my being at exactly the right place at the right time with the right name, and the correct Jack Howard *not* being here." He gave her a crooked smile. "If I had told you the truth, I would have had to leave, and I couldn't bear the thought of that. It would have been like being expelled from the Garden of Eden."

Meg gave an involuntary chuckle. "It was Adam and Eve who were expelled—the role you played was the serpent."

Jack's expression eased at her laughter. "Not the serpent—just a cuckoo who landed in the wrong nest and was too happy to want to be cast out into the cold, cruel world."

She bit her lip. "I wouldn't have cast you out if I'd known you had no place to go for Christmas."

"Then don't cast me out now, Meg," he said quietly. He held his hand out to her.

Hesitantly Meg accepted it, and Jack tugged her down onto the carpet next to him. This close to the fire, it was much warmer, quite cozy in fact.

He clasped both her hands in his. "Yesterday I said that I had something to say to you, and then a question to ask. Now you know what I was going to tell you. Have you been thinking about your answer to the question?"

"Just what was the question, Jack?" Meg asked.

His brows lifted. "Don't you know?"

"I thought I did, but perhaps I was wrong." The expression in his eyes made Meg feel rather breathless. It was really quite warm now, almost uncomfortably so. "You had better say exactly what you mean."

Jack smiled at her tenderly. "I want to marry you, of course."

"Is it because you want me to protect you from the dowager countess?"

"No." He grinned. "Or at least that's only a small

part of the reason. I want to marry you because I love you and will certainly go into a decline if banished from your presence." He lifted her hands and kissed first one, then the other.

Meg's fingers curled around his. "I'm dreadfully managing, you know. I would torment you unmercifully."

He looked hopeful. "*Please* torment me, Meg. You can't imagine how much I look forward to that."

She could not stop herself from laughing. "Are you never serious, you absurd man?"

"I am when I say that I love you." Suddenly solemn, he met her gaze. "Were you serious last night, Meg?"

She blushed and nodded. "I've never been in love before. This morning I felt like a bit of a fool when I realized that I'd fallen in love with a cuckoo."

Jack laughed and drew her into his arms so that her head tucked under his chin. Meg relaxed against him, thinking how very large and comfortable he was.

Jack murmured into her ear, "You still haven't answered my question. Will you marry me?"

"I'll never make a proper countess."

"All it takes to be a proper countess is to marry an earl, and I'll take care of that part of it," he said, laughter in his voice. More seriously he continued, "With your warmth and wisdom, you'll make a countess such as Hazelwood has never known before."

Weakly she summoned the last argument she could think of. "We've known each other for only three days."

"But I've been looking for you all my life."

Meg caught her breath; it was easy to believe that he was a military hero, for he certainly knew how to destroy one's defenses. "Is it really that simple?"

"It is for me, Meg." He brushed her hair with one large hand. "And if you do love me, it should be simple for you too."

With a slow flowering of joy, Meg's hesitation dissolved. "It really is that simple, isn't it?" she said in a voice full of wonder. "Yes, Jack, I'll marry you."

He gave a whoop of delight and fell back onto the carpet, pulling her with him so that she was sprawled across his chest in a perfect position for serious kissing. For the next several minutes, guests and Christmas were utterly forgotten. Then came the faint squeaking sound of a tiny door opening, followed by a clear, "Cuckoo, cuckoo!"

They stopped kissing and counted. "Nine o'clock," Jack said with satisfaction. "The clock is working just as it ought. Do you think your father would be pleased?"

"Good Lord!" Meg clapped her hand over her mouth. "I had completely forgotten about the deed and Peacock Hill. We must go tell the others. What an unforgettable Christmas this will be!"

Jack stood, then assisted Meg to her feet. "It already is."

As she made a token attempt to restore her appearance to that of a decorous older sister, Meg said mischievously, "I never realized that the cuckoo and his foster family might become attached to each other in spite of their differences. But then, I never met a Christmas cuckoo before."

Laughing, Jack put his arm around his ladylove's shoulders and escorted her to the door of the parlor. But just before leaving the room he gave the cuckoo clock a salute—as a mark of respect between two birds of a feather.

The Best
Christmas Ever

by

Mary Balogh

"I wish for an army of tin soldiers," Peregrine Milford said very deliberately, fixing his eyes on the holly draped over the high marble mantel above the crackling fire. He made sure that his voice was loud enough to penetrate to the farthest corner and the most remote uncle and aunt in the drawing room.

"A whole army, not just a company or regiment," Sir Peter Milford, his father, said dryly. "Well, when one makes a wish, one might as well make it a grand one, I suppose."

"I wish for a porcelain doll," Peregrine's sister Harriet said with equal distinctness. "With golden ringlets and blue eyes."

"Predictable, thank heaven," Lady Sophia Milford murmured to her husband.

"I wish for a cricket ball and bat," Aubrey Dermott blurted uneasily, out of turn, "although I shan't be able to use them until summer. But I say, this is a foolish game. I am too old for this."

Lord Hodges, his father, seated somewhere behind the semicircle of children about the fire, laughed. "Until you are twelve, Aub, it must be done," he said. "It is family tradition. And you are only eleven and seven months."

"The children of this family have always made their Christmas wishes about the fire the night before Christmas Eve," the Countess of Crampton,

147

Aubrey's grandmother, said. "And by the strange miracle of the season, their wishes are almost always granted."

The Earl of Crampton wheezed in such a manner that it was impossible to tell if he were laughing or coughing. "And many an addled parent has had to hare into York on Christmas Eve for a spot of last-minute shopping, too," he said.

"My love, please," the countess scolded, *sotto voce.* "The children!"

The earl's wheezing this time was definitely a product of amusement.

"It is Julie's turn," the countess said. "What is your Christmas wish, dear?"

Edwin Gwent, Baron Radbrook, the only son of the earl and countess, fixed his eyes on the child indicated and frowned. She looked rather like the porcelain doll her elder sister had just wished for. She was flushed and starry-eyed with all the excitement of the approaching Christmas in her face. But Lord Radbrook did not listen to what she requested.

What about Anna? he thought, his eyes straying to his own five-year-old daughter, who was sitting cross-legged on the floor with the other children, staring dreamily into the fire. What did she want for Christmas? And how was he to know? How was he to prevent her disappointment and disillusionment on Christmas morning when her wish did not come true?

It was all very well for the other parents to encourage a continuance of this family custom, which had been observed for as long as he could remember. The chances were that their children had been dropping hints for long enough that they had already been able to purchase the wished-for items. And as his father had just suggested, there was always York a mere seven miles away on those occasions when a child had kept his wish a secret until the last moment.

But what about Anna?

"Anna?" The countess spoke in the softened tones she always reserved for this particular granddaughter. "It is time to make your wish, dear."

Anna turned to look up at her grandmother with the large dark eyes that would make her a beauty when she grew up, her father thought. Marianne's eyes. Her mother's eyes. But at the age of five the eyes seemed too large for her thin, pale face, and the dark hair, dressed in ringlets, seemed too heavy.

She turned back to gaze into the fire again while the members of her family, gathered in the drawing room at Williston Hall, maintained a polite silence.

I wish for a new mama for Christmas, Anna thought, articulating the words very clearly in her mind. *Please, a new mama. I don't want her to be pretty, like Miss Chadwick, or always talking and stooping down to tell me how pretty and how good I am and then smiling at Papa and forgetting about me. I want someone not so pretty, and someone quiet. Someone who will love me and not try to take Papa away from me.*

"Have you made your wish, dear?" her grandmother asked, breaking the silence around her.

Anna closed her eyes very tightly. *A new mama for Christmas, please,* she begged an unseen power once more, and opened her eyes and turned her head to look up into her father's unsmiling face.

"She has," he said quietly, and he smiled at her. And felt his heart ache for her. He had noted the tightly closed eyes and compressed lips and knew that a very particular wish had been made.

What was it? he asked her with his eyes. *What*

*is it that you want, Anna? A doll? A new dress?
A parasol? A muff?* All four were upstairs in his
room, wrapped carefully and tied with bright ribbons, waiting for Christmas morning. But what if
on all four counts he had guessed wrongly?

"Stephanie?" the Countess of Crampton said in
her more normal voice, turning her eyes on her
niece Marjorie Fotheringale's daughter. "What is
your Christmas wish, dear?"

Anna liked her cousins. She liked all her relatives, in fact. There was a wonderful feeling of security about being at Williston Hall, at her
grandfather's house, surrounded by people who
belonged to her and who accepted her. She loved
Christmas in particular and all the decorations and
spicy smells and rich foods. She loved the way the
children were allowed downstairs to mingle with
the adults so often during the days of Christmas.

And she loved the activities of Christmas—the
long walks outside and the rides when there was
no snow, like last year, and the sleigh rides and
the skating when there was snow. Two years before, her papa had taken her up into his arms—she
could remember it though she had been not quite
four years old—and skated about the frozen lake
with her, and she had felt as safe as could be, even
though her older cousins had been shrieking and
falling all over the place. Papa had not fallen even
once.

And the indoor activities—charades and blindman's buff and carol singing while Aunt Sophia
played the pianoforte, and a whole host of other
things.

There was only one thing wrong with family
gatherings. Stephanie, Angela, and William had
Aunt Marjorie to fuss over them and scold them
and praise them and tuck them into bed at night.
Peregrine, Harriet, and Julie had Aunt Sophie.

Even Aubrey, who was too old to need a mama, had Aunt Patricia.

She did not have a mama. She had had one once. In fact . . . But no. Her thoughts were always pulled to an abrupt halt at such moments. She had had a mama, but she could not remember her. She *would* not remember her.

She had Papa. And she loved him totally. He was her world and her universe. She was going to stay with Papa for the rest of her life. When she was grown up, she was going to go to India with him and to America and Brazil. And to Bath too. She was going to go all over the world with Papa.

But for some time past she had longed for a mama. Ever since last summer, in fact, when she and Papa had been at Grandpapa's and she had watched Aunt Marjorie undress Stephanie for the night and brush out her long blond hair and laugh with her as she drew the hair into various grown-up styles with her hands. And then Aunt Marjorie, seeing Anna staring wistfully at them, had come and done the same for her before Papa had arrived to kiss her good night. And Aunt Marjorie's hands had been slim and soft—not like Papa's—and she had smelled of roses.

The flames of the fire were dancing before Anna's eyes. She had not heard Stephanie's wish, or Angela's or William's, though everyone was doing a deal of laughing over William's wish and Aunt Marjorie was saying "Mercy on us!" and looking appealingly at Uncle Humphrey.

"We will have to hope that York is a miracle city," Uncle Humphrey said, and bellowed with laughter while Aunt Marjorie said "Mercy on us!" again.

Anna got to her feet and left the semicircle of children. She went to her father, who picked her up and set her on his lap, and she burrowed her head beneath his coat and against the warm slippery silk of his waistcoat.

"Did you make your wish, Anna?" he asked her. "Can you let Papa know somehow? Will you draw me a picture?"

But she shook her head and burrowed deeper. Wishes did not come true if one told. That was why all the children were instructed to think aloud to the fire. They were not telling anyone. They were merely thinking. That was what Grandmama always said, anyway, and Anna believed her implicitly. Her wish would not come true if she told Papa. And she wanted her wish to come true. More than anything.

But please not Miss Chadwick, she thought. *Please, someone very quiet and ordinary. Someone who smells of roses. Someone with soft, slim hands.*

Lord Radbrook lowered his head and kissed the dark ringlets clustered on his child's head.

What he should give her for Christmas, he thought, was a new mother. That was probably what she needed more than anything else. She had been without Marianne for well over two years— for almost half of her young life.

Roberta Chadwick? She would be arriving on the morrow with Mr. and Mrs. Shelton, her sister and brother-in-law, and several other guests who were not close enough family to have been invited for the full week before Christmas.

Should he do what he had been steeling himself to do ever since the previous Season in town and offer for her? Should he tell Anna on Christmas Day, if he had the reply he expected, that she was to have a new mama?

"Children?" Marjorie Fotheringale was on her feet and clapping her hands. "Time for bed. And there is no point in groaning and looking hopefully at your papa, William. If you are to be up and

bright for Christmas Eve, you will need your sleep.
To bed!"

"Yes, you too, Aub," Lord Hodges said firmly.
"You will be an old man next year when you are
twelve, and will doubtless be allowed to stay up all
night and all the next day too if you so wish. This
year you are only eleven. Off you go."

Lord Radbrook got to his feet, his daughter in his
arms. "I shall take Anna up," he said. "I'll be back
soon."

The Countess of Crampton sighed as her son followed the children from the room. "Dear little
Anna," she said. "Will she ever talk again, do you
suppose?" She was addressing no one in particular.

"One day she will, Mama," Lady Sophia said.
"But the shock is very deep-seated. She was only
barely three."

Lady Patricia shuddered. "Dear Lord," she said,
"I hate to think of it. I still have nightmares about
it. Watching her mother drown like that, trying to
retrieve her ball from the river, and no one else
about to save her. And the child's screams. Merci-
fully I did not hear them, but Edwin described
them graphically enough. Screaming for two whole
days until she lost her voice."

Lord Hodges patted her hand. "There is no point
in torturing your mind, Trish," he said briskly.
"This is Christmas. Children are resilient. Anna
will talk again, mark my words, and laugh too."

"Roberta Chadwick would be good for her," Lady
Sophia said. "She is so very lovely and always so
sunny-natured. Will Edwin ever come to the point,
do you suppose?"

"Anna would be eclipsed by Roberta," the
countess said quietly. "She would draw all of Edwin's admiration. And remember that Anna has
had him all to herself for almost three years." She
sighed again.

"Sophia," the earl said severely to his elder daughter, his voice rumbling out of his chest, "to the pianoforte, girl. Is this Christmas or is it a funeral? Play something lively, something we can all sing to."

Lady Sophia rose obediently to her feet.

"Williston Hall at last?" Miss Hannah Beynon peered from the carriage window as the conveyance turned sharply and passed between two high and imposing stone gateposts. "And about time, too. We would both be blocks of ice, Emma, if we had much farther to go. Is the driveway long? I cannot recall. I have not been here since Peter's wedding to Sophia. Was that eight years ago or nine?"

"Nine," her niece replied, turning to smile at the red-nosed figure of her aunt, huddled from chin to toes beneath a fur-lined robe. "The driveway is no longer than a mile. We will be there in no time at all. I am sure there will be a fire in every room to greet us, and doubtless plenty of hot tea as well."

"Christmas Eve," Miss Beynon said with some indignation. "It is quite inhuman, Emma."

"Yes," her niece agreed, "it is bitterly cold. But those clouds are going to drop a load of snow before the day is out, Aunt Hannah. We are going to have a white Christmas. That will be a rare treat."

"And a body will not be able to set a toe outdoors without slipping and sliding and breaking every bone in her body," her aunt complained.

Emma was not feeling the cold. She was feeling something far worse. Dread. Nausea. Panic. A terrible nostalgia. A bitter regret that she had not stood against her aunt and refused the kind invitation of the earl and countess, as she had done the year before. Last year it had been easier, of course. She had still been wearing black for her mother. This year there had been no such excuse.

And her brother Peter had been eager for her to accept, as had her sister-in-law, Sophia.

No, it would have been near-impossible to have refused to come. The house, large, rambling, a curious mixture of architectural styles spanning several centuries, came into sight as the carriage rounded a bend in the driveway, and Emma felt a final lurching of the stomach.

Yes, that was what it looked like. She remembered now as if it had been yesterday. In truth, it was nine years—nine years last summer. Peter and Sophia's wedding, when she had spent a whole month at Williston Hall with her parents. She had been eighteen at the time. Only barely eighteen. A child. And yet old enough to make the decision that would set the course for the rest of her life.

Old enough to ruin the whole of the rest of her life.

"Brrr!" Miss Beynon said as the carriage drew to a stop before the horseshoe steps leading up to the main floor of the mansion. "I do not want to come out from beneath this robe, Emma."

Emma smiled. "Just think of those fires," she said, "and that tea." She turned and allowed a footman to hand her down onto the cobbles. The main doors were open, she saw in a glance upward. Peter was there, and Sophia, and the earl and countess. No one else. Just the four of them. She felt enormously relieved.

"You are the last to arrive," the Countess of Crampton said a few minutes later, having hugged both ladies and welcomed them to Williston Hall. "And just in time, too. The snow is going to fall at any moment. Wagering is loud and lively and fortunes are about to change hands on the exact moment when we may expect the first flake. Do come upstairs, my dear Miss Beynon. You will wish to freshen up, I am sure. And tea will be ready in the drawing room as soon as you are. Do come too,

Emma. How lovely to see you wearing colors again, my dear. The last time I saw you was at your poor dear mama's funeral.''

The drawing room was full, Emma found to her vast relief less than half an hour later, when she and her aunt had changed their frocks and washed their hands and faces and combed their hair. There were far more guests than she had expected. She had anticipated a family gathering, extended to include the families of in-laws.

She did not look about her. She allowed her brother to take her arm, answered his queries about the journey, greeted Sophia's younger sister, Lady Patricia, and her husband, Lord Hodges, and took a seat beside the former, far from the fire and the center of activity. She hoped that with her pale lavender frock and white lace cap she would blend unnoticeably into the background. Almost all of the other ladies were far more becomingly dressed, and several of them were younger and far prettier than she.

She kept her eyes focused on the small group of people close to her and Lady Patricia.

"Ah, here come the children," Lady Patricia said, looking across to the doorway and smiling. "They have been chafing at the bit all afternoon, waiting for the promised moment when they might join the adults in the drawing room for tea. I don't know how you feel about having a room invaded by infants, Emma. I am sure some of our guests will be horrified. But what is Christmas without children?"

There were several of them, Emma saw. All of them had obviously been released from a nurse's care only moments before. There was not a curl or a bow or a shirt cuff out of place.

And looking across the room, Emma noticed for the first time all the signs of Christmas—the holly and ivy looped about the walls and draping every

painting and mirror, the evergreen boughs decorated with large green and red bows of satin, the
silver bells and the candles. And the elaborately
decorated kissing bough at the center of the room.

One small girl stood still just inside the door,
looking about her. She did not immediately proceed to the side of a parent as the other children
did. She was a small, solemn child, too thin and
too plain for the heavy dark ringlets that covered
her head. They were all wrong for her, Emma
thought absently.

And then the child looked directly at her, and
Emma could see even across the room that the
child's large dark eyes took away her plainness and
gave her a strange, unexpected beauty. Emma felt
herself smiling as the child held her gaze.

And then she realized in some surprise that the
child was crossing the room toward her, never removing her eyes from her.

"Hello," Emma said a little uncertainly when the
girl stopped in front of her. "What is your name?"

The child said nothing, but looked up at her solemnly and steadily.

Emma felt a little uncomfortable. She had never
had a great deal to do with children. Lady Patricia,
she could hear, was talking to a gangly young boy
who was complaining about something.

The little girl reached out a hand and touched
Emma's knee before withdrawing the hand. Emma
leaned forward and smiled.

"I am Emma Milford," she said. "Would you like
to shake my hand?" She extended her hand. The
child's eyes dropped to it, and she laid her own
slowly in it. Emma closed her hand around the
child's and shook it. "I am pleased to meet you,"
she said. "A happy Christmas to you. May I know
whom I have the pleasure of meeting?"

The child looked up into her eyes again and then
suddenly—Emma did not quite know how it came

about—she was on her lap, sitting still and straight-backed, her legs dangling above the floor.

"Well," Emma said, pleased and not a little flattered. "What a lovely welcome indeed. I have been traveling all day and am in a roomful of near-strangers, and suddenly I have a friend. Are you ready for your tea? I certainly am."

Two large dark eyes looked up at her from a thin and strangely familiar face, and then the child leaned sideways and all those dark ringlets were against Emma's breast. She closed one arm about the child, startled, and hugged her close. She felt near to tears for no reason that she could fathom except that she was an old maid with two nieces and a nephew who had never been very partial to being held and cuddled by a mere aunt.

Who was this strange, silent little child with the dark, beautiful eyes and thin, familiar face?

But of course! The answer came to her in a rush even as someone came to stand in front of her, cutting off her view of the rest of the room and everyone in it.

She raised her eyes with a physical effort to look into gray eyes that were much like his daughter's in the rather narrow face that he had also passed along to the child. She had forgotten the bump in his nose, where he had broken it as a boy, a feature that destroyed all chance he might have had of being classically handsome, though it made him impossibly attractive, she had once thought. And she had forgotten that the thickness of his dark hair made it somewhat unruly.

He had not changed in nine years. Not really. There were perhaps more years, more experience, more character in his face. He had been only twenty-tree at that time. A very young man.

"Hello, Emma," he said.

"Hello, Edwin."

Unconsciously she held his child closer. She

should have called him Lord Radbrook, she thought. But then, he should have called her Miss Milford. She was very conscious of her simple frock and lace cap, of her plainly dressed hair—all of them planned with him very much in mind. To show him that nine years had passed, that she had not come with any silly notion of renewing an old romance, that she had come merely because his parents had invited her and it would have been uncivil to have refused.

"I see you have been making friends with Anna," he said.

"Yes."

"She does not talk, you know," he said.

"I know."

Her new mama was not pretty, the child was thinking. But she had a sweet and a kind face, and when she smiled, one knew that the smile was not meant for herself, to make herself prettier or to draw attention her way, but to make the other person feel good.

Her hands were soft and slim. And warm. And her bosom was warm and comfortable. She felt just exactly as Anna had expected a mama would feel.

She did not smell of roses. The scent was something not quite as strong or as sweet. Anna closed her eyes for a moment and breathed in. Violets. That was it. Her new mama smelled of violets.

Emma Milford. That was what the lady had called herself. And Papa had called her Emma. But Anna did not need the name. She was Mama. Anna had known it almost as soon as she had stepped into the drawing room.

She had thought it out for herself the night before while lying in bed waiting to fall asleep. And she had thought the same way again that morning. If her wish was to come true, then surely it would come true today, on Christmas Eve, not on Christmas Day. Grandpapa and Grandmama were

expecting several new visitors today, but none tomorrow.

Her new mama would come today.

And so she had entered the drawing room with
a mingled confidence in Christmas wishes and
anxiety lest this be the very one that would not
come true. She had looked about her carefully at
all the ladies. Miss Chadwick, looking prettier even
than usual, was laughing up at her papa, so that
he did not immediately notice Anna's entrance.
There were several other unknown ladies, a few of
them of the approximate age she expected her new
mama to be. But none of them had seemed right.
She had felt no recognition for any of them.

Until she had spotted the lady at the far end of
the drawing room, close to the great windows,
seated on a low chair near Aunt Patricia. The quiet
lady in a lavender dress and wearing a lace cap on
her smooth brown hair. A lady who was neither
pretty nor vivacious. A lady who smiled at her in
a thoroughly kindly and comfortable manner from
across the room.

And walking toward her across the drawing
room, with not one twinge of uncertainty or unease, Anna had felt sorry for her cousins, who
had one more night of excitement and suspense
to live through before they would see the fulfill-
ment of their own wishes, while hers had been
granted on Christmas Eve.

She was contented, she thought, her cheek nestled against her new mama's bosom, her nostrils
drawing in the warm and subtle scent of violets.
She was happy. It was going to be the best Christmas ever.

"Anna," her papa was saying, "let me take you
over to the tray for mince pies and lemonade. It
looks as if the children are being allowed to go first.
Miss Milford will need both hands for her plate and
her tea."

But Anna did not move, and her new mama did not relax her hold on her.

"Anna?" her father said. He sounded perplexed.

"Please," the lady said. Her voice was soft and musical. Anna had noticed that right at the start. "Let her stay if she wishes. I have so little chance to be with children."

Anna's eyes looked up to her father, though she did not raise her head. He was standing very still, his hands clasped behind him. He was feeling it too, she thought, smiling without ever moving a facial muscle. Papa could feel it too. As of course he must. He was going to have to marry her new mama.

"Very well, then," he said. "But please don't allow her to annoy you. You must be tired after your journey."

His words suggested a concern for her comfort, Emma thought. But his jaw was tight. A pulse beat there. And when he turned to walk away, it was with abrupt, rather jerky movements. He was angry.

As well he might be. She had been at Williston Hall for less than an hour, and already she held his daughter in her arms, and the child had refused to go to him.

Anna Gwent had not spoken since the horror of her mother's death almost three years before, Sophia and Peter had told her. Father and daughter were virtually inseparable. And he doted on her as if she were the only item of value in the universe.

Yes, she could hardly blame him for being angry.

"Shall we share a plate?" she asked Anna when a footman offered her one and then displayed a plate of cakes and pastries for her selection.

The child nodded.

"Which one would you like?" Emma asked.

Anna pointed to an angel cake smothered in white cream, and the footman set it on the plate with the mince pie that Emma had chosen.

"Oh, Christmas goodies," Emma said with a sigh. "Are we going to get fat, Anna?"

The child stared solemnly up at her before reaching for her cake.

Emma raised her eyes and looked unwillingly across the room. He was talking with a very pretty blond young lady and looking over the girl's shoulder quite directly at her. Or at his daughter. It was hard to tell which.

The evening of Christmas Eve began with a lively banquet, at which thirty family members and guests sat down. The children ate upstairs, though they were to join the adults in the drawing room afterward for games until the carolers would arrive from the village. Their visit was traditional and always eagerly anticipated. Then those children who so wished would go to church with their parents. They were always given the choice, though no self-respecting child beyond the age of three ever went to the warmth and coziness of his bed when there was a chance to endure all the self-inflicted torture of staying up until after midnight.

Lord Radbrook found himself seated beside Roberta Chadwick at dinner. She was dressed in a delicate white confection of a gown in defiance of the season and looked as pure and as lovely as a lily—a lily sparkling in the sunshine. There was always a brightness about Roberta that drew eyes her way quite regardless of her blond beauty.

He had never seen her without the sparkle, Lord Radbrook thought. She would be a constantly cheerful companion throughout life, even if her conversation was far from profound. She would bring light and gaiety into Anna's life, and those were qualities his child needed more than anything.

She would accept him, he was sure. He sensed that she favored him, though she was not so ill-bred as to openly fawn upon him. Indeed, she spent as much time during dinner conversing and laughing with the young Viscount Treadwell at her other side as she did with him.

He talked when he was able with Miss Beynon to his left. And when his head was turned her way, he could see Emma at the far end of the table. She was wearing blue tonight, the dress simple and high-necked and long-sleeved. Her head was bare of the cap she had worn that afternoon, but her hair was dressed as simply, drawn back smoothly over her ears and knotted at the neck. Her face looked serene as she talked with Colonel Porchester beside her.

He had a sudden and unbidden memory of that same face full of life and laughter and that brown hair cut short and curled about her face. He saw that same body lithe beneath light muslin, tripping lightly across the park and beside the lake, her hand in his. That same slim hand that now held her fork.

She had changed. She had aged. And not for the better.

He felt his jaw tighten with anger. How had she lured Anna onto her lap at teatime? Had she hoped to impress him? Anna was shy even with her relatives. She almost never had anything to do with strangers.

He put the thought from his mind and turned to Roberta, who had finished her conversation with the viscount and was smiling his way.

But his irritation returned when the gentlemen joined the ladies in the drawing room after being left to their port for a short while. The children were already downstairs, but Anna did not even notice his arrival. She was standing in the center window with Emma, holding her hand and gazing at her with the look she normally reserved only for him. Emma was stooped down beside her. Amid all the noise and laughter in the room, the two of them seemed set apart in a little world of silence and contentment.

Almost unwillingly he strolled toward them.

Anna had sat patiently upstairs while her nurse recurled her hair into its myriad ringlets, and she had smoothed her hands carefully over the pink silk frills of her second-best dress—the best was to be reserved for Christmas Day—so that the creases would fall out. But inside she had been bursting with excitement. She had had to be reminded to eat her dinner, and she had scarcely listened to the chatter and arguments of her cousins.

When the children had been summoned to the drawing room, she had flown down the stairs with the others instead of holding back until last as she usually did. And she had glanced about the room with bright eyes, ignoring—indeed, not even see-ing—the gentle and welcoming smile of her grand-mother, and darted across the room to take the hand of her new mama.

"You have made a friend, Emma," Marjorie Fotheringale said with a laugh. "I noticed that Anna sat on your lap at teatime." She smiled fondly down at the child and touched one of her ringlets. "Anna is very special in this family."

But Anna was not prepared to become a third party in an adult conversation. She tugged on her mama's hand, drawing her toward her very favor-ite spot in the house at Christmas, the Bethlehem scene that was always set up in the central win-dow.

"Ah," Emma said, "a Nativity scene. It is a very lovely one, too."

Anna looked up at her. She did not know the

word her new mama had used. But yes, it was
lovely. Someone had made it especially for Grandmama. She pointed to the baby Jesus in his manger.

She loved the baby Jesus because he looked like
a real baby. One chubby arm waved aimlessly in
the air while the baby sucked on the thumb of the
other hand. His chubby legs were bent. All his
limbs were free of the swaddling clothes, which
was not the idea of swaddling clothes at all, Aunt
Sophia had said once. But Anna did not care. She
loved this baby far more than the one at church,
with his arms stretched out as if to bless the world,
Uncle Humphrey had explained, and the halo
about his smiling face. That baby did not look real.

"He is a very happy baby, is he not?" Emma
said. "I wonder if the straw is scratching his skin."

Anna looked up at her again. She had always
wondered the same thing. It was the only thing
about the whole scene that had bothered her.

"But I daresay it is not," Emma said. "He does
not look upset, does he? And I am sure his mama
would make sure he is comfortable. She has eyes
for only him, see?"

Mary was bending over the manger, gazing down
at the baby Jesus. But her hands were not clasped
in prayer, as were the Virgin's at the church. She
was holding to the edge of the manger and smiling.
She was not worshiping the baby; she was loving
him. Anna touched the shoulder of the figure and
smoothed one finger down its back.

Emma stooped down beside her. "I think she is
very proud of her baby, don't you?" she said. "But
what mama would not be proud of her child?" She
released the child's hand and set an arm loosely
about her thin waist, watching the small finger
smooth lightly over Mary's robe.

"Anna," a voice said from behind them, "you

are keeping Miss Milford from the company. It is not very polite."

Emma looked around sharply and dropped her arm from the child's waist. "We were looking at the Nativity scene," she said foolishly, and was aware suddenly of a little hand taking hers and drawing it about her waist again.

"Yes," he said. "Anna has always been fascinated by it. I think it is because the sculptor emphasized realism rather than the idea that this is the Holy Family."

Anna took his hand in hers and pointed to the figure of Joseph.

He chuckled. "Ah, yes, poor Joseph," he said. "Always in the background." He stooped down on his haunches and looked more closely. "But this one is more human than most, is he not? He looks rather pleased with himself actually, and he definitely looks as if he would take on the world to protect mother and child. I do believe that he is about to hint quite firmly to the shepherds that it is time to take themselves off back to the hills."

Anna held to her father's hand and rested one cheek on Emma's shoulder as they all gazed silently at the Nativity scene for a while.

"Snow," Lord Radbrook said at last, looking beyond the stable and its silent figures to the uncovered window beyond. "It has set up a furious debate about whether we should go to church in the village or not. My father's head groom has given it as his opinion that the fall is not yet thick enough to make carriage travel hazardous, though doubtless by morning we will have to travel by sleigh or by foot. What about it, Anna? Shall we go?"

A head nodded against Emma's shoulder.

"Yes," he said. "It would not be Christmas without the church service, would it? Miss Milford?"

"Yes, my lord," she said. "I shall go with Peter and Sophia and my aunt."

"Oh, my lord," a sweet light voice said from behind them, "the carolers have come and are in the great hall preparing to sing. Adrian was wrong, you see, and they have come despite the snow." She laughed merrily. "I believe you won that wager. Will you come?"

"Yes," he said, straightening up. "I will lead you out there if I may, Miss Chadwick." He extended an arm for hers. "Anna?"

"Oh, yes," Roberta said, her eyes sparkling. "Do come along and hear the singing, Anna, dear. Will you take my hand?"

But Anna shook her head and clung to Emma's skirt. She watched her papa's jaw tighten and knew that he was annoyed with her. But she knew too with all the optimism of childhood that it would be a perfect Christmas after all. She had felt it moments before when Papa and her new mama had been stooped down on either side of her and the three of them had gazed at Joseph and Mary and the baby Jesus—one family gazing at another.

She had felt that she was as happy as Jesus, and the little matter of some brittle straw tickling her skin would not mar her joy either. She had felt that her new mama was hovering over her with as much warmth and love as Mary was lavishing on Jesus. And she had felt that Papa was there like Joseph, loving the two of them, protecting them from the world.

Papa was angry and he was walking into the great hall with Miss Chadwick on his arm while Anna walked behind, her hand in her new mama's. But she was not worried. Although her wish had been granted already, it was not quite Christmas yet. Tomorrow was Christmas.

Tomorrow would be the best day in all the world. The best day ever.

* * *

Emma was in the bedchamber beyond the nursery that was shared by Anna, Harriet, and Julie.
Harriet and Julie were in the nursery listening to
Marjorie Fotheringale tell a story, despite the lateness of the hour—it was past midnight. But Anna
had not wanted to listen. She had wanted Emma
to undress her and tuck her into bed.

Emma did not know whether to give in to the
temptation to hug to herself this rare day of joy or
to feel all the embarrassment of what had happened since her arrival at Williston Hall.

Anna had not left her side all evening. They had
stood hand in hand listening to the carolers in the
great hall and watching the cider and hot punch
and wassail being handed around afterward while
everyone chattered and laughed even more gaily
than they had at dinner. Emma had felt guilty. The
child should have been with her father and Miss
Chadwick, to whom he appeared to be paying
court. And Miss Chadwick had looked to Anna
kindly and spoken sweetly to her.

Emma had felt even more guilty when it came
time to go to church and Anna had stubbornly refused to go with her father in Mr. Shelton's carriage. She had clung to Emma's hand even when
Emma had stooped down and assured her that she
would see her in church.

It had ended up with Emma's riding in the Shelton carriage too, Anna on her lap. To say she had
felt uncomfortable was to understate the case. And
somehow Lord Radbrook had been separated from
Miss Chadwick outside the church and he had entered with Emma, Anna between them, clinging to
a hand of each. They had sat side by side and knelt
side by side throughout the service, the world
shrunk to a small space, Emma's awareness of father and child overwhelming even the much-loved
atmosphere of the Christmas service.

And then when they had arrived home and the overtired, overexcited children had been shooed up to bed by Marjorie, who usually took the lead in such matters, Anna had shaken her head when her father had stooped down to pick her up and had turned to lift her arms to Emma.

"My dear Emma," the countess had said with a laugh, "I have never seen Anna so enchanted with anyone except Edwin. Do carry her up, if you would be so good, dear. There will be warm chocolate awaiting you in the drawing room when you come downstairs."

Her words had been drowned out by a shriek from Miss Chadwick and a great deal of laughter from several others as that young lady was caught beneath the sprig of mistletoe in the great hall by Viscount Treadwell and soundly kissed.

Emma was at a loss to know what her appeal was to Anna. She wished that it could have been some other child. But even so, there was an ache of something in her heart as she undressed the child and clothed her in a warm flannel nightgown and turned back the bedclothes. Anna's regard was a Christmas gift she would not ignore or easily forget.

Anna handed her a brush and settled herself before the narrow mirror of the small dressing table beside the bed.

Emma brushed through the soft ringlets until the child's hair was smooth and free of tangles. In the mirror she looked suddenly far more like the tiny, fragile child she was. Emma brushed the hair back from the child's face and gathered it into one hand at the nape of her neck.

"It would look very pretty braided," she said. "You have lovely shiny hair, Anna."

The child looked at her in the mirror with large bright eyes. Emma smiled, though the smile faded when another figure appeared behind her.

"Time for bed, Anna," he said firmly. "You have kept Miss Milford from the drawing room long enough."

Anna jumped to her feet and dived into bed. Emma turned away as Lord Radbrook leaned over the bed, tucking the blankets up about the child. But his voice stayed her.

"Anna wants to say good night," he said, without turning his head toward her.

When she looked back it was to see his daughter, her arms held out toward her, her eyes eager, her cheeks flushed with tiredness.

"Good night, Anna," she said, bending past the still figure of the father, embarrassed again, feeling the child's arms close about her neck. "Happy Christmas."

But she was not to be released so easily. Anna clung as she raised her head, and her puckered lips coaxed Emma's head down to kiss them.

"Sleep tight," she whispered, and turned and fled out through the nursery and along the upper hallway and down the stairs to the safety of the other adults' company.

But he caught up to her just before she reached the drawing-room doors. His hand clamped on her wrist was not to be denied. He drew her past the drawing room without a word, past the doors of the music room, and on to the library. He drew her inside and closed the door behind them before releasing her. There was a fire in the grate and a single branch of candles on the mantel.

He leaned back against the door and crossed his arms over his chest. "What is going on?" he asked. His voice was tight and cold.

"With Anna?" She turned to face him. "I don't know. She seems to have taken a fancy to me for some reason. She will have forgotten by morning. I am sorry, my lord."

"Anna does not take fancies to people," he said.

"Since her mother died she has clung to me for comfort and reassurance."

"What can I say?" she asked after a short and tense silence. "You must have seen that I did nothing to lure her away from you. Why would I do such a thing, anyway?"

He pushed away from the door. "She might have been yours," he said harshly. "You might have had a right to her affection. But you would have none of me nine years ago. You did not even answer my letters. And now you want to take my child?"

"Edwin!" she said, shocked. "I refused your offer—twice. I gave you my reason. It was improper of you to write afterward. It would have been improper for me to answer."

"Propriety!" he said, his voice a sneer. "Did you ever do anything spontaneous in your life, Emma? I was mistaken in you. Youth and beauty and the summertime and the nuptials of my sister and your brother deceived me into thinking you a warm and a vibrant girl capable of love and laughter. I had a fortunate escape. Look what you have become!" His eyes moved over her.

She clasped her hands tightly in front of her and swallowed the lump in her throat. "I have become a twenty-seven-year-old spinster," she said. "Not a creature to be scorned, Edwin. I told you that I must remain with my parents, that they could not get along without me. That is what I did."

"You were cold, heartless," he said. "Without backbone. You would not see that they used you, that had they loved you they would have gladly given you over to the care of someone who fancied himself in love with you and had the means to support you. Though I suppose you would have fought them hard enough if there had been even half as much life and love in you as I thought I saw. I was a fool."

"And I was young," she said, stung. "I was

barely eighteen. You were the first man I had ever
been acquainted with. I was frightened, bewildered
by the feelings you aroused in me. It was safer to
cling to the life I knew."

"The first man!" he said, raking her from head
to toe again with his eyes. "The only man, Emma.
You are as cold as the grave, aren't you?"

She swallowed several times but could not trust
her voice. She wondered again what had been in
those three letters he had written. Her father had
told her about them, but they had been unseemly,
he had said. He had destroyed them. She had
ached over the years to have just one of those letters to keep.

"We are off the point," he said. "I married Marianne two years after your rejection. She was my
wife, Emma, for four years. We had Anna together.
I have lived through the agony of her death, when
she foolishly tried to rescue Anna's ball from the
river, knowing that she could not swim. You are
so far in my past that you count for nothing at all
with me. Nothing! Do you understand me?"

"Why must you say this?" she asked. "It was
many years ago, Edwin. I refused you. Why would
I expect you to feel anything for me now? What is
it I am to understand?"

"I don't know how you are doing it," he said,
"but you are trying to get to me through Anna. It
cannot be done. I would not touch you now with a
ten-foot pole if you were the only woman left on
earth."

Her chin came up. "And I would not allow you
to," she said, "if you were the last man. Do you
really believe that I have come here to snare you?
Do you think I am bursting with frustrated emotions just because I am twenty-seven years old and
have never known a man? I chose my course in
life nine years ago and have never regretted it. I
am content." Oh, liar, her heart told her.

He strode toward her and took her shoulders in a bruising grip, a fact that made mockery of his statement about ten-foot poles, one part of her mind told her.

"Leave Anna alone," he told her. "I don't want you near her, do you understand me? You might have been her mother, but you chose not to be. Her mother was Marianne. I was fond of her. And when it comes time for Anna to have a new mother, then I will choose her with care. I will choose someone who can bring light and youth into her life. Not you, Emma. You had your chance and you chose to scorn me."

"I did not scorn you," she said. "Never that. You know I did not, Edwin. I was eighteen years old. Can you not use that fact to soften your hatred of me?"

"Hatred?" he said. "You flatter yourself, Emma. I have no feelings for you at all. None. I don't want you in my life or in my daughter's life."

His hands felt as if they were about to break bones.

"I shall stay away from Anna tomorrow," she said quietly. "You are hurting me, my lord."

He released her immediately.

"Emma," he said. His voice sounded hurt. "It lasted only seven years, your chosen course. Your father died within a year, your mother within seven. At the age of twenty-five you were all alone with a lifetime yawning ahead of you."

"Yes," she said.

"Why have you not married?" he asked. "Twenty-five was not such an advanced age. Neither is twenty-seven, despite the spinster disguise you have put on."

"As you just said," she replied, "it is my chosen course."

"Well," he said, his face and his voice weary, "it is your life, I suppose. I never did understand you,

although I thought I did for that month. It was foolish to believe after little more than four weeks that
I knew you well enough to pledge you my heart for
the rest of a lifetime.''

"Yes," she said.

"I suppose we were both too young to handle the
situation sensibly," he said.

"Yes."

"You must be ready for a warm drink," he said.
"Go along to the drawing room, Emma. Forgive
me if I do not escort you. I am going to remain here
for a few minutes to see if I can recover my temper."

She left the library without another word. But
she climbed the stairs to her room rather than enter the drawing room, from which sounds of merriment were still coming.

Lord Radbrook was feeling somewhat more
cheerful the following morning, even though he
had slept poorly. He had successfully avoided both
Emma and Roberta Chadwick at breakfast and had
had a satisfying conversation with Colonel Porchester.

By the time breakfast was over, all the children
were up despite the fact that they had been so late
to bed. It was ever so on Christmas morning,
though, he recalled from his own childhood. On
Christmas Eve one always fell asleep almost ill with
anticipation and quite convinced that one would
not sleep a wink at all. And then came the relief of
waking in the morning to find daylight pushing
past the curtains and of knowing that the long wait
and the interminable suspense were finally at an
end.

Yes, the children were up, of course. And sending urgent messages downstairs to announce the
fact. The custom was for them to be taken into one
of the salons with their parents and grandparents

for the opening of their gifts. Lord Radbrook could, therefore, look forward to that particular ceremony. He would have his daughter indisputably to himself. His anger of the night before, he admitted ruefully, had been occasioned as much by jealousy as anything else. It was a disturbing admission. Would he have been jealous of Marianne had she lived?

Anna was waiting for him in the nursery and held her face up for his morning kiss.

"But what is this?" he asked her, laughing and turning her about to see the back of her head. Her hair was combed smoothly back from her face and coiled into a braided coronet about the crown. Unexpectedly, considering the plainness of the style in contrast to her usual ringlets, she looked pretty.

"She would insist on it, my lord," Anna's nurse said, flustered. "She would not let me near her with the curling rod. She showed me what she wanted done. I shall do it again quickly the right way if you wish, my lord, but you must tell her so. Miss Anna can be as stubborn as a mule when her heart is set on something, voice or no voice."

Lord Radbrook picked his child up and kissed her cheek. "No," he said. "Anna looks quite beautiful the way she is."

As his daughter's dark eyes settled on his, he had a sudden memory of Emma's holding back the child's hair the night before and brushing it smooth at the front. Was this her influence? But he pushed the thought away. Nothing was going to spoil his Christmas morning.

Anna sat quietly on his lap in the salon while her cousins tore wrappings from their gifts and exclaimed excitedly over their contents. She opened her own gifts more carefully and gazed up at him as each was revealed. She clutched them all in her arms, refusing to allow him to set them on the table beside the chair.

She seemed pleased. She seemed not to be looking about her for more. He breathed a sigh of relief. Somehow he must have guessed her Christmas wish and satisfied it. It was the doll probably. She had kissed it when she unwrapped it and set it carefully on her lap. She kept touching its crisp orange curls with one finger.

"Have you had what you wished for, sweetheart?" he asked her softly as Peregrine unwrapped his tin soldiers and whooped with delight.

She nodded solemnly and reached up one arm to catch at his neck. He lowered his head to kiss her puckered lips.

She pushed herself off his lap and he watched, amused, as she slid her new fur muff up one arm almost to the shoulder, arranged the ribbon of her new parasol over her wrist, folded her new blue satin dress over her arm, and settled the doll comfortably against the inside of her elbow. And then she reached up with her free arm and took him by the hand.

"Where are we going?" he asked, laughing as he got to his feet. "To show Grandmama?"

But she led him to the door and from the room. She wanted to go back to the nursery? Already? On Christmas Day, when the children drew out all the tricks in their not-inconsiderable arsenal to stay away from it?

But he knew almost immediately that he had guessed wrongly. And he knew where they were going. For one moment he considered stopping her, picking her up, taking her back to the salon, thinking of some way to distract her attention. But how could he? It was Christmas Day. It was her day. And he loved her to distraction.

Most of the guests were in the morning room, chattering brightly. One table of cards was in progress.

"Ah, there is Lord Radbrook," Roberta Chadwick said gaily. She looked extremely pretty dressed in warm pink. "Everyone is saying that we can go for sleigh rides later, my lord. But the snow is deep and very fresh. I say a sleigh will tip and hurl us all into a snowbank. What is your opinion?"

He grinned. "That would be a disaster only if one were hurled in alone or with the wrong company," he said outrageously.

But he was not allowed to pause to join in the laughter that greeted his words. He was drawn by his daughter's hand across the room to the window, where three ladies were talking quietly together.

Anna released her father's hand and held up her doll for Emma's inspection.

Emma looked up sharply and met the inscrutable eyes of the child's father.

"A doll," she said. "How very beautiful she is. She has ringlets just like yours. But, Anna . . ." She looked more closely at the child and smiled despite herself. "You do not have your ringlets today. You have a braided coronet. How very lovely you look, for sure."

Anna held up the doll until Emma took it. And then she laid the dress across Emma's lap and wrestled with the parasol until she had opened it.

"What a fortunate little girl you have been," Emma said. "These are lovely gifts, Anna. And the muff too?"

Anna lifted it and rubbed it against Emma's cheek. And then she raised both arms.

Emma looked uneasily up at Lord Radbrook. But she had no choice, he was forced to admit as he stared mutely back. He could hardly accuse her this morning of having lured Anna into her arms—any more than he could have the day before, he supposed. She had been right. For some reason Anna had taken a fancy to her.

"She wanted you to see her gifts," he said lamely as Emma hesitated and then leaned forward to lift his daughter onto her lap on top of the new dress.

Anna took her doll in her own arms again and snuggled against Emma's bosom.

Seeing her there, Lord Radbrook was reminded of the scent of her he had noticed on several occasions the day before—when they were at the Nativity scene, when they were beside each other at church, when he had stepped close to her in the library. She had smelled of violets as she had always used to do. He had been almost overwhelmed with a feeling of nostalgia as soon as he had stooped beside her to take a closer look at Joseph.

Now Anna would be breathing in that scent.

He swallowed. God, he had loved her. It had taken him months even to be aware that the sun was still rising each morning. It had taken him years to get over her.

Perhaps he never had. Perhaps if he had, he would not hate her so intensely now.

"Shall we go back to the salon, Anna?" he asked.

But she shook her head, as he had feared she would, and burrowed closer to Emma.

And Emma looked up at him with worried eyes.

"Do you mind?" he asked her.

She shook her head.

"I had better see if I can settle this question of the sleigh rides, then," he said, turning abruptly away.

Emma did not believe she had felt either so happy or so miserable for many years. She sat in one corner of the drawing room after a light luncheon, holding Anna asleep in her arms. The child's head was pillowed on her breast, her mouth open, her breathing deep and even.

Emma ached with a maternal tenderness that had never been allowed to awaken before. There surely could be no more wonderful feeling than just this, she felt, unless perhaps it were to hold a tiny baby to one's breast and feel it suckling there.

It was a Christmas to remember. This in contrast to the agony of the night before and its sleeplessness after all the hurtful things he had said to her, after her realization anew of all she had lost in that foolish, youthful decision she had made all those years ago.

Anna might have been hers, he had said twice. Emma might have had a right to the child's affection. Emma had completed the details herself during a sleepless night. He might have put Anna, or another child, inside her through the intimacy of married love. She might have had the joy of having his child growing in her for nine months. She might have held the child from the moment of its birth and suckled it herself. She might have had a great deal more than this brief agony of pretend motherhood when the child was already almost six years old.

She might have. And she might have had his love for the past nine years.

But she had decided otherwise. Enchanted, exhilarated, and finally terrified by that month of fun and friendship and blossoming love, culminating in his passionate outpouring of love for her and offer for her hand, she had turned to her parents for advice. She had been so very new to life and womanhood.

Why had they both been so vehemently opposed to the match? she wondered. She had been eighteen, after all, of marriageable age, and Edwin could hardly have been more eligible—a baron in his own right, wealthy, landed, heir to an earldom and an even vaster fortune. Papa had been only a baronet of moderate means. It would have been a brilliant match for her.

But they had, she knew, felt some humiliation at

Peter's marrying so far above himself. Pride, yes, but humiliation too at being unable to match all the lavish spending on the nuptials that the earl had indulged in. Perhaps they had shuddered at the thought of having to go through it all over again with their daughter.

Papa had been a proud man.

And then, of course, Mama had always been of a delicate constitution and had always leaned heavily on her daughter's care. They needed her, Papa had said. They could not spare her for this or any other marriage. Not for another few years, at least.

And so she had refused Edwin. And when he had pleaded with her, caught her in his arms and tried to persuade her in other than words, she had torn free of him and raced back to the house and refused to talk with him before her parents had taken her away the following day.

And she had regretted her decision perhaps every day since then. And still regretted it, now more than ever. And yet she wished herself a million miles away, she thought, smoothing a gentle hand over the side of his daughter's sleeping head.

"I don't understand it, Emma dear," the countess said in a whisper, despite the buzz of conversation going on all about them, seating herself briefly in the chair beside Emma's. "There must be a magic about you. Anna will not let you out of her sight." She patted Emma's arm with one ringed hand. "It is almost enough to set me to promoting a match between you and Edwin. Indeed, we thought one was in the making many years ago when Sophia married Peter, but nothing ever came of it."

Emma looked at her, horrified.

"Oh, don't worry." The countess chuckled before moving off to join another group for a few minutes. "I never have been a matchmaker, dear. I would not so embarrass you. And I do believe Ed-

win has his heart set on the little Chadwick girl,
though I am not at all sure that Anna will approve
his choice.''

But Roberta Chadwick would be perfect for him,
Emma thought determinedly. She would bring
laughter back into his life. He had used to laugh a
great deal. They both had. They had spent a month
laughing. And talking. And walking and running
and riding and boating. And kissing for that last
week. Kissing over and over. He was the only man
she had ever kissed.

Strangely, she had been very free of chaperones
during that month. They had been alone a great
deal.

''Emma.'' He was stooped down on his haunches
before her suddenly, the hostility of the day before
gone from his face—for the moment, anyway.
''Shall I take her from you? It is not fair that you
be so tied down.''

Tied down!

''If you wish,'' she said, her heart sinking. She
realized that tears had sprung to her eyes only
when his face blurred before her. She stared at his
blurred image, aghast. ''But perhaps she will
awake. She needs the sleep, I think. She was late
to bed last night and quite early up this morning.''

''Emma, what is it?'' he asked softly. She shook
her head. ''I am sorry about last night,'' he said.
''You have been remarkably kind to her. She has
not known a mother figure for a long time.''

''Leave her here with me,'' she said. ''I do not
mind.''

''The sleigh rides are to be delayed until later,''
he said, ''and are to be for the adults only.'' He
grinned. ''They are far too tame for the children.
They are going to sled down the hill by the lake
after it has been judged—doubtless by Marjorie—
that their luncheons have had long enough to set-

tle in their stomachs. I will be going with them, as
Anna doubtless will wish to go too."

"The fresh air will be good for them," she said.

"She is going to want you to come too," he said.
"You do not have to, Emma. It is cold out there,
and there is a longish trek to the hill. I warn you
now so that you can have a plausible excuse ready
for her."

"Yes," she said.

He searched her eyes with his own. "Unless you
want to come," he said. "You must do what you
wish to do. Disregard what I said last night. Will
you, please? I was in a foul mood and believe I
spoke many words for which I owe you an apology."

"No," she said.

"Well." He looked at her uncertainly and
straightened up again. "Anna will be pleased if you
come, Emma, even if only for a short while."

She did not answer him, but looked down at the
child who might have been hers.

He was gone when she looked up again.

Aubrey and Peregrine had set themselves up as
leaders of the sledding party, each sitting at the
front of a sled, a smaller child behind and clinging
to his waist as if for very life.

Anna would not go with either one. Lord Radbrook could hardly blame her. The hill was long
and fairly steep, coming to an end on the wide path
and lawn before the bank of the frozen lake. The
snow was fresh and thick and the boys reckless
and not the best of steersmen. Nine times out of
ten the sleds tipped before they reached the bottom and spilled out their two occupants into a
snowbank.

The other children seemed not at all perturbed
by the frequent spills. There was a great deal of
shrieking and laughing and a large number of in-

sults being hurled about. Lord Radbrook and Emma at the top of the hill and Marjorie at the bottom wisely decided to be deaf for the occasion.

"I know what it is going to be," Lord Radbrook said, looking down at his daughter, who was gazing wistfully at her laughing and snow-covered cousins but clinging to Emma's hand. "I am going to have to take you down myself, aren't I, Anna? And if I tip over halfway down, I will be the laughingstock for the rest of our stay here." He was grinning. "Will you come down with Papa?"

She looked up at him eagerly and nodded her head.

"This may be certain suicide," he said to Emma, "or may result in a few broken limbs at the very least."

"Admit it," she said. "You have been waiting for just this moment."

There was high color in her cheeks, he saw—and at the tip of her nose. Her eyes were dancing, her lips curved into a smile. He felt a sudden jolt of recognition. She really had not changed such a great deal after all.

"Aubrey!" he yelled, turning away sharply. "I am going to need that sled so that I can teach you a lesson about descending a hill without making yourself into a snowman on the way."

"Oh, famous!" Aubrey cupped his hands about his mouth and bellowed at all the other children. "Uncle Edwin is about to make an idiot of himself. Gather around, one and all."

"Impudent puppy," his uncle said. "Come along, Anna. You can sit in front between my knees."

Anna was big-eyed and solemn as he settled her on the sled in front of him and the other children gathered around to laugh and cheer and jeer.

"Here we go, then," Lord Radbrook said, launching them down the hill at the same moment as a snowball from William's hand landed with a splat against the back of his coat.

He felt like a boy again. And Emma had been right: he *had* been waiting for this moment, hoping that somehow he would find an excuse to take to the slopes himself. He was laughing by the time they arrived—safely—at the bottom. The children were all jumping up and down at the top of the hill, cheering, Emma off to one side of them. He picked Anna up, hugged her in his arms, and made their distant audience a theatrical bow.

"Now we have only two adult chaperones and one extra little boy," Marjorie said, clucking her tongue. "However will we manage? And when you go back up there, Edwin, tell William to tie that scarf about his neck or I will throttle him with it when he comes down. This is not the middle of July."

Anna was wriggling out of his arms and turning without a backward glance to run back up the slope. She was making straight for Emma, who stooped down and held out her arms as she neared the top. Lord Radbrook narrowed his eyes and watched them.

"It is most peculiar," Marjorie said from beside him. "But it was very sporting and kind of her to come all the way out here with Anna, when most of the real parents had a thousand and one excuses for remaining indoors. Is Roberta upset about it, Edwin?"

"Roberta?" he said. "Why should she be?"

She looked at him. "Are you not about to offer her the position of second mother to Anna?" she asked. "Or am I being precipitate?"

"You are, rather," he said.

"Am I?" She smiled. "But you paid her such marked attention in town last spring, you know, Edwin, and you did join a party at her brother-in-law's for a few weeks during the summer. And then they were invited here. You surely cannot blame me—and not only me, either—for putting two and two together."

"And coming up with five," he said.

"Oh, Julie," Marjorie said, her eyes going back up the slope. "She shrieks like a hoyden even if she does look like an angel. And I told Peregrine the last time he was down that if he did not lean sideways he would not tip over so often. There they go into a snowbank."

But Lord Radbrook was not watching the one sled come to grief on the slope. He was watching Anna draw Emma by the hand toward the other sled and Aubrey hold out the strings to her.

What the devil? She surely was not intending to come down? But she was. Anna had already climbed onto the front and Emma was lowering herself carefully behind her.

He had a sudden mental image of Emma as he had first seen her the day before, quiet and demure in her prim lavender frock and white lace cap, the very epitome of a fading spinster. But the image was almost immediately replaced by the memory of Emma, her straw bonnet cast aside, her short curls in riotous disarray about her flushed and laughing face, rowing furiously in a boat race across the lake with him, splashing herself with water at every undignified and unskilled pull of the oars. And of her finally climbing out of the boat and dropping to her knees beside him, where he lay at his insolent ease on the grass, having finished his race many minutes before. She had been giggling like a girl and accusing him of every form of cheating imaginable before he had drawn her head down and kissed her long and soundly.

"Mercy on us," Marjorie said, "here comes Emma. The world has gone mad."

She was shrieking and laughing helplessly. The sled teetered from one side to the other but miraculously held on course until it slid to a stop just a few feet from where the other two adults stood.

She was bent forward over Anna, Lord Radbrook saw as he took the few steps toward them, still laughing helplessly. And not laughing alone. Anna too was shrieking with high-pitched delight and leaning back into Emma.

"We did it," Emma said, gasping. "That will teach those nasty boys to mock us. Papa will be proud of you."

But Lord Radbrook was standing transfixed. God. Oh, God. She was laughing, her face that of a sunny-natured child. She was making sounds.

Anna bounced to her feet, silent again, and wrapped her arms about his waist. Emma was staring up at him, the laughter dying from her face. She got up slowly.

"She was not in any danger, I assure you," she said. "If I had tipped the sled, we would have landed in soft snow."

She had misunderstood the look on his face.

"She was laughing," he said, his voice curiously tight. But he had to bite on his lip suddenly and turn sharply away so that she would not see the humiliation of his tears.

He climbed back up the hill afterward while Emma and Anna stayed at the bottom with Marjorie. It was well over half an hour later before they arrived back at the house and Marjorie shooed all the children up to the nursery to comb their hair and wash their hands before tea.

Lord Radbrook was stooped down dislodging a particularly stubborn knot from Anna's scarf. She was still holding to Emma's hand, he could see, though Emma was at arm's length and had clearly intended to proceed on her own way upstairs.

"There," he said at last, straightening up. "The deed is accomplished. Upstairs with the others, then, Anna, to get tidied up if you want some tea."

But she looked up at him with eager eyes and across to Emma, who still stood a step away. Anna looked back to him and deliberately up to the ceiling above Emma's head.

"Ah," he said with a sinking of the heart and a strange churning of the stomach. And he knew from the suddenly stricken expression in her eyes that Emma had just realized too. "I have caught Miss Milford under the mistletoe, have I, Anna? How clever of me."

His child released Emma's hand finally and clung to her skirt instead. And her free arm came about his leg. She gazed upward at them.

"I have a well-trained daughter," he said as lightly as he could, setting his hands on Emma's shoulders and taking the step toward her. "She held you prisoner until I was ready to capture you myself." And he lowered his head and kissed her swiftly and firmly.

And was immediately engulfed in the delicate perfume of violets and in impressions of summertime and warmth and youth and laughter and young love. And in memories of Emma and what she had meant to him before all the dreary months and years of pain had made him hate her. And of what she had continued to mean to him despite all the pain and all the hatred. And of what she still meant to him and always would mean to him.

At least, he thought, raising his head and looking into dazed hazel eyes, he had meant the kiss to be swift. He had no idea if it had been or not. Anna, he realized, was still gazing fixedly up at them.

"You are beneath the mistletoe too," he said, stooping and kissing her. "And now that that nonsense is done with, perhaps we can proceed to our tea. I am starved."

They ascended the stairs in silence, the three of

them, Anna between them, holding to a hand of
each.

They were to keep country hours, the countess
had announced that morning, and have their
Christmas dinner early. Partly it was so that the
young people with their boundless energy would
have plenty of time both to go for their sleigh rides
and to join in the dancing planned for the drawing
room later in the evening, and partly so that the
servants could have some of the evening to themselves after the great banquet was cleared away.

Sleigh rides were always better after dark, anyway, someone said, especially as the storm had
cleared away completely and there were likely to
be moonlight and starlight by which to drive.

Emma would not go. She had decided that at
teatime. It would not be seemly. She was not either
one of the young people or half of a couple. She
was merely an aging spinster, in the same cate-
gory as Aunt Hannah, who had sat beside the fire
all day, nodding genially at all the merrymaking
proceeding about her.

Besides, if she went on a purely adult party,
without the presence of Anna to excuse her, he
might think that she expected to accompany him.
There were three sleighs apparently, each of them
large enough to accommodate only two passengers.

"Another reason why evening is the best time
for the rides," one young gentleman had said,
smiling warmly at a blushing young lady.

He might think that she expected to be taken
with him. Her cheeks burned at the thought. And
they burned again, and her breath came in uneven
gasps, as she remembered that kiss in the hallway
beneath the mistletoe and the way her lips had
clung to his instead of jerking away as soon as a
semblance of a kiss had taken place to satisfy

Anna. And the way she had swayed against him so that her breasts had come against his coat and she had felt all the male hardness of his upper body.

And she had stood beneath that mistletoe for all of a minute before the kiss, held there by Anna's hand in hers, not wanting to hurt the child by breaking away. But to him it must seem that she had waited patiently there until he had noticed where it was she stood.

She squirmed with embarrassment at the thought.

No, she would not join the sleigh rides. She would not dance later that evening, either. She would remember again who and what she was and behave accordingly.

But other people had other ideas.

"You are not joining the sleigh rides, Miss Milford?" Colonel Porchester asked her loudly from across the table at dinner, when she had just said as much to Lord Hodges beside her.

Emma swallowed a mouthful of goose. "No, sir," she said with a smile. "I do believe I will give in to sanity and stay indoors where it is warm."

"Ah, yes," he said. "You went cavorting with the children this afternoon, did you not, ma'am? Most sporting of you, I must say."

"Not going sleighing, Emma?" Peter said from three places down the table, leaning forward so that he could see her. "Nonsense! The snow will probably be melting by tomorrow or the next day and we will not see it again for another two years or so. Of course you must come. You may squeeze in between Sophia and me."

"I would not dream of it," she said.

"Emma," Sophia said with a sigh from even farther away, "Peter and I have been wedded for longer than nine years. We no longer need the romance of a sleigh ride."

There was general laughter from their end of the table.

"We can find it in other, ah, cozier places," Peter said.

His words were greeted with far heartier laughter.

The colonel coughed. "It goes against all the laws of gallantry to allow a lovely young lady to ride in a sleigh sandwiched between her brother and sister-in-law," he said. "Ma'am, I shall dust off these aged bones and air out these ancient lungs in order to take a turn with you myself if you will consent to trust yourself to my care."

Emma smiled. "Thank you, sir," she said. "That would be very pleasant."

So much for melting into the background, she thought ruefully as the conversation moved on to other topics. And so much for aging, decorous spinsters.

A schedule had been worked out, since there were only three sleighs and twelve couples who wished to ride in them, so that nine couples would not be standing outside for an hour or more getting no more pleasure from the evening than cold feet and reddened noses. Miss Chadwick and another fortunate young lady were to ride twice, since there were two gentlemen eager to escort each.

Emma was to ride with the last group. In the meantime she played blindman's buff with the children.

The ride when it came was very sedate and almost anticlimactic. While Lord Radbrook drove away with Miss Chadwick in the direction of the lake, and another young gentleman took the lady of his choice toward the pasture, the colonel took the ribbons of their sleigh and set the horses to moving slowly along the cleared driveway to the gates, out onto the highway for a mile, and back again.

It was very pleasant. The moon and stars made the night bright, and the slight breeze, which had made the air brisk during the afternoon, had died down so that it hardly felt cold at all. Of course, Emma thought, she had a heavy lap robe tucked about her, and her hands were snug inside her muff. The runners of the sleigh squeaked across the snow.

"Christmas Day," the colonel said. "There is always a special feeling about it, is there not? I remember . . ." And he was off on a series of reminiscences about Christmas and his military experiences. Emma relaxed and enjoyed the journey.

They arrived back at the house at almost the same moment as Lord Radbrook and Miss Chadwick.

"Ah," the colonel said, having helped Emma to the ground and turned about. "The freshness of youth. I swear that your eyes shine as brightly as the stars, ma'am." He bowed over Roberta's hand and took it in his. "And I will wager you are preparing to dance the night away."

"How could I possibly resist, sir?" she said gaily, linking her arm through his and proceeding up the horseshoe steps and through the main doors with him.

Emma felt a hand on her arm as she prepared to follow.

"Come for a drive with me," Lord Radbrook said quickly, and before she knew quite what was happening, she was seated in the other sleigh, its heavier lap robe about her knees, and he was setting the horses in motion. The bells on their bridles jingled.

She turned to look at his profile in the darkness and looked away again. They seemed very much surrounded by darkness and emptiness. The house seemed already far behind them.

She thought for a minute that he must have something very particular to say to her, perhaps a repetition of last night's tirade. Perhaps after all he had resented her going sledding with his daughter that afternoon or joining in the sleigh rides this evening. But he said nothing as he took the sleigh over the already well-worn tracks toward the lake.

"She has not spoken or made a sound or smiled or laughed since Marianne died," he said abruptly at last. "Not, at least, since her voice gave out after almost two days of nonstop screaming."

She thought of that afternoon, when Anna had shrieked with laughter on their near-disastrous run down the slope. At the time she had not realized the significance of what was happening—not until he had spoken and she had seen the tears in his eyes. She had thought at first that he was furious with her.

"It will all come back," she said. "It is bound to."

They rode on in silence.

"I almost did not come this year," he said jerkily, "when I knew that you would be here. I thought of taking Anna into Italy. But the pull of family is always too strong at Christmas."

"Yes," she said, the pain in her chest making it difficult to draw breath. "Peter and Sophia and the children were coming here. And Aunt Hannah wished to come. I did not have the heart to insist on staying away. If it had not been for her, I would have."

"Yes," he said. "As you did last year. I was relieved."

They lapsed into silence again. A long silence until suddenly, when they were on the path high above the lake at its eastern end, making the turn to return to the house along its other bank, he drew the horses to a halt and cursed expressively into the night. Emma clenched her hands into hard fists beneath the robe.

"Do you know where we are?" he asked her, speaking through his teeth. "For God's sake, Emma, do you realize where we are?"

She looked about her, startled. And her eyes widened. The high point of the lake, with bare trees falling away to the frozen water below. Trees laden with green leaves during the summer. Blue water, a darker shade than the sky. Warmth and the smells of trees and grass and wildflowers and water.

"Yes," she said, and the word trembled out of her.

It was the place where he had kissed her lips red and swollen until she had moaned and arched into him. The place where he had poured out words of love and asked her to marry him and told her what he wanted to do with her for what remained of a lifetime.

The place where she had said yes and then no and then she did not know, until he had laughed with lighthearted confidence and agreed that she should consult her parents. He must speak with her father too, he had said. He had not yet done so. But there had been no cloud of uncertainty in his face.

He had already been living in the happily-ever-after.

"Yes," she said again.

"Emma." Her name was a groan on his lips, and then one arm was about her shoulders and the other hand was turning up her chin, and his mouth was on hers.

Not his lips. His mouth. Open. Warm. Moist. Tasting faintly of wine. The kiss of a man of experience, not of the very young man with whom she had lived out a summer of innocent love. Or so she supposed. She knew nothing of men of experience. She felt his tongue against the seam of her lips, hard, demanding, confident—or desperate.

She pushed him away, resisting with every ounce of willpower in her the urge to jump from the sleigh and run and run.

"This is not why I came here," she said. "I did not come for this. I would not wish you to think . . . Just because Anna . . . Edwin . . ."

"No." His voice was calm. Expressionless. He was picking up the ribbons of the horses again and slapping them into slow motion. "Of course not. And neither did I. Forgive me, please, ma'am."

"Edwin," she said, reaching out to touch his arm, distressed.

"You will get cold," he said. "Pull the robe up over your knees again and put your hands back inside your muff. You must already be chilled after two successive rides."

"Edwin," she said, her voice pleading.

"Christmas will be over soon," he said. "Christmas always does strange things to people, does it not? It gives one dreams of perfect peace and love and amity. Ridiculous, really, though I suppose it is a pleasant myth. One worth perpetuating. In another few days we will be going our separate ways, ma'am. Next year I will try Italy, and the year after, perhaps Austria or Spain or America. I suppose there are enough places in the world for all the Christmases remaining in my life and yours, are there not? For nine years it has been relatively easy to keep our paths from crossing. I am sure that with a little ingenuity we can manage it for forty years or more longer."

She pulled the robe up about her and slid her hands inside her muff. She directed her eyes at the latter.

"I don't suppose you have ever visited Carlton House, have you?" he asked.

"No," she said.

"Good." His voice was brisk, cheerful. "I shall describe it to you. If we are still not quite at the house when I have finished, I shall describe the Pavilion at Brighton as well. I suppose you are unacquainted with that monstrosity too?"

"Yes," she said.

"Good." He launched into speech.

The children were allowed to stay up well past their usual bedtime, despite the lateness of their falling asleep the night before. Christmas came only once a year, after all. And no child was about to argue with that profound adult pronouncement.

They were herded upstairs from the drawing room to the nursery only when the adult sleigh rides were finished and the countess declared that it was time to have the carpet rolled up and the room prepared for the dancing.

It was high time to go upstairs anyway, Aubrey said, flushed with excitement and indignation. If he had to kiss one more of his female cousins beneath the kissing bough, he would run away to sea, see if he did not. And he had no desire to stay to watch the silly dancing, either. He condescended to slap a hand on the shoulder of the younger Peregrine and suggest that they set up a battlefield with the tin soldiers.

Anna was not so eager to go up, since neither her papa nor her new mama appeared with the return of the last of the sleigh riders. But she took her Aunt Marjorie's hand obediently and allowed her grandmama to kiss her cheek, and she climbed the stairs to the nursery without complaint.

She even played for a while with the other girls and their dolls. But when her papa finally came, she took his hand and led the way into her bedchamber. The others were not going to bed, but she had no wish to stay up longer.

"Tired, sweetheart?" her papa asked, sitting on

the edge of her bed while she undressed without her nurse's help.

She nodded and allowed him to unbraid her hair and then tuck the blankets up under her chin. She raised puckered lips for his kiss.

"Good night, Anna," he said, cupping one of her cheeks with a warm hand. "It has been a good Christmas, has it not?"

She nodded.

He leaned over her and kissed her again before leaving.

She lay very still on her back, staring upward. Yes, it had been a good Christmas. She had had the best Christmas gift ever, and her wish had been granted. She had the most wonderful mama of all—better than Aunt Sophia or Aunt Patricia. Better even than Aunt Marjorie.

Better than her own mama? She could not remember her and usually tried very hard not to do so. But she thought of her now and found that she could not remember her clearly at all. Mama had drowned. She knew that. She had seen it. But she had not pushed her. She had been afraid that they would say she had, but Papa had told her over and over and over again that she had not, that Mama had simply leaned over too far and fallen in. Yes, it was true. She tested the memory in her mind and no longer felt the old terror.

She could scarcely remember her mama. Except for a warm feeling. Mama had been warm. Just like her new mama was.

Except that there was something else with her new mama—a tiny feeling inside that she could not quite express. A tiny pain or emptiness or panic. She could not put a word to it.

Were Christmas wishes sometimes granted for Christmas only? She had never thought of that before. She had been given a new mama, but perhaps she was for Christmas only. Perhaps tomorrow she would not be Mama at all. Perhaps she would be just Miss Emma Milford.

Perhaps Papa would never marry her. And unless he did, then the gift could not last longer than Christmas. Papa had kissed her beneath the mistletoe and she had kissed him back. And clinging to them both, Anna had had a wonderful feeling about it all. She had expected when Papa had stooped down to kiss her too that he would tell her that they were to be a family.

But he had not done so. And when the adults had come into the drawing room after dinner, her papa had immediately taken himself off to talk with some of the gentlemen while her new mama had played with the children. And then, when they had both gone outside for their sleigh rides, they had not been together. Papa had taken Miss Chadwick on his arm, and her new mama had been with the elderly gentleman with the white hair and mustache.

They had not come back afterward, either of them. And though Papa had come upstairs to say good night to her, Mama had not.

She had been so sure that it was to be the best Christmas ever. She had been so certain that today it would all be perfect. Tomorrow Christmas would be over. Wouldn't it? Was it still Christmas tomorrow? She did not think so. Not really, though everyone would still be there and the decorations would still be up, and there would still be all the good foods to eat.

But Christmas would be over and not quite perfect after all.

Anna continued to stare upward. After a while one tear spilled from the corner of an eye and ran down the side of her face and into her ear.

Emma was doing without the services of a maid, though the countess had offered her one. She had laid out her green silk gown, her most becoming one, before going down to dinner, intending to change into it for the dancing.

But she hung it back inside the wardrobe and took out her lavender frock instead. She drew it on slowly and deliberately, smoothing the sleeves down over her wrists. She took the pins from her hair and brushed it out. She parted it carefully down the center, combed it back over her ears, and knotted it tightly at her neck. She set her best lace cap on the smooth crown of her head.

She looked at herself in the mirror, hesitated, and rejected the idea of putting on her pearls. She turned away and went downstairs and seated herself in a shadowed corner of the room beside her aunt, who was having a comfortable conversation with the elderly sister of the countess, Marjorie Fotheringale's mother.

She was almost the last person down, she saw, looking about her once she was safely seated. Sophia was already at the pianoforte, practicing quietly. The carpet had been removed.

It was Christmas night. The room was warm and festive, with its loops of holly and ivy and its decorated pine boughs, with the dozens of candles in the chandeliers, all brilliantly lit, and with the ornate kissing bough hanging from the center of the ceiling.

The ladies were dressed in all their silks and laces and feathers and finery. Most of the gentlemen wore satin knee breeches and brocaded waistcoats and coats.

It was Christmas, the most wonderful and most joyous season of the year. There was a buzz of anticipation as the Earl of Crampton led his countess onto the floor to begin the dancing, and a wave of laughter as he kissed her smackingly on the lips when they paused beneath the kissing bough, waiting for Sophia to begin to play.

"No," Emma said, distracted a moment later as she watched the couple begin to dance. She looked up at Lord Hodges. "I do not dance, thank you."

"But you really ought, dear," her aunt said in a loud whisper after his lordship had turned away to claim another partner. "You are not quite an old maid, and you know that you always like to stand up at the assemblies at home."

"It has been a busy day, Aunt Hannah," she said with a smile. "These aging bones of mine are weary."

Miss Beynon tutted and the countess's sister chuckled.

Lord Radbrook was dancing with Roberta Chadwick. He had not intended to single her out for the first dance, but somehow it had happened. And he smiled down at her and wondered if he should control his reckless mood or give it free rein. It would be the easiest thing in the world to guide their steps to the center of the room, claim his kiss, steer her to the door and out and into some quieter room to make his offer.

He had come to Williston Hall half-determined to do just that. And she was an extremely pretty and amiable young lady. Such an outcome of the Christmas holiday was half-expected by others in the room too, he believed.

"It has been such a wonderful day," she said, looking up at him with shining blue eyes, a blush of color high on her cheekbones. "I have never been part of such a party at Christmas before, my lord. There is so much to do at every moment of the day."

"It has been our pleasure to have you join our family," he said, smiling down at her.

Good God, he was thinking, trying to focus both his mind and his eyes on the young girl in his arms, if someone wished to paint a portrait of the typical, quintessential spinster, he could hardly do better

than paint Emma as she was now. That prudish
virginal dress. That ridiculous cap. That murder
done to thick, youthful hair.

He wanted to tear the dress off her, hurl the cap
into the fire, drag the pins from her hair. He wanted
to shake her until her neck snapped. He wanted to
do violence to her.

"And it is not to end soon," Roberta was saying,
her face bright with youth and vitality and Christmas. "Viscount Treadwell has invited my sister
and brother-in-law—and me of course—to spend
the New Year in Norfolk. He has sent off an invitation to Mama and Papa, as well."

"Then all of London must suffer from your absence for even longer than expected?" he said.

She laughed, a light, infectious sound. "I am sure
no one will miss me," she said. "My brother-in-law
Adrian says that there must be some significance
to the fact that Mama and Papa are being invited
too, but I think that is just silly. I am no one of any
great importance, after all."

"On the contrary," he said. "I seem to recall that
you are the young lady who took the *ton* by storm
during your first Season last spring."

She laughed again. Lord Radbrook was careful
to avoid the center of the room for the remainder
of the set.

He danced with his mother, with Maria Shelton,
with several of the other ladies. And he felt irritation build to anger and anger to fury as Emma continued to sit quietly in the shadows, her hands
folded primly in her lap, making herself one with
his aunt and her own.

He felt fit to do murder as he laughed at something one of his partners said while he led her back
to her chair at the end of a dance.

Emma had rejected offers to dance with Lord
Hodges and Colonel Porchester. She had even re-

fused her brother, though he had been more insistent and openly derisive of her cap.

"I would have given you half a dozen for Christmas if I had known you were so partial to the things," he had said. "You forgot to bring your knitting downstairs, Emma."

She had pulled a face at him, and he had gone away eventually.

Sophia had just announced a waltz. There had been several. It seemed to be a favorite dance of most of the younger people and of some of the older onces too. Emma had danced it once at a local assembly and had liked it, though the general opinion had been that it was fast and a little vulgar and best left to those people who liked to frequent London, which always encouraged all that was fast and vulgar.

"Ma'am?" A lace-covered hand was held out for hers. "Will you dance?"

"No." She looked up, startled, and felt her face grow hot. She had thought that he would stay as far away from her as possible for what remained of her stay at Williston Hall. "Thank you, but I do not dance."

"Do not or will not?" he asked. His hand was still outstretched. His voice was cold, abrupt. She did not see what his expression was. She found herself unable to lift her eyes beyond his neckcloth.

"Both," she said.

"Well," he said quietly, "you will make an exception on this one occasion. Come and waltz with me."

She could not believe his breach of good manners. Both her aunt and his were interested spectators, she was aware. Yet there was something in his voice and in the tension of his body that suggested to her that even another refusal would not

daunt him. He might just create a scene if she refused yet again.

She got to her feet.

Sophia was already playing. Couples were already dancing. She raised one wooden arm to his
shoulder. He took her other hand in his. She realized that her own was cold only when she felt the
warmth of his.

"Have you waltzed before?" he asked.

"Once," she said.

They danced in silence. She had not realized on
that previous occasion just how intimate a dance
it was. All attention was focused inward, within the
circle of their arms. Had she been a little taller,
perhaps she could have looked over his shoulder,
watched the other dancers, felt less held by a certain spell, a certain tension.

"Don't worry," he said quietly after a couple of
minutes, when she had caught the rhythm of the
dance and moved smoothly to his lead. His voice
was cold again. "I shall keep us well away from the
center of the room."

She did not answer him. The diamond pin nestled in the folds of his neckcloth caught the light
of the candles in whichever direction they turned.
She fixed her eyes on its brightly changing rainbow bursts.

He swore softly suddenly, and she looked up,
startled, into his eyes. They were as hard as ice.
His jaw was tight, his face pale.

"You are coming with me," he said, dancing her
toward the doors that led into the hallway. "We
are going to have this out. Don't make a scene,
Emma."

She had no intention of doing any such thing.
But she knew that he was on the verge of doing
so, and would do it, too, if she made one false move.
She did not resist when he opened one of the doors

and ushered her out, one hand at the small of her back. He closed the door behind them.

"The library," he said curtly. "There will be a fire in there. And candles too, probably."

It felt a little like reliving the past, stepping inside the library again, as they had the evening before, waiting for him to rip up at her. She walked halfway across the room and turned calmly to face him. He stood with his back against the door, his hands behind him, still on the handles. His eyes passed slowly over her from head to foot.

"I want to tear it off your back," he said viciously while her eyes widened in surprise and something like fear. "And that." He pointed an accusing finger at her head. "I want to . . . ." He drew in a sharp breath and strode toward her. "And I am going to do it, too."

He snatched the cap from her head, dislodging a couple of pins as he did so, and strode to the fire with it. Emma turned to watch him with shocked eyes as he hesitated, looked back to her, and dropped her best lace cap into the flames.

"Are you cold to the very core?" he asked. "Is there no warmth in you at all?"

She said nothing. She determinedly blinked back the tears that would have blurred her vision.

"What is it about me?" he asked her through his teeth. "What is wrong with me, Emma?"

She swallowed.

"I always thought myself eligible," he said. "I still do. Even apart from the title and the fortune and the expectations and all the other trappings of wealth and privilege, I would have thought myself eligible. I have always known I am no Adonis, but then, I am no gargoyle either. I have some education, some conversation, some breeding. What makes me so unacceptable, then? Or is it not me? Is it you? Are you cold to the very heart?"

"Edwin," she said, clasping her hands in front

of her, "don't do this. Please don't. There is nothing wrong with you. And I am human."

"What, then?" he said. "Why do you prefer this to me?" He gestured at her lavender frock.

She shook her head. "It is what I am," she said. "I dress to suit my station in life."

"God!" He whirled suddenly to pound one fist against the mantel. He stayed facing away from her, both hands gripping the high mantel, his eyes gazing down into the fire. "I was a fool. A total fool. I made myself an abject, ridiculous figure, pleading with you, crying over you, writing those letters. How could you have been cold enough to ignore them so totally, Emma? The whole fragile and broken heart of a young man was in them, ridiculous as they were."

"My father destroyed them," she said. "I never saw them."

He turned his head to look at her over his shoulder, his expression cynical. "Would it have made a difference if you had?" he asked.

"I loved you," she said, her voice dreary. And then, more impassioned, "I loved you, Edwin! If only I had loved you less, I think perhaps I would have fought against them and married you."

He pushed himself away from the mantel and turned to look at her fully. "What sort of nonsense is that?" he asked.

"I had never been from home," she said. "I had never met any man but the ones I had grown up with. I fell in love with you so totally, Edwin, that I was terrified by the power of my own emotions, terrified by what you did to my feelings and to my . . . to my body. I wanted you and what you had to offer more than I wanted anything else in life. I also wanted the safety and familiarity of home. I was afraid of my own awakened womanhood."

He stared at her, his expression stony.

"And then they advised me against it," she said.

"Indeed, my father said that he would not give his consent. He said it was wrong, that I was not ready, that it would be ungrateful and unfilial of me to leave my mother so soon and when she was in such delicate health. He said so many things that bewildered me. So many things that I hated to hear and yet that strangely comforted me. I could crawl back into the life I knew."

"For the rest of your life," he said, his voice a sneer. His eyes raked over her again.

"Yes," she said. "But I have regretted my decision every day since and will regret it every day for the rest of my life."

He laughed without amusement. "Then why have you not married?" he asked. "You are not going to tell me that you have not had chances, Emma."

"But none of them was you," she said softly.

He laughed again and stared broodingly at her.

"I am the love of your life, I suppose," he said. "You have carried me in your heart for nine years and will continue to do so to the grave."

"Yes."

"Strange," he said, the sneer back on his lips. "Do you pull away in panic and revulsion from the love of your life when he tries to kiss you, Emma?"

She swallowed. "Edwin," she said, "I was eighteen. It was nine years ago. You were the first man to kiss me. And the last. You have changed. You did not kiss me like that nine years ago." She flushed. "I am a spinster of almost thirty years. You frightened me. As you did when I was eighteen, I suppose, but this time in a purely physical way."

He stared at her.

"I was frightened," she said again lamely.

They stared at each other in silence.

"Come here," he said at last.

"Why?" She was clasping her hands very tightly to stop their trembling.

He stretched out a hand toward her. "Let me see if I can do it without frightening you," he said. "Come to me, Emma. Please?"

She took a couple of hesitant steps toward him and then walked steadily into his arms until they closed about her and her face was buried against the velvet of his coat.

"There has only ever been you," he said. "You know that, don't you? I meant everything I said to you during those days, and time has not changed anything. I loved you for a month, went through hell for you for a year, hated you for eight, and have been through hell again for two days. But there was only ever you. You know that, Emma, don't you?"

She swallowed against the lump in her throat.

"I was fond of Marianne," he said. "I will not dishonor her memory or lie by denying that it was so. She was sweet and kind and I was fond of her. But there has really only ever been you." His arms tightened about her. "Emma, what is it to be? Another year of agony before somehow I gather myself together again to live on? Or is there to be the happiness that lasted for only a month the first time?"

She drew her head back from his coat front and raised her face to look into his eyes.

"Edwin," she said, "so much time has gone by. So much time has been lost. I am no longer young."

He smiled. "Nine years ago I was five years older than you," he said. "How old are you now?"

"Seven-and-twenty," she said.

"Ah," he said, "what a strange coincidence. I am two-and-thirty, still five years older than you." The smile faded from all but his eyes. "Do you still love me enough to marry me?"

She bit her lip. "You cannot possibly want me, Edwin," she said. "It is just the memory of me that you want. I am an old maid."

"You have been doing a fair imitation of one," he admitted. "This ghastly dress is a masterpiece of disguise—at least it was until I touched you. But your acting skills have not been flawless. Who was it that came rushing and shrieking down a hillside on a sled this afternoon and almost stopped my heart with fear that she would overturn into a snowbank?"

She smiled unwillingly at him.

He lowered his head and kissed her slowly and gently, with closed lips.

"Will you marry me?" he asked.

"Yes," she said. And when she closed her eyes and the silence stretched, "Yes, I will." She opened her eyes again. "Will you do it as you did it out at the lake earlier, Edwin?"

"Like this?" he asked, lowering his head, opening his mouth over hers, and brushing his tongue across her lips.

She gulped. "Yes, like that," she said, her voice breathless.

He grinned at her. "Very well," he said, "but only because you are my betrothed, Emma. I am glad I had the foresight to turn the key in the lock when we came in here. This is going to get quite unseemly, I warn you."

"I want to learn," she said.

"Oh, you will," he said. "That I promise you, my love. You will surely learn. Now, open your mouth for me."

She looked up at him in surprise and obeyed as his mouth approached hers again.

And then she was clinging to his lapels and flinging her arms up about his neck for better support as his head angled against hers and their open mouths met and his tongue thrust all the way into her mouth. Long before he finally lifted his head away in order to drop soft kisses on her nose and cheeks and eyelids, she had pressed her body to his from bosom to knees to save herself from sliding to the ground. At some unspecified moment she seemed to have lost control of the parts of her legs below the knees.

"Lesson number one," he murmured. "The rest come after the banns have been read and the marriage ceremony performed. Before the end of January."

"So long?" she said. "How many lessons are there?"

"Five thousand, three hundred, and fifty-seven," he said, trailing kisses down over her chin and along her neck to the base of her throat. "Give or take half a dozen."

"Oh," she said. "And a month to wait for the second? With a warm and empty room, Edwin, and a locked door?"

"Lesson two may frighten you again," he said, returning his lips to hers and talking against them. His eyes were open, watching her. "It involves this." His hands were at her breasts, cupping them through the fabric of her dress. His thumbs found her nipples and brushed over them until she shivered.

"Oh," she said, her eyes closed, her head thrown back. "Edwin?"

"And then," he murmured against her throat, "lesson three involves the removal of the top half of your dress for the same process. But you definitely would not want to proceed to lesson three tonight, would you? It would be very improper."

"Improper," she said, dazed. "What is that?"

"Of course," he said, finding the buttons at the back of her dress, "it is Christmas, Emma, and people do all sorts of improper things at Christmas, like kissing each other in the middle of crowded drawing rooms just because there happens to be a sprig of mistletoe above their heads."

"Yes," she said, "it is Christmas."

"And it is a hideous dress," he said.

"Yes."

"Mm," he said before raising his head and hers with one hand behind it and kissing her open-mouthed again, "and you look so very much lovelier and feel whole universes more feminine without it, Emma."

"Do I?" she said while she still could. Her voice became a moan. "Edwin!"

All the other children had gone to bed long ago and fallen asleep long ago. Anna's nurse had come to her twice, once offering to fetch her a drink and bringing her doll and tucking it in beside her when she shook her head, and once asking if she wanted her papa sent for.

Anna continued to stare upward as she shook her head.

"Do you want the lady, then, lovey?" her nurse asked softly so as not to waken Harriet and Julie. "Miss Milford? Do you want her to come and say good night to you? Would you sleep then?"

Anna shook her head more slowly.

But she hoped that her nurse would send for one of them anyway. She felt so very alone and so very sad, though she felt guilty for the sadness, since her Christmas wish had been granted in such a wonderful way and Christmas Day had been the very best one ever.

She was glad when she heard their voices in the nursery, talking to her nurse. Both of them. They had both come. She was glad. She wanted to hug her mama—Miss Milford—one more time before Christmas was over. She did not think Christmas could be over yet. Surely it was not quite midnight.

And then they came into the bedchamber and

along to the side of her bed. Papa's arm was about
Mama's waist, she saw immediately. And when she
looked up into her mama's face, she held her eyes
there in wonder and hope.

There was something. Her mama's hair was un-
tidy, as if it had just been grabbed and pinned back
without benefit of brush or mirror, and her lips
looked red and swollen, as if she had toothache,
though not quite like that either. And her eyes—
oh, there was something about her eyes.

"Anna?" she said. "You can't sleep?"

"What is it, sweetheart?" Papa asked. "Has the
day been too exciting for you?"

There was something about him too. A certain
brightness about his eyes and a certain curving of
his mouth. Anna could hear her heart beating in
her ears.

Her new mama sat down at the edge of the bed,
and Papa's hand transferred itself to her shoulders. And Mama leaned over and hugged her.

"Poor Anna," she said. "It is wretched to be unable to sleep, is it not?"

Anna put her arms up about her new mama's
neck and closed her eyes.

"Mama," she whispered softly.

She was saying good-bye in her mind, behind her
tightly closed eyelids. Good-bye to the loveliest
Christmas ever. She did not notice the curious little silence.

"What?" Papa said, also in a whisper.

Perhaps there was hope. Perhaps if she could just
get him to see Mama as she saw her . . .

"Mama," she said again.

And then Papa was crying. He turned sharply
away from the bed and Anna could tell that he was
trying to control himself, but he was crying nevertheless in noisy gulps.

She should have said his name too. She did not
want him to feel left out. She did not wish it to be

just Mama and her. She wanted it to be the three of them.

"Don't cry, Papa," she said.

And then he was on his knees beside the bed, his face against her stomach, his arms about her tight enough to crush the breath from her.

"I still love you too, Papa," she said, pushing her fingers through his hair. "Even though I have a new mama."

He looked up at her suddenly, and up at her new mama, and he was laughing although his eyes were wet.

"A new mama?" he said. "What little bird has been up here ahead of us, telling you that?"

"I knew," she said, looking up to see that her mama was smiling back at her, her eyes wet too. "It was my Christmas wish."

Papa looked thunderstruck. "Your Christmas wish?" he said. "Emma was your Christmas wish?"

"She came early," she said. "Yesterday, not today. I knew her as soon as I saw her."

Papa got to his feet and ran a hand through his hair. He looked down at her and down at her mama.

"Would someone care to tell me if I am dreaming?" he asked.

They both looked silently up at him.

"Anna," Mama said, cupping one of her cheeks as Papa had done earlier, "I will be very honored to be your new mama, dear."

"Are you going to marry Papa?" she asked.

Her mama nodded. "At the end of January," she said.

Anna looked up to her papa, whose hand was resting on her mama's head.

"I won't ask you if that will make you happy, little imp," he said. "You have been playing determined Cupid since yesterday, haven't you?"

Anna did not know who or what Cupid was, but Papa looked pleased. She smiled.

"Oh, Anna," he said, gazing at her, and he looked for a moment as if he were going to start crying again. "My little Anna."

"May we have a baby?" she asked.

He looked dumbfounded. Her mama turned scarlet. Had she said something wrong?

"A brother?" she said. "Everyone has a brother except me."

"I tell you what," Papa said, stooping down again and kissing first Mama and then her on the lips, "you go to sleep, Anna, and leave Mama and me to discuss your suggestion. We will work on it during the next year. And perhaps next year your Christmas wish can be for a brother."

Anna moved her head about on the pillow until she was comfortable and burrowed her arms beneath the blankets while her mama pulled them up under her chin. She sighed with contentment and closed her eyes.

All was well after all. She had had her wish and it was all quite, quite perfect. Christmas, she decided, was the best time of the year. And perhaps next year there would be a real baby in a cradle just like the baby Jesus in his manger, and Mama bending over it on one side of the cradle and Anna on the other, just like Mary downstairs in the drawing room. And Papa would be standing just a little distance away loving them all and keeping them safe from all harm, just like Joseph.

Next Christmas.

"Or perhaps a sister," she said, opening her eyes briefly. "I would not mind a sister instead."

"We will see what we can do," Papa said. "Won't we, Emma?"

"Yes," Mama said. "We will see what we can do, Anna."

Home for Christmas

by

Melinda McRae

1

A thrill of excitement ran down Ashby Sutton's spine when he spotted the twisted, blackened hulk of the old oak beside the road. It would not be much longer now. He urged his horse onward, oblivious of the chill breeze that swept down the road. He had traveled so far to reach this place; he only wanted the journey over. Only two miles to home.

Home. The word conjured up a myriad of images, not all of them fond. But the place he had once hated now sounded more glorious than any exotic pleasure dome he had seen in all his travels. Sixteen long years had passed since he had last set foot on the island. Sixteen years since he had seen the English countryside, breathed in the fresh English air. Sixteen long years since he had enjoyed an English Christmas.

It had taken a long time, but now, finally, he was free of the bitterness that had kept him away for so long. He had made peace with the past, and was no longer afraid of it. Coming home would put the final seal on all the old wounds.

For a moment a twinge of apprehension disconcerted him. Perhaps he should have written that he was coming home. Then he shrugged. Christmas was the time of surprises. And his visit would certainly be that, he had no doubt.

Ash slowed his horse to a walk as they passed between the two posts marking the entry to Thorn-

ton. He could not yet see the house, but he could
picture it easily in his mind: the front steps rising
to the entry door, the pale weathered stone walls
contrasting with the sparkle from the many windows. This time of year, the front hall would be
festooned with evergreens, their loops held in place
with bright bows of crimson. Ribbons and clumps
of greenery would cling to the long, curving ban-
isters.

The family would be gathered in the front drawing room. That chamber, too, would be decorated
for the season, the carved twin mantels dripping
with entwined ivy and yew. And above it all, hanging from the chandelier, would be the gaily decorated kissing bough. Christmas.

As he reached the head of the tree-lined drive,
Ash caught his first glimpse of the white stone
house. Then the road curved to the right and
Thornton was there before him.

Puzzled, he examined the darkened exterior. Odd
that no glimmer of light slipped from beneath the
drawing-room curtains. Was it later than he
thought? Ash grimaced at the thought of ruining
his grand entrance with the necessity of rousing a
sleeping household. Then he saw a brief flickering
of light from an upstairs room—the schoolroom—
and he smiled with relief. If the children were still
awake, it was all right.

After dismounting and tying his horse carelessly
to the pillar, Ash bounded up the front steps and
yanked the bell rope beside the front door with un-
feigned enthusiasm. He could not wait to see the
look on old Harriman's face when he opened the
door. It would take a week for the butler to recover
from the shock.

Impatient at the long wait, Ash again jerked the
bell rope. When that summons brought no response, he reached for the door handle. He started
back upon discovering it locked. Perhaps the

household was asleep after all. Scowling, he stepped back. Best to try the kitchen door next.

The slightest trace of disquiet niggled at his brain when that entry, too, was locked. In a short time he would be reduced to pitching stones at one of the bedroom windows if he could not find another way in. Then a grin of remembrance swept over his face. How many times had he slipped in through the terrace doors after sneaking out at night? With any luck, the latch had not been changed.

His pocketknife worked as well on the flimsy latch as it had all those years ago. Stepping into the darkened room, Ash stood still for a few moments, allowing his eyes to adjust to the darkened chamber. He *thought* he could make out the outlines of the door on the far wall. Hesitantly he took a few careful steps forward and immediately sent a small table crashing to the floor.

"Damnation," he swore, righting the table and moving on more warily.

The door was flung open and a bright light stabbed at his eyes.

"Don't you move, now," a commanding voice warned. "I've got this here shotgun trained on you and it won't take much to make me pull the trigger."

"Harriman?" Ash queried, for the voice did not sound at all like he remembered.

"Mr. 'Arriman's not the one speaking to you. Now, move slowly, toward the door."

"I am not a housebreaker," Ash said, holding his hands carefully at his sides. "I'm Ashby. Ashby Sutton. Lord Denby's son."

"And I'm the Prince of Wales," the man holding the gun retorted. "Lord Ashby's been gone from these parts for years. He was in North America, last time anyone heard."

"Well, he crossed the ocean from North America

and he is now standing in front of you," Ash retorted with a hint of exasperation. "Now, will you please put that gun down? Take me to my father; I am certain he will identify me."

" 'E's not 'ere."

Ash started. "Where is he?"

"If you're 'is son, shouldn't you know where 'e is?"

Ash grimaced with vexation. "As you pointed out, I have been in North America. How should I know where he went?"

"The 'ole family packed off to Dorset for Christmas."

"I knew I should have written," Ash said ruefully, shaking his head. Now they were all at his uncle's. "Did they take Harriman with them? And who are you, by the way?"

"I'm Paul, the head footman. Mr. 'Arriman's gone off to visit some relations in the north."

"Is Mrs. George still the housekeeper?"

"She is, and she ain't here neither."

"Well, after a good night's sleep I promise to leave too. Could you move that blasted light so I am not blinded? And is there anything in the house to eat? I dined at Helmsford, but that was at midday."

Ash waited with growing impatience while the man deliberated. What an unbelievable homecoming. If he were not staring down the barrel of a shotgun, Ash would be tempted to laugh.

The footman finally lowered the gun and motioned for Ash to follow him into the corridor.

"If everyone is gone, what was the light I saw in the schoolroom window?" Ash asked as they walked toward the kitchen.

"That's Miss Norris," Paul replied. "She's governess to the young 'uns."

"Who else is here?"

"Most of the 'ouse staff. A few left to visit their families until the marquess returns."

"I hope there is someone in the stables. I left my horse out front."

"I'll have someone take care of it." Paul looked at him with a quizzical expression, then added, "m'lord."

Ash laughed at the unfamiliar title. "No one's called me that in years."

"Cook's abed," Paul announced when they reached the kitchen, "but I can get her for you."

Ash shook his head. "That is not necessary. Some bread and cheese will do. I can prepare it; you make arrangements for my horse. And have my bags brought in." He ran a hand through his hair. "Lord, I do not even know which room I should sleep in. I used to be at the north end of the hall upstairs. Is that a guest room now?"

"I think so," the footman replied. "I'll have one of the maids make up the bed."

Later, sitting back in his chair with booted feet stretched out before him, his hunger assuaged, Ash shook his head at how all his plans had gone awry. Well, perhaps "awry" was not the word. They were merely postponed. He still had plenty of time to rejoin his family before Christmas. Yet he felt a twinge of regret knowing he would not be spending Christmas here at Thornton. It would not be quite the same, somehow, at another's house. But surely Uncle Richard's would be equally festive. And his family would be there. That was what mattered.

Yawning, Ash stretched and rose. He half-wanted to explore the house, but there would be time enough for that in the morning, before he departed. He picked up the candle and made his way to the entry hall.

It would have been foolish for his family to have decorated the house when they were to spend the holidays elsewhere, but the absence of the anticipated greenery in the great hall disappointed him. The bare marble floor did not offer the welcome he had sought. It reminded him all too well of the home he had left—cold, austere, and rigid.

He was halfway down the corridor to his room when he remembered the light in the schoolroom. The governess, the footman had said. Curiosity drew Ash to the stairs. He should make his presence known, at least.

The second-floor corridor was as chilly and drafty as he remembered. What a haven the schoolroom had been on those long-ago winter days, when a fire was always merrily blazing in the grate and there were cups of steaming chocolate after the morning lessons. The shocking contrast between such homey comfort and Eton's grim austerity had soured him on school from the beginning. He hoped this lady maintained a cheery atmosphere for his nieces and nephew.

Rosalie Norris stepped back to examine her handiwork. Satisfied that the hanging loop of evergreens matched its predecessors, she moved her ladder along the wall.

It was foolish for her to go to such lengths to decorate for her solitary Christmas. But this year, more than any other, she needed this reminder of the season. For without it she might forget the holiday altogether.

Not that this was her first Christmas alone. Christmas had always been that way, for as long as she could remember. There had been little Christmas cheer in the home of her aunt. Christmases spent at school, in the company of only a teacher, had not been exciting. Even on those few occasions when she had accompanied a classmate home, Rose had never felt part of the celebration. These last few years, with younger children under her charge, she had been able to gain an appreciation of the magic and wonder of the season. She sorely missed the preparations this year.

So to cheer herself, to remind herself that even those who were alone in the world could enjoy their simple pleasures, she had spent the last two days gathering evergreen and holly. She would create her own festive corner of the world. She, Rose Norris, was going to celebrate Christmas. Even if it was by herself.

"I think it should be a few more inches to the left," a voice drawled.

Rose started at the strange voice, nearly toppling from her precarious position. The ladder swayed dangerously before it steadied beneath her feet. She turned her head to look down at the stranger whose secure grasp on the ladder had saved her from a nasty fall.

Except he was no stranger. Despite the fact she had never met him, or heard his voice, she knew exactly who the tousle-haired, blue-eyed man was. His hair had darkened to a sun-streaked brown, and his face was leaner, more defined. But she would have recognized him anywhere. The one person on earth she had never thought to see.

"Lord Ashby!" she exclaimed in shocked recognition.

Ash looked up into her wide sapphire-hued eyes, which blinked at him in surprise. "I did not mean to startle you," he said apologetically. "Miss Norris, I presume?"

She nodded silently, still maintaining her white-knuckled grip on the ladder. He stood below her, one foot planted solidly on the first rung of the ladder, his clear blue eyes lit with suppressed amusement.

"Perhaps you would like to climb down?" he suggested gently.

"Oh," she said, flustered at her dull-wittedness. In those first moments of shocked recognition, rational thought had fled her mind. Carefully she felt her way backward down the rungs.

Ash appraised the gray-clad woman on the ladder. She was tall and slender, and her unbound black hair reached nearly to her waist. As she descended the ladder, his grin widened at the revealed glimpse of her trim ankles. Not at all the sight he had expected from a governess.

"That is much better," Ash said when she stood before him. "It nearly made me dizzy having to look up at you like that."

She laughed. "A sailor with an aversion to heights?"

He smiled widely, but less from the irony than in appreciation of the dark curling locks that lay tumbled about her shoulders in a most ungovernesslike manner. "That is precisely why I am the captain—so I can order others up into the masts. But tell me, Miss Norris, how it is that you are so well-acquainted with me? For I am very certain we have not met before."

She saw the scrutiny in his eyes and she self-consciously brushed back the long strand of hair that fell over her ear. What an ignominious manner of meeting!

"Your portrait," she said simply, gesturing to the far wall.

Ash turned and frowned at the painting hanging there. Frozen in time forever, an arrogant, willful boy of fifteen looked down on him with haughty disdain. He shook off the cold chill that passed through him at the sight of his former self.

"I should perhaps take insult in the fact that you can see the resemblance between myself and that insufferable brat," he said, forcing lightness into his voice.

Since first setting eyes on that seventeen-year-old portrait, Rose had been fascinated by the story of Lord Ashby, the son who had rebelled against his aristocratic family and fled from home in bitter anger. She admired him for having the courage to follow his dream, and had invented a larger-than-life image of the man that painted boy had become. It had seemed a harmless enough pastime. Yet now suddenly he stood here before her, living, breathing flesh, and she could barely regard him without embarrassment. She stood in tongue-tied discomfort.

Ash glanced about the room, breathing in the fragrant scent of the carefully draped swaths of fir and holly that adorned the walls. At least one person in this house had not forgotten it was Christmas. This was what he had come home for. It was almost as if she had anticipated his need.

"Are you planning a celebration, Miss Norris?" He regarded her with an amused half-smile.

Her expression grew sheepish. "A rather solitary one, I am afraid. But the house looked so forlorn without any decoration."

"My thoughts exactly," he agreed. "Although I can quite understand why no one bothered, since the family is not here. Why are you not in Dorset with them?"

"I have a fortnight's holiday," she explained.

"You are going to spend it here alone?" Ash stared at her with growing incredulity. Why would anyone choose to be alone for Christmas? "Why do you not go to your family?"

"I do not have any family," she answered quietly. "My intentions were to visit a friend near Bath, but her mother took ill."

"How unfortunate," Ash said, noting the faint trace of regret that crossed her face. His curiosity had only reminded her that she was spending Christmas by herself. Berating himself for his clumsiness, he examined her decorating efforts more carefully. "You have done a nice job," he said, seeing that she had nearly completed her self-imposed task. "May I assist you in finishing?"

"There is no need for you to trouble yourself," she began.

"But it is no trouble," he insisted. "I want to."

Rose suddenly realized the keen disappointment he must feel at discovering his family's absence. He had come such a long way, only to be met by strangers. She knew exactly what he wanted—a few moments of conversation and reassurance. Even a stranger could provide that.

"Then you are more than welcome to help," she said with an inviting smile.

Ash picked up the ladder and moved it a few feet further along the wall. "I think it would be best if I did the reaching," he said, forgetting for a moment that his action would deprive him of the chance to see those ankles again. With a regretful sigh he nimbly stepped up the rungs, reaching down for the greenery Miss Norris handed him.

"I was not aware you planned to return home," she said, watching him with discreet concern. Had his parents deliberately ignored his impending visit?

"It was rather a whim of the moment," he said, carefully tacking the bough in place. He turned and flashed her a rueful grin. "As you can see, I am paying the price for my rash behavior. It never occurred to me that the family would go elsewhere for the holidays. I received an adequate comeuppance for my arrogance, I assure you. It took me several minutes to convince the footman that I was who I said I was."

"It will not take you more than a day to reach them," she pointed out.

"Oh, I realize that," he said, turning back to his task. "I will be off again in the morning."

A stab of sadness sliced through her. She would have him near for only a short while. Yet she had no cause for complaint, having never thought to see him at all. Rose observed him closely while he tacked the last few strands of greenery into place. He looked every bit as handsome and masculine as he had in her imaginings. Broad shoulders, a trim form, and muscled legs all bespoke an active man. His clothes, while not the skin-hugging apparel favored by those of the highest *ton*, were well-tailored.

"Will that do?"

He looked at her with such an expression of eager appeal that she realized how important this simple task had been to him. It was a decided shock to think that Lord Ashby was as needful as she of the trappings of home and tradition. Surely a man who had made his own way in the world for as long as he would have reached an accommodation with that. But then, something had driven him to come home at last. Perhaps this was a piece of it.

Whatever the cause, she was loath to have him leave her company yet. "Would you like to have a cup of tea?"

"That would be welcome," he said, smiling easily. Perhaps she sensed his desire for company. Or perhaps she had need of company as well.

He watched while she prepared the tea from the kettle atop the schoolroom stove. Her manner of dress was plain, eminently suitable for a governess. Yet those lively blue eyes and cascading tresses painted the picture of a more lively spirit. He doubted she had been a governess for any length of time. He felt a sudden need to know more about her.

"Have you been here long?" he asked.

"Three years," she replied, carefully pouring the hot water into the flowered china pot.

"Is this your first post?" A roundabout way to

ascertain her age. She hardly looked old enough to be a governess.

Rose laughed. "No, I fear I am not as green as all that. Your nieces and nephew are my third group of charges."

He wanted to ask her if she was content being a governess, but knew it too personal a question from a total stranger. He accepted the proffered cup with gratitude.

"Did you have an easy journey here?" she asked, her interest genuine. She had spent too many hours studying his portrait to think him a stranger.

"Hardly. Crossing the North Atlantic at this time of year is never easy. But I have seen worse. Once I set foot on solid English ground again, it was all worth it."

"This is your first time back?"

He nodded. "I never felt any desire to, before. Then this year . . . It is odd, but I had the strongest feeling that I *needed* to be here. At Christmas." He ran his hand through his thick hair. "We sailors are a superstitious lot. I decided not to ignore the feeling." He took a long sip of tea. "And it is past time that I came home."

Rose both envied and sympathized with his need. She, who had no family, knew what a precious thing it was. He realized it as well. "Thank goodness it hasn't been frightfully snowy this winter," she said. "You will have an easy journey to your uncle's."

He nodded but remained silent for a moment, deep in thought. His barely suppressed doubts returned. At last he spoke. "How do they go on?"

Seeing the eagerness in his eyes, Rose felt an onrush of sympathy for Lord Ashby. She could only imagine his crushing disappointment at finding his family gone after such a long journey. "They are all well. Your father's gout plagues him on occasion, and they say he is not as active as he once was. I believe your brother is taking up more of his duties. Your mother is quite well."

"It is sometimes difficult to believe it has been sixteen years," he said, shaking his head in amazement. "I have lived apart from them for half my life."

"I am certain they will be pleased to see you," she said with calm reassurance.

He grinned wryly. "I wish I shared your optimism. But I fear there will be no fatted calf for this prodigal son."

"Perhaps a small goose?"

He laughed at the teasing look in her eyes, appreciating her attempt to restore his spirits. She had an uncanny knack for saying just what he needed to hear. "What of you, Miss Norris? Is there no other place you could go besides Bath? It seems a dreadful shame that you must spend your fortnight here alone."

Rose tilted her head to one side, considering. "It is not so bad. I find I quite enjoy the peace and quiet."

A solitary Christmas, Ash thought. Lord, how many of those had he spent down the years? Christmases in exotic locales like Delhi and Canton, where the crisp, clean scent of evergreens was only a fond memory. Or in places like New Orleans or Charleston, where the spirit of Christmas seemed strange and alien against a backdrop of warm weather and Spanish moss. He was quite familiar with solitary Christmases. But he had never grown accustomed to them.

No matter how hard he tried to recreate the celebrations he remembered from his childhood, his efforts always failed. For he was never able to capture what had made them special—home and family. It was that feeling that he found himself longing for. It was that feeling that had led him home at last. It was that special part of Christmas that Miss Norris would not have.

Rose watched him carefully while she sipped her tea. It would not be quite the same for him, to celebrate Christmas at his uncle's house. But at least he would be with his family.

Lord Ashby's quick laugh startled her into attention. She noted the way the skin around his eyes crinkled when he smiled.

"I fear I am not a voluble companion this evening," he said with a quick grimace. "You must find me intolerably rude, Miss Norris."

"I am certain you are tired from your traveling," she replied.

"I am at that," he acknowledged. "More from excitement than the journey itself." He offered her a self-deprecating grin. "I fear I anticipated this family reunion with a good deal of mixed feelings."

"I think you worry yourself unnecessarily," she said. "They are always relieved when they hear from you. The children are always entranced with the presents you send. We often use them as a basis for a geography lesson."

"And so I will always be associated with the boring drudgery of the schoolroom."

"I did not mean—"

"I am roasting you, Miss Norris. I am pleased the little trinkets have some use. Lord knows I have enough of them cluttering up my rooms, with not nearly such a useful purpose."

"Where do you make your home?" she asked.

"I have rooms in Salem now," he explained. "Since the war ended . . . it is comfortable for an English sailor there again."

Yet it had still taken him three more years to make the trip home, Rose realized, suspecting it had been a long-fought battle within himself. She was glad his longing for home had won out at last.

"I fear I am keeping you from your bed," he said

politely, not truly willing to end their *tête-à-tête*, even if their silences grew longer than their conversation. He felt surprisingly comfortable in her company, as if they *had* met before.

Rose admired his skillfully worded method of escape. "I do confess that the hour grows late. And even if I am free of my charges for the time, it will do me no good to grow slothful in their absence." She rose, forcing Lord Ashby to scramble to his feet.

"I thank you, Miss Norris, for the tea and conversation." He meant it sincerely. It had been an age since he sat sipping tea with a proper English lady, governess or no. It was a rare treat. A most suitable welcome to England and home.

"And I thank you, Lord Ashby, for your help tonight," she said with a trace of wistfulness. "I wish you Godspeed on the rest of your journey."

Bowing in his most polite manner, Ash exited into the corridor, closing the door on that cozy corner of Christmas. With reluctant steps he made his way to his room.

The chamber had been completely redecorated, he noted without surprise. Where once his rocks, stuffed birds, and Roman artifacts had been the despair of the housemaids, there was now merely a bland, serviceable guest chamber.

Stifling a yawn, he wondered briefly where his old possessions were. Had they been relegated to the attic, or tossed on the rubbish heap in the first flush of anger at his departure? Perhaps he would ask his mother. There might be a few things he still wanted.

Undressing quickly, he donned his heavy winter nightshirt and climbed thankfully into the warmed sheets. But tired as his body was, he found his mind unwilling to cooperate. His thoughts kept drifting back to the festive schoolroom and to Miss Norris.

He had no illusions about the reasons behind the lavish decorations in the schoolroom. In her own way, she was doing what he had done in so many out-of-the-way places—making Christmas for one. The fate of lonely people.

A deep sadness filled him. Despite the fact that he had turned his back on them years ago, he still had family. He was far luckier than Miss Norris, who was alone in the world. She most likely would never have a family Christmas.

Rose carefully snuffed the candles in the schoolroom and dampened the fire before slipping into her room.

What an amazing night. As if conjured from her own dreams, Lord Ashby had stepped into her world, a man more dashing and exciting than she could even have imagined. He looked very much as she had expected, yet somehow different.

It was his eyes, she decided. They were still the same brilliant shade of blue, but the look within them had altered over the years. He was no longer the boy in the portrait. That painted boy was a spoiled, petulant youngster, at war with the world and himself. At fifteen he had looked out with the arrogance of a duke and the anger of a second son who had little control over his destiny. There was no trace of that now. Instead, she saw a mature man, comfortable with his life, but looking for something as well.

There was loneliness in those eyes, the loneliness of a man who had not been close to anyone for many years. The loneliness of a man who would take any manner of risk to be home with his family for Christmas. She could only pray that his reunion would be a happy one.

Rose was grateful that he had not written ahead and discovered his family's plans. For if he had, she never would have made his acquaintance.

While she carefully wove her long tresses into a thick braid, she pictured his face again in her mind, wishing she was more skilled with her pencil, so she could capture a permanent image of the man. In the morning, when he was gone, she would almost wonder if it had been a dream. Perhaps it had been.

2

Ash woke with the dawn. Mariner's hours, he thought ruefully, surveying the cold hearth. On frigid mornings like these, it was easy to contemplate settling on one of the Caribbean islands, where cold winters existed only in memory.

Still, he had much to accomplish today, and he could not lie abed long. Grimacing, he threw back the covers and swung his feet onto the floor. Sprinting across the room, he quickly shrugged himself into his clothing and hurried downstairs to the warm kitchen.

Fortified by breakfast, Ash set out on his tour of the house. He needed to see it now, while he had the opportunity, for he did not know when or if he would be back again. He peered into each and every room, feeling something like a naughty child while inspecting the bedrooms of his absent family. He lingered only in his father's room. Its uncluttered, austere interior reminded Ash of the man—harsh and direct.

Shaking off the unbidden memories that rose within him, Ash descended to the floor below. He was less uncomfortable in the common rooms. They did not reflect any one personality. And, in truth, there was very little in them that looked familiar. Wall coverings, furniture, and draperies had all been altered since he left. Only the library looked as he remembered it, and since he had spent little time there, he drew no comfort from that.

In fact, he thought while he completed his circuit of the ground floor, this house felt very little like the Thornton he had idealized during his years away. A deep gloom descended upon him. Would it be the same when he finally saw his family? Would they have changed too, out of all recognition?

He looked one more time about the drawing room, trying to picture it as it had been sixteen years ago. But the only images that came to mind were those of the room decorated for one of those long-ago Christmases. Swaths of evergreens, bright red bows, and glittering candles had turned the room into a special place. Much like Miss Norris' schoolroom.

Ash's eyes brightened as the idea grew. He would do it. He still had plenty of time to reach his uncle's before Christmas. One day's delay would not cause any harm. And he could see at least a part of Thornton the way he imagined it. He was certain Miss Norris would be willing to help—she, of all people, would understand. Quickening his steps, Ash took the stairs to the schoolroom two at a time.

Waking slowly, Rose blinked to clear the sleep from her eyes. She spent some minutes staring at the ceiling, sleepily recalling that strange and wonderful visit from Lord Ashby. She was reluctant to leave the warm cocoon of her bed, as if by leaving it she would finalize his departure. But delaying her rising would not make Lord Ashby's absence any less real. Like tucking away a treasured trinket, she put her memories of last night into a special place. She would draw them out one day when she needed comfort.

Upon making her way to the warm kitchen, Rose

was surprised to find the cook up to her elbows in flour.

"Baking so early?" Rose asked, helping herself to a cup of tea.

"The quality," Cook replied, shaking her head dolefully. "Think all we have to do is respond to their every whim. Mince pies, he says, as if I weren't going to be baking them in two days. Goose, he wants. You would think he was lord of the manor."

Rose's heart skipped a beat. "Who asked for all this?"

The cook uttered a snort of derision. "Lord Ashby, that's who. Seemed to think he needed his own Christmas dinner right here in this house. Couldn't wait until he reached the viscount's, where they will have twice the food and more hands to fix it." She grimaced as her hands worked the dough. "Even wanted my pudding, but I said to him there was no way he was going to get my pudding before Christmas. He can find his own pudding if he wants one so bad."

"Lord Ashby is staying for dinner?" Rose's spirits rose at the thought that she might yet see him again.

"Christmas dinner for all, he said. Them that's downstairs, and dinner for two upstairs." She sniffed and eyed the governess suspiciously. "You wouldn't be knowing who he plans to entertain, would ye?"

Rose flushed. "Perhaps he plans to invite an old friend from the neighborhood." He certainly did not intend to dine with her.

Shrugging, Cook went on with her work. "There's cold toast and marmalade on the table there. I won't have time to fix you a tray for luncheon or dinner, so you'll have to come down to get your meals today. Gotta prepare this feast for his lor'ship."

"I do not mind," Rose replied with a friendly smile. She knew the kitchen staff best of all the household servants. Cook was never loath to prepare special tidbits for the children, and for their governess from time to time.

"Is there anything I can do to help?" Rose asked. "Here or upstairs?"

Cook shook her head. " 'Tis no business of yours. Trot back on back to your schoolroom. Best you keep out of the way."

Rose nodded, her desire to see Lord Ashby again warring with her feeling that it was better if she did not. But oh, how she wished to talk to him one more time. To ask more about the mysterious Orient or the massive continent of North America. Sadly she finished her light breakfast and turned toward the back stairs, hoping she could salve her disappointment with a brisk walk.

"Ah, there you are, Miss Norris."

Lord Ashby stood above her on the stairs, his blue eyes bright with delight. "I have been looking all over for you."

"You have not left," she replied inanely, praying he could not hear the hammering of her heart.

"No," he replied. "I thought to delay my departure one more day. I found there was something I wished to do while I was here."

"Cook said you were planning to entertain tonight," she said in a subdued tone. "I hope you have an enjoyable evening."

"I certainly hope so too," he said, his grin widening.

The merriment in his voice puzzled her. Last night he had sounded so eager to be off to his family. Rose looked away quickly, before he saw the longing in her eyes. She was foolish to think he would want to spend the evening with her. With effort, she gave him a friendly nod and started to brush past him on the stairs.

He reached out and touched her arm. "Miss Norris?"

She turned, surprised at the eager tone in his voice. "Yes?"

"It would give me great pleasure if you would dine with me this evening." He was surprised to find he held his breath, waiting for her response. It made him realize just how much he looked forward to her company again.

"Me?" she whispered in awe.

"Well, yes, you." He smiled encouragingly. "I thought you might like to share a formal Christmas dinner. Cook said we could not have the pudding, but she is making all else for us, down to the mince pies."

Rose stood silently, torn between desire and caution. It was more than she dared to wish for, yet she feared every moment spent in his company would make his eventual departure even more wrenching.

"Come now," he said. "It is difficult enough to have a festive Christmas dinner with only two people. It would be utterly impossible were I forced to dine alone. And," he continued, fixing her blue eyes with his own, "I feel I must return the favor you extended me last evening."

"I did not do anything," she protested weakly.

"Oh, but you did, Miss Norris. You welcomed me home."

"It was hardly the welcome you expected," she demurred, absurdly elated at his commendation. "A greeting from a total stranger was not much when you were anticipating your whole family."

"But you helped to ease my disappointment," he said lightly, watching her closely. "And I do not like the idea of you celebrating all on your own. I am certain that if the family had known your plans for Bath were canceled, they would have invited you to accompany them."

"It is not necessary—"

"It is, Miss Norris. I have spent too many Christmases of my own alone. I cannot allow you to do the same." He drew himself up and in his most commanding captain's voice ordered, "You will assist in the decorating of the drawing room, Miss Norris. And you will join me for dinner."

She could not stifle the smile that crept over her lips. "As you say, Captain."

He tilted his head back and laughed. "You learn fast, Miss Norris. Would that all my crew members were so accepting of my authority. I expect you to meet me in the drawing room at one so we may begin."

"One?"

"It is a rather large drawing room," he noted dryly, then smiled. "It will take us some time to decorate. I wish it to be complete before dinner."

She shook her head in disbelief, but could not stifle the smile that crept over her lips.

Ash returned her smile, knowing he had overcome her protestations. "I know, you are thinking it is only typical of the rash and impetuous Lord Ashby. Humor an Englishman during his first visit home in sixteen years."

"It would be churlish of me to refuse you," she acknowledged.

"I should be back from the village by one. I will have some manner of cold collation brought up to the drawing room for our luncheon." He grinned broadly, then turned and loped down the stairs.

Rose gripped the banister to keep her legs steady. Lord Ashby wanted to entertain *her*. Even in her wildest dreams she could not have imagined such a turn of events.

Matters were occurring much too quickly for her to absorb. It was a chill day, but a long walk in the crisp, clear winter air would be welcome. She could use the solitary time to think. Rose grabbed her cloak from the schoolroom and slipped out into the park.

She had always prided herself on her ability to keep her dreams separate from the reality of her life. Dreams were merely a temporary escape, deliberately fanciful. Yet now dreams were colliding with reality and the lines between the two blurred. Rose shivered, and not from the cold December air. She sensed that she was walking straight into a disaster. It was easier to face the life that stretched before her if she did not have a firsthand sample of what she would be missing. An afternoon spent with a handsome man, an evening during which she would be treated like a guest in the house would make it all the more frustrating to take up her governess's mantle when he left.

She had rarely railed against the chain of circumstances that directed her in this life. It was a pointless effort, and she knew only too well that she had been luckier than many. But her relative contentment rested upon her deliberate avoidance of situations that would remind her clearly of what she was not. As today most surely would.

She could have said no. His disappointment would not have been great. It would have been the safer course. But she did not quite have that strength of character. She *wanted* to pretend, if even for only a few hours, that she was not Rosalie Norris, governess. That it was not exceptional for her to be in the company of Lord Ashby Sutton. Like an actress in a play, she would take on a new role. Until he was gone again.

Ash drove the gig home from the village, a smug smile upon his face. He had found everything he needed in the village: red ribbons for bows, candies as a childish whim, and the all-important goose. In an impulsive gesture, he'd purchased several lengths of blue ribbon that looked to be an exact

match for Miss Norris' eyes. Most important, he
had found the one last missing symbol of Christmas, now tucked carefully into his jacket pocket.
That had been an even more frivolous whim, but
he could not resist. It would not be Christmas without the kissing bough.

He thought Miss Norris uncommonly attractive
for a governess—or had all the ladies grown lovelier during his long absence from England? It
would be pleasant to spend the rest of the day in
the company of such a comely woman. It had been
an age since he had last done so.

Promptly at one, she joined him and the two
footmen in the drawing room. Two enormous piles
of evergreens and holly awaited them.

Ash turned hopefully to her."How exactly does
one construct a garland, Miss Norris?"

Rose stifled a laugh. How like a man to under-
take a project with no idea of how to go about it.
She patiently instructed the three men, then
turned her attention to making bows while they
worked.

Lord Ashby insisted on handing the decorations
himself, wanting everything to be exactly so. Rose
sat and watched, controlling her mirth with some
effort. She grinned widely as he clambered up the
ladder to move a garland a fraction of an inch or
to increase the hang of a loop. She wondered if he
had decorated for Christmas before. Perhaps when
he was a boy, in the last years before his departure.
And maybe in other lands. Certainly people cele-
brated Christmas in Salem. She hoped there were
families there that he knew, who invited him for
the holidays and allowed him to join in their merrymaking.

When at last he decreed everything was just so,
he dismissed the footmen. Ash leaned against the
mantel, arms folded across his chest, watching
Rose skillfully turn the flat strips of ribbon into

fanciful bows. It was a much more pleasant sight than observing grizzled sailors knotting ropes.

"Do you wish to place your own bows, or can I be trusted with such a task?" he asked.

She laughed. "I fear I dare not volunteer, for I know you will be darting up the ladder after me, insisting that I have put my bow a half-an-inch too far to one side or the other. By all means, Lord Ashby, let the task be yours." She held out the first bow to him.

When the bows were nearly gone, he took her hand and drew her to her feet. "You must place at least one or two," he insisted.

Eschewing the ladder, Rose chose to bestow her bows among the holly bedecking the mantel. One particular bow proved most unwilling to nestle among a cluster of red-berried greens. It took Rose both hands to secure it tightly, and she became snared by the sharp-pointed leaves.

"Ow!" she exclaimed, jerking her hand away.

"Are you all right?"

Rose nodded, stepping back. "I merely scratched my hand on the holly. 'Twas clumsy of me."

"Let me see," Ash demanded.

He snatched up her hand, and the real concern in his eyes surprised Rose.

She had lovely hands, he thought. Small, delicate, and well-shaped. Very ladylike hands. Marred now by the bloody mark left by that damned plant. It was his fault. He should have put the blasted bows up himself. He raised her hand, brushing the scratch with his lips.

The touch of his lips upon her skin jolted her. Rose kept her eyes lowered, not willing to look at him until she had herself firmly under control.

This was what came of all her flights of fancy, she chided herself. She had thought her images of the mysterious Lord Ashby were safe dreams, for what chance was there that he would ever return?

Now he had, and he was more powerful in the flesh than in all her fervent imaginings. She must guard her emotions carefully.

The poor man would be mortified to know that he had been the object of a foolish governess's fantasies, the hero of the wishful dreams of a woman who began to confront the inevitability of her spinster future. Rose felt suddenly awkward and reticent, and was no longer certain that sharing dinner was a good idea.

"There," he announced, releasing her hand at last. "I do not think you will be permanently scarred."

He was wrong in that, she thought. The touch of his lips would mark her hand forever.

Ash stood back and surveyed the drawing room. "It does not look half-bad, does it?"

"It looks very nice," she said, looking up despite her apprehensions and catching his eye upon her. She forced a cheerful smile. "You have done a superior job, Lord Ashby."

"Pardon me, Miss Norris, but I grow terribly tired of 'Lord Ashby.' No one has called me that in an age." He took a long breath. "Could it not be simply 'Ash'?"

"Ash." The name felt familiar on her tongue. In her mind, she had called him that many times.

"And it seems deucedly formal to continue to call you 'Miss Norris.' I am certain you have a perfectly lovely given name."

"Rosalie," she said with a shy blush. "Rose."

"Rose," he repeated, savoring the sound of it. "An English rose, brightening the winter with its bloom. How appropriate."

She felt suddenly embarrassed, hearing her name on his lips. It had been years since anyone called her that. "Rose" had disappeared a long time ago, along with her parents.

Ash glanced to the mantel clock, once again trying to still the odd sensation he experienced whenever he glanced in Rose's direction.

It was her vulnerability that made him so susceptible. He had always had a soft spot for women in uncomfortable situations. And she touched him more than most, for it had been a long time since he had conversed with a gently bred Englishwoman. Despite her status as governess, she had been raised as a lady. Probably the daughter of an impoverished squire who had left her without a competence at his death. No doubt she had been forced to become a governess to survive.

What would she have liked to do if she had not had to make that choice? Marry, no doubt, and raise a family of her own. He could tell she liked children; he could hear it in her voice when she talked of her charges.

"We should perhaps change for dinner," he said at last, covering the awkward silence that had befallen them. "I am certain that you are efficient in your toilette, but I fear I am woefully out of practice at formal dressing."

"Yes, perhaps it is time." She stood, shaking out her skirts. "But do not expect an elegant evening gown, Lor . . . Ash. Governesses do not possess such things."

"By formal, I meant I shall attempt a cravat." He smiled ruefully, chagrined that he might have caused her embarrassment. "I think there is one somewhere in my luggage. Sadly wrinkled and shapeless, I am certain, but then, that will be its state when I am finished with it anyhow."

His self-deprecating laugh eased her worry. It had been foolish to think that he would expect her to look like a London fashion plate. He was not dull-witted.

There was no question it would have to be her maroon silk, she mused as she trod up the stairs. It was the best gown she possessed, and the only one which was not suited to the schoolroom. It was three years out of style, but Ash would not be so aware of that, she hoped. In a burst of feminine vanity, she wanted to look her best.

Rose lingered long before her mirror, combing and recombing her hair into a variety of styles before she was finally satisfied. Years of experience allowed her to dress her own hair with ease. Just for this evening, she allowed herself the indulgence of wearing it in a softer manner than usual. She encouraged a few curling tendrils to escape and frame her face. A man as dashing as Ash would not want to eat with a woman who looked like a governess.

Satisfied with her hair at last, Rose smoothed down her skirts and gave herself one last glance in the pier glass. She pinched her cheeks to add a spot of color to her pale face. Silly girl, she chided herself afterward, but secretly she was pleased with her appearance. She would not give him cause to flee the room in fright. For a governess, she looked well.

Carefully she pinned a cameo brooch to her dress. It was her only piece of jewelry; her only remembrance from the woman who had been her mother. Rose wore it for only the most special occasions.

Uncertain of exactly when she should go down, Rose paced impatiently about her room. She did not want to be the first downstairs, for she did not want Ash to think her too eager. Yet she did not desire him to wait impatiently, thinking she was a frivolous thing. Finally, when she could stand the suspense no longer, she gathered up her warm woolen shawl and proceeded down the stairs.

Ash turned the moment he heard the drawing-room door open. He had been relieved to find she was not yet there, for he knew he had spent an inordinate amount of time tying that blasted cravat. Normally he was not so vain about his appearance, but he wished to look his best for Miss . . . Rose. He did not want her to think he had tendered this invitation to dinner lightly. He truly wanted to give her a pleasant evening.

"You look very lovely, Rose," he said truthfully, feeling his cravat constricting around his neck. The gown did wonderful things to her form. The loose, curling tendrils of hair softened her face, making her look even more vulnerable.

Her wide blue eyes lighted with pleasure at his words. "And your cravat looks very presentable, Ash," she replied. As did the rest of him. Clad in form-fitting pantaloons and a well-tailored jacket, he looked as elegant as the son of a marquess should. Very much the kind of man who had little in common with a simple governess.

"Should you like a glass of sherry before dinner?" He turned to the sideboard, once again struck by how her nearness affected him. He felt like an awkward schoolboy in her presence—and not because she was a governess. He was not accustomed to dealing with a lady.

"Thank you," she replied, gracefully taking her seat in one of the chairs before the blazing fire.

He handed her a glass and picked up his own, seating himself across from her. He looked at the shooting flames. "It is not quite an official Yule log, but it will have to do," he said at last with a hint of apology in his voice.

"It is most warming," she said, before they lapsed into a hesitant silence. She did not think he would care for idle female chitchat, yet she was reluctant to pester him with more questions about his travels. Perhaps later, after dinner . . .

They both looked up in relief when a footman appeared to announce dinner.

"You are in for a special treat," Ash promised after they were seated. They watched the footman ladle the soup into the bowls. "We shall have dinner with a hint of the mysterious East."

"What are we having?" Rose asked, eyeing her bowl with curiosity.

"Several curried dishes," Ash replied. "Very common in India. I nearly had to wrestle the cook away from her pots, but she finally allowed me to add some seasoning."

Ash watched eagerly while Rose tasted her soup, but her wide-eyed look of surprise and her hasty fumbling for her wineglass told him he had erred. Jumping from his seat, he grabbed the wine decanter from the sideboard and hastily refilled her glass as she sat gasping for air.

"That was," she said finally, after several more generous swallows of the cooling claret, "a most unusual experience."

Ash looked chagrined. "I forget that it can be overwhelming for someone who is not accustomed to the taste."

"You mean it is possible to become accustomed to that?" she asked in disbelief, taking another sip of her wine.

He grinned. "It does seem impossible at first, doesn't it? But one adjusts. I found it roundly ironic to have such hot food in India's heat. But nothing else can take the chill off a freezing cold Salem evening."

Rose toyed with her spoon, unwilling to attempt another taste. "Is this the most unusual food you have encountered on your travels?"

Ash, eagerly partaking of his soup, shook his head. "You do not even wish to know some of the things that pass for food in the East, Rose. Things no self-respecting Englishman would ever eat. Yet many are quite good, in fact. Mongoose is quite a delicacy. As are roasted chicken's feet."

Rose surveyed him carefully, suspecting he was teasing her.

"I am perfectly serious," he said, grinning at her disbelief. "I've eaten rat, snake, all manner of birds and fish, peppers so hot they make this curry taste like bread pudding." He leaned toward her in a confidential manner. "Even tasted whale blubber." He made a face. "Nasty stuff."

Rose laughed, shaking her head at his wild tales.

"I am sorry about the soup," he apologized. "I advise you not to eat the carrots either."

"Thank you for the warning," she said. "I trust the goose will be fit for British palates?"

He nodded. "Deucedly difficult to cover a whole goose with curry powder. Although cut up, in a sauce . . ."

Rose rolled her eyes in mock dismay and they both laughed.

The remainder of the dinner passed uneventfully, with Rose carefully heeding Ash's warning about the carrots. He attacked each dish with relish, and not until he had finished his second serving of mince pie did Ash again grow talkative.

"Now I feel that I am truly home," he said, tossing his napkin casually onto the table. "This is the best meal I have eaten in years. Even without curry on the goose."

His delight at being home pleased Rose. She wanted him to be happy. As happy as she was to be in his company.

"I see no need to sequester myself here while you retire in lonely splendor to the drawing room," he said. "You do not mind if I join you with my brandy?"

"Of course not," she replied. She knew this truly would be their last time together, and she did not wish to be parted from him for even a moment.

"Should you care for a glass?" he asked. At her rapid declining, he laughed. "I guess it would not be at all the thing, to have a brandy-swilling governess. Some port? Or Madeira?"

"A small glass of port would be acceptable," Rose replied, knowing she had already consumed far too much wine while extinguishing the curry fire in her mouth. But she felt relaxed, and warm, and content.

"Tell me a bit about yourself," he encouraged when they were seated in front of the blazing drawing-room fire again. "You know so much about me, yet I know so little of you."

"There is not much to tell." Her smile held a hint of regret. "I have not lived a very exciting life, I am afraid."

"Sometimes I wish I had led a life with a little less excitement," he confided. "Where were you born?"

"In Lancashire," she replied.

"Goodness, you have come a long way to Kent, then." He struggled to keep his questions from sounding like an inquisition. But there was so much more he wanted to know. What had happened to her family? Why had she become a governess? What were her hopes and dreams and fears? "Did you spend your childhood in Lancashire?"

She shook her head. "My parents died when I was quite young. I lived with an aunt for several years; then she sent me to a ladies' seminary in Somerset when I was ten."

Even he had not left for the hated Eton until he was twelve. He suspected a girls' school could be equally ghastly for a young orphan girl.

"And have you been a governess for many years?"

"This is my third post," she replied. "I stayed at the school for two years, teaching. I had two short-term posts following that before I came here." Rose took a deep breath. It was more than she had said to anyone about her past in a long time. His comforting presence encouraged confidences.

She glanced quickly at him and was taken aback at the mingled look of sadness and pity she saw in his eyes.

"It has not been so dreadfully bad," she announced, unsure whom she intended to convince. "As a governess, I have a great deal more freedom than I ever did at Miss Blanford's Seminary. And certainly children are much more cooperative in their own home than when away at school."

"That I can believe," he said, rolling his eyes. "I was a holy terror at Eton."

"Sent down at fifteen, if I remember right," she teased.

He gave her a shrewd look. This English Rose seemed to know a great deal about him. "And I could not shake the dust of Eton off my feet fast enough. God, how I hated that place. Always cold, always hungry, and always miserable."

"It might have been better at another school."

"No," he said. "I was relieved when my father said there was to be no more school ahead of me after that last, final prank. Book learning seemed like a tremendous bore at that age. And truly, I cannot say that I have been hurt by the lack. Latin and Greek are very useless subjects."

"Why did you leave?" she asked, suddenly wondering how his story would match up with the others.

Ash ran his hand through his hair, taking a slow sip of brandy. "It was quite simple, actually. My father and I could not agree on my future career. The church was obviously inappropriate, so that left the military. Had he suggested the navy, I would have eagerly complied, but he had his mind set on a guards' regiment." He took another swallow of brandy, a larger one this time. "I often wondered whether he intended it deliberately, knowing of my passion for the sea. I think it was his final attempt to beat the disobedience out of me."

"But it failed."

He nodded. "I went along with him for a while. Even traveled to London to fill out all the papers at the Horse Guards. But the night before I was to join, I slipped out and headed for the docks. I was at the mouth of the Thames, aboard a ship bound for India, before my father even knew I was gone."

"Do you ever regret choosing the sea? Or leaving your home, and England, behind?"

"Never," he replied quickly. "Oh, I regret the manner in which it was done, and the rift between myself and the family. Mayhap I can do something by way of patching that up now. But I will never for one moment regret choosing the sea. It was what I had always wanted to do."

"I envy your ability to follow your dream," she said wistfully.

"What of you, Rose? What is your dream?"

"Oh, my dreams are not very grand," she said. "A home of my own, perhaps."

"With a husband? And children?" he asked.

Embarrassed to see any more pity in his eyes, she focused her eyes on her lap and nodded.

"Those are admirable dreams, Rose," he said softly. "I hope they come true for you."

He took a long sip of brandy, watching her toy with the ribbons on her dress. Her dreams were not so far removed from his own. For was it not his all-consuming need for his own family that had driven him across the raging sea? The two of them had more in common than one would think.

"Do you play the pianoforte?" he asked suddenly.

Rose nodded.

"Do you know any of the old carols? 'God Rest Ye Merry, Gentlemen' or 'On Christmas Day in the Morning'?" He wrinkled his brow in concentration, then gave a frustrated shake of his head. "I cannot remember any more."

"I have music for several," she said, setting down her glass and crossing the room to the instrument. She leafed through the music sheets.

"Do the waits still come by?"

Rose shook her head. "They are not very common anymore." She saw the disappointment reflected in his face.

"That is one of my most vivid memories," he explained, leaning against the pianoforte. "In the days leading up to Christmas, there would be two or three groups singing in the night."

"I think the war changed many things," Rose replied softly. "Not as many people are eager to keep up the old ways."

" 'Tis a pity," Ash said.

Rose selected some sheets of music and sat down before the keyboard. "Your eldest niece and I were practicing these the other day," Rose said. " 'Rejoice, Our Savior' and 'Whilst Shepherds Watched.' "

"I will try to sing," he said. "Although I may be best employed at turning the pages." He flashed Rose a rueful smile.

Rose struck up the opening chords, pleased when Ash chimed in. He had a pleasant voice. They sang their way through all the songs she knew, with Ash turning pages and peering over her shoulder to recall half-remembered words and verses. Not until she started picking out the more somber notes of "The Coventry Carol" did he step back, to lean against the side of the instrument once more.

Ash listened in rapt fascination to the old tune, oblivious of Rose's hesitating fingers and missed chords. This was what he had been looking for in this mock Christmas—a recreation of the celebration he remembered from his youth. It was Rose who had answered his yearnings so well. Did she need this as much as he?

Rose glanced up to find Ash gazing intently at her, a mixture of longing and some other emotion she could not discern in his eyes. She sat frozen for a moment, unable to turn away from his scrutinizing look. Even if it meant he would see her own yearning in her eyes.

A warm, comforting smile spread over his face. "That was exactly what I needed, Rose. Thank you."

She looked down again, flustered, gathering up the sheets of music in order to avoid those clear blue eyes again. This was, after all, merely an elaborate play. Rose stood hastily, but Ash took the music from her hands and set it down on the piano. He took her hand in his and led her back to their seats by the fire, where their sham Yule log burned merrily. A restoring sip of the port calmed her senses.

As they sat in companionable silence before the fire, Ash could not recall a recent evening when he had felt so comfortable. It was not just being in his childhood home. It was Rose herself who made him feel so at ease. In her presence he felt all the things he had missed for so long—companionship and understanding. He realized with surprise that he was glad his family had not been home. For then he would never have had the opportunity to sit and be with her like this. He sought another excuse to draw the evening out.

"It is a pity we do not have a third party," he said finally, draining the last of his glass. "If there were someone else to play the pianoforte, we could dance."

"I am not much of a dancer," she replied, but Ash saw the wistful look in her eyes.

"Neither am I, but perhaps we could stumble along together. I can hum a creditable waltz. Do you know how to waltz, Rose?"

"A little," she confessed.

"Then we shall give it a try," he said, drawing
her from her chair and into the center of the room.
"No Christmas party is complete without dancing."

Rose found the feel of Ash's bare hand on hers
unsettling. Perhaps this was a mistake. Perhaps
this whole crazy evening was a mistake, a mis-
guided journey into a world that she would never
be a part of. In the very secret recesses of her heart,
she had a place left for dreams, but she was most
realistic about the impossibility of their fruition.
An evening such as this, a glimpse of the life she
would never have, brought those hidden yearnings
too far into the forefront.

She started to draw away from him, but he continued to lead her through the patterns of the dance
as if he did not notice. Each time they drew together, his hand resting lightly about her waist
formed an exquisite torture for Rose. She closed
her eyes and tried to shut off the warning clamor-
ing in her mind.

Ash was glad there was no accompanist in the
room, but only himself and Rose, sweeping across
the floor in the graceful moves of the dance. She
was smooth on her feet and light in his arms. It
required all his concentration to keep humming the
tune that allowed him to hold her so. She fitted his
arms perfectly and he knew without a doubt that
if he pulled her close, her head would nestle comfortably against his shoulder.

He longed to pull her against him, to hold her
tightly for only a moment. To feel, if only for a
fleeting second, the warmth and comfort of a real
English lady. The type of woman he would have
teased and flirted with, had he stayed at home. The
type of woman he would have taken for carriage
rides and picnics. The type of woman he might
very well have married, had he not left England all
those years ago. A proper English lady.

Regret washed over him as he realized how he sorely rued missing that part of his life. At first it had been a grand adventure. While his school chums recited Latin to a bored master, he was scrubbing decks under a blistering sun. When they struggled over Greek during torturous spring afternoons, he learned about women in the back streets of Delhi and Canton.

Yet now, while he sailed his ship back and forth from one port to another, those long-ago friends were settled and married, bouncing children on their knees, content within the circle of family. And he had no family. No wife. No children.

"Ash?"

He started at Rose's voice, suddenly realizing he had stopped humming, had stopped dancing, and merely stood there with her clasped in his arms. A slow smile spread across his face when he realized where they paused.

"There is one other Christmas custom we have yet to experience," he said softly, smiling into her wide blue eyes. He had seen seas that color. In places far distant from here.

Rose looked at him in confusion.

"It cannot truly be Christmas without the kissing bough," he said with a trace of huskiness in his voice. It suddenly seemed imperative to him that he kiss her, here, in the one place where it would not be improper. For friendly kisses under the kissing bough were very much a part of Christmas.

He saw both wariness and curiosity in her eyes. "Merry Christmas, Rose," he whispered, and lowered his mouth onto hers.

If ever one could die of happiness, it would be now, Rose thought when his lips brushed against hers. Warm and soft, they felt like nothing she had ever experienced before. For it was her first grown-up kiss, her first kiss from a man not her father, or uncle, or pupil. A man's kiss, a thing she had always been curious about. And now she had received one that felt far more wonderful than she could have imagined.

From the very moment their lips touched, Ash was instantly on his guard. He realized how very much he wanted to kiss this English Rose, to explore her mouth, to pull her close—so close that her soft shape pressed against his. And that he could not do. He was a gentleman, after all, and she was a lady. A chaste kiss under the kissing bough was all that was permitted him.

He drew back, intending to release her as he ought, but the sight of her face, her closed eyes and gently parted lips, made him forget his good intentions. He kissed her again, and this time he lingered, savoring the taste of her, reveling at the feel of her in his arms.

He pulled away a second time, and her eyes flicked open to stare at him in wide-eyed wonder. His face crinkled in a smile. "A most pleasant custom," he said, planting a soft kiss on her brow before he reluctantly released her from his arms. "One of the best things about Christmas."

Rose struggled against the confusion of sensations coursing through her. She longed to be in his arms again, longed to be far away in the safety of her room. For she was suddenly fearful of this real man, who could wreak such havoc on her usual well-ordered mind. She was afraid she had already spent far too much time in his company. Now, having been held in his arms, having felt his mouth on hers, she would always know what it was like. Would always know what she could not have.

Tears of despair stung at her eyes. She had played the game too well, for the game was blurring into reality. And the reality was too painful to contemplate. She thought only of the sheltered haven of her room. She would be safe there from his

mesmerizing spell. Safe from her desperate longing for what she could not have.

"You will wish to depart early tomorrow," she
said, fearing he would hear the tremor in her voice.

"And you are going to point out to me that the
hour grows late," he said with a short laugh. "How
nice it is to have another looking out for my wel-
fare. I could grow quite spoiled with someone to
look after me."

He realized the truth of his words the moment
he uttered them. He *would* like someone to look
after him, to take care of his comforts as well as
his needs. Someone to cajole or bully if necessary,
to make certain he did as he ought. Someone like
Rose.

"Allow me to escort you up the stairs." Without
waiting for her reply, he lit a taper and took her
hand, reluctant to be parted from her so soon.

They climbed the stairs in silence. Rose fought
to control the turbulent emotions welling up inside
her. So she was almost grateful when they reached
the door to the schoolroom, which led into her
chamber beyond. He entered first, carefully light-
ing the candle on the near table before setting his
own down and turning to face her.

"I will say good-bye now, Rose, for I will be leaving early." Sadness tinged his smile. "You cannot
know how deeply I regret that my family is elsewhere, for I would like to stay."

"You have been far too kind by remaining as
long as you have," she said quietly.

"You deserved more than a solitary Christmas
in the schoolroom," he said, wishing with all his
heart that there was more he could give her.

"You have already made it a special Christmas,"
she told him. "I will never forget it."

"Neither shall I," he replied. Taking her hand,
he pressed a kiss on her palm, then folded her fin-

gers over it. "It has been a most enjoyable home-coming, Rose. Thank you."

He sketched an elegant bow, took up his candle, and departed.

Ash returned to the drawing room, to snuff the candles and bank the fire for the night. Satisfied that all was well, he turned to go, then paused. Grabbing a chair, he dragged it to the center of the room. Cautiously stepping onto the seat, he reached up and untied the clump of mistletoe that he had so carefully fastened to the boughs earlier that day. He tucked it into the pocket of his jacket. It would be a reminder of this special Christmas celebration and his English Rose.

3

Ash frowned at the open trunk before him. How he wished he could delay his departure for Dorset. But he could not, not if he wanted to arrive in time for Christmas. With a deep sigh, he recommenced packing the bag he would take with him. His trunk would have to trail behind him again.

He hated the thought of leaving Rose here alone. If only he could take her with him. He would have to hold on to his memories of their short time together to sustain him through this reunion with his family.

At least he could leave her some token of his gratitude. The ribbon he had bought her in town seemed more of an insult than anything. She deserved far, far more. He had brought back a trunk full of trinkets for his mother, sister, and nieces. There must be something in that mishmash that was worthy of Rose.

Ash's frown deepened as he scrabbled through the trunk. Everything seemed so ordinary. Then his eyes lit on one of the bolts of silk he had collected on his last trip to China. It was the same hue as the ribbon, the same hue as her eyes. She would look magnificent in it. He dismissed the knowledge that a governess would not have the need for such an elegant dress. Even if the cloth sat in the bottom of her wardrobe forever, he wanted her to have it.

One of the assembled fans caught his eye. Of delicate carved ivory, it featured an intricate painting of a Chinese scene across its silken face. An item of rare beauty. Totally useless for a governess. She would have it also.

With a widening grin, Ash looked more carefully through his assembled treasures. This fringed shawl would complement the silk. Rose could store whatever trinkets she possessed in that aromatic sandalwood box. His hand passed over, then returned to hover above a velvet bag. He reached down and picked it up, untying the knot at its neck, and slowly let the cascade of pearls fall into his hand.

He had intended them for his mother when he found them in his possession after a high-stakes card game in a long-forgotten hellhole. But they would look exquisite on Rose, with her flawless white skin and ebony-black hair.

They were the most inappropriate gift of all. And the one he most wished to give her. She would be aghast at the idea—and would insist he take them back. He must make certain she did not see them before he left. For although they had cost him nothing, they would be worth a pretty price if she sold them. They could provide modest security beyond the reach of even the most generously paid governess. He wanted to leave her that.

Well-pleased with himself, Ash set aside his intended gifts and returned the other items to the trunk. There were still plenty of presents for his family. He repacked his own personal belongings, setting out those things he would need in the morning. He half-wished to see Rose again before he departed, but knew it would be better if he left before she awoke. What could he say to her that he had not already said last evening? Better to leave quietly. Perhaps she would realize, when she saw the gifts he had left behind, how much their special Christmas celebration had meant to him.

Rose awoke to a still-darkened room. She stumbled to the window and peered out between the heavy curtains. The first rays of light streaked the sky. Morning was here and Ash would soon be gone, if he had not already left.

She resolved to remain in her room until she was certain he had departed. Seeing him again would only do her greater harm. Now she could still almost convince herself that it had all been a marvelous dream.

She crawled back into the warmth of her bed. How much longer would she need to lie here to make certain of missing him? Would he tarry, wanting to say good-bye again? A foolish thought, she chided herself. Had he not said his good-byes last night, for the very reason he wanted an early start? He was eager to visit with his family. She hoped he would not regret the time he had lingered on her behalf.

Hearing the faint crunch of hooves on gravel, Rose bolted from her bed and raced to the window again, pulling the heavy drapery aside. The dull ache within her grew while she watched Ash ride down the drive and out of her life.

The deep, despairing reality of her situation swept over her. Just as 1819 waited around the corner, each succeeding year would roll into the next, blurring in their unending sameness. Her charges would grow and change, but her duties would not. Her employers might change, but her situation would not. She would watch herself grow old and gray in her mirror, knowing that no other future stretched before her.

Tears glistened in her eyes, but Rose dashed them away with the back of her hand. She was too sensible for this kind of nonsense. It was only the sentimentality of the season that made her so susceptible to such blue-deviled thoughts. That, and Ash's unexpected appearance. For in his presence she could no longer convince herself that she was totally content with her situation.

Sighing, Rose wrapped her robe tighter around her and entered the schoolroom to start the tea. She stared in surprise at the bundle lying atop the table. Hesitantly she stepped forward. Atop lay a letter, inscribed to "Rose."

Her heart lurched. He had been here before he left. How she wished she had run out into the schoolroom and flung herself into his arms for one last embrace.

Shocked at her thoughts, she gathered up the heavy bundle and carried it into her room. Setting it upon her bed, she unfolded the letter.

> Rose,
>   Please accept these as a simple sea captain's token of appreciation for a most pleasing welcome home, and a memorable Christmas. I wish you a safe port on your own journey through life.
>
>   Ash

Rose carefully unwrapped the paper, staring in amazement at what lay beneath its folds. On top was a most gorgeous shawl, a mass of clustered flowers in every hue of the rainbow, trimmed with a delicate fringe. Below it, an ornately carved box, its sweet-smelling scent permeating the room. At the bottom, wrapped in a rough cloth of nubby yellow and tied with a blue ribbon, lay the most exquisitely beautiful silk cloth she had ever seen. She rubbed her hand across its shimmering surface, almost fearful to touch such loveliness. Oh, what a beautiful dress it would make!

Setting the material aside, Rose turned her attention to the box, running her fingers over the intricate inlay of wood and ivory. Its fragrant scent hinted of the exotic Orient. Lifting back the hinged lid, she exclaimed in surprise at the fan nestled inside. It looked too fragile to even touch. Beneath it there lay a lumpy velvet pouch. With trembling hands she drew it out and untied the silken cords at the neck. She poured out the contents, gasping aloud at the milky-white luminescence of the strand of pearls that pooled in her hand. She unfolded the note that came with them.

Yes, Rose, they are real and as valuable as they look. Keep them, in remembrance of the impetuous and slightly mad sea captain with whom you once shared an early Christmas. Should you ever have the need, they will fetch a pretty penny.

Ash

He *was* mad, she thought, to leave such a valuable gift for a lady he barely knew and would never see again. It was completely impossible for her to own such a valuable necklace, yet she knew he would be mortally insulted if she insisted he take it back. Carefully slipping the pearls back into their velvet pouch, she replaced them in the box, laying the fan carefully atop. Shutting the lid, she set the box to one side and sank back onto her pillows.

Christmas was a time of miracles, it was always said, and she was half-disposed to believe that now. For why else had she been blessed with such a magical two days? If the family had chosen to remain home for their celebration, she would never have had more than the fleetest of conversations with Ash. If he had written ahead to tell of his arrival, he would have traveled to his uncle's. Had her friend's mother not been ill, she would have not been here when Ash arrived. But a mystical combination of events had contrived to bring them together for a very few hours, and in so doing had wrought monumental changes in her life.

Those captivating moments spent with Lord Ashby had brought back all the long-buried dreams of young girlhood. Dreams of love, and marriage, and family. All the things that were denied her. The things that, despite her efforts to convince herself otherwise, she wanted most of all. But now, having pulled her dreams out into the open once gain, it was difficult to put them back again.

Because this time the dreams had a focus, a real person on whom to center themselves. Her fascination with Lord Ashby had been a safe occupation when she thought she would never be faced with him. Now she had, and it only showed how dangerous her curiosity had been.

He was not the larger-than-life figure she had conjured up in her dreams. If he had been, perhaps all this would not be so difficult. It was precisely because he was who he was, a man with the same needs, wants, dreams, and fears as any other, that made him so appealing. She wished he had still retained the arrogance of that sulky fifteen-year-old captured in the schoolroom portrait. She could have disliked him then. She wished he had been condescending in his manner toward her, as befitted her post, for then she would not have spent much time in conversation with him. By treating her as an equal—nay, treating her almost as a guest in his home—he had only increased the damage. Because she could now put a flesh-and-blood man at the center of her dreams. And those kinds of dreams could not be casually brushed aside.

Rose absently fingered the patterned blue silk. Someday she would have it made up into a dress— when she could wear something so fine without arousing comment. She smiled at her thought. She could only imagine herself a stooped white-haired old lady parading about in the shimmering material. A retired governess dressing like a princess. It would land her in Bedlam for certain.

Sighing, Rose carefully rewrapped the fabric and set the bulky bundle carefully in the bottom compartment of her chest of drawers. But she could not bear to hide away the box as well, and set it atop the table, where she could look at it and remember.

The emotions churning within Ash as he neared his uncle's were nothing like the ones that had plagued him three days ago when he reached Thornton. The ones today were less acute, less desperate, as if the edge of his need had been taken off. Seeing Thornton again had done some of it, for the house was as much a part of his past as his family.

Yet even so, there was more to it than that. It was his unexpected meeting with Rosalie Norris that had also dulled the sharpness of his desire. He now knew, even if his own family was less than enthusiastic at his return, that he had received the kind of welcome he wanted from at least one person in England. That made whatever reception he was about to receive less critical.

Still, as his uncle's house at last came into view, an edgy apprehension arose within Ash. The moment was here at last—the time when sixteen years of estrangement would be either dismissed or perpetuated. At least the matter would be decided once and for all.

Ash guided his horse to the stable block, knowing it deliberately delayed his entrance. But once he handed the reins to the groom and pulled off his bags, he had to carry this through to the end. Resolutely he set his steps toward the front of the house.

The footman who took his coat and bags visibly

started when Ash declared his name. Was he such a figure of notoriety in this house as well as his own? He held out a staying hand as the footman reached for the drawing-room-door latch.

"I will announce myself," Ash said. He could not resist the temptation to make the dramatic entrance. With a mental squaring of his shoulders, he opened the door and stepped into the room.

It took all his willpower not to explode into mirthful laughter at the varied reactions his appearance elicited. His brother glanced up from his book to ascertain the identity of the interloper, then lowered his gaze, only to rapidly turn his eyes again when he recognized the man who stood near the door. Ash's mother, deep in conversation with her sister-in-law, did not even look up until she grew aware of the hushed silence that had descended upon the room. She looked about in quick confusion, her eyes narrowing as she spotted him, then growing wide with shock and surprise. Lady Denby half-rose from her chair, her embroidery dropping to the floor.

"Ashby," his mother whispered.

Ash hastened to her side, suddenly realizing the shock his sudden appearance had given her. He took her hand in his and smiled a welcoming grin. How tiny she was! And old. Somehow, in his imaginings, he had forgotten that his own family would have aged, just as he had.

"Hello, Mama," he said.

"Is it really you?" she asked, as if disbelieving the sight before her. "After all these years . . ."

"Like the proverbial bad penny, I managed to turn up," he said lightly, though the tension in the room was palpable. Without releasing his mother's hand, he turned to his brother, Edmund, Lord Wakefield, who had also risen from his seat.

"Hello, Edmund," Ash said, shocked at the change time had wrought in his older brother.

When he had left, the seven-year gap between them had placed Edmund in his prime. Now Ash saw a man of middle years with a growing paunch and thinning hair.

"Ashby," his brother said, the surprise evident on his face. "How the deuce. . . ? What brings you here?"

"Isn't Christmas the time for families to be together?" Ash's tone was light, but he remained tense, still uncertain of his reception.

"Why did you not let us know you were coming?" his mother asked in a manner more hurt than accusatory. "Have you been to Thornton?"

"Yes," Ash said. "I found everything there to be in fine order."

"Your father is in the library," she said. "I will summon him."

"I shall go," Lady Hoxworth, Ash's aunt, announced.

"Have you just arrived in England?" Edmund asked.

Ash nodded. "I had thought to be here earlier in the month, but the storms were fierce in the Atlantic."

"You are still in North America, then," Edmund said.

"It is a most convenient situation for me," Ash replied, relieved that his mother had recovered from her surprise enough to sit. His own legs were none too steady. "There is plenty of business plying goods along the coast to keep me as busy as I wish."

As if all their questions had been answered, his mother and brother fell silent. Ash glanced across the room, noting for the first time the fair-haired lady who sat there.

"We have not met," he said, smiling apologetically.

"Of course," Edmund replied. "Caroline, this is my brother, Ashby. M'wife."

Ash nodded in greeting. "It is a pleasure to meet you at last. I cannot wait to see your children. I spoke with Miss Norris while I was at Thornton. She seems a very capable lady."

"We have been pleased so far with her services," his sister-in-law replied in a languid tone. "One can never find exactly what one wants in an employee, but she is adequate."

Ash cringed at her words.

"I thought Norris was going to Bath," Edmund said, giving his wife a puzzled glance.

"Now, dear, you recall that her plans changed at the last moment."

"Then why did we not bring her along?" he grumbled. "Are we not paying her to watch over those rapscallions?"

"We had promised her a holiday," she reminded her husband. "And we do not have to pay her while she is not working."

It was enough to cause Ash to clench his fists. Rose had said nothing to indicate that her situation at Thornton was anything less than ideal. But after listening to his sister-in-law, he began to have his doubts. There was no question that Rose was firmly cast in the position of inferior.

"Well," boomed out a hearty voice from the door. "The wandering son returns home at last. Ready to give up the sea and keep your feet on land like a proper Englishman?"

"Not yet," Ash replied, hoping he heard a jest in his father's words. He strode across the room and clasped the older man's hand. "It is good to see you again, sir."

"Hrumph," mumbled his father. "Looks like the years have been good to you," he said, taking the measure of his son. "You've grown apace." He patted his protuberant belly. "So have I, but in the wrong places."

They all took their seats, looking about a bit awkwardly.

"Ashby is here to spend Christmas with us," his mother said, breaking the silence.

His father raised a brow. "Getting sentimental in your old age, eh?"

"It has been many years since I enjoyed an English Christmas," Ash confessed.

"That will teach you to wander off to heathen countries," his father retorted. "Would have had any number of English Christmases if you had gone into the army."

Ash did not want to reopen all the old wounds. "The sea has been good to me," he said quietly.

"The children do so enjoy the presents you have sent them," his sister-in-law announced. "Miss Norris has cleverly used them to further their learning in geography."

"Yes, she mentioned that," Ash replied. "I have several more things for them, when my trunk arrives. It has been following a day or two behind me ever since I reached England. I am only sorry we cannot be at Thornton for the holiday season."

"If you had given us some indication of your plans, we could have done just that," his father said testily.

"I thought it was better this way," Ash said quietly. "I was not certain of the reception I would receive."

His mother looked pointedly at her husband.

"Well, I cannot deny that there was a bit of an upheaval over your departure," he said finally. "But what is done is done, my boy. There is no denying you have greatly pleased your mother by returning at last."

"And you?" Ash asked, looking determinedly at his father.

"I am more concerned with my gout these days than with the way you chose to disoblige your family all those years ago," he said. "You are my son, and will always have a place in the family."

Ash felt the palpable relief at knowing they accepted him back into the fold. Grudgingly, but his father would never do it any other way. "Thank you." He looked to Edmund's wife. "Now, where are those nieces and nephew of mine? I have half a mind to quiz them to make certain those geography lessons have sunk in."

"They will join us in the drawing room later this afternoon," Edmund said.

"Perhaps, then, you will excuse me while I change from my traveling clothes." He smiled quickly at his mother. "Forgive my rudeness at appearing in such a state, but I did wish to see you."

"Quite so," his mother replied.

Ash rose and kissed her proffered cheek. In the corridor a footman waited to show him to his room.

Not until he was private behind the closed door did Ash let out a deep sigh of relief. It had gone well—better than he had anticipated. They had not greeted him with fawning enthusiasm, but neither had they turned him away at the door. The awkwardness they felt in each other's presence would fade over the next days as they grew reacquainted.

He wished he could tell Rose of his reception. She would be pleased for him, he knew. Perhaps he would write to her in a few days to let her know all had gone well. Or he could stop at Thornton on his way back to London, after he completed his visit with his family. He could tell her himself how well the visit had gone. The thought cheered him.

Following dinner, Ash's family gathered in the drawing room. A sense of unreality settled over him. It was difficult to believe that he was here with his family at last. Or that they accepted his presence with such nonchalance. They acted as if it had been sixteen weeks, not sixteen years, since they had seen him last.

He sighed imperceptibly, swirling the ruby-red claret in his glass. It was arrogant of him to have expected more. Yet now, as they all stared uncomfortably at each other, he began to wonder if they cared at all that he had returned.

"Well, how does it feel to be back in England at last?" His uncle broke the disconcerting silence.

"Disorienting," Ash replied. "It all looks familiar—yet so much has changed."

"You will soon feel comfortable again," Edmund said. "By spring you will think that you never left."

Ash looked down at his glass for a moment, then met his brother's gaze. "I have no plans to stay until spring," he said. "In fact, I've a cargo to take back to Boston after the New Year."

"You can come back after that," Edmund persisted. "We will get you set up right and tight, take you up to London and find you a wife. Caroline will be in alt at the thought. Do we need to find a rich heiress or are you settled comfortably these days?"

Ash glanced at his sister-in-law, who looked as though she were already mentally evaluating prospective candidates.

"You realize," Caroline said, "that your past mode of life will make things more difficult."

Ash shook his head in amusement. "I'm not ready to come home for good yet. Years from now, perhaps. I like the sea too well to leave it."

"Pity you didn't choose the navy," said his father.

"Yes, sailing the seas for his majesty is less disgraceful than sailing for my own profit," Ash said, a trace of resentment in his voice. His father had refused to buy him a naval commission all those years ago.

Lady Denby glanced between father and son and

asked hastily, "Will you be making more trips to England in the future? If you were here more often, you might feel more comfortable about staying."

"It may be possible to increase my voyages here," Ash said carefully. It was an eventuality he had not thought much on, yet it would be easy to bring cargoes to England.

"It would give you the opportunity to visit Thornton," Edmund announced.

"I did that on this trip."

"I meant with the family there."

"Goodness knows, it must have seemed a very dismal place with only the servants," Caroline said. "You must give us more warning next time, so we may welcome you properly."

"I received a nice-enough welcome from Miss Norris," Ash said with some irritation.

"But it is not as if she is family," Caroline pointed out. "It does sound as if she was pushing herself forward to have made her presence known to you. I find I much prefer servants who remain unobtrusive."

With difficulty Ash strove to keep his temper in check. "On the contrary, Miss Norris was all that you would wish, Caroline. It was I who intruded upon her. She was very gracious about the disruption."

"Should have brought her here to watch over the children," Edmund mumbled. "A fortnight's vacation indeed."

Ash turned to his mother, desperate to rein in the discussion of Rose before he caused her irreparable harm—or throttled his brother's wife. "I wondered, Mama, what became of my things. I slept in my old room, but it did not seem the same without them. Are they somewhere in the house?"

She thought. "I am certain they are. I believe I had everything placed in boxes in the attic." She turned to Caroline. "Do you recall, my dear? I believe the children are in the attics often."

Caroline thought. "Charles dragged some indescribable mess from the attic into his room—a crumbling bird's nest and moldy feathers." She shuddered at the memory. "I had the lot tossed out."

Ash sank back in his chair. It did not matter, really. He really had no need of such things. They would have been old and falling apart. Yet they had been his, and their careless disposal only irritated him further.

He should not expect more considerate attention. After all, he was the one who had fled without a word. He still marveled at how graciously he had been welcomed back into the fold. He should not be looking for miracles. He had found what he came home for—hadn't he?

Christmas Eve morning, Rose eagerly accepted Cook's commission to walk to the village with her shopping list for the dinner tomorrow. She found she preferred to be alone with her thoughts these days.

Ash should have arrived at his uncle's home the previous day, Rose calculated. How she wished she could know if the meeting had gone well. She would discover the outcome eventually, she hoped, although she could not go to Lord or Lady Denby and openly ask. She would have to wait and hope enough was said to give her an inkling of the reaction to his reappearance.

She was surprised to find the remaining house servants busily decorating the servants' hall when she returned. They had always asked her to help in past years. Rose stood in the doorway, confusion upon her face.

"May I help?" she asked.

The footman turned toward her. "We thought

you might have had your fill of Christmas decorating," he said with the trace of a sneer. "Seeing as how we don't have any lords helping us."

"After associating with the quality, we thought you might find our humble *servants'* celebration beneath your dignity," one of the maids said.

Rose settled herself against their thinly veiled hostility. She knew that as governess, her place in the servants' hierarchy was an ill-defined one. But she had gone out of her way to be friendly in the years she had been here, and had shared many meals and celebrations—two Christmases, in fact—with these people. Why did they turn on her like this? She forced a smile.

"I would not dream of missing the celebration," she said. "Christmas is always special."

"Some people begin putting on airs when they start thinking they're part of the family," the maid said with a disdainful sniff. "A governess ain't no different than a scullery maid, when all is said and done. We're both workin' for wages."

"And I ain't never yet seen a governess marry into a household," the footman interjected.

Rose struggled to rein in her anger. Is that what they thought? That she had been casting out lures to Ash? Their ill-informed gossip threatened to destroy her memories of one of the happiest days of her life. How could they place such a label on such an innocent evening?

But he did kiss you, a tiny voice reminded her. Rose shrugged off the memory. It had been a friendly kiss under the mistletoe. A proper Christmas kiss, with no deeper meaning. For him, at least.

"I assure you I have no designs on Lord Ashby." Rose surveyed them with ill-concealed vexation. "I was merely being polite by accepting his request to share his dinner. He was very cast-down at discovering his family's absence."

The maid gave another audible sniff, but said no more. Rose crossed the room with a determined step and picked up a sprig of holly. She would join them no matter what they thought.

She glued a placid smile onto her face, but inside, the pain of their pointed remarks cut deeply. Rose needed no reminder that when all was said and done, she was merely a servant in this house. She knew just how wide the gulf between herself and Ash was. He was the son of a marquess, and she . . . she earned her bread taking care of other people's children. He was as unobtainable as the moon, a subject only for wistful dreams.

And she had spent too much time of late indulging in those. It was time now to reassert her authority over her mind. Later today she would help prepare the Christmas boxes for the tenants. She had very many things to keep her busy. There was no spare time to dwell upon Ash.

4

Ash looked out his window on Christmas Eve to the ever-darkening landscape outside, reluctant to join the assemblage in the drawing room. He resented the fact that the house would be filled with strangers—friends and neighbors of his uncle's. He wanted this to be a family Christmas.

Shrugging, he pulled on his coat. It was not for him to say what his uncle could or could not do. Ash resigned himself to a less-than-perfect evening.

Dinner was an elegant and sedate affair, but as the evening wore on, the party grew more boisterous, assisted by liberal helpings of the oft-refilled bowl of lamb's wool. Ash played charades, joining in the laughter at his side's preposterous attempts to act out Byron's poem *The Corsair*. More lamb's wool followed the games, and the talk and laughter grew louder.

Ash stepped away from the center of activity, content to watch from afar. He felt more and more out of place with each passing moment. It was the very thing he had come home for, an English Christmas celebration. Why could he not enjoy himself more?

"Ashby, here is a young lady I should like you to meet." The voice of his sister-in-law turned his thoughts away from his musings. Caroline was all smiles as she drew the girl at her side forward.

"This is Lord Newnham's middle daughter, Lady Susannah Forest."

"My pleasure." Ash took her gloved hand in his, bowing low. He strove to keep his lips from twitching. Despite his disclaimers of the night before, it was apparent Caroline was proceeding with her own plans for his future.

"Lady Wakefield has been telling me about all your exciting adventures," Lady Susannah began. "I should dearly love to hear more."

Ashby carefully scrutinized the girl who stood before him. Small, blond, and done up in a confection of pink lace and ribbons, she looked the very picture of English beauty.

"You must tell me the types of stories you like," he said, nodding in feigned gratitude to Caroline as he drew the girl away. "Do you wish the fierce, terrifying ones, or the exotic, amusing ones?"

"Oh, amusing, please." She pouted prettily. "I do not wish to be frightened."

Ash smiled inwardly at the situation he found himself in. But he gallantly squired Lady Susannah about the room, describing several of his more innocuous journeys in lively detail. He managed to elicit a few tidbits of information from the girl—she was seventeen, making her come-out in the spring, and looking forward to that immensely.

Her mindless chatter registered only dimly on his brain. Ash suspected there were any number of men who would be impressed by the girl's easy manner and attractive looks. But not he. She would want to live a life in the giddy social whirl, which would bore him in a week. She would not be the type of wife who would contently sit at home while her captain husband was off to sea.

His attention had wandered and he was forced to scramble to concentrate on Susannah's lively chatter.

"I think it would be exciting to sail away on a

ship," she said eagerly. "There must be so many exotic places, with warm breezes and palm trees . . ."

"Ah, but with the palm trees comes a blistering hot sun," he said, deliberately wanting to dampen her enthusiasm. "One so fair as you would suffer mightily, I am afraid."

"Bonnets and parasols would protect me," she insisted.

"Have you ever sailed?" he asked. " 'Twould be dreadful to discover you were prone to seasickness at the start of a six-month voyage."

The thought gave her pause; then she brightened. "I am certain a conscientious captain would take care to sail only on the smoothest seas."

Ash smothered a laugh. Sailing on only the smoothest seas, indeed! The poor girl did not have an ounce of sense. There undoubtedly would be men who found her brainlessness adorable. But not he.

At last he managed to extricate himself from her presence. From his new vantage point, leaning negligently against the far wall, he watched his mother fanning herself against the heat. She, his aunt, Edmund's wife, and a few other ladies of their generation sat along the sides of the room, watching over but not participating in the fun. It was the younger set who took the lead tonight. And that meant the guests who were younger than he, he noted with a pang. He had never thought himself old at two-and-thirty, but faced with the bouncing enthusiasm of those in their late teens and twenties, he realized there was an indefinable line between them and him. He was no longer a child.

The thought chilled him, and in that instant he recognized it was precisely that which made this Christmas somehow dissatisfying. He had been looking upon it with the eyes of the child he had been when he last spent the season in England. He now looked out on the world with the eyes of an adult, and it changed his vision. That which he had sought to recapture was already irretrievably lost.

But it would have been lost anyway, whether he had remained in England or not. It was not his leaving that had wrought the change, but his growing and maturing. Even if he had not left home sixteen years ago, his parents would still be old, his brother middle-aged. And he would still be . . . alone.

He had come home to find his family. Yet in finding them he now recognized how much had changed between them as well. They no longer moved in the same world. He had no regrets over that. He was content with the course he had chosen.

It also made him realize that he could not count on his family to provide him with the feeling of peace, home, and security he sought. That had been a boy's view of life, cherished over the years by the man he had become. They were still his family, but Thornton and England were no longer his home. That he would have to make on his own.

He watched the lively Susannah, laughing and talking with her sister. Her curled blond locks lay in carefully arranged disorder about her face, which was dominated by that perfect rosebud mouth. She was a delicious picture. Why did she make so little an impression upon him?

Because he had been unconsciously comparing her with another, whose company he had enjoyed far more. Susannah's light blue eyes paled when compared with Rose's brilliant sapphire ones. Even in her fashionable dress, Susannah did not look as elegant as Rose had in her simpler gown. Rose had grace and refinement, an air of distinction that a wigeon like Susannah would never have.

The younger members of the party cajoled one of their members to play the pianoforte for dancing. Ash smiled wistfully, recalling how he and Rose had done the same. What was her Christmas Eve like? Were there games and dancing in the servants' hall, or was she sitting alone in her festively decorated schoolroom? Did she think of the Christmas celebration they had shared?

He looked up, startled, to find Susannah grabbing his hand and pulling him into the forming set. He put up a forestalling hand, but she ignored his entreaties. Over her shoulder he saw his sister-in-law beaming at him. Bumbling his way through the dance, he resisted the girl's pleas for another. Let her save her flirtations for a more receptive audience.

"Caroline is moving quickly, I see." Edmund made a move to refill Ash's glass.

"Tell me, Edmund, have I changed so drastically, or were the girls always so featherbrained . . . and young?" Ash grimaced. "I feel like the chit's father."

Edmund laughed. "Newnham's girls are giddier than most. Give Caroline time; she is bound to find more suitable candidates."

Ash shook his head. "I am beginning to realize just how out-of-place I feel here." He glanced about the room. "I fear I have been in America for too long. Those revolutionary ideals are beginning to affect me. Caroline herself said it," he continued. "I toil for my living. That is something the son of a marquess is not supposed to do."

"I hardly think—"

"Over there, no one cares who my parents are, or that my money is earned, not inherited. I am accepted for what I am, no more and no less."

"I think you put too much trust in Caroline's nonsense," Edmund said. "Once you settle in, no one would question your background."

"They would if I kept sailing the seas," Ash said. "Can you see a girl like Susannah being content with a husband who is gone for months at a time? Her head is filled with balls and fetes."

"Yet you need to take a wife," Edmund persisted. "If anything happens to Charles, you are next to inherit."

"Nothing will happen to that scamp," Ash said, horrified at both prospects. "I am no more cut out to be a marquess than you are for sailing my ship."

"Ashby, Edmund," Caroline trilled. "It is near midnight. Throw open the doors and see if we can hear the bells."

Ash lifted a rueful brow at the interruption, and followed Edmund to the doors. Ignoring the blast of cold air, the assemblage gathered around, listening to the faint strains of the village church bells ringing in Christmas Day. It was a mark of hope and comfort.

As the guests began to take their leave, Ash took the opportunity to make his own escape to his room. He had accomplished all he had set out to do on this trip. Yes, it was good to be with his family again. But it was no longer enough. He needed more. A home of his own, where he would be comfortable and at his ease. Like he had been at Thornton with Rose.

He sat very quietly, hardly daring to breathe. It was a preposterous thought. He had spent little more than one day in her company. Yet the more he argued against his idea, the more convinced he grew. It was not Thornton that had so set him at ease, it was Rose. She had welcomed him warmly, understood his situation, given him encouragement and strength.

He already cared deeply what became of her. Why else had he left those pearls? Yet now he wanted to give her something more substantial, more permanent, more personal. Himself, if she would have him.

Still, could one dare call it love after an acquaintance of such short duration? He could not believe that they had spent so little time together. From that first meeting in the schoolroom, after they exchanged greetings, they had settled down to chat like old friends. He had told her things he had never expressed to another—his regret over the estrangement from his family, his eagerness to repair the break, and his fears that they would not be receptive. He had opened up to her, a perfect stranger, and had felt no embarrassment or discomfort. And she had talked with him also, of things he suspected she rarely discussed—her memories of her parents and her lonely life in school. It was as if they both needed to confide in the other.

Yet would she be willing to leave the security and respectability of a governess's life for the disruptive existence of a captain's lady? His thoughts must be fogged with lamb's wool to think she would even consider such a thing. Perhaps he was a slightly mad sea captain after all.

Yet his brain would not let go of the idea, and he kept turning it over and over in his mind while he slowly drifted off to sleep. He would laugh at his foolishness in the morning.

Yet when he awoke at his usual early hour, Ash found that the idea had taken hold of him stronger than ever. A long, cold, and wet tramp about the grounds of his uncle's estate did not dampen his interest. He had to see Rose. Had to know if she felt as he did.

He could reach Thornton in a day—if he left immediately and rode hard. Yet what would his family say if he departed so soon? Particularly if he said he was leaving to spend Christmas Day with their governess? They would think all that sea air had unhinged his mind. But the thought of Rose, all alone on this day of days, tore at him.

How could he think she would even consider such a rash proposition? He wanted to know if the faint longing he had seen in her eyes matched his own. The longing for home and family. The need to *belong* to somewhere and somebody. He no longer belonged in England, or with his family. And Rose had not belonged to anyone or anywhere for a long time. They had only themselves. Together, they would have each other.

Ash scrawled a hasty note for his father. There would be time for further explanations later, if his plan prospered. He said only that he had gone to visit a friend. If she laughed him out of the house, they would never know. And if he stole their governess . . . well, it would not be the worst thing he had done in his life.

Impatience gnawed at Ash while the groom saddled his horse. The weather was chill and damp, and it would be a long, cold ride, but unless it rained hard he would be able to make good time. He could reach Thornton by early evening if he rode steadily. He could have Christmas with Rose.

Rose awoke on a Christmas Day that seemed strangely diminished in importance. She knew she should be uplifted by this annual opportunity to celebrate the glad tidings of the Savior's birth, but she found it unusually difficult to find much inspiration. Perhaps at church she would be in a better frame of mind to appreciate God's great gift.

Ash would be with his family now. She prayed the reunion had been a pleasant one and his family had welcomed him back eagerly. He deserved to find what he had sought this Christmas. He was entitled to peace and contentment. She only wished she could find some of it for herself.

The vicar's sermon did little to restore her spirits. Certainly the Son of God was a symbol of hope for all the world. But however wrong, her hopes were centered on more worldly matters, and the words brought her no personal comfort. Hope had very little place in her life. Dreams, not hope, were what sustained her.

Her spirits rose in the contagious gaiety of the servants' hall. By the time they sat down to their Christmas dinner, Rose had been restored to their good graces again. But she could not so easily forget their hostility of the previous day. As always, she was well aware of her precarious position in this house.

"That's a mighty well-cooked goose, if I say so myself," Cook announced to an assenting chorus.

"Too bad we can't eat like this every week," grumbled the footman.

"You'd soon be bursting all those waistcoat buttons you're so proud of," the maid teased him.

"And you wouldn't be able to bend over and scrub your floors either," he retorted. He reached across the table to snag another slice of goose, but Cook whacked his hand with her spoon.

"Like grubby children you are," she admonished. "Mind your table manners. Miss Norris will be right justified if she starts taking her meals upstairs if you go on like that."

"Why, I think I shall help myself to more goose as well," Rose said lightly, snatching a piece with her fingers. They all laughed with her. That simple act had accomplished more than all her verbal protestations.

"Better watch her at snapdragon," the footman said in an admiring voice. "She's got quick fingers."

When the flaming pudding was carried in they oohed and aahed in chorus. Rose remembered how Ash had wanted one for their dinner four nights ago. She took an extra bite for him.

When the last platter of food had been returned to the kitchen and the table cleared at last, out came the platter for snapdragon. Amidst much laughter they braved the fire to capture their prizes. Rose scorched her finger snatching the heated raisins from the flaming brandy.

It had been a jolly Christmas. Trooping down *en masse* to church, the servants had been a cheerful group. It had almost seemed like a family gathering as they all helped Cook prepare dinner. Rose had felt a renewed comradeship with them as they shared their afternoon. But now she wished to be alone for the rest of her Christmas Day. She slipped up the back stairs to the privacy of the schoolroom.

After preparing a pot of tea, Rose closed the draperies and pulled her chair closer to the fire. Staring into the flames, she wondered how the Christmas festivities went at Viscount Hoxworth's. They would certainly be sitting to a more elegant table, with course upon course of every seasonal delicacy. She hoped Ash was enjoying himself. Christmas with his family had meant so much to him. She could picture him at the table, joking and laughing, his eyes crinkling in merriment.

Rose allowed herself a moment of envy, wishing, as she rarely did, that she, too, had a family to spend Christmas and the New Year's celebrations with. A home where she would be welcomed, where she belonged. A home of her own. With a loving husband and gamboling children, a home of hopes and dreams and a future. All the things that she knew she wanted, and knew as well she would never have.

Absorbed in her reading, she jumped with a start when she heard a knock on the door. She was growing as goosish as the fictional heroine in her book. "Come in." Her eyes widened in surprise at the sight of the man who entered.

"A merry Christmas to you, Rose." Ash bowed low.

Rose stood up, filled with dismay. He would not be here unless the meeting with his family had gone poorly. Poor man! She extended her hand in greeting, and was shocked at how cold his was.

"You are like ice," she said, turning hastily to pour him a cup of the still-warm tea.

"It was a long, cold ride," he said, gratefully accepting the cup. He clasped it with both hands, warming them against the heated china.

She glanced at him with sympathetic eyes. "Did things. . . ? Was your family not pleased to see you?"

"Oh, they were a trifle taken aback at my sudden reappearance, but they took it in good stead." His mouth quirked into a smile. "We had a lively reunion."

Her expression clouded. "Then why are you back here at Thornton?"

Ash set his cup down on the table and took her hand in his. "To see you, Rose," he said slowly. "I wanted to spend what little there is left of Christmas Day with you."

Rose stared at him. Why ever would he wish to do such a thing?

"May we sit?" He looked eagerly at the blazing fire.

Rose nodded, still dazed and confused by his unexpected reappearance and puzzling words.

"This is better," he said, stretching his legs out before him and basking in the warmth. "It was deucedly cold out there." He stared into the fire for a few moments, gathering his courage, then turned to face her. "I learned a great deal in the past two days, about my family and about myself." His gaze grew intense. "Mostly I learned that one cannot go home after sixteen years and expect nothing to have changed."

She nodded. "Everything changes with time."

"I know that," he said with a rueful smile. "And had I not been so filled with this idea of coming home and seeing my family, I would have realized that things would be different." He shook his head at his folly. "But it took this entire trip for that idea to sink into my thick skull."

Rose eyed him with concern. "You said all went well."

"Oh, it did. At the same time, I realized I am not the same person I was sixteen years ago."

"I should hope not." She flashed him a winsome smile.

His eyes met hers with a grateful look. "I have changed," he said. "And in such a way that I no longer am a part of all this." He gestured with his arm. "When I left, I was the son of a marquess. A second son, mind you, and not a very dutiful one, but that was my role. Now I no longer fit that description."

Rose twined her fingers together, sad that his dreams had been dashed. "It is not always so easy to face reality."

He ran a hand through his hair. "In actuality, it bothers me little. It only altered my way of thinking about the future. I had thought, perhaps, that I would like to come back to England someday. Perhaps I still may, but not for the same reasons." He hunched forward in his chair, leaning closer toward her. "Wherever I have been over the last sixteen years, I always carried the thought with me that back in England there was a place for me. It was shattering at first, when I realized that was no longer true, but the more I thought on it, the more pleased I grew. It freed me from the last vestiges of my childhood. I am my own person now, and wherever I choose to call home is my choice."

"You will stay in North America, then," she said quietly. She would never see him again.

"Yes," he said. "It would be a good place to raise a family. That was the other thing I discovered—I cannot depend on my parents and my brother to provide me with a family. I have to make one of my own."

She smiled with a touch of sadness, knowing full well how deeply that longing could go. "I am certain you will do a good job of it."

"I am not so assured." He looked down at his hands. "Rose, I . . ." Looking into her deep blue eyes, he was suddenly unsure. Would she call him foolish? Mad? "I know this seems a bit precipitate after such a short acquaintance, but would you . . . would you come with me when I go, to help me make my home? Our home?"

She stared at him, too stunned to utter a word. She watched helplessly while he took her hand in his.

"I have had the strongest feeling, ever since I first met you, that we had much in common. We have both been without family for so long, and I think we have both been searching for that sense of belonging. And it is with you, Rose, that I feel I belong. Not with my family." He offered her an encouraging smile. "All the time I was with them, my thoughts kept returning to you. I need you, and I thought you might need me, as well."

He looked at her still-stunned expression and his smile grew wary. "You do think me the mad sea captain, do you not?"

"I do not think you mad," she said carefully, finding her voice at last. She swallowed hard. What he proposed was not possible. It could not be. It was too much what she wanted. Rose averted her gaze. "How can you possibly feel that a stranger like me—"

He grabbed her other hand, squeezing them

tightly in his. "But we are not strangers, Rose. Do you not feel it as well—this sense of connection, of rightness between us?"

Rose nodded as she returned her gaze to his face, drawing courage from the eager pleading in his eyes. "You are right, I do sense it. I only thought it the result of my foolish imaginings about you."

His eyes widened. "About me?"

She looked away again, embarrassed to make her confession. "The day I discovered that painting, I was drawn to it. You fascinated me. You had the courage to leave everything behind and make your own way—and be a success at it. I admired you for being all the things I was not—brave, daring, independent." Her blue eyes locked on his again. "When you appeared before me, it was like a dream come to life. Then, as we talked, I realized that you were not the pasteboard figure I had created, but a real man. A man who was nervous, unsure, and intimidated at the prospect of seeing his family again."

"How lowering," he said with a weak laugh, "to find I did not live up to your lofty expectations."

"Oh, it was not that at all," she said hastily. "It was only that the fictional man I created was much safer than the real one."

"Safer?"

She blushed. "A real man reminded me of all I was not, and of what I was—a foolish governess who had not quite left her girlish dreams behind her."

"What were those girlish dreams, Rose?" he asked softly, stroking the back of her hand with his thumb.

"To find love, and marry, and raise a family," she whispered.

"And what of the woman you are now?" he asked. "Does she still have the same dreams?"

She nodded, not trusting herself to speak.

A slow smile spread across his face. "Then come with me, Rose. I can give you all those things, if you will let me. We can travel to those exotic lands you yearn to see. There will be children, if we are lucky—a family that *we* create, that is yours and mine alone."

What he offered was so tempting. But he could do so much better than an orphaned governess. There were elegant ladies aplenty in England who would not disdain to wed one such as he. And equally suitable ladies in America as well. In a few weeks, or months, he might regret this rash act.

"You doubt my certainty," he said, as if reading her mind. He reached up to stroke his fingers along her cheek. "Rose, I have never been as certain of anything as I am of the rightness of this. Fate threw us together, but we can decide here and now to remain together." He tightened his grip on her fingers. "I need you, Rose. I need you to restore my sense of belonging, to watch over me, to care for me. I need you to need me, to want me, to love me."

"I do need you," she said softly, knowing the truth of it as she uttered the words. "And I think I have been in love with you for a very long time."

He pulled her toward him, settling her on his lap, clasping her to him in a tight embrace. He looked down into her smiling face and grinned. "We do not need the mistletoe this time." He bent to gently brush her lips with his. Then his kiss deepened, as he sought to drive away any lingering doubts and reassure her of his words of hope and promise. "We will be happy," he whispered against her hair. "So happy. I love you," he said simply, holding her tightly and kissing any doubts away. "With you I found what I came for—a home. Wherever we shall be, wherever Christmas may find us, as long as we are together it will be home.''

Yes, Rose decided, secure in the encirclement of his arms, Christmas *was* a time of miracles. For the season had brought her a man who loved her. He would give her everything she wanted—a family and a home. A home—for Christmas and ever after.

The Dark Man

by

Edith Layton

It was a perfect lovers' night. The moon drifted over London like a great phosphorescent excursion balloon—so close to the earth it drowned even the gaslights in its eerie radiance. The night was bright and still and clear, uncommonly warm for late autumn, but just chilly enough so that a lady might take a shivering step closer to a gentleman, so that he might put an arm around her without feeling like a cad. And then, of course, anything might happen, from a stolen kiss to an honorable proposal. So then it was odd that when the tall, broad-shouldered gentleman accompanying Miss Swanson led her out onto the balcony at the ball, and after a moment passed staring at that incredible moon finally began to make his proposal to her, she'd the nervous notion that it was somehow inappropriate.

It might have been because of her nervousness.

She was very anxious. She'd been expecting his declaration while at the same time doubting that it would come, with equal certainty. Or it may have been because she'd felt a kiss would have been more appropriate than words at that moment, and he'd never kissed her. Or it could have been because of the way he finally said it. For he didn't ask it, he said it . . . that was the crux of it.

Of course, she didn't think so at that moment. She wasn't thinking at all just then. Only waiting her turn to speak. And she knew that time had come when she realized he'd fallen silent and was waiting for her reply.

It took only a second's hesitation before she answered, and it was nothing like the second a drowning man was supposed to experience; not even a fraction of her life flashed before her eyes. There wasn't very much of it to review anyway—she was only just twenty years old, however long in the tooth that might be considered to be for an unmarried maiden of her class. And she'd done little enough in that brief time, except for being a devoted daughter, a splendid sister, and a very good friend to all those she called friend. That might have been many more people if she'd done all those excellent things in London rather than in the countryside where she'd grown to her present great age. But at eighteen her come-out had been forestalled by a distant uncle's demise, and at nineteen by an absurd outbreak of chickenpox that had involved all the children in the nursery, including, humiliatingly enough, herself.

But now she was here, unscarred by either event, in London and in fashion, and only recently introduced to society. And here was Francis Dayne Sutherland, Earl of Poole, Viscount Acton, himself, standing before her, putting every inch of his impressive six-feet-plus of spectacular manhood forever at her service by begging her to do him the honor of becoming his wife. Everyone had told her he'd do just this for days now, but she still couldn't quite believe it—hence the second's pause, which was hours longer than any other woman in London would have hesitated.

Her odd, niggling doubts drowned in the radiance of his smile as she gazed up at him and said, "Yes."

Only to be born again when he pressed his lips

to her forehead and murmured, "Thank you, my dear. You'll not regret it, I promise you."

Because he didn't promise anything else, by word or deed. He only took her gloved hand in his and in his more usual tone of voice asked lightly, "Shall we announce it tonight? After all, I spoke with your father this morning, and have already sent in the notice to the *Times*."

"But what if I'd refused?" Miss Swanson blurted, because there might have been something to that folktale about madness in the night of the full moon.

He laughed as answer. It was such a lovely sight, she forgot the reason for his doing it. But really, the moon favored him; its glow turned his thick fair hair silverine and his white teeth shone in its light, and his odd rain-colored eyes were transmuted to purest quicksilver tonight.

So, moon mad enough to drown her doubts and bewitched into forgetting that little spurt of anger she'd felt at his laughter, flattered by the knowledge that she'd caught *the* catch of the Season, because this silver-etched gentleman was the most elusive gentleman in the *ton*, and realizing that her parents were in expectation of hearing the gladsome news, she laughed with him. It wasn't at all like her to let her doubt and anger go. But then, there was that other reason for it as well. She was, moonstruck or not, very much in love with him. And had been from the moment she'd laid eyes on him.

He'd been exactly the size and shape of the hero of all her daylight dreams, and when he'd first spoken, she'd known his voice from all her nighttime dreams as well. There was nothing in him not to like: for though he was said to be a ladies' man, he was not precisely a rake, and though he was known to drink and gamble, he was neither a sot nor a gamester, and if he was a bit toplofty, he was an earl, after all, and so in all things not so much different from any man of fashion. Except, of course, anyone could see that he was far handsomer than most, and was said to be more intelligent too—or so at least it was said; it was hard to judge, for he wasn't a man to pass time in conversation with many people. Not even Miss Eve Swanson herself.

But there wasn't any help for that; when they'd met at balls and musicales, there'd been time for only brief bright comments and passing references. The morning calls he'd paid had been full of necessary social chatter. Their drives through the park had been punctuated by commentary on the weather, their carriage, horses, and surroundings, before always being periodically interrupted by the greetings of his many acquaintances. The one chance she'd had for private speech with him, that delightful evening at Vauxhall, she'd gotten tipsy on the rack punch she'd begged from him, and he'd been as amused as sympathetic to her difficulty managing any coherent conversation.

But she'd never known him to say a foolish thing, and if he never precisely roared with laughter, his lips quirked with suppressed laughter often enough, and a ready sense of humor was the best gauge of intelligence that she knew.

The most astonishing thing, she thought dazedly as she put her hand on his arm and he led her back to the ballroom, was that it seemed he'd actually chosen her to be his wife. There was no doubt of it, even if she thought she was still dreaming, for she heard him say it to her mother, and then her father, and then when there was a pause in the dancing, and they'd signaled the orchestra to silence, she heard her father announce it to all the world. Incredibly enough, she was to wed the earl in the spring. She'd heard it with her own ears.

She appeared to be the only one staggered by the news. Everyone else present commented on how

fitting it was: both young persons were of fair face
and fortune, breeding and position. He was seven
years her senior—if decades older in experience—
but that was only commonplace. She—if at twenty,
a bit elderly for an *ingénue*—was still obviously
dewy fresh and new to London. It was much discussed, but it wasn't to be wondered at. Except by
Miss Swanson herself.

Late that night, when finally alone in her room—
a luxury she enjoyed only this Season in London,
since at home she had to share with her sister—
Eve was still at it.

On the one hand, she thought, sitting up in bed
with her arms wrapped around her bent legs and
her chin on her knees, she'd a quantity of hair. Not
the most glorious color, perhaps, but thick as
cream and easy as pie to manage, or so her maid
always said. Whereas the inky tresses she coveted
were usually coarse as horse hair, and the silky
blond stuff she envied was fine as dandelion clocks,
or so the same wise maid had sworn. Brown wasn't
dramatic or ethereal, but it suited her fair complexion to a nicety and it sometimes stole a glint
or two of gold from the sun, and hadn't John Hayes
called it "mink" in his dreadful but flattering poem
to her? The earl had never mentioned it at all, but
if he hadn't liked it he wouldn't have offered for
her, would he have? He'd scarcely care to chance
a horde of brown-haired children if he didn't like it
. . . but that thought led to thoughts of how those
children would be begotten, which led Eve to admit that her figure was considered especially fine
too.

She peered down at herself and couldn't avoid
seeing two firm reasons why her form was so admired, because she was really extraordinarily
buxom, although slender almost everywhere
else, pleasing both fashion and the gentlemen.
Which was as it should be, she decided with **sat-**

isfaction, since she'd worked so hard for it, giving up pastries and sweetmeats until the longing for them made her ache. But not so much as the thought of how she'd look if she indulged as she wanted to. She'd been a very plump little girl, and never forgot that—or at least none of her siblings would let her.

On the other hand, she thought, frowning, although she'd neat, even features, and eyes to match her hair, there was nothing stunning about her looks. And he was as handsome as he could hold together . . . Ah, but he was in love with her, and that clouded one's senses, she thought on a deep, satisfied sigh, sliding down under her bedcovers again. Obviously. For he'd talked with her and danced with her and then chosen her, above all others, to be his only wedded wife, because he'd seen beneath the surface as well as that which was apparent. He'd seen her spirit, her sense of humor, and her honesty—the things her parents always told her were her especial virtues—and he'd liked what he'd seen everywhere. No, he'd loved what he'd seen. As she loved him, and that was that, and she buried her doubts beneath her pillow with her head and tried to convince herself she was only suffering last-minute bride-doubts early . . . before she surfaced to avoid smothering. And passed the rest of the night wondering when she'd see him again, in order to stop wondering why he'd asked her to marry him.

In the clear light of the breakfast table, Eve saw her doubts as the foolish fancies they'd been. Because Mother and Father were in ecstasies. Quiet, well-bred ecstasies, to be sure, but there was no doubt they were both in raptures. They paid not half so much attention to their bacon, eggs, and porridge as to the courses of humble pie and crow they envisioned Uncle Cyrus and Aunt Mary would be dining upon this morning. Uncle Cyrus had the title, Aunt Mary the fortune, and between them they'd also the manor and the town house, the position in London society, and all the airs that went with it. But they also had seven daughters, not one of whom as yet had made nearly so good a match as Cyrus' younger brother's daughter had just done, although they'd been gotten the best husbands money could buy. Eve could understand her country-squire father's delight at besting his lofty brother and sister-in-law at last. But, she reminded herself fairly, since her cousins were as famous for their lack of charms as looks, there really was no reason for her to feel smug.

"First one out of the gate too," her father was chortling. "Ho, just wait until our little Beth has her chance in two years—our Goldilocks might just get us a duke! The little charmer will have 'em eating out of her hand . . . not that Eve couldn't have had three dukes if she'd a mind," he added quickly, manfully suppressing a yelp at the force with which his wife's slipper met his shin beneath the table, and, avoiding her more keenly cutting glance, he went on, "but why should she, when she's already got the brightest, best-looking catch on the market right off the bat?"

"Poole is more than handsome and clever; he's a man of taste," his wife put in smugly. "I daresay Mary tried to interest him in any of her girls for some time now—she must be seething. Oh, my," she said with a sigh of purest satisfaction. Then she recalled herself and exclaimed, "Look at the time! Eve, do get dressed! Put on that charming sprigged muslin—the white with blue trim. We'll be inundated with well-wishers soon and you'll want to look your best. Not puffed-up or filled with self-consequence, of course," she warned, "but it's permissible to appear elated and just the smallest bit charmingly overset—as you seemed last night,"

she said, as though Eve had any idea of how she'd
looked last night after the earl had spoken for her.
"Yes, the white with blue will do very well, I
think—it's stylish but demure."

So of course Eve dressed in her green frock, the
one with the alarming neckline that her mother
had been wary of having her wear in company, no
matter what the modiste said, because it made her
daughter look far more sophisticated than any well-
bred young woman had a right to be. It was more
than a gesture, it was an indication of how Eve's
natural independent spirit was beginning to reassert itself. She'd been truly overset last night, and
still dazed this morning, but she was as unaccustomed to humility as she was becoming weary of
it. The earl had offered for her, she'd accepted him,
and she refused to act as though the king had offered his crown to the beggar girl. Her family
mightn't be rich, but they were by no means poor;
she mightn't be dazzlingly beautiful, but she was
no antidote. She might often have been stunned to
polite monosyllables while in her fiancé's company, but she usually had a thing or two to say
about most things, and it was certainly time for
her to do so now.

She scarcely had the chance.

The first wave of visitors were the defeated, as
anxious to show they were good sports as they
were to offer their congratulations. Dashing Harry
Fabian and his friendly rival Charlie Bryant made
their bows and left their regrets with their best
wishes, as did young Viscount Billingsly and John
Whittaker. Lord Dearborne went so far as to leave
a sonnet with his farewell, but she took no more
note of it than she did of the Baron Bly's sly in-
nuendos as he took his leave of her. Some gentlemen considered a married lady fairer game than a
single one, and Eve didn't need her mama's frowns
to take their measure. The sonnet went on the fire

and the memory of the leer was consigned to more eternal ones as soon as its donor's shadow had lifted from her drawing-room door.

Amy Carson and the Welling sisters, the Honorable Miss Merryman, Miss Pruett, and other fashionable maidens came to praise her, not to celebrate her, for their chagrin was as obvious as their envy. They eyed her with surprise and dismay, as though, Eve thought, she were a lapdog that had bitten them. She was heartily glad when a second wave of visitors arrived to displace them, for though they were fewer in number, they weighed more with her because they were her friends and true well-wishers.

"Imagine! You'll be a countess!" shy Miss Protherow breathed, as Elizabeth Foy giggled, "Indeed, and I doubt she'll speak to any of us peasants again."

"Oh, never! That is to say, I shan't, never again," Eve said haughtily, and then laughed with them so loudly she won a startled glance from her mama from where she sat in a clutch of other mamas discussing her good fortune.

The morning passed quickly, Eve taking the good wishes with the bad, and enjoying both very much, for she was, after all, only human. The only cloud on her horizon was caused by the absence of one glowing figure, and she found her eyes going to the door and her heart sinking lower as each new arrival proved not to be him. But, she thought, as the morning went on without her fiancé's presence to brighten it, she supposed he'd a great many things to do this signal morning, and perhaps as many well-wishers to contend with as she did. Or so she imagined, for she knew very little of his private affairs except for the address of his town house and the names of his closest friends. But not, as soon became obvious, all of them—houses or companions.

For Cousin Harriet was all too pleased to advise
her as to the whereabouts and identities of both.
Uncle Cyrus and Aunt Mary had finally arrived, as
though for a funeral rather than an intimate family
luncheon. They'd one of their married daughters
and her unhappy spouse, and two unwedded ones
in tow: the remainder of their daughters being var-
iously indisposed, either with envy or indigestion,
as was claimed. And as Harriet was closest to her
in age, it was she that bore Eve off to a corner for
a "nice quiet coze" while her parents and sisters
sought to swallow down their chagrin with their
sweetmeats and cordials immediately after that
awkward meal.

Harriet wasn't the handsomest of her sisters,
even though that wasn't much of a competition.
The sharp expression in her close-set eyes and her
thin pursed lips ruled even that small honor out.
Nor was she the best-natured, because she thought
herself clever and good-looking and resented the
fact that no one else did. But she was, if not the
cleverest either, the wisest of them all. She knew
a thing or two because she made use of the hours
she passed warming chairs and propping up the
wall at balls and dances. She listened to everything
said in her vicinity, and forgot none of it. And used
all of it when the occasion called for it: whenever
she felt ill-used, out of sorts, or mean-spirited, as
she usually did, and she especially did today.

"And so then where will you live after the happy
day?" she asked Eve at last, when they'd settled
in adjoining chairs and she'd discovered as little as
Eve herself knew about plans for her wedding day.

"Why, I expect at Poole House in Kent, of
course," Eve answered, "and in the Season, here
in town."

"In which house?" Harriet said, and tittered.

"His house, of course," Eve snapped, promptly
losing patience with Harriet, as was usual. She'd

known her all her life and could honestly say that
they'd never shared a commonality. In fact, she'd
have been horrified if they had, because she held
Harriet in lowest esteem, although she always—or
at least, she admitted, since adulthood—tried to
conceal it. Not the least of Eve's sins was her short
temper. She knew and regretted it. The only sav-
ing grace was that she genuinely disliked hurting
people, no matter how richly they deserved it.
Which was why her best cuts were said only inside
her own head, and why, for example, she'd com-
plimented Harriet's mustard-colored hat and gown
today, although she'd yearned to say that they
matched her complexion rather than suited it.

Harriet narrowed her eyes, a most unfortunate
and unnecessary mannerism in her case, Eve
thought uneasily, glancing away.

"Oh, but shall you live in his great house on
Grosvenor Street? Or in the smaller one on Curzon
Street?" Harriet asked sweetly, lowering her voice
to a whisper.

It was the fact that Eve had never heard of the
house on Curzon Street that alerted her, and the
whisper and smirk that made her wish she could
restrain her curiosity, not rise to the bait, and hold
her tongue for once. She knew it for a vain hope
from the second she thought it, for a heartbeat later
she heard herself asking, with considerable dread,
"What house on Curzon Street?"

"Why, the one where he keeps his mistress, Maria Bliss," Harriet said in conspiratorial tones,
and went on, "A diamond of the first water, tall and
Spanishy-looking, with hair and eyes like fire and
jet—as Lord Dearborne says, and a form that delighted the gentlemen from the pit to the balcony
when she danced, as Sir Bennett commented that
night at the Duke of Torquay's musicale. Of course,
she's not so handsome as Lucille la Poire, his previous light-o'-love, but she, as you know, was get-

ting long in the tooth, and Poole prefers them
young these days. Why else do you think he broke
with that Turner woman, when even her husband
thought they made a pretty pair?'' she asked in the
same sweetly inquiring tones as she'd asked Eve's
opinion of her hat when she'd come in, as she
watched Eve's fair complexion become alabaster.

"I've no idea," Eve said promptly, scarcely caring if her reply made sense, she was concentrating
so hard on keeping her face still and calm. She'd
rather consign her eternal soul to damnation than
admit she knew nothing of any of this to Harriet.

"Well, some said it was because the Turner
woman was so notorious," Harriet said chattily,
"but I have always believed it was because he
found Lady Cadge more amenable, if less attractive. *Her* husband, after all, was entirely dead, and
that Turner woman's was only dead, as they say,
from the neck up," Harriet tittered again.

Eve smiled. Enigmatically, she hoped. But it
looked more like she'd gotten a sudden cramp. She
hadn't known about any of the earl's women,
though she'd heard their names in similar sorts of
gossip before. Still, although she had been raised
in the country, it was not beneath a cabbage leaf.
She was aware that single gentlemen often had
their familiars, and single noblemen more than
their share. He'd just become engaged to her, she
reasoned quickly, and what he'd done before that
was a thing she could fret about after—at least after Harriet left—and so she simply shrugged.

"Ah, ancient history," she managed to say in
nearly normal tones.

"As ancient as yesterday," Harriet, thwarted,
snapped, "for that's when he was last seen leaving
the flat on Curzon Street."

"Precisely," Eve said on a yawn that was really
a suppressed scream, but she'd played cards for
straws before she'd come to town, and had always

wound up with a haystack in front of her, and now she was playing for a great deal more. "As you say, he was *leaving* it. He did offer for me, you know," she added, hoping she sounded smug, not deadened, as she felt.

"You believe that makes a difference?" Harriet asked in a vehement whisper, leaning closer. "Listen, my dear country cousin, why do you think he offered for you? With all the beauties of rank and position available to him? He needs an heir. He decided it was time to wed, and you happened to be there at the right moment to fill the bill. It's as I heard Lord Dartmouth say to his cronies at the Cumberlands' ball, when he thought no lady was near: 'A gentleman needs a wellborn, well-bred innocent to act as hostess when he decides to toddle home every now and again, and provide an heir to commemorate each time. But something less than a lady and more than an innocent to entertain him betweentimes.' All the gentlemen cried, 'Hear! Hear!' till he hushed them," she said with a bitter reminiscent smile.

"Otherwise," Harriet said with great conviction, for it was a thing she needed to believe, "Poole would have offered for someone more up to snuff. Why, did you think him smitten with undying love for you?" she asked on a laugh that was so near to a cackle that even her sisters stopped talking to stare over at her.

"I think you ought to learn to dance, Cousin Harriet," Eve said with cold fury despite her brittle smile, "and give your feet exercise and your ears rest for a change."

She arose with as much majesty as a severely shaken young lady could manage. And smiling, left before Harriet could realize she hadn't answered her question. For though she could manage a small credible falsehood or two to save her face, Eve couldn't bring herself to utter such a complete lie

as she'd need now to save her soul—which she felt
she'd just lost anyway. Because no, she thought
with absolute honesty at last, it was extremely un-
likely that he loved her . . . at all, much less un-
dyingly. And it was time she faced it, and admitted
it, if only to herself—for now, at least.

She was very beautiful. Not exactly fire and jet,
Eve thought sadly, but there was little doubt Miss
Bliss was a beauty. There were other women present tonight who had black hair and eyes and with
their spectacular forms snugly fitted into dampened gowns, this being a theater audience, after
all. But no other had been the object of Harriet
Swanson's pointed stare, and once Eve had noticed her too, Harriet's smug smile was as good as
a nameplate being affixed to the woman's impressive chest. But by not so much as a flicker in his
light eyes did the earl show that he'd seen her in
the audience beneath his box—probably because,
Eve thought glumly, he was so used to seeing her
beneath him in other circumstances.

It was a singularly depressing evening for Eve.
The newly engaged couple had made their first
public appearance *en famille*, and so various ill-
assorted Swansons shared the box with them. Harriet didn't have to utter so much as a word
throughout the evening; her little close-set eyes
pointed the way to all sorts of unhappy consider-
ations easily enough. Eve soon saw that the notorious Turner woman was there, and the slender
honey-haired female that the earl acknowledged
with a nod and Harriet with a smirk was probably
either the widow Lady Cadge or some other fine
lady who'd enjoyed his company; she was far too
elegant to be a common courtesan.

By the second act, which she'd not paid the least
attention to, Eve finally reflected that she ought to
have been morally indignant instead of wildly cu-

rious as to how the earl must feel: sitting high in a box in the theater with his fiancée, knowing that at least three women present were ones he'd known in the most intimate fashion. She watched him, marveling at his calm. What was going on behind that cool, polite expression and those light eyes that reflected everything and gave nothing beyond their surface back? Was he remembering the feel and taste of the women? Or had he really forgotten them as he seemed to have done? But how could he? How could he and they be so casual about it? she wondered, for it seemed to her, from all she'd heard, that they'd shared the most intimate thing imaginable together.

He seemed to feel the force of her stare at last, and turned his attention from the stage to gaze at her. And whatever he saw in her eyes was the only thing to disturb the smooth surface of his face, for she caught something suddenly live in those odd looking-glass eyes before she turned her head away and pretended to watch the play.

In all, she supposed, after he'd kissed her hand and handed her back to her father at their door again later that night, he'd handled the whole thing extremely well. She went to her bed, and he, she supposed, to his own, either alone or with his mistress, or mistresses—the whole lot of them, she neither knew or cared, she thought defiantly. But of course she did. Which was why she sat up late into the night planning on how to tell him their brief engagement was at an end. Because it was.

She had only to decide on how to tell him. It was several hours later, deep in the dwindling night, when it dawned on her that it was odd to have to plot a way to approach him privately and rehearse what to say when she did. After all, he was the man she'd promised to spend the rest of her life with. It made her see the wisdom of her decision. For she realized he frightened as much as at-

tracted her, and it was hard to think of a way to be
natural with him. He was as intelligent as he was
handsome, and that was considerable, but more
elegant even than that. The thought of his anger
was as disturbing as the thought of his disapproval. Fair and immaculate, poised and correct,
he might be only seven years older than she was,
but he made her feel like a schoolgirl, and she'd
the unnerving notion that he'd always be as un-
approachable as he seemed right now. She wanted
to look up to her husband, but not because she
always had to bow down to him. That, she mused,
was certainly part of the reason for her decision in
itself. But not all of it, by any means.

In the end, she decided after hours mulling it
over, it wasn't because of anything he'd done, not
really: not his past mistresses or even his keeping
one into the present, or planning to acquire more
in future—for all she knew. Because not by word
or deed had he acknowledged any of it, and all of
it was merely commonplace in his set anyway. No,
it was what he hadn't done.

For early this evening she'd greeted him quietly,
she'd eaten little of her dinner and spoken less, said
not a word to him in the coach on the way to the
theater, and had sat still as a mouse from the moment she'd taken her seat beside him there. He'd
finally tried to engage her in conversation on the
way home, discussing plans for the coming holiday season with her, and still she'd stayed mute,
or answered in a grudging, almost surly fashion.
She'd never precisely been a prattlebox with him
before, but there was no way he could have missed
the way she'd avoided him, then ignored him, and
then finally sulkily shut him out. But he had. And
that, she decided, was the last straw. She could
forgive him anything, she supposed with as much
sorrow as outrage, except for Harriet's being right
about him.

The Earl of Poole was thinking of his fiancée as he dressed for dinner, and that was odd, because he wasn't planning to see her tonight, and actually disliked the thought of seeing her soon again. For he'd passed a part of the afternoon with her, and she'd been about as comfortable with him as a head cold. Which meant that she'd been even more uneasy than she'd been at dinner the night before and at the theater two days before that, and he hadn't thought anything could be more uncomfortable than that. It was making him wonder if the words "Will you do me the honor of becoming my wife?" hadn't been some sort of magical incantation, transforming her from a charming little companion to a gauche and tongue-tied clod. Of course, it might only be that she was vexed with him for some reason, although he couldn't think of anything he'd done to overset her; and as they'd scarcely spoken to each other since, he knew it couldn't be anything he'd said.

She'd seemed to be such a merry little lady, as pretty-mannered as she was looking, which was to say, she was an engaging little armful, bright-eyed and quick-witted. Her lovely lips promised more than the sweetness they obviously held, because they were often quirked with inner laughter and seemed half-closed against all sorts of mischief. He'd the suspicion she was even brighter than she appeared, which was nearly as daunting as it was delightful—he'd almost given up on finding an eligible female with brains as well as beauty. She was obviously attracted to him too, which was beyond delightful; it would be very good to have a wife it was as easy to make love to as respect.

He'd been looking forward to his marriage, which both surprised and enchanted him, for he'd never anticipated that. Given his parents, and the set he traveled with, his own experiences, and the sort of

female he knew he'd eventually have to offer for,
he had never expected to make a love match. The
sort of women he amused himself with weren't
worthy of love, and the sort he was expected to
wed didn't think love a worthy consideration when
it came to something as financially and socially
important as marriage. But she'd seemed different.
He thought perhaps it was because she'd been
country-bred, or maybe because she was older than
the run of available young women, or possibly just
because she was truly unique. He didn't know how
he'd been so misled, but it hardly mattered anymore.

At least she was of good family, so it wasn't a
misalliance; it could have been far worse; at eighteen he'd been tempted to run off with an opera
dancer. Fortunately she'd run off with someone
older and less wise first. Now all he had to do was
to put up with the sort of marriage most men of
his class had to—as his father had done—one of
necessity. He sighed; he'd always thought to avoid
that, but he supposed it was inevitable and that in
some part of his mind he'd always known it, and
deluded himself in order to get the thing settled.
Now that it was, his winsome brown-eyed doe of a
girl had turned into something more of a dairy cow.
But it was done and he'd go through with it, and
he supposed he deserved it for deceiving himself.

His inadvertent shrug at the thought made his
valet frown because it disarranged his neckcloth
just as it was being tied. But before the valet could
decide to repair it or begin to construct another
snowy creation for his master's chin to rest upon,
there was another interruption.

"A young lady to see you, my lord," the butler
said from where he'd suddenly appeared, hesitant,
in the doorway.

The earl stood still, considering the matter, as
though it were not altogether extraordinary. A

young lady never called at a bachelor's house, unless there'd been a death in it, and it looked as though there might very well be one soon, since he noted that his valet was so thunderstruck he'd actually stopped breathing. His butler would never have disturbed him for anything less than a true lady's summons, but neither had he announced who it was. Still, there was something in the man's eyes that begged him to say no more. He'd known both his butler and his valet forever—the one was the soul of discretion and the other thrived on every indiscretion.

"Very well," the earl said calmly. "I won't need you just now, Jeffries," he told his valet dismissively, and shrugging on a jacket with a carelessness that made Jeffries wince as much as did his dismissal in the face of something obviously deliciously noteworthy, he went down the stair to the sitting room, where the butler murmured that his unexpected guest awaited him.

Eve Swanson spun around from contemplating the fireplace as he entered the room, and he noted that her chin went up and her eyes held a challenge, and she looked altogether the girl he'd first been fascinated with. He'd a moment to wonder if she were a victim to morbid changes in personality before she burst into speech.

"I came because there was no other way I could discover to speak with you alone," she said in a rush. "Every place we meet there are chaperones and company," she complained, "and I suspect it will get worse as time goes on, and I have to speak up before it's too late. I came alone, but no one need know, because I slipped away while everyone was resting up for dinner—as though there were a reason to rest in order to eat," she disgressed with a grimace of disgust, for so many London manners still annoyed her, before she remembered her mission and said quickly, "because I wanted to be able to tell you that I have reconsidered and I no . . . no longer wish to be b-betrothed to you," she concluded, her voice dwindling as she looked up to see his reaction and saw that for once he'd lost his air of calm. He blinked, before the light in his eyes flared.

But all he said as he watched her was, "Really?"

"Well, yes," she said in a grieved voice, fidgeting with her glove, "b-because we should not suit at all, you know."

"No, I didn't," he said conversationally as he strolled into the room. "Why not?"

She hesitated.

"Come, now," he said with a small smile, "you've been very valiant until now. I suspect this has been brewing since the night at the theater, it's why you haven't said 'boo' to me, isn't it?"

"So you did notice!" she exclaimed with wonder.

"I am not three weeks dead, of course I noticed," he said lightly. "Now, come, tell me the rest."

"Well," she said, diverted, "that's part of it, because you ought to have told me you saw something was amiss."

"You're quite right," he said after a brief pause, nodding, "I ought to have."

His confession, made in a clam, uninflected voice, agitated rather than soothed her, and she perversely wished to see some fierce emotion on his face.

"That's not all, of course. I am not so petty," she said haughtily, and grew still, closing her eyes with dismay as she remembered what else it was. Still, remembering gave her the courage to blurt, "No, it's not only that. And not just because of Miss B-Bliss and all your other mistresses, which I do understand gentlemen have and ladies aren't supposed to notice, although how I am expected to ignore a stunner like Miss Bliss beneath my very nose, I don't know," she said, opening her eyes to show the hurt there before she raised that insignificant nose higher and said, very much on her high ropes, "It is not what I'm used to, my papa never looked at another woman . . . Well, he does, now and again," she admitted, "being only human. But only that, I assure you, because everyone knows everything in the countryside and we'd know if he had. But he doesn't want to do more than look. You see, he takes marriage far more seriously than London gentlemen do. And so do I.

"And," she added in a less militant, very sad little voice, "there's also the fact that telling you this is the h-hardest thing I've ever done," she said with a catch in her voice, "for I never stammered before I met you. And one cannot marry a man one is afraid to speak with, and that is a thing I know for certain, my lord.

"So," she went on determinedly, "since I know that as a gentleman you cannot be the one to call the thing off, I must, but as I haven't told Mama and Papa yet, I must ask you to place the notice in the *Times* under my name, for I'm sure you'll know just how to word it. And I shall reimburse you for it if you'll just advise me as to the cost," she concluded, and grew still, looking very pale.

"I'd rather not," he said softly, advancing until he stood inches away from her. She heard him sigh, but resisted the urge to look up and see his expression.

"I'm sorry," he said quietly, "truly, I am. I didn't think you'd find out about Miss 'B-bliss,' " he explained with a smile in his voice that made her eyes fly up to his, "and no, you're not supposed to know or speak about her, but I think I chose you for my wife because I'd the feeling you would speak about her if you did know about her. I'll sever that connection forthwith—and it won't be a wrench, I assure you. Not now," he said gently, "not now that

I've found the real Miss Swanson, after all. I'd like to be as faithful a husband as your father, in the countryside or not, but I beg you to bear with me for now, if only because unlike you, I'd no good model to follow. My father never deceived my mother, precisely," he said with the traces of a not-very-amused smile. "They didn't care for each other very much, so there was no deception involved. Only relief on both sides when I arrived to free them from their marital duty.

"I'd like to make it easier for you to speak with me too, and I'd think it would be if you knew me," he went on without a trace of humor, real or assumed. "We've not begun very well, but we can do better. Can we give it a little more time, please?"

She stared up at him, but before she could speak, his arms went around her and he said, mistaking her jolt of surprise for protest—when she was only trying to catch her breath and decide whether to push him away or step closer to him—"Not until spring, if that seems too long a trial to you. I'm confident enough that we'll suit to make it a matter of weeks—until the New Year, shall we say? But I must dare risk a trial of my own first," he murmured, and kissed her.

It began as a tentative, light, comfortable touching of lips, but the sparkling sensation that Eve felt as he met her mouth with his must have been mutual, because it soon became a great deal more, and involved more than their lips, or hands, or other delightfully obvious things that were called into play as it went on. She'd never known anything like it, and from the wondering look that suited him so well when he drew back at last, she could almost swear that for all she knew better, neither had he.

"Yes?" he asked. "You'll give me until the New Year to try to change your mind?"

"Yes," she said, and won another kiss for her clever answer.

Then he held her very close and whispered, "B-bliss, my love. That was pure b-bliss."

She pulled away an inch. "You oughtn't to jest about such a thing," she said worriedly.

"No, my love, I ought. Think about it. My not mentioning it would be the thing for you to be alarmed about. Now, I'd best smuggle you back home before you're discovered and you *have* to marry me, willy-nilly," he laughed.

But her look of dismay at that prospect sobered him. As much as he wanted to give her his lips again, he gave her only his arm, and led her to his door. He'd been shocked and displeased at finding her so lost to propriety as to visit him alone, but now was glad she'd dared. It would be an interesting few weeks, and he was looking forward to them. For he'd told her the entire truth. He was very confident of their outcome. Nor was he being vain or smug. Simply, he knew his own worth. And now he knew her expectations. Even better, he thought, gazing down at her with pleasure, now he knew her possibilities. He didn't see how he could fail—but then, that was pardonable, if not admirable or wise of him. Because for all his wide experience, he'd never felt the stirrings of love before and so couldn't understand that such total confidence was in itself a failure.

He told her about his infancy between dances at Almack's. And they laughed at tales of his school days at Astley's Amphitheater. She learned about his grand tour over ices at Gunther's. And realized he'd done more than touring when they met up with his good friend the Viscount Talwin there and she suddenly recalled the viscount's reputation as a spymaster. Then she realized some of the countries her fiancé had mentioned were ones he couldn't have visited safely or comfortably in those years. He didn't deny it, but made little of it, and laughed off her admiration, calling it all sport. Eve had to add "brave" and "patriotic" to "hand-some," "clever," and "kind" and found herself de-fying the laws of gravity and reason by falling more deeply in love with him each time they met.

Which made each night after they'd parted even harder for her to bear. It wasn't only the desire that kept her wakeful, though it was true that he'd got-ten as free with his kisses and caresses as he had with his speech, and she found herself longing for him in the most shocking ways in the most shock-ing places. But there was something else that was like a bur that clung to her conscience, so prickly it hurt as much to try to dislodge as it did to let it remain.

She'd wanted to dance every dance with him at Almack's, but after a few he'd steered her to others and taken other partners himself. Because, he'd said, they couldn't disregard the others: it was just not done.

She'd wanted to sit right at ringside at Astley's so she could feel as well as see every nuance of the wonderful equestrian performances. She knew it was childlike, but the place made her feel like a child again. But he'd gotten them front seats on the second tier instead, and there they remained, because, he explained, that was where persons of their sort sat.

At Gunther's he'd laughed off her request for cream puffs with her ices as a jest, and ordered her a dish of ices with a slender wafer beside it, which, he'd said, was what all the ladies enjoyed.

They were little things, to be sure, but they loomed large in her nights because she couldn't help but feel that they were symbolic of a great deal more. She'd rejected him once for not caring enough for her; now, despite all his efforts—or perhaps because of them—the notion Harriet had planted wouldn't go away. Perversely, the more she loved him, the less she felt deserving of his love, and so her doubts as to his love for her grew even as her pleasure in his company did. Because for all he'd done the socially acceptable thing in becoming engaged to her, she knew he could have done better, and for all his kisses and caresses, he said nothing that led her to believe he thought he couldn't have, as well.

It was the canker in the rose. She'd discovered that once a defect is noted, no matter how small, it increases in size each time it's noticed—which becomes all the time. She consoled herself by reasoning that was only so because, like the startling sight of a blemish on the cheek of a great beauty, the merest flaw looks hideous in the face of perfection. And that she was a fool to quibble, and possibly a coward as well: a shrinking virgin overwhelmed by her good fortune and mastered by her missish fears, seeking disaster in the arms of a miracle.

But now there was not even rationalization to comfort her. Now it was as plain as the smile on his handsome face before her. Because now he was saying, in his usual calm, amused tones, that they'd go to the Driscolls' ball Christmas week, even though she'd just said she would not.

"No," she said again, thinking perhaps he'd not heard her right, and shaking her head for emphasis, "I don't want to go."

"But we'll be at the Kents' for dinner, and at Torquay's afterward, and the Driscolls' town house lies just between the two houses, just as the time of the ball is between the two engagements," he said reasonably, still smiling as he tucked a flower that she'd shaken from its place above her ear back into her heavy hair, and kissed that exposed ear as he

did, which caused her to lose her wits more surely
than she'd loosed the rose.

They stood alone in the entry hall of her family
town house. Her parents had gone to bed soon after they'd all returned from the opera, and the footman, prodded by the butler, signaled by her
mama's eye, had found an errand backstairs as Eve
bade her fiancé good night. They were an engaged
couple, after all, and entitled to some few moments
of privacy. And he was a gentleman, and there
wasn't much they could get up to in a hallway—at
least not in the five minutes they'd been granted.

"I should like to go," he whispered now, his
tongue done touching her earlobe, his breath dry-
ing the slight moisture he'd left, chilling it, so that
she trembled, and began to give way, without
thinking, as ever. For his words had done as much
as his touch had. She found it hard to deny him
anything that would give him pleasure. Until he
spoke again.

"And we'll be expected," he added softly as he
focused on her lips.

Which parted with a swiftly indrawn gasp. She'd
been lulled into acquiescence. But now she was
thinking again, and lulled, she thought angrily,
was not the same as gulled. Harriet had told her
who the honey-haired beauty she'd seen that night
at the theater had been, and it had been no widowed lady, but Lady Driscoll, whose husband was
very much alive, if dead to all decency.

"But I do not wish to go to the Driscolls' ball,"
Eve insisted, stepping back a pace.

"Why not?" he asked bemusedly, letting her
take the step, but not letting her go from the circle
of his arms.

"Because," she said, goaded by his indulgent
smile, "that Turner woman will be there, she's
Lady Driscoll's cousin. And . . . and . . . and," she
said with stunning bravery in the face of his sud-

denly sober face, "I hear that L-Lady Driscoll herself was once . . . once, your m-mistress too."

"M-my, m-my," he said, letting his arms drop to
his sides. "Someone has been busy! Eve, child,"
he said after a moment in serious but gentle tones,
"that was then. This is now."

"But . . . but then, if that is so, why do you want
to go so badly?" she asked.

"Ah, well, I don't," he admitted, sighing as he
drew her back to him. With his hands around her
waist and her lower body pressed close against his,
he looked down to her face and the white glow
where her frock exposed her shoulders, neck, and
breast, to see where he'd place his lips next, as he
lectured softly, "But we shall be expected, because
everyone will be there. And as everyone will know
where we were earlier," he said, placing a light kiss
on the tip of her nose, "and where we'll be after,"
he continued, feathering one on her lips, "it will be
remarked upon if we don't show up." He subsided
as he felt her body stiffening instead of melting, as
usual, into his.

"What's wrong with that?" Eve asked coldly.

"You're joking," he breathed, drawing nearer to
her lips again, until she pushed him away so
sharply he staggered, and he realized she was not.

He'd been trained for action, and knew what to
do when startled, but was totally unaccustomed to
puzzlement.

"What?" was all he could say, feeling as foolish
as he knew he sounded.

Her lovely lips were trembling, but he didn't feel
in the least like kissing them when he heard what
they shaped themselves to say next.

"I don't want to go," she said, "whether or not
you believe it is the thing to do. There it is," she
said distractedly. "There it is again. Everything we
do is determined by what you consider to be ac-

ceptable—from where we sit at Astley's to what I eat at Gunther's."

He began to smile, and realizing how childish mentioning horse shows and ices sounded, she went on a little desperately, "You may think it's socially acceptable for me to watch you do the pretty with your former mistresses, but I cannot enjoy it and I don't believe you'd ask me to witness it if it weren't 'what's expected.' "

"You refine too much on my previous liaisons," he chided her, his light eyes shining, because for all he knew she was suffering, still he was only mortal, and considering how she'd once refused his suit, such ardent jealousy was a lovely thing to see. "I've told you that's all over and done. And mentioning it to me isn't at all the thing, you know . . ." he said, stopping abruptly as he realized what he'd said.

"Just so!" she cried with bitter triumph. "There it is again."

"Now, look, my dear," he said with some impatience at himself as well as her, "we live in a real world. A man doesn't expect his bride to keep dredging up his past and throwing it at him—"

"And she doesn't expect him to keep reliving it before her very eyes!" she said, raising her voice as she saw his indulgent grin again, "whether or not it's 'done.' Not if it gives her pain. There it is," she said in a wavering voice, but with curious dignity. "You care more for how life is expected to be lived than how it is lived."

"And you, my child," he countered in exasperation, because he saw her point, and yet couldn't avoid the fact of his social obligations, "seem to expect it to be lived as in some fairy story. Come now," he coaxed her, "I've admitted I had certain connections before we met, as have most of the gentlemen you know. Living as we do, I'll likely meet some of those women again from time to

time. Should I cut them dead? That would be need-
less and cruel. A smile and a pleasant word are
only civil. What do you expect of me?"

"I'd hoped," she said at once, answering what
he'd thought was a rhetorical question, "that you
. . . cared for me . . . per-perhaps loved me enough
to care for my opinion more than the world's."

He gave her a tender smile. "I do care, but you
have to grow up and understand the way of the
world and the way things are done, Eve, my darling . . ." He paused, seeing a newly sprung tear
glistening on her cheek.

That was unfortunate. Because he was about to
go on to tell her how none of it mattered to him—
not just the world around them—since his love for
her made everything he'd done before he met her
seem pointless, and every liaison he'd had then
seem remote and incidental now.

But she spoke up first. "I'd hoped," she said with
as much sorrow as accusation, "for a husband who
cared for nothing but me."

"Ah, you were looking for a care-for-nothing,
were you?" he quipped, trying to lighten her mood,
never thinking of the dual meaning that would be
attached to his light jest.

She pushed back an errant strand of her heavy
hair and eyed him silently. She found love to be an
uncommonly messy emotion, making her lose all
control, causing her to feel hot and confused, so
achingly unkempt in spirit it surely must show in
her face and form. But he looked so damnably cool
and complete, from his black evening jacket to the
perfectly fitted breeches which showed his strong
legs. He was all in black and white tonight, everything about him was clear and unruffled, just as
she always saw him. But then, she'd always kept
her eyes closed when they kissed. Now she yearned
to prod him to some sort of emotion.

"Oh, I expect so," she said bitterly, "and I don't

doubt there are many girls who'd agree with you.
My cousin Harriet, Miss Merryman . . . oh, so many
others, but I'm sure you know that far better than
I."

"Do you think me a rake?" he asked tenderly. It
was unfortunate that he found that notion as en-
dearing as he did flattering. For the one emotion
she did recognize in him now seemed very like
preening.

"No," she snapped, "I don't. I think you care
more for your consequence than you do for any
vice."

"Eve, I don't think you understand," he began
with weary patience, choosing to overlook her insult, attributing it, correctly, to her chagrin at his
not declaring his love for her. He was about to rem-
edy that, but didn't speak up quickly enough, having never encountered her temper before.

"Oh, I do understand!" she cried before he could
speak. "It's you who don't. Because you can't do
anything that hasn't been done before!"

He checked at that.

She was stung by being told yet again about the
way things were done, and only half-believed that
was his real reason for inflicting his beautiful ex-
mistresses on her in public, and was also furious
at his amused, exquisite patience. She finally lost
control. Her eyes blazing, her cheeks flushed, her
remarkable bosom heaving, she put her small fists
on her hips and glared up at him. He was as surprised as enthralled, for Miss Eve Swanson losing
control was a notable thing to see. And then he
was aghast, for she was even more so to hear.

"Why . . . why, I don't think you'd even have
had a mistresses if everyone else didn't! No, truly,"
she said as she saw his head go back as though
she'd slapped him, "I doubt you would have done
if everyone else didn't think it the thing for a young
gentleman to do. If they all became monks, why,

so then, I think, would you. I don't believe you've ever done a thing in your life that wasn't correct, whether it was moral or immoral, for right and wrong don't figure into fashion at all. Or a thing that you thought up for yourself, either. Why, from the clothes you wear to the clubs you wear them to, to the women you take them off for," she raged, oblivious of his widened eyes and sudden pallor, blind to everything but the thrum and surge of her hot temper now, "everything you do is done for 'everyone else,' isn't it? Well, I don't believe I can live that way. Now and again I need to be myself."

"Indeed?" he asked with icy calm, though she noted as her vision began to clear of the smoky red cloud that had enveloped her that the end of his finely shaped nose was so pinched it seemed sharpened. "I begin to think it ought to be more often than 'now and again.' I'm sorry I'm not a rebel, my dear. Or a clown, for they're the only others that have no concern with what's done and no fear of wearing their breeches on their heads and their hats on their bottoms if it pleases them."

She gasped. It was beyond indelicate for him to mention "breeches" in her presence, and as for "bottoms," it simply wasn't done! Then she colored; she certainly couldn't rail at him for doing what wasn't done, not now. But she had to strike back. She didn't want to hurt him so much as she needed to even the score, and needed even more to be reassured as to his care for her. But she could scarcely ask for that now. So she lifted her chin and cast all her cards down on the table in one last desperate gamble.

"There it is. I fear I must again ask you to give notice of the termination of our engagement to the *Times*," she said loftily, "since obviously we do not suit."

"Since you don't care for society's opinion," he

snarled, clapping his hat on his fair head, "do it yourself!"

He wheeled around and strode to the door.

She trembled with fury. Though she gazed long-ingly at a great Chinese vase in the corner of the anteroom, she knew her limitations. There was nothing small enough for her to throw at his head near to hand, except for an insult.

"Be damned, sir!" she shouted, shocking herself badly.

"Delightful," he said, casting her a withering backward glance. "So speaks the rebel, eh?"

But she didn't speak again.

She only moaned, "Oh, Lord," when he'd gone, realizing that whether it had really been a winning one or not, she'd overplayed her hand, and so had lost the entire game.

It was hard to leave London as the Christmas season approached, whether you liked the city or not, Eve thought sorrowfully. Because that was the time the city put on its best face, even though it may have been a false one.

The shops were suddenly filled with marvelous things. Just seeing them available was such a treat that half the citizens of town didn't care if they could afford them or not, and the other half bought them whether they could or not. There'd been such an influx of street musicians that it seemed every street corner was filled with music. It was possible to walk from square to square going from Haydn to carols to music hall, from trumpets to Jew's harps to drums, as though getting round town was some wondrous new musical game. It was such a roisterous holy season that even druids might en-joy it, for there was an entertainment at every the-ater and church, as well as parties everywhere for the rich and poor and anyone who could resemble one while being the other. It was a bad time to leave

town, unless, of course, you were off to the countryside for even better amusement.

And it was hardest to leave, Eve thought on a
sigh that fogged her coach window, when you'd
been sent away—to exile. Or Doncaster, whichever
came first.

"I don't know why you should lament," her
mother had complained bitterly, "when we were
the ones to bear the brunt of your folly. Imagine!
Casting away a gem like Poole. For no reason."

"For good reason," Eve had argued. "He offered
only because he needed an heir. Everyone knew
it."

"That beastly Harriet," her mother wailed as her
husband grumbled.

"And how should I tell everyone why our daughter threw him over? Should I say because he only
wanted an heir?" he asked with awful sarcasm.
"Ah, yes, and have half the *ton* and his brother
dying of laughter, for why else should a man
marry?" he answered himself.

He conveniently forgot why he'd married her
pretty mama, Eve thought, and Mama why she'd
wedded a slim, unfashionably red-thatched younger son with even more slender expectations. But
she said nothing, for though she'd inherited her
mother's delicate looks, she knew only too well she'd
her father's terrible temper.

"She'll have to go into hiding for a space. She'll
go to Grandmother Swanson's in Sussex until this
blows over," her mother said heavily, because she
wanted Eve to be punished as well as incommu-
nicado, and though her husband's widowed
mother had a mansion, there was no more ghastly
company she could think of on earth.

Neither could Eve or her father. But she only
sniffled at hearing her fate, and he was as unwilling to admit it as much as he was unable to see
her suffer even if she deserved it. Like most hot-

tempered persons, he relented just as quickly as he'd been enraged, and sighed, "No. Better she goes to your mother, in the North. Too many people in Sussex."

"But Mama and Aunt have some rather odd notions . . ." her mother protested, for she'd not forgotten that Sussex was well-populated, and knew her old home was not, and hadn't wished to punish Eve quite that much.

"Odd notions!" her father thundered. "I remind you, madam, that your daughter has her share of them too!"

There was silence until Eve spoke again.

"He didn't love me," she said in a small voice, and turned her head so they wouldn't see the treacherous tears that insisted on slipping from her eyes whenever she thought about it. As she'd been doing little else since it had happened, they were remarkably red eyes now. They, or the words she'd uttered, silenced her parents completely, and they exchanged uneasy glances.

"Well," her mother finally sighed, "we shall wait and see. No need to say or do a thing until the thing is in the *Times*. Perhaps he'll reconsider."

But he hadn't. After Eve passed two anxious weeks in indoor exile in London, her father had finally got the official news with his morning paper. The announcement was printed up in the newspaper of record. And Eve was off to Doncaster to see out the old year in solitary state and eminent disgrace, like Napoleon on his rocky little isle. Only with no dreams of a triumphant return.

And now she'd been riding for days, her mood darkening as the signs of human habitation in the landscape around her grew lighter. Sheep, she thought morosely. The North is populated only by sheep. But so is London, or so you said, she reminded herself, and dabbed at a tear that surprised her by trickling past her nose, because she'd thought she'd used up her store of them for the year.

A light snow began to flutter down from the milky sky, and though Eve would rather it had been a sullen rain, to match her lowering mood, she had to admit it lifted her spirits somewhat. Because it did look lovely, sugaring the hedgerows and giving the naked trees something sparkling to wear for the approaching holidays. And if it kept up, she thought with a surge of hope, she might not be able to reach her grandmother's house. She might have to pass another overnight at an inn tonight, and maybe the next night too, and perhaps there would be congenial company there, and . . .

And then the coach rolled to a stop.

"We're here," her maid said softly.

It would have suited Eve better if her grandmother's house had been some decaying Gothic manse, brooding high on a jagged hill over a seething sea. But it was as charming as she remembered it to be from her childhood: a warm red-brick home set in a graceful park full of towering evergreens behind walls of still-green-leaved rhododendrons, so that it carried the remembrance of spring far into the winter. The house was so nicely proportioned that it seemed neat for all its great size; all eccentric corners and coppices, with snow swagged like icing on its eaves now, it looked very like the gingerbread house of her favorite fairy-tale story.

It mightn't be so bad at that, Eve thought as she left the coach and stood gazing up at the house. It seemed a magical sort of place. Here she might yet even forget what she'd been sent here to remember and regret. She climbed the stair to the great Christmas-wreathed front door, only to find it swinging open to receive her before her footman could so much as lift the bronze head of a satyr that served as a knocker. She stepped forward. And

halted in her tracks as an eldritch screech froze her
in place.

"No, wait!" the agitated voice shrieked. "Not another step! No, no! *Right* foot first. Right foot only
when you enter a new domicile. For luck," the
voice commanded.

Eve carefully stepped in on her right foot and
sighed as she was enveloped in her grandmother's
arms. For now she remembered what the outward
charm of the place had made her forget, and exactly why it would be a true term of exile for her.

"It is not superstition," her grandmother said
comfortably as they sat at the dining table that
night. "Superstition is mindless folly. It is folk wisdom, which is only good common sense. I daresay
you'd not have had any trouble at all with that
young man if you'd have come to us at once. A bit
of daisy root beneath your pillow, a lover's knot for
him to wear, and a betrothal toast of elderberry
wine with a pinch of forget-me-not and rosemary
. . . ah, well, but what's the use of repining over
what was not done?" she said briskly, seeing Eve's
face grow that still and shuttered look that suited
her so ill. "Do have some more of the mutton, my
dear, the sauce is superb."

She gave a twinkling look to her sister, who returned it. The ground acorns and dried leaves of
bristly oxtongue that flavored it were a specific for
broken hearts, and wouldn't do the girl's hair a bit
of harm either.

Well, and they could have put adder's tongue
and mouse toes in it for all she cared, Eve thought,
dutifully taking a mouthful of the mutton, even
though she knew they'd laced it with something
that gave its gamy taste an acrid flavoring of
weeds. "The two weird sisters," Papa had always
called them. They were too plump and sweet-
looking to remind anyone of certain scenes in
Macbeth, and they were as good-hearted as they ap-

peared to be. But there was no denying that they were two ladies of considerable age and oddity. As Eve chewed her mutton beneath their approving stares, she recalled the first time she'd gotten a ginger cookie from them. Even after all these years she remembered her shocked surprise at finding something sharply sour in her mouth instead of the sweet and spicy treat she'd expected. "We added an herb—hot arssmart . . . it makes little girls grow wise," Great-Aunt Alice had said smugly. It had only made her grow ill, she remembered now.

Eve sighed. Her grandmother and great-aunt nodded and looked at each other again. She heaved an even more heartfelt sigh then, since that look obviously meant she'd be dining on henbane and bachelor's button or some other such treat tomorrow night. It was three weeks until the New Year, and she very much wondered if she'd be alive to greet it. For if her well-meaning relatives didn't put an end to her suffering by trying to ease it, then surely the heavy lump that had once been her heart would sink her entirely by then.

Because neither wreaths of rowan nor ropes of myrtle nor enchantments muttered by the light of the fullest moon could make her forget his smile, nor infusions of pennyroyal and rue his voice, nor all the holly berries and mistletoe on earth his kiss. No, nor all of that and a human sacrifice besides, the last look of loathing he'd leveled at her. For now, too late, she realized that for all his faults— his worshiping the great gods of convention and his lack of understanding of her jealousy and hurt—she loved him all too well. And wiser, from great-aunt's hot arssmart or not, now too she knew that she wouldn't love him if he were perfect, as she'd wanted him to be. Because like called to like, and she was not perfect either—oh, all too obviously, she thought on a barely audible whimper that won her a week's worth of exotic vegetable and mineral infusions. Oh, decidedly, she was not.

"Freedom is a glorious thing, is it not?" Lady Driscoll asked softly, tapping the gentleman lightly with her fan to get his attention.

There'd been a time when all she'd had to do was flutter her eyelashes as lightly to claim all his notice. Now she wondered if she'd need a hammer and chisel. She'd been standing next to him for a long while, reasoning that he'd catch the sound if not the shimmer of her silken skirts rustling so close to him. She'd leaned toward him until he must have got the scent of her signature perfume, if not the unspoken message as she let her breast accidentally graze against his arm. But he wasn't stirred, nor had he. The Earl of Poole stood still as stone, his glass of champagne in hand, watching the dance reel by him. Nothing in his handsome face moved but his cold light eyes, following the dancers as a cat watched empty air, as if waiting for some vital unseen thing to appear. But he'd heard her spoken question.

"Is it?" he answered, though his gaze never left the dance floor.

"I have always found it so. As I recall, you did too. Heavens!" she said with mock humor. "Have I trodden wrong? Has your heart been broken along with your engagement to wed?"

It was a jest. He'd been free for weeks now and had been seen in all his old haunts: the clubs and gaming houses, theaters and brothels, boxing salons and parties that all the gentlemen of his set congregated at. But he hadn't been over her doorstep, and seeing him again tonight, so poised, handsome, and remote, had given her a desire to renew their intimate acquaintance. They'd been lovers once, had parted on amicable terms; there was no reason now that he was so obviously at loose ends not to find an interesting way to knit them up with him.

"My heart broken? Why, yes, I believe it was," he answered so expressionlessly that for a moment she almost thought he was being serious. Then he turned his odd bright empty gaze upon her and said, "And so I think I'll take my leave now. Good night and Happy Christmas, my lady."

Then he bowed and left, so that she never knew if he'd meant the bizarre thing he'd said or not.

It had to stop, the earl reasoned as he strode down the street to his next appointment. Sooner or later, he knew, he'd have to start feeling something apart from this curious emptiness and unease. She'd said they wouldn't suit, and she was entirely right, and so why, then, he wondered as he walked almost fast enough to flee his thoughts, could he not forget it, and her? There were dozens of eligible young women in his world, as well he knew, just as she'd told him. But though he'd danced with almost every one of them in the weeks since he'd severed his betrothal, it was as if he'd been dancing with himself all the while, and he'd felt just as foolish doing so. As he'd felt, in other ways, just the other week when he'd finally decided to bury his lust for her in some more suitable fashion, and had taken that girl from Madame Felice's to her silken lair. That had been so unpleasant he'd not lusted after any female since. Except for Eve Swanson. She'd never been that pretty, witty, or wise; it must be the novelty of being scorned, he decided as he mounted the stair to another of his friends' town houses to give them his best greetings of the season.

But the Duke of Torquay was difficult company for him tonight, if only because the duke's gaze was always on his lovely wife, as were also, obviously, his thoughts. So it was with his invited guests as well. For most of them had come two by

two, and seemed newly wedded, no matter how
long they'd really been wedded, so that the brightly
lit, evergreen-decked house seemed like some great
ark sailing through the snowy London night,
bound for the New Year on some mythical bridal
voyage. The earl drank his host and hostess's
health and took their hands, and then his leave of
them as soon as he could.

But he'd gained an escort. The Viscount Talwin
accompanied him out to the snowy streets, and
stayed a moment to chat. The slender, middle-
aged, affable viscount hadn't been accompanied by
his wife, but then, theirs had been a modern marriage even in earlier times; they appeared together
for ceremonial purposes only. The sort of female
the viscount was most frequently paired with was
the sort that would have been as wildly out of place
at the Torquays' as the earl had felt there.

"Ah, me," the viscount sighed, his breath gust-
ing a puff of white steam through the whirling
snowflake-filled night air, "my merry men are one
by one becoming merrier married ones. If I'm to
trace the little corporal on his adventures, I'll have
to find a few new adventuresome chaps. Happily
married men acquire a new sense of caution along
with innumerable tea sets when they wed, it
seems. And too much caution can be the death of
a man in my service, as surely as none at all can
be. Torquay, and now, it appears, North and Little-
ton too . . . females have broken into my ranks
more than Boney himself has."

"You still have me, sir," the earl murmured, his
spirits lifting, thinking that going abroad mightn't
be a bad idea at all—and then realizing it with such
sudden glee that his eyes shone in the glistening
night.

But his companion, a man who knew rashness
as his worst foe, gazed at him sharply before he
turned his head and said mildly, "Ah, yes. But I

almost lost you too, didn't I? The little Swanson chit, the one from the right side of the family, wasn't she? Taking little thing she was too. Too bad it didn't work out."

"Not at all," the earl muttered. "Still, as you say, I'm free. And rather at loose ends right now. Since I won't be reeking of orange blossoms, the sight of chestnuts in blossom in the spring would suit me admirably. Do you need a man on Avenue Napoleon, or do they call it Avenue du Roi again now?" He chuckled.

"You seemed so admirably suited," the viscount mused. "No, I don't think I can send you. Sorry, my boy. A fellow nursing a broken heart is as incautious as one dreaming of returning to his beloved. I've nightmares enough from when things went wrong when all else seemed right to dispatch a fellow wearing his heart on his sleeve. It makes too easy a target, you see."

The earl's head shot up. His eyes glittered in a way that might have alarmed men stronger and younger than the viscount.

"You've been misinformed," the earl said through clenched teeth. "My heart's intact, and precisely where it belongs."

"As for where it belongs . . ." The viscount shrugged. "But I've known you a long while, Francis," he said, reminding the earl by the use of his Christian name that he'd known him since he'd been given it. "You've been acting differently of late. You didn't dance with Lady D. when you stopped at her house earlier tonight, for example, and it was her ball."

"A little thing," the earl said, shrugging some of the snow from one broad caped shoulder.

"Ah, yes, so it was. But not for the Earl of Poole." The viscount laughed. "You always do the correct thing, my boy, and so when you don't, however little a lapse, I take note of it, since it would be large in anyone else. It's noting behavior that minutely that—''

"I always do the correct thing?" the earl echoed in a strange voice, cutting him off.

"Of course," the viscount said. "You're known for it."

"Surely not," the earl protested heatedly. "Why, I . . . I've not always been sociable—as you said, take tonight and Lady D. for example—and I've gamed, and had intrigues, and . . ."

"But snubbing is an art in our circles, my boy, and the fellow who doesn't have affairs of the body, if not of the heart, would be much remarked upon. And who does not game? If you didn't, you'd be wondered at. No, no, you are, in all things, a fellow who always does exactly as he's expected to. Every time and everywhere. That's what made you such a good agent, I think—at least until the Frogs caught on that there was a vogue for some of our most correct young noblemen to spy as well as play in Paris.

"Ah, well," the viscount went on as the younger man stood staring at him, "but that was before Miss Swanson tiptoed into London and out of it again."

"She's gone?" the earl asked before he could stop himself.

"Oh, yes. Into exile. Like Joseph in Egypt. Only this time it's Eve in Doncaster. Didn't you know?"

"I hadn't seen her," the earl said gruffly, as though he hadn't looked everywhere for a glimpse of her in the past weeks, seeing her everywhere as well—before he'd turn to see it was only another girl who laughed with almost her sort of music, or a sudden play of light that had brought a glance of something in another's face that was nearly her. "I'd thought she was merely avoiding me."

"Oh, no," the viscount said blithely. "You're a big chap, Francis, but she didn't have to go all the way to Doncaster to do that. She was sent away to her grandmother's as punishment for throwing you over. Her parents were quite miffed with her, I understand. There's not much to do in the North this time of year, unless she's a great reader," he mused.

The earl stayed so still the snow settled on his lashes. It had been bad enough to think of her mewed up in her house for fear of meeting him, or staying away from her usual entertainments because of him. But exile? And such loneliness? He began to wonder about how long it might take him to travel north. He thought he remembered that he had a friend in Doncaster, or was it Lancaster? No matter. It was only a matter of a hundred miles. He could arrange to be in the area, he thought with growing excitment. He could say he was sightseeing, or buying sheep . . .

"Of course, they quite dote on her, you know," the Viscount Talwin continued, "and so they soon managed to put all the blame on you. The squire and I were schoolmates, and he's not changed much since then, I imagine. Like a whistling teapot, as quick to heat up as to cool down. Because then they hied to Doncaster to see in the New Year with her. In fact, they're giving a great party there as apology to her, I understand," he said, as though he hadn't an invitation to it in his study at that very moment. "Everyone is going . . . such a lot of important people won't have converged upon the North since the Vikings invaded there." He smiled. "If peace ever comes, Francis, I'll be demoted from patriot to prattlebox, for I've a way of hearing all the gossip, whether it's to do with national security or a young girl's broken engagement. But it's all the same to me. I can't afford to miss a word of any of it."

Well, then, thought the earl with as much of a pang of pain at hearing of her pardon as he'd felt at hearing of her punishment, she won't suffer for it, after all. In fact, she'll likely be lauded for her good sense. She's likely laughing at her good fortune now. She'll soon find herself some fellow she can laugh with too, if she hasn't already. A gala party, is it? She needs neither my pity nor my presence.

"Oh," Viscount Talwin said as he raised his hand to summon a hackney cab, "yes. Be sure I'll tell you what transpired there when I return. Hold a moment," he said, pausing as if much struck, and wheeling around to stare at his young friend. "There'll be dozens of people you know there. I'd enjoy your company and am sure a guest of mine would be admitted . . . Ah, but I don't know if it would be at all the thing, and you'd hardly wish to do the wrong thing, would you?"

But by this time the earl had recovered himself.

"It's not a matter of right or wrong. I didn't receive an invitation. But neither am I interested," he said coldly, touching a gloved hand to his snowcapped beaver hat. "Fare thee well, sir, and a Happy New Year to you."

Ah, well, the viscount thought sadly as he settled himself in the coach, at least I can tell my friend Squire Swanson that I did all I could. I prodded and teased as much as I dared. But the pretty little chit had the right of it, he sighed as he saw his young friend's tall form disappear into the whirling snow. You can always count on Poole to do the correct thing, damn his eyes.

It was the novelty of it that was the making of it, or so everyone said. The North was unfashionable at this season, and Doncaster always was. The location was as inconvenient for the guests as the setting was unfamiliar to them. Which was why every rake and rattle, pink of the *ton* and tulip of the town, as well as their ladies, discovered themselves enchanted to come to the house in Doncaster to see the New Year in with the Swansons. For fashion doted on inconvenience, and novelty was even more valued, and besides, everyone who mattered would be there.

Almost everyone, Eve thought as she smiled at all the company.

She wore a red gown for the festive season, a white rose at her breast for the New Year, a nosegay of holly and ivy for her grandmother's and great-aunt's sake, and a smile for her parents'. but for all that she was truly the belle of this ball, she wished she were anywhere else, because she could see him in her mind's eye as clearly as she could hear his name in every conversation she overheard, and in the subtext of every word her guests had with her.

He was in London this New Year's Eve, doing the things a gentleman was supposed to do. There were a dozen gentlemen at the party who would have done the same, a dozen more who would have tried to, and even more who'd not enough interest in London tastes to care at all for fashion. And so Eve wondered why it was that she longed only for him, even here, especially now. But his conversation had been wittier than any other gentleman's, and his face dearer, and above all, there'd been that about him which called to her and defied all explanation. And for all his serving fashion, his perfect manners had been belied by something in his eyes, those remarkably mirrored eyes that saw so much and gave back only what he wished you to see— which was nothing of his soul, damn him, Eve thought. And raised her head higher, and went off to the dance on the arm of another gentleman who'd suit her very well if she could only stop thinking of the one who wouldn't.

The house was so filled with holiday that it seemed incredible her spirits were not as high as

she pretended them to be. It was wonderful that
her parents had forgiven her, and come, with all
their greetings, gifts, and friends. Grandmother
and Great-Aunt had received them all with glad
welcome, and unknown to them, less usual sorts
of hospitality. They'd hauled half the forest into
the ballroom, and every room and salon was simi-
larly bedecked. The guests might think it only holiday with them, but between the rowan and the
mistletoe, the oak log and the holly berries, the ash
twigs within, and hawthorn boughs without, the
dried white heather and the fresh pine cones, the
house was protected from evil-wishers, nightmare,
witches, and for all Eve knew, cohorts of ancient
Romans and dragonshipfuls of Vikings as well.

But the London guests were enchanted, and the
local ones bemused, and so the impromptu party
was a wild success. Eccentrics, after all, were the
pets of fashion, and gossip the very breath of it. So
Great-Aunt and Grandmother enjoyed a certain
vogue among the guests, even as Eve herself, a
young lady who'd whistled the most eligible gentleman in London down the wind, was an object of
awed fascination. Eve and her family were the
heart and soul of fashion this season. But she didn't
give it much thought, knowing society to be as
fickle as her current fame was fragile. The *ton*
could just as easily have pilloried her for her unusual behavior, and laughed at Grandmother and
Great-Aunt as easily as lionizing them for their
rustic oddity. She supposed it had been a dull season that accounted for it, for all she knew it might
have been the effect of all the magical charms. And
she cared less than she knew. It was almost over.

Christmas had come and gone, and now the New
Year was upon them. Pots and pans and bells were
in readiness for the guests to beat and swing, not
only for their merriment but also for chasing bad
spirits from the vicinity. Barrels of pitch on the

grounds were ready for firing, for spectacle, and for encouraging the return of the sun to the land; and red herrings lay in rows on their platters for the guests to eat and ensure good fortune with. There was not a custom Great-Aunt and Grandmother neglected at this treacherous turning point of the year, for, as they'd lectured Eve, one could never be too careful when dealing with fate, and custom only became custom for good reason, after all.

Which was precisely what he would say on other matters, Eve supposed. And then sighed, wondering how many bells she'd have to ring and herrings she'd have to eat in order to rid herself of thoughts of him in the New Year. But she would, she resolved as she stepped into the dance. And if she didn't, she decided as she danced the old year out, then she'd learn to live with it, as she had with the fact that she'd never grow an inch taller—because she had no choice in the matter.

"No, my lord," the butler said sadly, shaking his head as regularly as the pendulum on the clock behind him was counting the New Year further in, "it's not possible. Impossible, I say," he said, raising his voice, trying to be heard above the merrymakers in the great house. "We can't admit anyone until Tom gets here, I'm sorry to say."

The earl's eyes glittered. He stood on the doorstep and glanced back to where his exhausted horse stood breathing almost as hard as he was, and paused for breath to demand a further explanation. He'd ridden out from London like a madman, leaving his good sense and his valet behind. But it had come upon him all at once, and all at once he'd known that he'd been a fool for letting her go, an arrogant one for waiting for her to change her mind, and a cowardly one for giving up when she hadn't. And the worst one of all for not realizing that she'd been right.

He'd been too concerned about his style to care about his substance. He'd cultivated charm, he'd courted popularity, he'd discovered a thousand ways to hide his heart from pain since he'd been an overly impressionable boy. And in so doing, somewhere along the way to adulthood had lost the sensitivity that he'd been so attracted to in her. She'd seen and deplored it, and yet had given him a chance to change. But the habits of a lifetime had been stronger than his love for her. Had been. "Had been," he'd repeated to himself all down the long and lonely road from London. Because nothing had been stronger than his loneliness and the steadily growing realization that a lack of pain wasn't worth losing the ability to be hurt. His parents might have hidden their hearts away, some of his friends might truly claim to have none at all, but his own, for all its protection, had pained him so that he'd had to rip the armor off so as to restore its steady beat. He'd woken in the night as Christmas bells rang out, but it had been his own heart calling that wakened him. He'd brooded long enough. She was the woman he loved, he needed her, and he'd have her however he could.

How that would be, how he'd apologize, how he'd convince her he was her slave more than fashion's, were things he hadn't reasoned out yet. But it made no matter. He'd thought to wait for her to return to town, but even that proved too much for him. He'd come to her. Only to be turned away at her doorstep. Half the *ton* was within the house with her: men he'd been to school with, gentlemen from his clubs, ladies he'd danced with, women from his past, and distant relatives too, no doubt, and he was not to be admitted in their company. And yet if he could believe the butler, it had nothing to do with his name. Only his face.

He'd ridden up the drive to the bright gabled

house in Doncaster, feeling like a prince come riding to the princess in the tower. Only to be told he
couldn't set a foot over the doorstep. Bedtime story
had turned to child's nightmare. He could hear the
sounds of laughter from within, and catch glimpses
of the rich company in their festive raiment as they
greeted the New Year. But he'd been cast back into
the darkness.

"I'm that sorry, your lordship," the butler said
with sympathy, for rural servants stood on less
ceremony, "but the old ladies wouldn't have it. Nor
would you wish to upset them, my lord," he added
nervously when he saw the earl's set face and the
size of his shoulders as he moved a step further
toward the door. "And that they'd be, because
they'd believe you ill-wished them for the coming
year if you was to come in before the first footer,
you see."

"First footer?" the earl murmured, his exhaustion making him wonder if he'd heard right, his
eyes seeking the rooms behind the butler, watching for a glimpse of her.

"Aye, that's right, my lord, the dark man, as I
said when you arrived," the butler said. "Tom
Jenkins it is this year, as last, and his father before
him. He's tall and dark as a Gypsy, for all his family's been here since the Flood. But he's well
made and merry as a cricket, and has a neat foot.
You see, my lord," he added, noting the weary confusion on the tall fair-haired gentleman's face, "it's
the custom here, and the ladies set great store by
it. The first person in the house after the stroke of
midnight of the New Year must be the dark man.
A tall, nice-looking bachelor, preferably. A dark fellow with a fine, high-arched foot. He carries a bit
of coal and a silver coin in one pocket, salt and a
bit of mince pie in the other. And a bottle of whiskey in his right hand, of course. He steps in on his
right foot and says:

" 'I wish you health,
I wish you wealth,
I wish you happiness and cheer,
Good luck in all you do,
And a healthy, happy New Year.'

"Then he drinks with the family," the butler went on, "and leaves by the back door, which is then locked up tight, to keep the luck in."

The butler sighed. "You're a good-looking chap, my lord, but fair as the dawn. The old ladies would have a fit, if they didn't die of fright thinking of what would happen in the New Year if I was to let you in before the dark man comes."

The earl consulted his watch.

"It's the New Year, and past it," he argued. "Where is the fellow?"

"Ah, well, as to that. See, we're at the outside of town and a bit back from that, my lord. And Tom goes everywhere in town first, as well as everywhere else on the way out of it, before he comes here. Expect him at the stroke of three, or later, or even near to first light. He has a toast with the master and mistress of every house he visits, you see," the butler added gently.

"You might ask at the inn first," the butler called as the earl strode back into the darkness.

Tom was staggered at the request. But then, he was staggering at everything by now. Lurching, actually, the earl noted as Tom tried to stand straight and stare him down. He was a handsome youth, with curly ink-black hair, a dark smooth complexion, and the sort of eyes that women called "romantic" but reminded the earl more of a devoted dog's than a poet's.

"Come with you . . . now?" Tom asked with such incredulity that he actually stopped weaving for a moment. "W' half the parish undone?"

One of his friends whispered something in his ear.

"Aye, well, maybe not," Tom agreed, nodding without letting up, as if once he'd got the hang of it he'd forgotten how to stop. "Not pre-cisely *half* undone, but it's undone they'd be if I went out to the old leddies' and forgot them who is along the way. I take my reshponsibilities keenly, my lord, I do. It's I that brings in the New Year's luck, me. It's a remark-remarkable foot, really," he said tenderly, looking down at his boot so fixedly he began to bend toward it until his friends, on either side of him, propped him up again so he could add, trying to focus on the earl, "See, it's not just the fach . . . face. It's the foot. Small and neat and with an arch you could shoot peas under, and there's a fact."

He grinned at his superior foot again as the earl shifted from one of his own weary feet to the other in his impatience. He held up a coin, and added it to the ones already in his gloved palm. Tom's friends looked at them longingly. They stood in the village street not far from the inn, where the earl had finally literally run Tom to earth, watching his friends picking him up from the cobbles so he could complete his rounds. He'd the face and the figure and the foot for the job, the other lads had confided, but not the hard head his father had. But he was young yet, they assured the earl. Now they stared at the coins in the earl's glove hungrily. But Tom was far too pleased with his world to want anything more from it. Gold was nothing to him; nothing was anything to him but his pride—and his expectations of the greetings he'd drink to at the next door opened to him.

"I'll come to 'em in proper turn, and'll be glad to have your company, m'lord, but not before time. S'matter of honor, y'see," he told the earl, and then, after beginning a bow his friends rescued him from completing on the cobbles, he staggered on down the street.

The earl pocketed the coins. By the time Tom was ready to be first footer at Eve's grandmother's house, it might be October. Or dawn. It was all the same to the earl now. He felt frustration and despair, emotions as alien to him as the pleasanter ones love for her had brought him. But it was that very life that she'd given to his perfectly correct numbed senses that was part of the wonder of her. And he'd let her slip away. Even now she might be straying further. She was there now, dancing and laughing. And if he came tomorrow, who knew what she'd have committed herself to by then?

New Year's was a sentimental sort of night, one made for endings as well as new beginnings. And she was there in the midst of the cream of London society, the gentlemen of name and fortune and note—and he was here alone on a village street, and all because his face wasn't dark enough to suit tradition. He supposed, he thought, smiling with grim weariness, that it served him exactly right. The gods were very clever with retribution. But he didn't care for custom any longer, or for what was done or was expected of him. That was the whole point of his journey—to let her know that, to let her see that . . .

The earl stood very still, and then suddenly wheeled about and made for the inn with a smile so wide and mad on his face that he startled passersby. One followed him to see what he was about. And then, when he saw what he'd purchased from the landlord and what he was doing with it, went running to his good friend Tom. The incredible news stung Tom into actually putting down the glass of whiskey he'd been given with such violence that he spilled a drop.

* * *

The clock had chimed twice, but no one heard it above the music and the conversation. It wasn't until the butler came to the door of the ballroom and announced it that Eve's grandmother and great-aunt called for the orchestra to be still, and then led the company to the entry hall for the last of the night's rituals.

"Ah, attend me, my friends," her grandmother cried in a thrilling voice as the company assembled before her in the marble-tiled hall, "it is the advent of the first footer. Open the door and let the luck come in," she commanded.

The door swung wide. The dark man took a step inside, his right glossy foot first. He wore a capacious smock over his form-fitting breeches, and swept off his high beaver hat as he entered the house, showing hair the color of ravens after midnight, and causing a shower of darkness to filter down all about him on the white marble floor. He was darker than the night he'd come in from, blacker than the coal he drew from one pocket, and his eyes glinted silver as the coin he produced from the other. The company, every one of them, stood transfixed at the sight of the tall dark man, for they'd never seen a darker one.

But however black the soot that covered him over so entirely, still Eve could never mistake those eyes. She gasped, hesitated, and then ran to him, and he gripped her hand hard.

" 'I wish you'd see what a fool I've been,' " he recited, looking down at her,

" 'I wish you'd note that nothing really matters to me but your good opinion.

" 'I wish you to know I love you more than I've ever loved anyone, always shall, and wish nothing more for myself than to be as true to you as I wish you'd be to me.

" 'Forever.

" 'Because I wish you'd say "yes" again, for if you did

" 'I'd never let you go again,' " the Earl of Poole said.

Then, his smile a white slash in his sooty face, he added, "I'm never a poet. But, ladies," he said, looking up to see his hostesses gaping at him, "at least, am I dark enough?"

"Well, it *is* the heart that counts," Eve's great-aunt said hesitantly.

"Oh, but be sure his is black enough," Eve said on a trembling laugh, looking up into his eyes.

And if the sight of the lofty Earl of Poole looking like a chimney sweep wasn't wonderful enough for the gossip-loving company, and the sight of him sweeping Eve into his arms and kissing her with a thoroughness that was in itself astonishing wasn't treat enough, the state of her face and his when they parted was. For Miss Swanson's blushes were covered over with soot, and she looked as if she'd crept up a chimney herself, and the earl was grinning like a boy.

Then the company was titillated by the sight of Squire Swanson's face. For it was as red as his daughter's gown was in those places where the obvious evidence of where the earl's hands had been during that kiss was not. And if that wasn't exciting enough, the earl's next words certainly were.

"I'm taking your daughter straight back to London with me now, sir," he said, "in a private coach I've hired for the occasion. So, you see," he said as the squire groped for a weapon of some sort, "she'll be compromised so thoroughly that she'll have no opportunity to change her mind about marrying me when we get there."

As the squire relaxed, and began to grin at the besotted look on his daughter's face, the earl added, "We'll be wedded as soon as may be. I wish

you a Happy New Year," he added to the assembled company. And his lady's hand tight in his, he
made for the door with her.

But even without the butler's startled warning,
he suddenly wheeled about and made for the back
door with her instead. Not because he remembered tradition in time, but because there was no
room to leave by the front door. Because by then
Tom's friends were bringing in the first footer—
horizontally, of course—but carrying him right-
foot-first.

The coach made marvelous speed because of the
hour and the emptiness of the roads on such a
night. And since, because whenever Miss Eve
Swanson drew back from her fiancé's embrace, his
face was such a terribly smudged thing to see, she
could scarcely be blamed for not drawing back too
often. It was somewhere nearer to London than
Doncaster when she did pull back from him with
a sudden startled cry.

"Oh! Ugh! Whatever is that?" Eve exclaimed in
disgust, her hand frozen upon him, her outsize
grimace of distaste discernible even on her sooty
face.

The earl grew very still. And then tentatively
put his hand over hers. And then laughed so hard
in his relief that the coach rocked even more than
it had been doing through all their wild ride.

"It's my . . . it's just a bit of my . . . mince pie,"
he managed to say, withdrawing some of the gluey
mass from his pocket before he pulled off his smock
entirely, wiped her hand with it, and cast it on the
floor. He drew her back in his arms immediately,
as if he couldn't wait for her to besmirch his dazzlingly white shirt with the last of the soot she'd
rubbed off him.

"I've given up the correct thing to do, but I don't
think we should mock all custom, my love," he

said when he'd finally gotten Eve settled against him once more, "for it did bring me luck. And you. Happy New Year," he said with gratitude, feeling free and whole as a boy again. "Happy New Year," he whispered to the look in her eyes.

"Oh, yes, it is, it is," she responded gladly, before she responded even more delightfully.